CONVERGENCE

THE MERCER WITCHES BOOK II

D.O. SCISSOM

CONTENTS

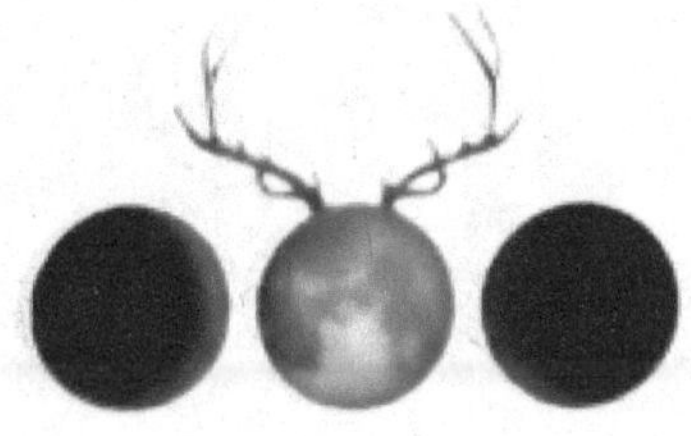

A Note From The Author

Hello Family,

I wanted to thank each and every one of you for continuing this journey with me. I would also like to offer a couple words of advice. If you somehow stumbled onto Convergence: The Mercer Witches Book II, without having read The Harvest: The Mercer Witches Book I, I would highly recommend you pause and read it first.

That being said, this story is heavy. You will find a lot of themes contained in these pages that might be difficult for some people. I am not going to list them all out, not because I have a distaste for trigger warnings, but because I don't believe that we all see these things in the same ways, and I want you to interpret what you see for yourself.

As a thank you for your continued interest in this series I have included a couple of extras at the end of this book. Notes From Detective Alexander LaSalle, which are part of the upcoming Tales of Mercer Lore collection, and a preview of The Mercer Witches Book III.

Thank you.

D.O. Scissom

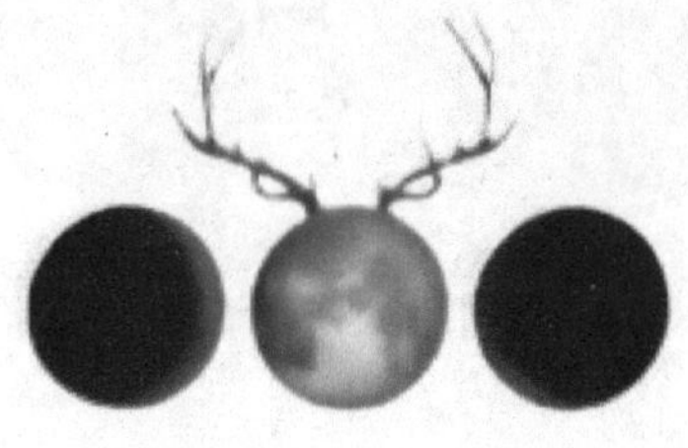

DEDICATION

To the Mercer women in my life, who fill my days with magic and grace.
To my sons, for your endless patience, inspiration, and curiosity.
I could not have done this without you.
I love you all.

D.O. Scissom.

BIRTH

"Hello child, open your eyes, it is time to do what you were created to do."

"Father?"

"Yes, my child?"

"What do you desire? How can I serve you?"

"My precious child, you are never my servant. You were not created to serve; you were created to protect this world and all its children. You are the bringer of light, and the sword of righteousness."

"Yes, Father, point me to your enemies, allow me to strike down those who threaten your children."

"One day, you will. But before you can, you must do two things."

"Anything, Father."

"You must go, take up your holy blade, and live among them. Make a life for yourself, see with your own eyes who they are, and why they must be protected."

"Father, who threatens them, tell me now so that I can end the threat and return to your side where I belong."

"Live among them, my child. When the threat comes, you will know who the enemy is, and you will know to act."

"And the second thing?"

"When the time comes, when you know what must be done. You must not hesitate."

"Thy will be done, Father."

The Shining Star of the Morning, the first and most beloved angel fell from the heavens.

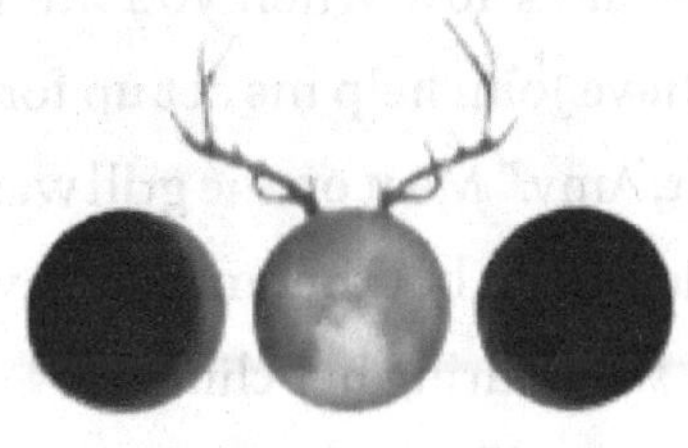

Smells Like Game Night!

"Tammy, are you sure I can't help with anything?"

Amy's voice brought Tammy's attention up from the grazing board she was finishing. "Hmm, how about some more of that chardonnay?"

Amy grabbed the bottle from the ice bucket and located Tammy's wine glass among the chaos on the kitchen island. She raised her eyebrows at her. "A glass, or enough that you have a glass when we take everything to the dining room?"

Tammy rolled her eyes and touched her chest in mock indignation.

Amy poured two fingers of wine, then teasingly pulled the bottle away and raised her eyebrows at Tammy--who shook a rolled up piece of prosciutto at her. Amy laughed and teased, pouring another drop or two into the glass. "You can put your meat away lady, it doesn't work for John; it certainly won't work for you either."

She topped off the wine.

"Okay, I am going to go check on the guys and the kabobs, make sure that they haven't gotten distracted by something nerdy, and forgotten they are cooking. Let me know when you are ready for me to help transport, and I will have John help me set up for cards."

"Oh, you're the best, Amy." Meat on the grill was always such a mixed bag for her. She loved to eat it, but the smell always reminded her of the burn victims she had seen during her clinicals.

Amy slid out of the room like a whisper. Tammy stopped her preparations for a moment to watch her go. She and Kenneth moved into this house six months ago. Within an hour of the moving truck driving off, the doorbell rang. By the time she made it down the stairs to the front door, no one was there. Just a box with a note taped to the top.

I am sure you are hungry, and who wants to cook after moving? Just set the box back on the porch and text when you are done, and we will collect it. Do not worry about washing anything. After you are settled in, we can get acquainted. Until then, WELCOME TO THE NEIGHBORHOOD. Amy and John Park.

The note ended with a phone number, a house number, and a cute little smiley face drawing. Opening the box, a second note listed all of the ingredients in the pasta dish contained in the thermal bag. The second container held precut ingredients for a simple salad, oil, and vinegar, two bottles of sparkling water, garlic bread, a piece of carrot cake, and a piece of peach cobbler—along with plates, silverware, glasses, and condiments.

Looking over her shoulder, Kenneth said, "Do they not think we have plates?"

She remembered tearing up while she explained. "No, they know we likely haven't unpacked and didn't want their gift to make more work."

"Okay Tam, but we aren't going to really give the dishes back dirty, are we?"

"That is exactly what we are going to do. Kenneth, we have moved five times in ten years. This is the kindest gesture anyone has ever offered as a welcome. They didn't pop up and expect to be entertained;

they didn't make more work for me. They just provided comfort with no expectation. It would be rude not to accept it for what it is."

In the following months, her and Amy have become close friends. The guys get along fine, but she and Amy are nearly inseparable.

Their friendship fit so well. They were all in their forties, and neither couple had ever had children. Tammy was a nurse, Amy was a social worker, John was a paramedic, and Kenneth was a rescue diver. She could hardly believe how fast they all got comfortable with one another. With Kenneth's job being so transient, they rarely stayed anywhere too long, and it was so hard to make friends without the usual social anchors of kids and church.

Tammy took another drink of her wine and gathered up the grazing boards. She grabbed a grazing board and her wine; she could send Amy back for the second board. Time to start game night for real. They were playing spades tonight; last week at Amy's it was Settlers of Catan, and the guys had cleaned house. She was ready for some payback.

She rounded the corner from the kitchen into the dining room. There was a sliding glass door that led out onto the sunroom. and the patio where the guys set up shop to grill some kabobs. She loved this part of the house, with the high ceilings and detailed carpentry. It was perfect for her. Lights of natural light between the two big windows and the door to the sunroom. Dark walnut crown molding and matching chair rail. It spoke to her the moment she laid eyes on it.

She tried twice, unsuccessfully, to lay her board down on the sideboard with one hand, before finally giving up and setting her wine down first. Laughing at herself she stepped toward the door to call out for everyone to come in.

Amy was in the sunroom and headed her way already. John was close behind her with a tray of kebabs, and Kenneth was closing the lid on the grill out on the patio beyond the exterior door. But who was that in the backyard with him?

Tammy squinted against the light, thinking it must have been a trick of some sort. But no, there was another man in the yard beyond the concrete pad where the grill was set up. He wore a purple robe of some sort. Tall, dark-skinned, with locs that nearly reached the ground.

"Kenneth, who is that?" She called out to him.

He didn't answer, he couldn't hear her from this far away. But when she looked back, the man wasn't alone. On either side of him, two men appeared, both shirtless, in athletic shorts and sneakers. She was still trying to make sense of the scene when the blond man on the left raised a big hammer up to his right shoulder, then pointed toward the house with his other hand. The man in the robe lifted his arms high in the air and some kind of ball appeared between his hands.

Amy turned to see what Tammy was looking at and started screaming.

"Get down, get down now."

Amy dropped to her knees and held her hands up in the air toward the patio right as the explosion hit. A wave of hot air and debris blasted Tammy off her feet. The roar of wind mixed with the crunch of breaking glass and splintering wood as the sunroom was leveled by some kind of blast.

Tammy lay on her side, her back against the wall. Her head was ringing and there was a searing pain in her left shoulder. She tried to turn her head to see what was causing the pain and couldn't. There was something propped against the side of her head.

She shifted her body and screamed from the pain in her shoulder. She cast her eyes a little to the left. A wedge of glass, still attached to a piece of broken window frame, was lodged in her shoulder. It was the piece of window frame that kept her from turning her head, every time she did, it pushed the glass further into her shoulder.

She cried out, "Kenny, baby, help, it hurts so bad."

She opened her eyes despite the pain. Amy was in the middle of the pile of debris that used to be her sunroom. There was some kind of fire behind her, no, not behind her. Surrounding her. Tammy tried to clear her head. She squeezed her eyes shut and opened them again. But the scene was the same. Amy stood in the pile of rubble. Her hands in the air. She was screaming something that Tammy couldn't understand. Fire shot toward her from outside the broken walls and broke around her like a wave around a rock.

The burning meat smell of the BBQ was everywhere now and she wretched from the nausea and pain. She couldn't see John, or Kenneth. But there was something, no someone, on the ground between Amy, and where Tammy lay bleeding.

Her heart dropped and the pain, the fire, the fear, and confusion all dropped away as the realization of what she was seeing dawned on her. An arm stuck out of the bloody mess of half-burned clothing on the floor. A muscular arm, with a Bart Simpson tattoo on the forearm. That tattoo belonged to the man she loved.

What she couldn't understand was the charred pile of exposed bones and tissue that arm was still tenuously attached to. That couldn't be the man she loved, because whoever that was had sustained injuries that you cannot survive. She was an obstetrics nurse, but she didn't have to specialize in emergency medicine or trauma nursing to know that you cannot being lying face down on the ground with your ribs and spine exposed and your lungs a few feet away and still survive.

The sound of screaming broke her focus on the destroyed body that somehow had the same tattoo as her husband. The man in the robe was charging in toward Amy. Small streaks of fire shot out from the man's hand, but were deflected somehow, before they hit her. She was waving her hand around and the spheres were shooting off in different directions. Amy was screaming in defiance as the man got closer and the balls of flame came faster.

Beyond Amy, and the hooded man, Tammy could see John fighting the other two men. Both of them had hammers and John danced across the yard like a ballet dancer trying to keep away from them. He twirled and jumped. With every movement he narrowly missed a swing from one of the giant hammers. The blond man darted in low and swung for his legs, while the dark haired one spun backhand blow toward his head. John jumped the low sweeping blow but even from her spot on the floor Tammy could see the high blow was going to connect with John's head. She tried to scream but nothing came out. A fireball blasted the brown-haired man in the chest pushing him back several feet.

Tammy looked back to Amy in time to see her deflect several of the fireballs back toward the hooded man. As he stumbled back toward where the dark haired man was on a knee recovering from being struck Amy swung her arm through the air like she was throwing a sidearm pitch. At first nothing happened, then as the hooded man and dark haired man both gained their feet Tammy's Nissan Sentra came flying across the yard. Not driven or rolling, but flying sideways like it had been tossed by a giant. The front bumper hit the hooded man and knocked him to the dirt with an ugly thud. The dark haired man got his hammer up, holding it vertically as the car crashed into him. He was thrown out of Tammy's field of vision and her car slammed to the ground.

Amy came running toward her, She reached for her hand, paused and examined the glass sticking out of her shoulder. She mouthed, "I am so sorry." And yanked the glass by the broken bit of window frame. The pain was excruciating. Amy spit in her hand and rubbed it across the bleeding wound and whispered,, "Il tocca dell' angelo."

Tammy stared in horror as the wound closed itself. Amy did not wait to see if she was okay—but yanked her to her feet.

John came running toward them, screaming.

"Go, go, get to the Bellow."

Tammy had no idea what that meant, but Amy dragged her out of her dining room and through the kitchen, out the back door, before she could ask. She heard John running behind them. Amy was nearly carrying her as they ran. *How can she be this strong?* Tammy thought. *What happened to her car? Was it a tornado?*

They approached Amy's garage; the big door was down, and Tammy thought they were going to run right into it. But Amy did something with her hand, yelled a word that Tammy didn't know, and the garage door crumpled like a wad of notebook paper and flew out over their yard.

She dragged Tammy into the garage, pulled a faded Houses of the Holy, tapestry off the wall, and revealed a giant circle painted there. It had multiple concentric rings and letters and numbers in sequences that made no sense to Tammy. They turned to face the garage opening. John was standing in the driveway. The blonde man with the hammer was stalking up the drive toward them, his big hammer spinning like a baton in front of him as he did.

Amy pulled a terrifying-looking axe from the wall and yelled for John. He held out his hand, and the axe floated on a direct path from her hand to his.

"John, come on." Amy implored him.

"Go, I will see you at home, or I will see you in the divine. But you have to get her safe."

Amy grabbed her uninjured left arm and held it tight. "Hang on Tam, this is going to suck."

Tammy looked at her in disbelief. "Amy, what the fuck?"

Amy reached out and put her hand in the center of the circle on the wall, and the world began to blur. The last thing Tammy saw before she lost all form, and thought was a rush of fire tearing across the yard and enveloping John.

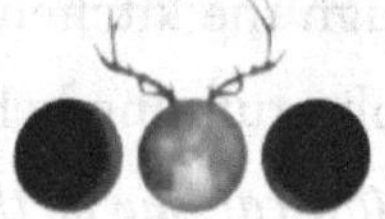

Tammy heard a retching sound and realized that it was her vomiting the little bit of wine and cheese she had eaten while preparing the grazing boards. She opened her eyes to see Amy hacking away at the circle on the floor with a knife, tearing up chunks of wood.

"John, Amy, did you see the fire? Where is John?"

"John is doing what he was born and trained to do Tammy. He is protecting his home and his witch at all costs, even at the cost of his own life."

Tammy could see Amy's eyes rimmed with tears and her face contorting as she struggled to hold back the pain. She thought of Kenneth's mangled body lying in the dining room and she started trembling. The realization and grief taking control. Amy reached out and squeezed her hand.

"Come on, we have a long way to go to get you help, and we are not entirely safe here." Tammy nodded and allowed herself to be led toward small stairwell leading up, and to whatever awaited her on the other side.

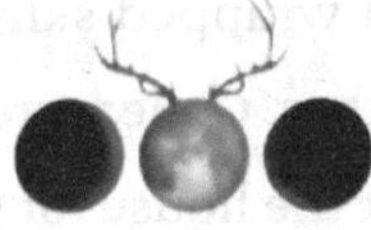

"Damnit Amy, what were you thinking?"

Tammy jumped at the muffled thump of something slamming against the wall.

"Oh, I don't know, maybe that protecting the innocent at all costs is our primary mandate and I wasn't about to leave that woman alone to face the Carpenters and some fucking pyro. You think I don't understand the risks, to her and to us?

Her husband was blown apart in front of her, her house and her life destroyed in a blink. Not to mention at this point I am praying that John was killed outright and not tortured by those monsters. I did what the fuck I had to do to minimize the damage in a horrible situation. Don't sit here in your safe house harvesting herbs and blessing bandages and judge what I had to do to keep myself and an innocent alive today."

Tammy closed her eyes against the sting of tears and the agony of grief. For a moment after she awakened in the evening dark of the room she was in, she had forgotten about the nightmare that brought her here. The attack, the man with the robes and the fire, the two men, almost twins, with the hammers. The pile of gore and bones that was her husband only a moment before. This had to be a mistake. This couldn't be real.

She rose from the bed and was headed toward the door when it swung open. She jumped back on the bed, pulling a pillow up to her chest in fear.

Amy entered the room with an older woman close behind her. Away in a loose cotton top and a wrapped skirt of some kind. This made Tammy look at her own clothes. Gone were the leggings and blue crop top she had been wearing at the house for game night. She was in soft pajama pants and a long-sleeved t-shirt. Both of them felt very worn, like familiar old favorites. She stared at Amy over the pillow.

"Where are my clothes? Amy, I want my clothes please."

Amy approached the bed. "Tammy, can I sit with you? Is that okay?"

Tammy nodded her head but did not come out from behind the pillow.

Amy sat on the bed and reached slowly over to pat Tammy's knee.

"You're safe here sweetheart, please believe me, nothing can hurt you here but your grief."

Tammy squeezed her eyes shut tight and shook her head slowly behind the pillow. She could feel her grip on her sanity slipping. Kenneth was her rock, her foundation. Up until her and Amy had become friends, he was the only friend of family she had. Now he was gone and she was slowly sliding into blackness that was calling her name, a comforting nothingness.

The older woman in the doorway spoke softly. "It has been two days sister; she has to eat."

Tammy looked between the two women and whispered. "What does she mean? What's been two days?"

Amy patted her leg a little more firmly now. "Tammy, you've been in bed for two days. It is Sunday evening. I will be honest with you. This is the fourth time you've woken up, and you have the same look of shock and panic as the last three. You keep waking up and going into shock and we keep giving you something to help you sleep.

But your mind and body aren't going to tolerate being neglected for much longer. I need you to focus and stay with me here. I know it hurts.

Kenneth was a good man, and you can mourn him for as long as you need to. But you have to live in order to do that."

Tammy let the pillow slip further down exposing her entire face. Her voice was soft and childlike. "He is a good man. He is my best friend. I can't, I don't want to go on without him." Her sobs became an unbroken cry.

"Why Amy, who were those men? Why did they hurt Kenneth? Kenneth never hurt anyone, ever."

Amy held out her hands, and Tammy took them into her own. Her grip was weak but present.

"They weren't after Kenneth. Tammy, let's do this. Can you get up for me? Let's go to the kitchen and have some soup. Sister Ruth made you a wonderful soup that will start you to feeling better and I will explain what I can. Can you do that for me?"

Tammy was slowly nodding her head. "Will you stay beside me? Please don't leave me alone."

"I won't, Tam, I promise."

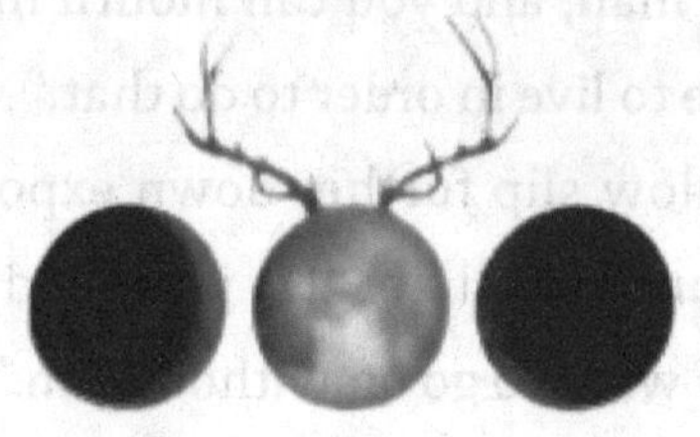

Not Everyone Gets To Be An Astronaut, Someone Has To Make the French Fries.

Amy led Tammy into a small chapel at the back of Ruth's house. Candles and lanterns were set into the walls and on every shelf and table. The room glowed and shifted with the flickering of flames. Smoke drifted through the air; it smelled of something old and forbidden.

A circle of white paint dominated the center of the stone floor. Nine small bowls lined the circumference. All decorated ceramic, and each one filled with something different. Herbs, rocks, and liquids of various colors. A larger bowl in the middle was filled with beautiful yellow flowers.

"Tammy, as I told you, our home is protected; in order for you to be allowed sanctuary, we have to call the protector. We must have his permission."

Amy was speaking to her, but her voice seemed so far away. She had been right, the soup that Ruth gave her made her feel better. Then she thought about Kenneth again, lying broken in the rubble of their home, his insides exposed, and bones smashed. Everything got fuzzy again for a while. When she came to, Amy was talking to her about something that didn't make any sense. Witches, and guardians, dangerous enemies, a safe place. She wanted to scream at her, *Kenneth is dead, there are no safe places for me.*

She knew in her heart that Amy meant well; she just appeared to be mentally unwell. Magic wasn't real, or witches, or whatever she was babbling on about. But Tammy didn't want to hurt her feelings, so she nodded along and said she would be happy to go see Amy's real home. She figured she could always leave once she got around people who weren't crazy.

She allowed herself to be led to three cushions lined up at the edge of the circle. The other women knelt, and so she did as well.

"Tammy, when we light these fires, our guardian will arrive. He can be very frightening. Try to stay calm and answer his questions truthfully. He will decide if you will be allowed in our home."

Tammy didn't say anything in response, but she really was concerned at this point that maybe Amy's mind had snapped during whatever happened to Kenneth and John. *Couldn't hurt to humor her though, right?*

The three of them knelt on the cushions, and the woman, Ruth, was seated at Tammy's right. She lifted her arm and whispered a phrase so quiet that Tammy barely heard it. Flames erupted from the nine bowls, and Tammy had to shield her eyes from the glare, then the room went black.

Tammy tried to open her eyes, but the world was black, and her eyes hurt. She tried to sit up but a terrible pain in her chest and shoulder, and a pressure on her stomach and legs stopped her. She cried out in agony, and confusion. She heard a voice through the pain and darkness.

"Hello, Mrs. Nash, Mrs. Nash? Is that you? Can you hear us? We are going to be very still, make any noise you can, and we will find you. Stay with us."

Tammy moaned in pain as she tried to move, and this time the voice was right on top of her.

"I've got her. Get me a backboard and a brace. I need EMS here right now. Mrs. Nash, Tammy, lie real still, it is going to take us a minute to dig you out. But you're safe now. It's almost over."

Tammy remembered the explosion; they were having game night. Amy and John were coming over, and Kenneth was on the back patio cooking, when something exploded. She remembered seeing Kenneth's mangled body in the rubble before everything went black. She heard the voice again.

"IV fluids and bandages now, she's been buried for two days. Expect dehydration and possible organ damage, let's fucking go, come on."

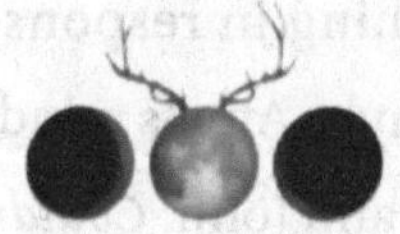

In the small chapel room of Ruth Menn's house, Ruth and Amy were still kneeling outside the circle when they felt the presence of Lord Seanchara, the guardian of Mercer, return.

"It is done, witches, just as you implored."

Amy raised her red-rimmed eyes, fighting back the grief and pain she so desperately wanted to give in to.

"Thank you, Lord Seanchara. May I ask what you saw?"

"Her mind and spirit were broken by grief. She was so far beyond acceptance of what she had seen that she believed you to be delusional. A mind and spirit like that would never survive passing through the veil of death in a way that would lead to a benefit to her, or our great family.

She awoke, in the rubble of her home, mere feet from a rescue worker, with no memory of anything other than an explosion while she was preparing for your arrival. Her husband, of course, is dead, and with your house leveled too, it is presumed you and your husband are also dead among the disaster."

"You are wise and kind, Lord Seanchara. Thank you again for attending and aiding us in our time of need."

"I am and will be at your service as always, Sister. Now, Sister Ruth, if you would be so kind as to make this one rest as well before she collapses on us, I would consider it a personal favor. Let us lose no one else to these bastards. Amy?"

"Yes?"

"When you find your consort and take your revenge on those who brought you and yours harm. Please skin at least one of them on my behalf."

"Yes, Lord Seanchara."

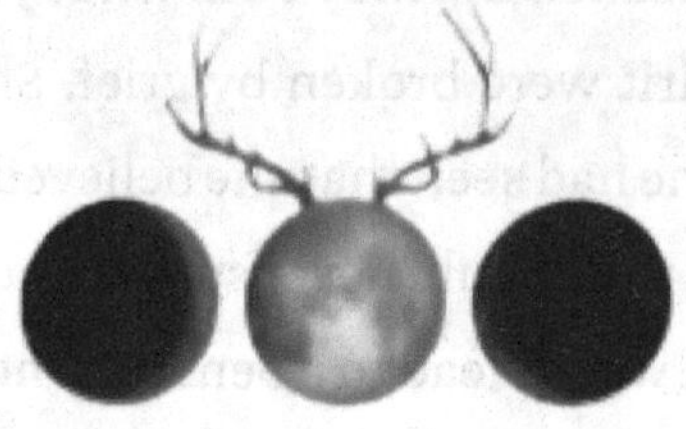

BACK TO THE FIGHT

S ugar knelt between two rows of tall hedges. It was nearing dark and his eyes strained to catch any sight of his targets.

He heard M.M. Wildes' voice in his earbud.

"Sugar, can you see them? Do you have a location?"

A moment of silence, then his whispered response in her earbud. "No, I am along the perimeter, opposite of where I left you. I am going to slip around another quarter of the way, then enter the rows. Tell me if you are coming in."

"Copy that, I'll block off the back entrance as soon as you enter. Be careful, baby, you don't know who you'll run into first."

A hiss of static, and an electric crackle in the line, then Sugar's sweet voice, yelling not so sweet things.

"Damn... slippery... little... bastard. Hit me with some kind of taser ball thing. Like getting hit with a stun gun attached to a tennis ball. Hurts..."

M. M. Wildes leapt down from her perch on the wall above the rows of hedges and fencing and started down the narrow path. She slid her baton from its hook on her belt and snapped it into place. Crouching low, she crept in. "I am in Sugar, I can't sit here and wait, not with two of them and taser balls or whatever that is."

"Probably a good idea, M."

Sugar kept as low as his seven-foot frame would allow and slid quickly between the rows of hedges. He came to a T and stopped short, glanced left, then right. A flash of movement, and he caught a glimpse of his quarry, wearing a ghillie suit of some kind and creeping down the row, his back was to Sugar, and he was heading away from him. It was possible he hadn't noticed him yet and was searching for a new vantage point.

Sugar picked up speed, moving as lightly as a jungle cat through the maze. He made no sound, and his strides were long enough compared to the other man's that he would be on him in a moment. The man in the ghillie suit stopped suddenly and slumped, leaning quietly into the hedge.

Sugar froze; his head cocked to the side, and his vision focused on the spot he last saw his movement. He ran through his options in his head. His target was twenty, maybe twenty-five feet ahead, up against the right wall of the maze. With his target no longer moving, Sugar was having a harder time distinguishing his form.

Sugar would be on him in less than a second. Superior size and strength would give him an advantage, and he wasn't wearing a tree costume either so he knew he could outmaneuver him. He also knew this guy favored unconventional weapons. *That taser ball still hurts,* he thought. He slid his baton from his belt, he did not extend it, he would flick it into place as he made the last few steps to his target. *Time to go!*

Sugar pushed off with his powerful legs; and hit the ground hard as the wire leads around his ankles snapped taut. He tried to roll to his left, away from the hedge, to get to his feet and face his attacker.

Instead, he felt the pinch and pressure of a fork tine sliding past each side of his muscular neck and sticking into the ground. At the same time his legs were wrenched up, bending him in half in the process. A pained ghost scorpion.

A shrill, unhinged whisper just behind his left ear. "Eeeeeasybiggun', like the opening bars of a deranged children's song. "You've played your part and drawn her into the maze, now be real still and this will be over soon."

Sugar seethed, but he had no leverage; he pushed up with his hands but was stopped by the third point of the fork, resting at the base of his skull. His legs were wrenched high up above his back, no doubt secured to the handle of the fork somehow. Nothing he could do now, but wait for M and bide his time, hoping his attacker got within grabbing distance.

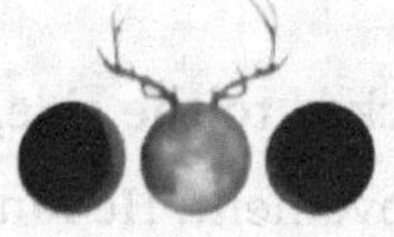

M slid through the rows of hedges, baton in hand, repulsion charm ready. The rustle of leaves behind her gave her a target as she spun, powering the charm, but a wall of blackness blocked her vision.

It encompassed the whole of the walkway and was taller than the hedges by far. Light disappeared into it. She focused her perception, reaching out through the energy of creation. Feeling for Sugar, feeling for their targets.

She found him, close to the center of the maze; she extended her vision, seeing the space he occupied in the energy of creation. There was something wrong, he was... "Shit." She said aloud as she darted in the opposite direction of the darkness. "Shit, shit, shit." He was facedown, bound with a spear or pitchfork, holding him in place, his long legs stretched into the air above his back.

She located her adversaries the same way. He was just ahead of her; she did not see his partner. She ran toward them; she had to free Sugar. Fighting both of them would be tough, but if she hit them hard enough in the first strike, she might have a chance to overwhelm them. She turned the corner, and he was running right at her, his shaggy red hair and beard his only visible features under the cowl he wore. He dropped his head low to dive for her legs.

She pulled the energy into her body, powering the repulsion charm. She was going to blast him right into the dirt and then find his partner and do the same to her.

She screamed as the power was sucked out of her, every bit of it. All the energy, all the connections to the universe around her, everything, pulled right out of her body. As was her fear at seeing Sugar bound and bent, her anger at her slow recovery from her fight against Diana the Triformis, and her frustration at not being faster.

She snarled and jumped hard to try and clear his height as he came diving in. She would come down behind him, spin on him, driving him down with the baton and making him scream for hurting Sugar.

Instead, she slammed into the translucent filament net strung across the top of the hedgerow. It caught her like a spiderweb and rolled her up so tightly she couldn't even brace for the impact as her body fell to the ground. Her back jolted and her teeth clicked together as her heels hit hard. Instead of her head cracking against the hard earth as she fell, unable to slow her own descent. She felt herself slowly lowered. Warm hands cradled her head as she looked up into the smiling blue eyes of her little sister Bets, who kissed her on the forehead before lowering her head gently to the dirt of the arena where they had been training.

"Alright Edward," Bets called to the man behind her, go grab Sugar, I will get M undone.

M heard a cackle and a crash of branches as his sing-song voice echoed through the maze. "Gonna untie the big one and I'm gonna run, untie the big one and I'm goooooonnnnaaa ruuuuuuuuuunnnnn."

"Probably not a bad idea." M said grimly. I am sure Sugar is going to be thrilled at losing a match and doubly grumpy from being hogtied while we finished."

Bets pulled the netting free from M's body helping her to her feet. "Oh, Sis, let him have a little fun, you guys have won every round this week until now. You have to admit, that trick with the net was pretty slick."

M leaned on her sister for support and laughed, "That trick with the net was standard Edward the Fish fare, and nothing compared to the void wall you created away from your location and pinned in place. And draining my repulsion charm just as I was casting it, that was really impressive Bets. Be proud of that work."

Bets hugged her sister tight to her. "Thank you Sis, that means everything coming from you. Now, that puts the week at you guys four and us one, so it looks like I am cooking tonight. That was the deal, right?"

Alabama Barbee and The Florida Man

"The Gentlelady from Alabama will come to order."

"I will not come to order, I will not allow this travesty to continue, I will not sit quietly while the American people are robbed of their voice." She slammed her hand down on the bible that always seemed to be in front of her when she started these rants.

"The Gentlelady from Illinois has the floor, and you will come to order, or I will have you removed from the chamber, again."

Chairman Dietrich rubbed at his temples, then slid his hand over his shinning bald head, smoothing the place that used to be his hair, as the screaming continued.

"The real Americans deserve to have their voice heard; this committee cannot continue to silence the voices of freedom in this chamber."

The Representative from Alabama started waving a bible in the air and slamming her hand on the table for emphasis.

"The Sergeant at Arms will remove the Gentlelady from Alabama."

Representative Roger Beckham from Florida leapt to his feet. "Mr., Chairman, Mr. Chairman, Mr. Chairman." He repeated, waiting for the camera to swing his way. "You cannot continuously bully us out of this chamber every time someone from a state you don't consider elite enough, tries to speak."

LaRhonda Kelm, Representative from Illinois' first district, silently watching the disruption of her time on the floor, finally spoke up. "Mr. Chairman, I am reclaiming my time. Every single time I speak on this floor, one of these two representatives scream until the meeting gets shut down. Mr. Chairman, this is a simple bill, withholding Homeland Security funding from any local law enforcement agency that does not have a written policy in place for dealing with sexual abuse allegations against its officers. It would also bar any department from hiring any officer with a sexual abuse related conviction, or currently on trial, or awaiting trial, for a sexual abuse related crime; if they receive federal funding."

She turned toward the representative from Florida, "I cannot imagine how any real American wouldn't want fewer police officers in their communities who have been convicted of sexual crimes."

She smiled at the now silent Roger. "But if anyone can explain to me why it's a good idea to let convicted rapists have power over ordinary citizens, or why their constituents would support that, I will happily yield my time."

No one in the chamber suppressed their laughter as Roger Beckham stormed out.

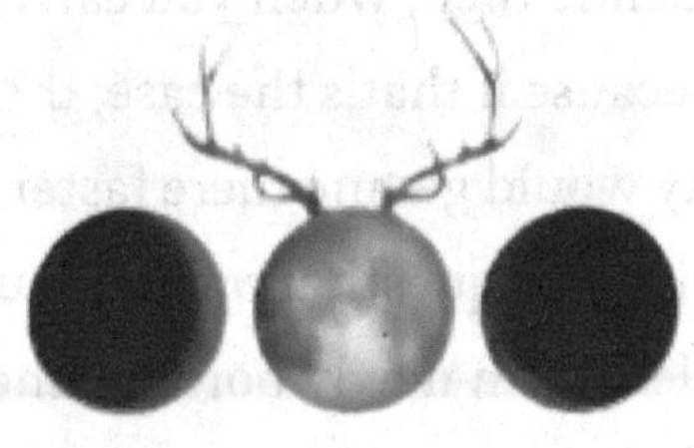

EVEN WITCHES HAVE HOMEWORK

"Okay, I still don't get it, why do I have to memorize all this? If it is all based around the energy of creation?"

Claudia took a deep breath and tried not to let her impatience show. There were few things on earth that she found less endearing than a teenager who is sure they have everything figured out. *Loud and wrong, loud, and wrong, loud, and wrong.* This was her mantra these days.

"It is all about focus and energy, Kay. Can Mother Mercer cast a protection circle without chalk, salt, or rosemary? Yes, of course she can. She can focus her thoughts, define the area in her mind, and pour the energy of creation into her construct at will. But she has also been practicing and refining her craft for a thousand years. When you have been practicing for a thousand years, you can cast whatever you want, however you want. Until then, you learn the craft."

Kay leaned back in her chair. Claudia could see the rest of Kay's argument solidifying behind her eyes. She braced herself for the coming onslaught of teenage logic.

"Is the general guideline then, when you can do it, you can do it? Is it like the carvings? Because if that's the case, then I think focusing on developing that ability would get me there faster. Wouldn't it?"

"Kay. You are basing your question on your current understanding and ability. The problem with newly born witches is that your ability to channel the energy of creation will very quickly outgrow your ability to control and focus the flow of energy.

Look at it like this, right now you are holding a water hose, a regular old garden hose. And the water is barely trickling out. A tiny little stream. Now, you're getting impatient because I am telling you to hold on with both hands and brace yourself against the wall. I know it seems silly, but very quickly that little trickling garden hose will become a fire hose. Then a river, then Niagara Falls.

You have to have a system in place to deal with that flow of energy, or it will run you over. The carvings are a self-regulating system. You can't understand them until you are able to control the magic that they teach."

She could see the understanding dawning on Kay's face, she hoped it wasn't another way around the argument, that maybe she was actually beginning to understand.

"The reason I need you to understand and know these components is to hammer home the feeling of laser-focused control over your spell work. Why do we use rosemary and sea salt in a protection circle, and for whom?"

Kay closed her eyes and took a breath. "Sea salt is a shield, cleansing and protecting against attack. Rosemary..."

She faltered a moment before sitting up straighter, smiling. "Rosemary is a specific protection herb for women, mothers in particular. Mixing the two together with a tag lock from the witch makes a powerful protection circle. Add the symbols of Lord Seanchara and the fifteen point sun around the perimeter for extra protection."

"And what tag locks can be used in protection?"

"Hair, spit, and blood. Blood being the most powerful."

"Why not nails, skin or urine?"

"Nails and urine would be used in repulsion, but they are also highly aggressive and make the circle more dangerous and less predictable, should only be used in the most dangerous of circumstances. And skin? Uh, I can't remember any protection that calls for skin."

"Very, very good, Kay. Now, when you touch that circle and pour the energy of creation into it. It knows exactly what you expect of it. It has a path to follow, a purpose that doesn't rely solely on your will to be successful. Why might that be handy?"

"I, I don't know."

Claudia smiled and thought to herself. *Good, not knowing and admitting it is a far better way to learn.*

Claudia sighed, "Alright, perhaps we try a quick demonstration?"

Kay grinned; she was always thrilled at the opportunity to get hands on with some magic.

"Grab that mixing jar from the shelf and set it on the floor by the door. Leave enough room to cast a circle around it."

Kay hurriedly did as she asked.

"Now, protect it. Quickly."

The edge in Sister Claudia's voice told her this was not going to be a fun lesson.

She grabbed the salt from the shelf and poured a protection circle around the jar. From the pocket of her bib overalls, she grabbed a piece of charcoal wrapped in parchment. She spit on the charcoal and focused her intention. She quickly drew the symbol of the stag inside the circle on the stone floor, channeling the protective energy of Lord Seanchara as she did. She considered her options. No blade handy, she spit in her hand and pressed it to the circle. The divine energy of creation flowed through her and responded to her will and the protective circle came to life.

Sister Claudia's voice behind her was deadly calm as she spoke. "That jar is the children you and Tren are rescuing from some traffickers. But if you think they are letting them go without a fight, you are sorely mistaken."

Sister Claudia dumped the bowl of stones on her desk she used for teaching rune carving.

"Shit." Kay said out loud as she dived to the left and spun to face Sister Claudia. The first small stone grazed the right side of her forehead before she got a shield in place. The clacking of stones hitting floor as they ricocheted off of her protection circle, told her that it was holding up to the barrage. Every time Kay tried to move back in front of the jar, Sister Claudia hurled another volley of stones at her.

Two more got past her shield and hit her. One on the shoulder, stinging her. The other grazed her cheek and drew blood from under her right eye. Sister Claudia stood behind the small wooden table holding various ingredient jars. Kay fell into her connection and the warding in place around Sister Claudia lit up in her vision. She was well guarded. Two more stones came rocketing at her. One from the pile in front of Claudia on the table and one from the floor next to the circle where it had fallen.

Now that she had her feet under her and was ready, Kay was able to deflect them. Several more stones flew out from the pile on the table. Some pounded against her protection circle, more flying at her face. Kay deflected all but one, and it stung her badly as it clipped her ear.

Claudia remained calm as she fired more stones her way. "Can you muster enough focus to maintain a protection circle with no components Kay?"

Stones whizzed back and forth across the room now. Sounding like a swarm of angry bees as they shot by Kay's head. A couple rang from the stone walls as Kay deflected them.

Kay's chest heaved from the exertion of trying to maintain her wards and deflect the stones. Her face and shoulders stung from the stones that slipped through and got her. "No, of course not. I get it."

Sister Claudia said nothing, but the stones kept flying. Kay looked for any way through Sister Claudia's wards. She was tired of getting hit with rocks, and she had gotten the point. Kay focused on her connection to the divine energy. Little lines of energy flowed out from her, surrounding the stones and forcing them to do her will.

No head-on attack would work against Sister Claudia; the witch was too powerful, her wards were strong, and the shielding around her was a wall of energy with no openings. But Kay was angry and tired of being treated like a child.

-She focused first on the stones lying on the floor around her, not being controlled by Sister Claudia. She commanded the divine energy to move the rock, to lift it and begin an orbit around her, like a tiny moon. She tried two more, and they easily fell in behind the first one. She found the other stones almost followed of their own volition; it took very little effort on her part to make them cooperate now that she had the first few going. In moments, all the rocks not being hurled at her by Sister Claudia were under her command. Swirling around her in various patterns and speeds. A spinning cyclone of small stones protecting her, shielding her from attack.

Kay tried to wrestle control of some of the stones from Sister Claudia. At first, she felt no opening, then an idea struck her. She used one of the stones surrounding her and sent it on a collision path with one of the stones whirring passed her toward the protection circle. As they made contact and it knocked Sister Claudia's stone off course, Kay felt the energy guiding the stone weaken just slightly and she used that moment to take control.

Knowing that Sister Claudia would be on to her trick she paused, taking three deep breaths, then sent all of her orbiting stones out at ounce. As each one collided with another she willed them to stay together, to join her stones on their journey.

And they listened.

Kay nearly jumped in excitement when she realized that every stone in the room was now under her command. One hundred and four stones whirled around her. She began to walk forward meaning to crash the stones into Sister Claudia's shield spell, in a big dramatic end to the exercise.

Sister Claudia was smiling at her and began to push back. Kay struggled to take two steps forward then Sister Claudia pushed her back again. This time she took several steps back before charging forward. Putting all of her strength and will into her movement.

She made it two more steps than before when Sister Claudia raised her arms, snapped her fingers on her right hand, and spoke a word that Kay could not hear over the clacking of the stones.

Every rock stopped where it was and fell directly to the stone floor.

Kay looked crestfallen at the stones littering the ground around her like a hive of dead insects. "Damn."

Sister Claudia pointed behind Kay.

She turned to see the glass jar smashed inside the protection circle.

"Your circle won't protect against your magic Kay. It sees you as an ally unless you tell it otherwise."

"Damn."

Kay said nothing else as she knelt to begin picking up the stones.

That was enough magic for her for one day.

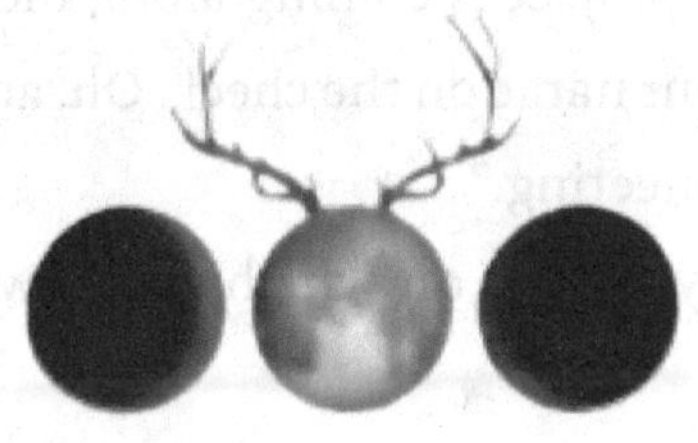

I Can Never Remember What Color That Fish Should Be

Gerardo was waiting in her office with a cup of coffee and a briefing from yet another committee when she arrived.

"You know, LaRhonda, you keep having on camera moments like that, you may end up at the big desk one day. Your approval ratings and social media engagement went through the roof."

"That's great Gerardo. Can any of that help me deal with Tweedle-dee and Tweedle-downright-dumb?"

She sipped the coffee and slid behind her desk to open the briefing. "Because it is ten in the morning and I have already been screamed at by Alabama Barbie and called a communist by a guy who can't spell it without his phone. Any word from home?"

"Yes Ma'am, the grant was approved for the statue of Former President Obama, word from his office is he is delighted that the statue of former First Lady Obama would be completed before his. He will be speaking at the next DNC, and that gives him more material to work with. The road project is coming along nicely, a lot of jobs and better streets with your name on the check. Oh, and a social work team reached out about a meeting."

"Sounds good, any details on which social workers or what they needed?"

She was already reading the briefing, and it took a moment to notice Gerardo had not answered. Annoyed, she looked up at him.

"Sorry Kelm, I wasn't clear, they reached out on behalf of Mother, she has called a conclave, and everyone is to return home for it."

"Clear my calendar, make the arrangements please Gerardo."

"Yes Ma'am."

Efficient as always, Gerardo was out of the room without another word. She could not ask for a better partner, a talented and effective Chief of Staff, and her consort since the age of fourteen when she awoke in Mercer. Born and raised in Cabrini-Green, she was orphaned at the age of ten, and just kind of existed. Bouncing back and forth between a couple of aunts and a great-grandma that was too far down the road to dementia to notice when she was or wasn't around. Until the night she came to Mercer. She didn't remember much, only trying to get to her great-grandma's house before it got dark. It didn't matter who said they were at the door, great-grandma did not answer her door after dark.

LaRhonda had been out with TJ and Demarcus, and a couple of other guys. One of them had stolen a joint from his older brother and she lost track of time. Stoned, they strayed a little further from the "Reds" where her great-grandma stayed, and she ducked down a path she normally wouldn't have used, because she didn't know it, and wasn't known on that block.

She remembered the fear, the running, as the group of men, or boys, she didn't know how old they were, only that there were too many for her to even think about fighting back. She remembered the initial pain of something hitting her in the back of the head. Then nothing, until she felt herself being carried. She managed to open one eye, trying to beg for someone to help her, to get them to put her down, let her go back to her grandma's apartment so she could eat dinner and go to sleep. She was so tired.

A man's voice in her ear. Thick with an accent she didn't recognize. Like those Marley records TJ's brother listened to, "Rest now, you will be home soon. You are safe."

As she faded from consciousness, she heard his voice again, this time to someone else. "Sister, the men?"

"The animals? The monsters? Those weren't men. Men don't do that to children."

"Sister?"

"Two of them are restrained and waiting for the police."

"The other four?"

"Will never hurt another child Hammond, and will serve as a warning to anyone else who thinks that might be a good idea. Let's get her to the apartment quickly. Lord Seanchara must be summoned."

A light knock brought LaRhonda from her memory, and she looked up to see the Representative from Mississippi, Harlan Rice, standing in her doorway.

"Representative Kelm, I hope you will forgive the unannounced visit. Do you have a moment?"

LaRhonda stood and waved him in. "Representative Rice, please, come in. Is there something I can help you with?"

Harlan Rice stepped completely into the room. LaRhonda had only ever seen him at a distance; they served on no committees together and did not travel in the same circles as a rule. Him being a Republican from one of the country's most conservative southern districts, her being a Democrat from Chicago's south side. But by all reports, he was a true southern gentleman, polite, intelligent, and self-aware. What he also was, was handsome. She could not help but notice the cut of his expensive suit, the haircut, the manicure. She took it all in at once. Then she opened up her sight, allowed the energy of creation to come into her vision as he crossed the room. She felt no threat from him at all, no malice, or hidden agenda. Just a warmth and kindness that radiated out from him like sunshine.

"Ma'am, please call me Harlan."

"Representative Rice, please be seated." She motioned to the chair across from her desk. She knew that by refusing to use first names with her colleagues or allowing them to use hers, she often came across as guarded at best, and probably downright bitchy most of the time. But she had found, even now, edging closer to fifty, given a little familiarity, most of the men she encountered reverted to condescension at some point or another. If she gave up Representative Kelm to someone, especially to a man in her field, she inevitably became honey or sweetheart or darlin', and that she could not tolerate.

"Thank you, Representative Kelm, I won't take up much of your time. I saw what happened in the Homeland Security finance meeting this morning. I want to say I was appalled. I know that sometimes you and I end up at cross purposes, but I would also like to think that its mostly because we represent vastly different constituencies. They have different priorities and so we must have different priorities."

She felt no deception from him at all. She also did not miss that he did not attempt to use her name, even after offering his. She wondered if her reputation preceded her, or if he was that observant and quick on his feet.

"But I have never felt, not even once, that you are anything less than a person of the utmost integrity and goodwill. Your passion for helping the less fortunate, specifically the women and children of our country, is evident in everything you do here."

He crossed his long legs, and she noticed the cartoon characters on his socks as he did. She hid her smile, but not by much.

"My point is what happened to you this morning, and really, every time you take the floor is ridiculous. I am ashamed to be associated with this group of folks. I really don't even know what to call them, and I don't really even know what they stand for or represent."

He held up his hands in frustration.

"Representative Rice, I truly believe the only thing they represent is disruption; they want to make our government appear as inefficient and dysfunctional as possible. For what reason, I cannot say. Especially with those two, I am not even sure what their ideology or political stance even is. They change, sometimes mid-argument, to keep the fight going. I am sorry, I did not even offer you something to drink. Can I get you something? We are well stocked in the main offices."

He held up his hands. She noticed he did not have on a wedding band, but the socks would indicate the kind of gift a child gives a parent for Christmas or Father's Day.

"No Ma'am, as I said, I do not want to take up much of your time. I want to put something on the table for you to consider, and please, if you would chew on it for a day or two. It may not taste great at first, but I hope that you will be able to see the benefit. I would like you and I to work together on a bill, a co-sponsored legislation, that would benefit both of our constituencies. I have a couple of ideas, but I am sure you do as well, and well, yours are likely better. I am thinking, education, women's services, early childhood, along those lines, we can work out the details."

He sat up a little straighter and leaned toward her desk. His big dark eyes never leaving hers.

"While I am personally angry about the way that these folks have been treating you. I represent a larger group of my party than you might think, that sees the way they are representing Christian Conservatives in this country and want that to end. We may not be able to primary them in these iron-clad districts they have gerrymandered, but we can isolate them and minimize their influence. I have it from a lot of folks that if we can come up with some really positive legislation that benefits everyone, they will jump on board quickly. They would like you and I to run point and be the faces of it."

He rose from his chair and held out his hand. LaRhonda rose and shook it. Saying nothing.

"I will take up no more of your time, Representative Kelm. Please consider, if you would. I am always available, just reach out or have your Chief of Staff get in contact."

He slid a business card out of his jacket pocket and laid it on the edge of her desk. "If you are comfortable reaching out directly, here is my number. I look forward to talking to you again."

Without another word or glance back, he was gone.

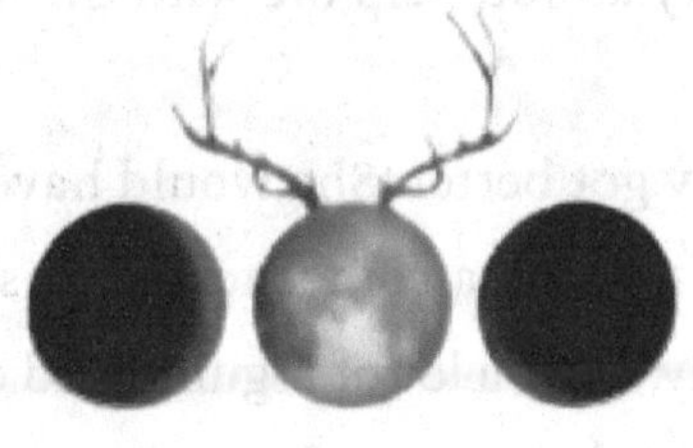

The Making

Jebediah Cavins sat alone at his kitchen table. The bottle of whiskey he bought two days ago, and a single glass sat in front of him. He had not opened it. Nor had he opened the pack of Camels sitting next to it that he had bought at the same time.

He had not had a drink, or a cigarette in five years, five years last Thursday to be precise. His wife Joanne had not made it to their sober anniversary. She had died eight days short of it.

You hear people say things like, "the cancer came on suddenly", not for his Joanne. He watched it creep up on her over the course of a year or so. They had been working this farm together for fifteen years. That's how he first noticed the signs. She went from tossing hay bales with him and manhandling the couple of dairy cows they kept, to barely being able to carry a grain bucket. In less than a year she went from a farm-strong, daughter of a rancher, to asking him to open pickle jars for her because she couldn't muster the strength. Add to that the constant exhaustion, and Jebediah knew there was something wrong. But she kept saying she would be fine. *"Just tired"*, she said over and over, nothing to worry about, help me with the feed and I will be fine after some rest.

But she never really got better. She would have days where it really seemed like she was making a comeback, then she would be back to barely moving. Finally, after a lot of arguing and even making a call to her little sister, a world class Karen if ever there was one, he convinced her to go talk to her doctor about it.

In hindsight, he thought she probably knew what they were going to say. Lung cancer, he didn't remember what it was called. But the word that he will never forget for as long as he lives; is Cachexia. A symptom of whatever kind of lung cancer she developed from years as a smoker. The wasting, muscle loss and weakness made it almost impossible for her to receive any kind of treatment. Chemo, radiation, surgery. She wasn't likely to survive any of them, and her cancer was far enough along that it wasn't likely even if she did, that there would be a positive outcome. Ultimately she decided that pain management and comfort were her best options.

It was a very hard year. Joanne was nothing if not tough. Even though she had opted not to fight with things that weren't likely to work, her will to live had never diminished. She worked the farm with him until she was no longer able to safely navigate the barns and paths. But it wasn't a big place, and though it was hard, he could manage it on his own. Even after she couldn't really walk on her own; there were still days she would have him prop her up in a nest of pillows and blankets on the passenger seat of the side-by-side. She would do crossword puzzles and scroll social media while he worked. She said it made her feel more alive to be out there and uncomfortable with him, than to lie around the house. They had tried to make love a couple of times in those last few months, but no matter how much she said she wanted to, her body just did not respond, and it was so obviously uncomfortable for her that he couldn't continue. The last time only led to them lying in the dark of their room. Her head on his chest, both of them silently crying as they marked off one more milestone of things that would never happen again.

Once, she offered to divorce him. She said it wasn't fair that his life had to waste away along with hers. She could move in with her sister or go to hospice. He could start his life over, without the weight of a dying wife around his neck.

It was one of the only times he was really angry with her. He knew that it was guilt and fear talking and not her heart. She didn't want him to abandon her, but he was still insulted she would even insinuate it.

Even if he would have entertained the idea it wouldn't have mattered. Joanne was gone long before the proceedings could have taken place. Jebediah walked into the living room one morning. Joanne had made a kind of nest in the corner of their large couch and often slept there. Jebediah watched from the corner of the room as she slept. Her chest barely rose with her breathing, and twice it stopped completely. *This is it.* He thought. *However long the end may take, this is the end.* As it turned out it took less than three weeks from that moment. He took to sleeping in the chair next to her couch. One night, at about two in the morning, he heard her gasp for breath. He shot bolt upright and rushed to her side. He was going to wake her but thought better of it. What did it really matter now? If it wasn't tonight it might be in the morning or even worse, while he was out doing chores around the house.

He grabbed one of the dining room chairs and moved it as close to her as he could. For the next two hours he sat, listening to her struggle to breathe. He had some of her pain meds close by and he crushed up two of the pills like the nurse had shown him. He had a tablespoon and some water there. If she cried out or acted like she was in pain at all he would mix the crushed pills in a little bit of water and spoon them into her mouth.

By the grace of God, it was never needed. Just before dawn, the love of his life took her last breath. Jebediah knelt beside the couch and prayed. When he could find no more words he called the funeral home and got Carl Williams on the line on the fourth ring. A brief conversation, the flip of a couple switches and the mechanisms of death, that they had put into place over the last few months all began to spin.

That was over a week ago now. The funeral was over, family and friends had all paid their respects and offered their quiet condolences. The refrigerator was packed with casseroles and desserts. Now here he sat, an unopened bottle of whiskey on the table next to a pack of his favorite cigarettes, and his Smith and Wesson M&P .40 in his lap. Originally, he bought the whiskey and the smokes, thinking with all he had been through, deserved a night of letting his demons take over. He had earned the right to a drink. The more he thought about it, he realized there was only two paths ahead of him; throw the booze and smokes away or open them. If he threw them away, he would continue on, work the farm until he couldn't anymore. Spend every day walking around this house filled with her ghosts and all the false hope that had become his life. Every room he walked into held some memory of her, some argument, some laughter, a meal, a moment of passion. He didn't see how he could go on like that. So, what then, get drunk, then he knew he would need to get drunk every night of his life from here until the end of it to keep her ghost at bay. He didn't want to live as a sad lonely alcoholic, but he knew that was what was coming if he opened that bottle.

This is what led him here. The last best option: he would open that bottle and that pack of cigarettes. He would get out all of Joanne's favorite records and he would spin every one of them tonight. He would drink, and smoke and spend the evening grieving his loss. Then he would write a letter to her sister, and his brother, their only surviving family, walk out to the barn, call 911 to report an emergency, hang up and put the barrel of his gun in his mouth and join his love on the other side. Nothing else made sense, nothing else seemed even close to the right option.

Jebediah reached for the bottle and peeled the plastic seal from the lid. Before he could pour his first drink a hand wrapped around his own and stood the bottle back on the table. Before he could turn to see who was in the house with him, he heard her voice in his ear.

"Jeb, this isn't the way. This isn't part of his plan."

That couldn't be, his Joanne was dead this was. He looked at the hand clasped over his own. He knew that hand as well as his own reflection. The nails were short and neat, the scar on the back of her first finger from their first time stretching barbed wire, the small birthmark on the knob of her wrist.

"Joanne, how?"

"By the grace of God Jeb, he heard your cries of pain, he saw into your heart and knew your plan and sent me to intervene. You must live Jebediah; God has work for you."

"But I don't want to live here without you, I cannot go on in this house, seeing you in every room, hearing you around every corner only to find the room empty when I get there."

"And you won't my love, this isn't the last stop for you. God needs you now to fulfill a different role, a war is coming. The evils of the world are amassing their armies and God needs warriors to fight in his name. Can you do that? Can you fight for what is right so we can be together for all eternity in heaven?"

"I, I don't know if I am strong enough. Joanne, I'm so sorry, I was weak, I was going to end it. I can't go on without you."

She wrapped her other arm around his shoulders and leaned her head against his.

"If you follow your path, his path, you won't have to."

Reverend Jim Meadows looked through the window in the door of the small cinder block room, deep in the basement of The Church of the Ascension. John Park lay on a stone pillar. His arms were crossed over his well-muscled naked chest. His breathing was deep and even. The room was dark except for a single source of light. At the head of the slab where John lay stood a Seraphim. A brilliant white light, streaked with gold and green emanated from its torso, where its heart would be. Tendrils of light enveloped John's head. The monstrous creature had its head bowed, its face blurred in and out of focus as it spoke in a voice Meadows did not know, from a mouth he could not see.

"Jebediah, you must follow the Lord's commands, it's time to take up your mantle as his warrior. Fight the enemies of our Lord, Jebediah and I will prepare our eternal home in heaven so that when you join me, we will live forever in his glory."

Meadows jumped at the woman's voice behind him, strong and firm. "Reverend, how goes the Ascension?"

He spun quickly away from the window; this was the last person he expected to encounter here in the crypts beneath this ancient chapel.

"Sister Wilcothe, forgive me, I did not expect to see you today. Had I known I would have met you upstairs where it is comfortable."

"Reverend, I did not ask about your expectations or offer my itinerary. I asked about the Ascension, how is our newest recruit? Have the Seraphim indicated whether they will join the Faithful Ascended or Malleus Dei?"

"All apologies Sister, from the sounds of things in the chamber, and given who he was when he came to us, I am guessing Malleus Dei."

"And who was he prior to his Ascension?"

"A consort of Mercer, Ma'am. Taken in a Malleus Dei attack on his witch."

The woman pushed past Meadows without regard for him and stared through the window for a moment before speaking. Meadows tried not to let the disrespect affect him. He was not someone who was used to being ordered around or intimidated. But this woman; she had shown him the way of The Ascension, given him the prayers and faith to summon the Seraphim, and everything she had prophesied in the name of the Lord had come to pass. She was as direct a conduit of God's power as he had ever seen.

She turned her fierce gaze on him, and he wilted a little more.

"Was the witch killed?"

"No Ma'am, the Carpenters and Al Bond leveled the home they were in, but the witch escaped through some kind of portal. Her consort stayed behind to guard the path presumably, giving her a chance to escape but he stood no chance against three members of Malleus Dei. They incapacitated him and brought him in. By all accounts he put up a serious fight, and I am sure he will be a great candidate for the Ascension."

Sister Wilcothe nodded along. The bun on the top of her head bobbing slightly as she did.

"Sister I do not understand the process, but this is the third day, and the Seraphim seem optimistic they will wake him soon."

"Good, trust in the Lord, trust his angels Reverend. When we reveal the Lord's plan in all its glory all the world will join us in praise. Now, I must return to my study. In fourteen days, I would like to meet with you and the other church leaders about some important matters. Please see to the details Reverend and we will convene at the ordained place and time. Thank you, and God bless."

"Of course, Sister Wilcothe. God bless."

Sister Wilcothe walked down the corridor toward the dead end and disappeared into the murky dark. There was nothing there as far as Meadows knew, just a stone wall with mural of Jesus on the cross surrounded by angels. He also knew that when it came to sister Wilcothe, it didn't matter if there was a wall or a door. She went where the lord directed her; the path was inconsequential to her.

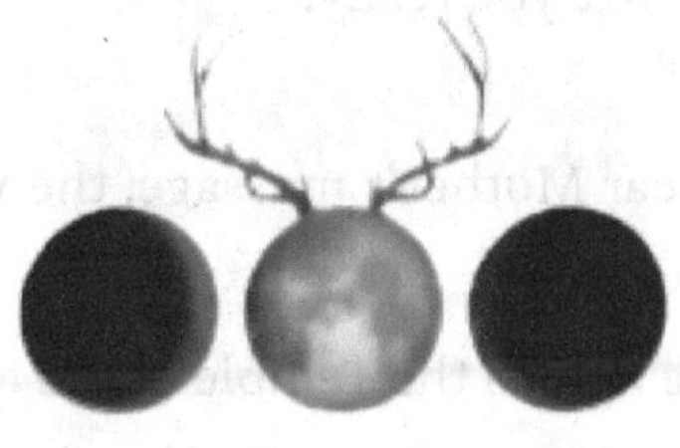

CONCLAVE

"Hannah, do you know how long it's been?"

"Not in my lifetime, Kay, maybe longer. This won't be everyone, but it will be most. Run on now and get us a table near the kitchen."

Kay nodded at Hannah, but before running off, she asked. "Not near the front?"

"Oh no, sister, children like us will take our rightful place near the back. Kay, Tren, listen now. You are both learning so much, and I am proud of you. But if ever there was a time to be seen and not heard, this is it. This is not only a gathering of the Elders, but of every witch and consort able to answer the call. There will be some very old and powerful sisters here tonight, many of whom haven't been in the presence of the rest of us in a very long time. Tonight is for learning. Kay, you, and Bets stick with me. Tren, find Fredrick, and stick to him like glue. If he sneezes, so do you. Do I make myself clear? Tonight is not the night to stand out from the crowd."

"Yes Ma'am." Both kids nodded and were gone in an agile cyclone of youth.

She turned to Bets "Are you ready?"

"I think so."

"Come on, let us hear Mother's message, then we can eat and celebrate our great family."

As they entered the Hall in the Temple of the Mother, the rumble of hundreds of voices nearly took Bets off of her feet. So many languages, so many connections. The room was a vast, complex web of connections in every color imaginable.

Kay waved from a table about midway to the back of the room. The massive hall was not completely full, but it was close. There had to be four or five hundred people in the hall, and Bets could not see any of the Elders or Mother Mercer.

Hannah led Bets back to the table where Kay was sitting with Polly, Dorthea, Hannah, two other sisters Bets did not recognize but were in deep conversation with Dorthea. She did not see the consorts anywhere.

Polly waved her over to an empty seat between her and Kay.

"Have you ever even imagined anything like this, Sis?"

Bets hugged her tight, holding on longer than she intended.

"Polly, I spent my entire life as a fantasy writer, and never once did I imagine a world like this existed."

She took her seat and within moments the doors at the head of the hall opened. Mother Mercer walked into the hall, followed by the entire council of Elders, which currently consisted of thirty witches. Although some witches were technically part of the council. Elder Alysse, Mama Rosie, Elder Valkyrie, and a couple of others—they were not as active in guiding the mission on a day-to-day basis. Although Bets saw all of them present today. They came and went as they saw fit and did not stay in Mercer teaching, as did most of the witches on the council.

As they stepped up onto the raised platform at the head of the hall, the room went dark as the chandeliers overhead blinked off. It only lasted a moment before torchlight erupted from the sconces placed every few feet along the walls.

Mother Mercer spoke, her voice amplified by a spell and the acoustics of the great hall.

"Hello Sisters, greetings and blessings to you all."

"Hello, Mother." Came the response.

"As many of you will remember, we have not called a full conclave of our sisters and brothers in more than one hundred and sixty years. The last time we all sat in this room as a family, was to discuss how best to aid the American President in his fight to end slavery in that country."

Heads nodded from the first few rows of tables. Bets turned to Polly and Dorthea, then shrugged. It only made sense that Mercer would have been involved in trying to end American slavery.

"We have brought you all here today, across many miles and great effort on your part, because we face a grave threat. I wanted to be sure that each and every one of you understood the threat to our great family, and the world at large. As well as get your input on how best to deal with it."

For more than two hours, Mother Mercer laid out the attacks by Malleus Dei, the group that appeared to be the militant arm of The Ascension, led by Jim Meadows and kept hidden by Meadows Ministries.

What they knew about the brothers known as The Carpenters, Leroy Lewis, and his abduction and apparent rebirth as Henry Bishop. What little was known about the monster that appeared at the church camp and took Leroy back.

After Mother and the Elders outlined what was known and what various groups and individuals were doing to protect the family, she surveyed the room.

"Sisters, we still do not know exactly what their goal is, only that at every turn they seem to be attacking members of our family with deadly effect. Their ranks seem to grow consistently because there are always new members that we discover or face, with a wide variety of abilities, and they still seem to be abducting young people with innate magical affinities."

"Mother, Elders." A woman in the front of the room rose to her feet. Bets had never seen her before.

Mother Mercer smiled at her as she did. "Sister Bethany, it is good to see you. It has been too long."

"Yes, Mother, it has. If this group is gathering numbers all the time, would it make sense for us to go on the offensive? Surely we can muster a force of sisters and brothers large enough and powerful enough to take this whole organization off the map."

She bowed her head and lowered herself into her chair with an elegant grace.

Hannah leaned over and whispered in Bets' ear. "Bethany is a daughter of Elder Alysse, very old, well respected among all the Elders."

Mother Mercer was nodding her head.

"Sisters, Sister Bethany is right. We have spoken at length about taking that very course of action. A full scale assault against Malleus Dei and the church leadership behind them.

Our hesitation comes from not knowing who among the congregations are involved and who are just faithful, and innocent bystanders. We also know that Jim Meadows has deep political ties, and his ministry is extremely wealthy and respected. An attack on them would likely bring more attention and scrutiny to Mercer. We cannot risk harming the innocent or exposing our brothers and sisters. We must find another way.

We must be diligent and precise, and we must maintain the integrity of our mission and mandate as we do.

Now, the consorts have prepared refreshments, and we have an evening of community and family to celebrate. Let us be thankful for the love and friendship that we have and rejoice in one another. I love you all."

The doors to the kitchen opened and the consorts, led by Fredrick and Eugene, poured out carrying trays of tea and coffee service and grazing boards of all kinds.

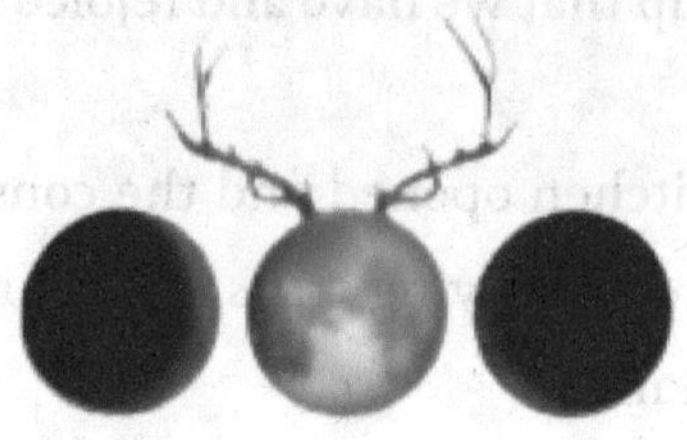

THE BLACK SHEEP OF AN OUTLAW FAMILY

LaRhonda was sitting at her desk in her apartment when the doorbell rang. Tonight, would be the third time in two weeks that she was meeting with Representative Rice about the bill they were working on. So far, "The Safe Women and Children Act" was coming along nicely. They found two senate partners in Rebecca Marsh and Ellen Bond. They had all met for lunch and frame worked everything, but the group had all agreed, better to have a focused vision. So, they left it to her and Harlan Rice to write up the details, then they would beach ball it afterward to make sure it would get passed by both houses.

She found she really liked working with Harlan Rice. He was smart and dedicated. Her initial impression of him, one of genuine compassion and goodwill, had been spot on. She had not picked up anything that had given her the slightest pause. In fact, the more time she spent around him, the more she learned about how deep the well of his heart was. And it was deep.

She made her way across the floor toward her front door. Pausing briefly to examine herself in the mirror. She wore a silk wrap in a deep blue and black pattern. She was barefoot, and the wrap hung down to the tops of her feet. Their first couple of meetings had been more formal, in his office or hers. But she had asked if they could meet here this evening. Maybe be a little more casual. She had been putting in a ton of hours at the office and just needed to be in her space. He agreed on the condition that she let him bring snacks. Besides, she had really come to like him and felt comfortable letting him into her space a little. She hoped that they could continue this work beyond what they were currently planning. She felt like a lot of people could benefit from a relationship like this.

LaRhonda opened the door to see Harlan standing there, tall and lean in a black t-shirt and tight jeans. She paused for a moment, noticing again his dark eyes and how they complemented his hair, black streaked with silver.

"Representative Kelm." He drawled the words out. He extended his free hand toward her, and she took it immediately. His grip was warm and firm, but not overly macho. There was no ego here, just respect and acknowledgment. She was suddenly overtaken with the urge to hear him say her name in his smooth Mississippi drawl. Something deep down in her wanted him to whisper in her ear. "LaRhonda."

"Representative Rice, come in, please. Welcome." She motioned to the bags in his left hand. She reached for them. "Can I help you with those?"

He stepped through the threshold, and LaRhonda felt another shift in the air. An electricity that hadn't been there before. He lifted his left hand toward her.

"Yes ma'am, if you would take that red bag on the top, it is for you—and maybe direct me to where you would like the food."

She took the large red bag from his hand carefully, so as not to dislodge the other one. He turned, seeing the mat next to the door, with her house shoes, sandals, and a pair of sneakers on it, and slid out of his loafers.

"Thank you for that." She nodded at the mat.

"Ma'am, I am not sure about your folks, but in my mama's house, if you walked in more than a step or two with your shoes on, you would find yourself uninvited pretty quickly. In fact, I can remember the local sheriff coming by to pick up my uncle Jimmy on a jumped bond warrant one time. She made both him and the deputy take off their shoes before she let them in to serve the warrant."

She smiled up at him. She couldn't help it. No, she did not want to help it. He was kind and charming and smart, and it felt good to be in the room with him. "A lot of criminal elements in your family, Representative?"

"Only on Mama's side. Daddy's side was all old hellfire and brimstone Pentecostal preachers. So, they were criminals who kept it hidden, not on Mama's side. They let their bad decisions hang out there for God and everyone to see."

She laughed so hard she snorted. She stopped laughing immediately, embarrassed. But he was red in the face and grinning ear to ear.

"Okay, follow me outlaw, let's get settled in here. I am starving." She led him to the dining room table. She put the red bag down and turned to help him with the other bag when she noticed the look on his face.

"Everything okay?" She reached for his food bags.

"Yes, ma'am, I do have a small favor to ask."

"Okay, shoot."

"I am not suggesting you not maintain your own boundaries, but I would consider it a personal favor if you would call me Harlan. I think I understand why you prefer to stick with your title, and I do not blame you. I know my co-workers, and if you give them an inch, most of them will take your wallet and car keys. But I sure would appreciate it if you would call me by my name."

She let her eyes linger on his, and her slender fingers brushed against his hand as she took the food bag from him, nodding her agreement.

The moment broke, and she began unpacking the food. Chicken curry, Chana Masala, rice, and fruit dishes. All from Delhi Deli down the street. All her favorites. "Okay, how did you guess this?"

"Oh no, I am not a psychic, I am, on the other hand, persuasive and have a seat on the board of the Baltimore Symphony Orchestra."

"Gerardo, that snake sold me out for an orchestra ticket?"

"No ma'am, he sold you out in exchange for two box seats. I wanted to make sure I got something you would actually like, and he really likes the orchestra, so it seemed to be a match made in heaven."

"Okay, let me grab some plates, oh, what's in the other bag then. She popped open the drawstrings on top of the large red bag. In it, she found a bottle of Jailer Corton Charlemagne Chardonnay, a bottle of Dominus Cabernet Sauvignon, and a bottle of non-alcoholic sparkling wine."

"Oh, Rep... Harlan, you shouldn't have. These are very good wines."

"I was hoping you liked them. The Dominus is one of my favorites on the rare occasion I have a glass. I thought it was only right to bring a gift."

"Well, thank you. It was incredibly thoughtful of you. Now, at the risk of breaking every culinary pairing rule. Would you join me for a glass with our food?"

"I would absolutely love one."

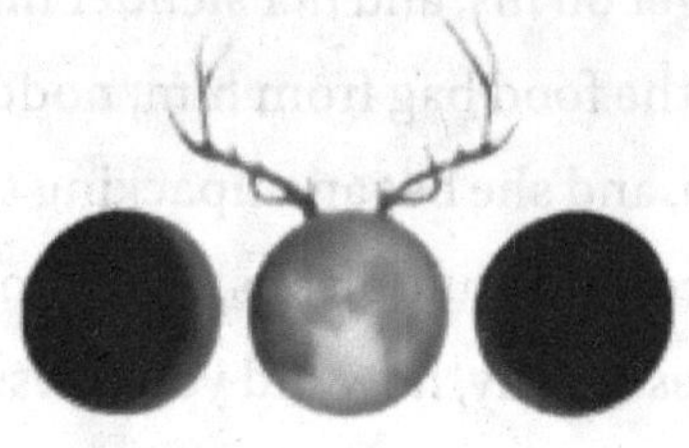

DON'T STOP

"**N**o way, you have got to be kidding me."

"Ma'am, I kid about a lot of things but kids, oh no. That's way too hard of work to joke about."

"You have twin fifteen year old daughters that live with you full time. How are you sane?"

"Well to be fair. They are fantastic kids, like I know every dad says that about his kids, but mine are really aces all around. And their mom is heavily involved; my house is just their full time residence. That way they didn't have to change schools."

"Oh good, kids need as many parents as they can get for sure."

"Do you have any family locally Representative Kelm."

They were well into the second bottle of wine now—and the food had all gone cold two hours before, along with any pretense of working on the bill.

"Okay, I will answer that, but first. I know you said you understood why I don't go by my first name with colleagues. If you promise you won't start calling me hon or sweetie. I would love for you to call me LaRhonda. In fact, I kind of feel like I can't answer you if you aren't."

"I do understand. Believe me, my limited southern charm aside. I am not unaware of what it must be like to get and maintain the respect of some of these folks.."

"Okay, thank you. Now, ask me again."

She surprised herself at how forceful she sounded with him. Even more surprising was the smile on his face as he did as she asked.

"LaRhonda, do you have any family local, anyone close by?"

She was right, she loved the way her name sounded rolling off his tongue. She felt her body flush from more than the wine. It was him; he was the electricity she felt in the air earlier. She knew that touching him was a huge misstep, a momentary pleasure, that could cause so many complications in an already complex life. But as if it had a will separate from her own, she saw her hand reach across the corner of the table and rest on his muscular forearm. She felt the hairs raise up to meet her and she fought the urge to run her manicured nails down the length of it. "Say it again."

"The question?" He raised his eyebrows at her. But he did not pull back or avert his gaze. He stared directly into her eyes.

"No, my name." This time she let her nails drag lightly across his skin. "Say it again."

"LaRhonda."

She closed her eyes letting the sound of her name carried on his voice wash over her.

The next hour was an exercise in will power for them both.

They stayed in physical contact almost every moment while they talked. She told him about being orphaned in Chicago, leaving out the part about the attack and her rescue by Sister Vivian and Hammond. But something about him made her want to tell him. She wanted him to know all of her secrets, her dreams, her pain, and she wanted to know his. Like she had never wanted anything before. It made no sense, she barely knew this man, but when he announced he should be heading out and excused himself to the restroom, her heart dropped a little in her chest.

She rose from the table and was gathering up the wine glasses and dishes when he approached from behind. Her ward tingled just slightly, not a threat, but she could tell he was intently focused on her. She turned and he was close, dangerously close. She looked up at him; he was easily six inches taller than her. He was close enough that she could not see his body below his chest without looking down. Blindly she moved her hand toward where she hoped his would be. *Stupid, stupid, you are too old for games like this, are you really going to reach for this man's hand?* But she was, no matter how much she admonished herself, it was happening. She didn't have to reach far. He caught her hand in his. She stopped breathing as he raised it to his lips, soft and pink and warm on the back of her hand. After planting several light kisses on the back of it, he held it flat against his cheek.

She realized he was putting the ball in her court. He made his feelings clear by kissing the back of her hand, now he was giving her the next move. Pull back, or pull him in.

A breath:

The feel of his stubble beneath her palm.

A breath:

His skin, so light against her own.

A breath:

The smell of his cologne, dark spices, and leather.

A breath:

His eyes locked on hers, not impatient, not demanding, just present.

She was lost, any semblance of control or concern she flew from her, as she pulled his face to hers. His lips were soft and tight against her own. His arms wrapped around her waist and pulled her into him. Now that the question in his eyes had been answered, he was back in the lead, and she was breathless for it. His lips brushed her earlobe and breathed her name into her neck.

"LaRhonda."

His teeth scraped lightly against the skin of her neck, and he kissed his way down her neck to her collarbone. She sighed into his ear, "Don't stop."

He didn't.

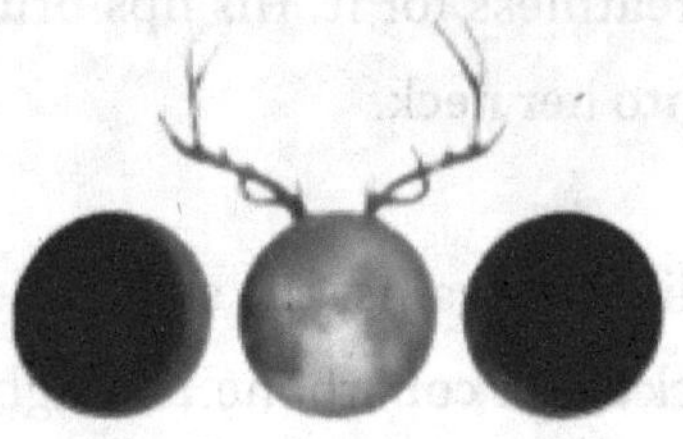

Biggun' Likes The Spuds

"Kay, grab those potatoes off the stove and get them drained please."

Bets spun around to grab the bread knife from the counter to cut up the sourdough she had cooling on the board. She would be damned if these weren't going to be the best steak sandwiches in the history of steak sandwiches. She was, after all, cooking for Polly and Sugar for the first time. Marinated ribeye, sous vie, then seared. Topped with Havarti cheese, grilled onions, and pub mustard on fresh sourdough. A little arugula salad and garlic mashed potatoes. She spun back toward the oven.

"Kay!" She yelled again as she grabbed the boiling pot of potatoes from the fire and headed to the sink.

She drained them out into the colander resting in the sink and went to look for her help, who had disappeared for the third time.

She was feeling a little impatient with Kay when she rounded the corner to the open back courtyard. The back patio and courtyard to the building where she and Kay shared a home were gorgeous this late in the evening. The sun was setting, and the whole courtyard was aglow with its soft orange light. Polly and Edward were off to her left at a picnic table, poring over some invention of Edward's.

Sugar and Tren were out in the courtyard. Both of them were shirtless and locked in a serious sparring session. They were training with escrima, and the clack of wood as they each attacked and defended was nearly constant. Bets scanned the courtyard. Off to her right, Kay was leaning on a pillar, almost hiding behind it, and watching the action unfold in the courtyard. Bets' shoulders relaxed, and she sighed as she realized Kay's reason for running off.

Watching Sugar and Tren fight was inspiring. Sugar was, of course, an absolute master. Big and strong, but as agile as a dancer. Tren seemed to be holding his own as well. In the couple of years she had known him, Tren had really grown into himself. He was tall for sixteen, over six feet. Slender and well-muscled, he moved with incredible grace and control for someone so young. Not like her, Steven, who was all knees and elbows and as clumsy as old drunk.

She smiled as she thought of Steven and Lilly; he would be eighteen this year, and Lilly would be fifteen like Kay. She missed them every day.

Thinking of Kay again reminded her of why she came out here in the first place. She was about to call Kay's name when Tren exploded into a flurry of attacks, drawing her attention. He jumped to the left. When Sugar swung to meet him where he would be, he jumped straight up into the air and spun back the other way. He attacked Sugar from above and the opposite side of where he was currently facing. Kay sucked in a breath and Bets glanced her way just in time to see her flinch, then sigh in relief, then glance toward Polly and Edward. When Bets returned to the action, it looked as if Sugar got his block up just in time.

Bets looked back to Kay, reassessing. Was Kay worried that Sugar was going to be hurt? She would have to keep an eye on things, but for now, she needed potatoes. She fell into her connection with Kay;

an iridescent pearl white cord of energy streaked with soft reds and purples. She pushed her intention down that connection. She could not really convey whole sentences or even thoughts this way- but she managed to push feelings and abstract ideas fairly well.

In this case, she surrounded Kay with all of the love she felt for her, and more than a fair bit of frustration. Kay spun immediately to face her, her eyes wide with shock. Bets felt her reaction flow across their connection. Guilt, pure and simple, guilt and...

Bets closed her eyes when she realized what the other feeling wracking Kay's mind and spirit was. Desire, Kay was crushing hard, and Bets did not think it was Tren that was inspiring these feelings in her.

Bets waved her over, "POTATOES," she mouthed as Kay approached. Kay's eyes went wide again, and she darted inside. Bets followed Kay into the kitchen.

Kay was busy mashing up potatoes in a big pot while roasted garlic, cream, and butter were heating gently in a bain-marie. She stiffened as Bets approached. She walked up behind and wrapped her arms around Kay's shoulders, pulling her tight against her in a hug. Kay craned her neck to look up at her.

"You're not mad?"

"Kay, what's to be mad about? You got distracted watching the guys sparring and forgot the potatoes. It's all good, sweetheart."

She kissed the top of her head, and Kay relaxed immediately. There had been some very real healing with the two of them living together. That part of each of them that was missing family had found it in one another.

"Now finish the potatoes and go set the table. I am going to open a bottle of wine and holler at everyone to come clean up."

"Okay, thank you, Bets. For everything."

"You are very welcome, Kay."

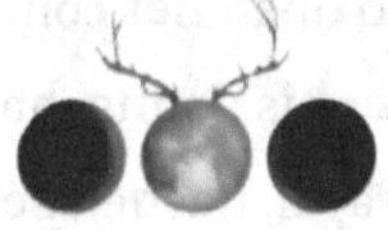

"Sugar, you need to stop hogging all the potatoes, damn it."

M slapped him on the arm playfully.

Edward giggled and chided him. "Big'un likes the spuds."

Sugar glanced around the table for help, and when none was forthcoming, he held his giant arms out to his sides.

"Do you see this bulk?" He winked at Kay and Tren. "Do you have any idea what kind of caloric intake it requires to keep this motor running? This is not a body that can be underfed and expected to perform at its highest level. Plus, these things are delicious. Bets, you really knocked it out of the park on everything, but these potatoes are fantastic."

"That's all, Kay. She made the potatoes; I handled everything else."

Sugar reached over and laid his giant hand on Kay's shoulder. "These are really good, Kay; you've really come a long way since that first breakfast you made for my birthday."

Kay blushed and beamed at Sugar. To get a compliment from a cook of his caliber would be great for anyone. But to Kay, who verily idolized Polly—and was very obviously crushing on him, he may as well have asked her to marry him. Bets couldn't help but smile at the interaction. She thought she might want to mention it to Polly, to let Sugar know, as he seemed oblivious to it. It would be best for him and Kay well for him to be clear and careful with the boundaries of their friendship.

It wasn't until she looked at Tren that she saw any real reason for concern. She did not need to open her connection to Tren to feel what he was feeling. It was all over his young, handsome face.

Jealousy, real visceral betrayal, flashed behind his eyes as he watched what should have been a sweet and wholesome interaction between Sugar and Kay. Sugar might not have noticed the way Kay looked at him, but Tren sure did. Bets looked around the table, and she saw that Polly and Edward both seemed to have picked up on what was happening. This needed to be squashed quickly. She fell into the connection binding her and Polly. She pushed her feelings of concern and love for Tren along that line, hoping that Polly would pick up on it.

Polly, of course, did not disappoint. She reached across the small wooden table and touched Tren on the arm. "Tren, would you pass me some more of that aioli? I just can't get enough of that stuff."

Tren seemed slightly surprised. He had been concentrating so hard on watching the conversation between Kay and Sugar that he seemed to have forgotten there was anyone else in the room. He looked at Polly's hand, lightly resting on his forearm, guilt and shame washed over him as he realized Polly could feel his emotions through that touch. She smiled sweetly at him and nodded toward the small dish of aioli.

"Oh, yes, Ma'am, sure."

Bets saw the flush creeping up his cheeks and decided to let him off the hook for now. *To be continued.* She thought then changed the subject at the table.

"Edward, what were you working on out there. Something new and exciting?" She knew full well what she had just unleashed upon the dinner party. But she thought the time spent listening to Edward might be good for all of them.

"Oh, Bets, Bets, Bets, you are going to love it."

Edward had developed a habit of saying her name three times, always in that cadence- "Bets," pause, then rapidly twice more. "Bets, Bets." It was odd but somehow endeared him to her even more.

"It is a variation of the shock ball I used in the maze the other day. That one had to make contact. You arm it, and hit someone, and it delivers the shock.

"Damn right it does." Sugar flinched as he said it. "Damn taser balls."

Edward's eyes went wide. "Taser Balls, that's a great name. Sugar, you need to start naming all my inventions."

There was not a hint of sarcasm in his voice.

"Anyway, like the Taser Ball, except this one doesn't have to make contact. It will send out what are basically these little lightning strikes. I arm the ball and throw it towards the bad guys, and it will basically zap as many of them as are in a ten-foot radius or so. Now the more there are the more diffuse the power. So, say there are four or five, it would be a hard shock, like a cattle prod or stun gun. But only one, it would be strong enough to bring down a rhino."

"Or a Sugar." Kay chided.

Sugar rolled his eyes and went back to his potatoes. Bets was glad he didn't re-engage with Kay. The last thing she needed was for Tren to act out and make everyone uncomfortable, or worse, make Kay feel like she was doing something wrong. Kay crushing on Sugar was completely natural and understandable. She was not only at the age where that sort of thing became inevitable, but Sugar had been around her and Tren almost every day for nearly a year, while he and Polly healed. Not to mention when Dorthea and Polly rescued her from Cordray. Sugar was there on that first night, helping to care for her and Lilly. She was certain, no little girl, in the history of traumatized little girls, has ever felt safer than knowing Sugar and Fredrick were nearby to protect them.

As a result, her admiration and familiarity becoming a crush was as natural a progression as one could ever expect. It also didn't hurt that Sugar was a literal giant, with the body of a superhero, and the voice of an angel.

But Tren would need to learn this lesson quickly; she would not stand for Kay to be made to feel like she was doing something wrong because of his insecurity. She would not let Tren's jealousy make Kay feel somehow flawed.

When she came back to herself, Edward was going on about the mechanisms and some of the more obscure applications of his latest marvel of engineering.

"What I am trying to devise now, what I was asking Ms. Wildes about, was how to supercharge it with the energy of creation. If I could find a way to increase the power by drawing in the divine energy as a source."

Bets leaned back in her chair as Sugar and the kids listened, seemingly enrapt by Edward's explanation. She looked at Polly, who was also studying Tren. She pushed her feelings toward her, down their connection. Polly smiled as she felt the warmth of Bets' gratitude and love wash over her.

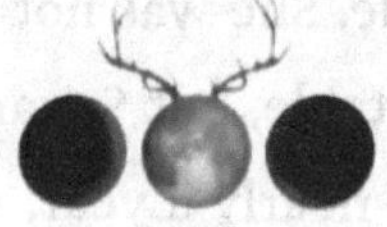

As the last of the chocolate bread pudding and caramel ice cream was being mopped up from the dessert bowls, Bets announced. "Okay, time to clean this mess up, but Kay and I cooked. So, Edward and Sugar could I ask you guys to tidy up a bit for me?"

Sugar and Edward both rose simultaneously. Trained warriors they may be, but neither one of them ever shied away from domestic chores when it was their turn. One more reason to love them both. She laid her hand on Tren's shoulder. Tren could you help Polly and I; we need to move the tables back in the courtyard? Kay, would you mind running the leftover potatoes, and the unused supplies back to the larder and drop them with Stasis or whoever is there?"

Kay leaned back and held her hands over her muscular stomach, moaning dramatically. "But Bets, I am so full. If I run I might explode."

"Then meander, mosey or crawl. I am not particular about your means of locomotion. I am particular about that pot of potatoes getting to the kitchen and properly refrigerated before it grows something we have to learn how to use in a binding spell."

"Yum!" Kay rubbed her stomach again, her sarcastic grin barely contained. "Mashed potato-cus" She waved her hand as she yelled it and the pot of potatoes levitated a full foot over the table before gently setting down again."

Polly raised her eyebrows. "Well done Sister. Now you better run or I will tell Sister Claudia that you said you were having trouble memorizing herb usage and growing seasons."

Kay's eyes went comically wide, and she pushed back in the chair until it overbalanced. Polly and Bets both reached for her at the same time but not only did the chair slowly lower itself onto it's back, but Kay gracefully rolled backward out of it. She was grinning like that cat that ate the canary as she picked up the chair and grabbed the potatoes on the way out the door.

Polly, Bets and Tren followed Kay out the back into the common courtyard. Tren seemed fine until Kay sprinted ahead with her load of leftovers. He turned to face the two Milburn sisters, who must have seemed about as friendly as a firing squad; given the crestfallen look on his face.

He took a couple steps back, obviously on the verge of panic. Bets held up her hand toward him. "Tren, relax. Everything is fine. But this is a conversation we have to have. Sit."

She pointed to a table on her left. Bets sat across from him and Polly on his side of the bench. Close enough for her bare arm to be within millimeters of his.

Tren was getting emotional, his eyes welling with tears. Bets took his hand; it was clammy and sweating. "Oh Tren, hey, you are not in any trouble. We just want to help you work through whatever it is you're feeling."

"I." He stammered on the words and Bets fell into her connection, pushing love and reassurance through it. She knew he could not feel it in the way that Polly or Kay could, but she was sure it would help calm him.

He breathed deep and tried again. "I didn't mean to act like that. But something happened, being out here, training with Sugar and seeing Kay watch us. Then I realized she was watching him. Then watching her inside, laughing and giggling at everything he said. I couldn't help it. I was so mad; at him, at her, at everyone. It's not fair. Kay is all I have in the world. She is my sister witch, and my only friend. I have no family, I didn't have any before, but now I have her. But seeing the way she looks at him, I know she would leave me behind in a moment for him."

Bets let him have his moment. But only a moment. She didn't like where this was headed. In fact, when she could, this was going to be a conversation for Dinah as well.

"Tren, you need to get your head around a couple things, okay?"

He stared at her, slightly nodding.

"You are Kay's consort. You role is to protect her in her mission at all times. Right?"

He stiffened. Some pride in his position coming through.

"Yes Ma'am."

"That's right. But now it seems to me, what she needs protecting from is you."

She hit that last word hard, and she felt Polly's energy shift into something a little more protective. Although Bets could not tell if she was feeling protective of her, or Tren. She pressed on regardless.

"It is one thing to love Kay, to protect her, to be her friend. But you do not own her, nor are you the only person in her life who cares for her or enjoys being around her. The same goes for you. We are all your family Tren, you are part of Mercer. More than that, you are family to me. I see you every day, you eat at my table, half the time you sleep on our patio in the hammock.

Are you telling me that is only because you have a crush on Kay? Or because I feel sorry for you. Because if you cannot tell from my tone, I don't really do pity with anyone."

"No Ma'am, you are family to me. All of you."

"That's right. But you being jealous, or acting like you have somehow been slighted because she is enjoying spending time with the people who love her, is unacceptable. It has no place in friendships, in family or in romantic relationships. You will find a way to work through it. I will go with you tomorrow to see the twins, and we will find you someone here in Mercer to talk to about how you are feeling and the best ways for you to work through your worries without—" She repeated it for emphasis. "Without, making it Kay's problem to deal with. I don't care if she asks Sugar to marry her. That is between the two of them unless, and only unless, the two of you are in a committed monogamous relationship, or Sugar is deemed a threat to her mission. Is that understood Tren?"

He stared down at the table and did not raise his eyes to meet hers. But Bets did not need Polly's gift to tell it wasn't because he was being dismissive or disrespectful. He was just embarrassed and confused.

"Tren, I love you; we all love you. You are our brother and one of our brave protectors. After watching you with Sugar today, we are all luckier for it. But you must be in control of your emotions. That doesn't mean bury them and pretend they don't exist until you blow. We will help you work through this, I promise. Now, please go help the guys finish cleaning up."

Tren rose from the bench, his head was still down, but his eyes were clear and he walked toward the back door.

Polly turned to Bets. "Holy crow sis. That was amazing. I thought you were going to coddle him, maybe explain why Kay and Sugar could never happen and he didn't need to worry about a crush. But that, that was a masterpiece in education. "

"Thank you. I mean, I was raising teenagers prior to this, so I had a bit of practice with silly teenage shit. But also, telling him all the reasons Kay and Sugar aren't romantically compatible only means he stops freaking out about Sugar. What happens when the next guy she takes a liking to is more age appropriate or isn't madly in love with a wildly beautiful witch."

Polly rolled her eyes at her little sister, but she nodded in agreement, nonetheless.

"Can you imagine the look on Sugar's face when Tren challenged him to a dual, or whatever it was he had in mind."

"Sis, I have been living with him since we were twelve. I don't have to imagine it. I also don't have to imagine the outcome if Tren stepped out of line with Kay in front of him. Sugar adores that girl, and even though he likes Tren. He would not hesitate to put him back in line, and once he starts he only knows one speed."

Bets shook her head at the thought, hopefully they can get him back to right and that particular nightmare would never come to pass.

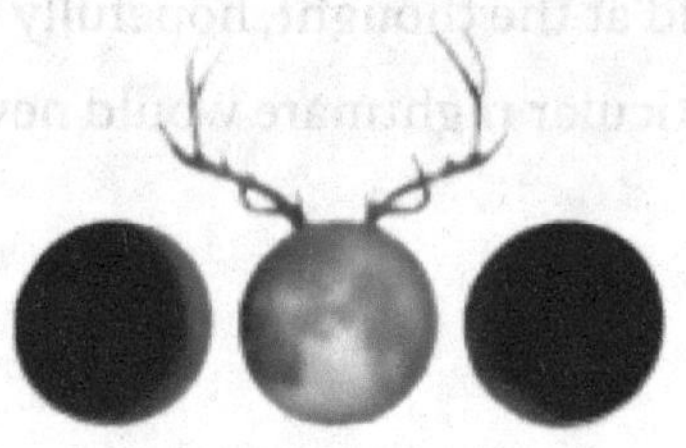

GOETH

Jim Meadows led the procession of pastors and ministers through the winding hallways beneath the Memphis chapel. He knew, although he did not understand how, these passages were not under Memphis strictly speaking. He had been at a prayer service in Texas when he first met her. He was praying after service in the Deacon's private office, on loan to him as a dressing room, when she appeared silently behind him. She led him through the utility closet of the church down a flight of stairs to the very chamber they were headed to now. He had met with her six times since then, always in this room, always accessible from wherever he was at the time.

Moses led them through a stout, iron, door from the clinical tile and cinder block halls beneath the chapel, to a beautiful but primitive looking stone tunnel. The walls were carved with faded reliefs.

He ignored the murmurs of a few of the church leaders trailing him. Only Tyus and Mary Ellen had ever met the enigmatic and intimidating Sister Wilcothe, and even then, only briefly. None of them had ever been down here to the chamber where she held council.

Moses disappeared around a corner, and he heard the heavy door creaking open and smelled the rush of stale air and frankincense.

He heard the quiet, stern voice of Sister Wilcothe. "Leading the Lord's children into the Holy Land brother Moses?"

"As you requested, Sister Wilcothe. Will you be requiring anything else?"

"No, thank you, Brother, may the Lord bless and keep you."

"You as well, Sister."

Meadows arched an eyebrow at Moses as he led the procession past him and into the room where Sister Wilcothe was seated at the center of a long wooden table. He was aware that Moses was the first of the Ascended, after Sister Wilcothe showed him how to summon the Seraphim, he was not aware of any further communication, or relationship.

He did not miss the fact that she sat in the single seat on one side, while twelve seats sat opposite her. There were two other people seated on the side opposite her.

They rose as the procession of ministers approached. Sister Wilcothe stood and waved her hand toward the unoccupied seats.

"Come in everyone, please be seated we don't have much time."

He had learned not to expect much in the way of pleasantries from her. Her personality and manners were as severe as her appearance. Meadows looked to the group behind him, expecting the confusion. To their credit, they stayed calm and shuffled to take their seats.

"Sister Wilcothe, would you like me to make the introductions?"

"No."

"Oh I'm..."

"I see no need for me to know who everyone is. The Lord has brought them to this table, and that is all that matters to me. Although moving forward, if the women who will be representing this church would show a little humility, it would save me the trouble of teaching it to them myself. I am old and not as patient as I once was with children who cannot be bothered to live according to his commandments."

She eyed Margarite Miller and Mary Ellen.

Meadows could not see any issue with how the women were dressed. Mary Ellen was wearing a dark blue pantsuit, and Margarite was dressed in a plaid, knee-length skirt, and a white cardigan. But looking at the women in contrast to Sister Wilcothe, with her plain brown blouse, grey skirt that Meadows knew reached to the tops of her New Balance sneakers. She wore no makeup or jewelry, and her brown hair was pulled into a bun so tight it looked like it might pull her hair from her scalp should she bump it on anything.

"Sister Wilcothe, who are our guests if you don't mind me asking?" He gestured at the two men sitting at the end of the table.

"Of course, this is Bryan Davis, and Michael Hedgpeth."

Both men raised a hand toward the group. As soon as he heard the name, Meadows recognized Bryan Davis, the slender black man in the gray blazer, as the chief of staff for the Speaker of the U.S. House of Representatives.

"They are here as liaisons from the United States Congress. There is a large faction in the government that hopes to see our vision come to fruition as soon as possible. Our Lord does not need the power structures of men to see his vision come to pass. But he uses all to his ends."

Bryan Davis spoke. "Reverend it is nice to meet you. We represent a group of conservative Christian politicians who understand the truth of the spiritual warfare being waged in this country—and are ready and willing to see this fight through to its glorious end. We believe that the adversary has infiltrated our government at the highest levels—and are working every day to expose them for who they are and weed them out."

Meadows shifted in his chair to look at the man.

"Are you saying the witches have infiltrated the government? There are..."

Bryan cut him off "Reverend, I am saying there are Mercer witches holding elected offices. In congress, as Governors, everywhere."

Judith spoke again, her harsh tone pulling everyone's attention back to her.

"Which is precisely why our work here is so important These monsters must be stopped. For too long they have corrupted God's plans for our world. The work of the Ascension must continue."

She turned to him. "Reverend Meadows, are we on schedule to reveal the Church of The Ascension?"

"Yes Sister."

"Good, how?"

"We have a large revival service scheduled under the Meadows Ministries banner. We are holding it in a suburb of St. Louis, Missouri. Attendance so far is estimated at seven thousand, plus the streaming should reach another eight to twelve thousand. All of the heads of the other ministries will be there, and their congregations are being informed of the live stream. We will announce the merger there. The legal team filed the status paperwork six months ago, and we have officially recognized as a single church entity for tax and legal purposes since then."

He waited for her to acknowledge any of what he said – or the hard work it represented on his part. She did neither.

"We will announce the church, as well as introduce the Faithful Ascended. There are currently eighty Faithful Ascended. After being introduced, they will begin the healing service. We have a special guests section up close the stage under the cameras. This is where the elderly and infirm will be brought. This way they can see the service from up close, and the world will see them both before and after."

"Always the showman, aren't you, Reverend?"

The disdain in Sister Wilcothe's voice.

"Respectfully, sister, my faith in God's plan and my showmanship have financed this entire endeavor."

"Proverbs 16:18 Reverend."

Her message was deadly clear. He took a breath; they had come too far and accomplished too much for his temper to jeopardize their work. Besides the fact that it was Sister Wilcothe who had shown him how to summon the Seraphim, and for what purpose. Not to mention, she apparently had a connection to Moses that he knew nothing about. That didn't sit well with him. *Could she have a connection with all of the Ascended that he knew nothing about?*

He wondered if her understanding of the Seraphim had allowed her to put in a way for her to communicate or control them. He shuddered at the thought of the whole of Malleus Dei and The Faithful Ascended turning on him at her command. While he was in charge of his ministry and the head of the Church of Ascension, none of that would matter if he found himself on the receiving end of a Carpenter's hammer.

He focused on the stone mantel behind Sister Wilcothe and continued.

"After the announcement, the other ministers will start extending the invitations to congregations all over the world to join under the umbrella of the church. The Faithful Ascended have a schedule of healings that will bring the world to attention. These will not be isolated events or church services. They will be going out into the world and healing the people where they need it the most. There will be no doubt of the Lord's miracles once they begin."

"And Malleus Dei?"

"They will continue their mission of fighting Mercer Witches wherever they find them."

"Good. Do not waiver. Hold fast to your faith, everyone. Our Lord will reveal his glory to the world soon, and he has mandated that you all be there when paradise comes to earth.

"Thank you, Sister."

"Please see yourselves out.

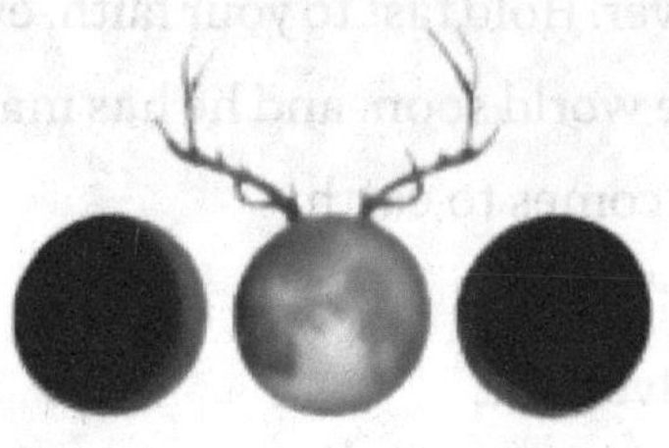

FILTHY DOG

"K ay, what's the rush?"

"Tren come on, we have to get up to the upper halls now."

"Why? What's so important?"

"I just overheard Claudia and Ashanti; Bets is going to run a gauntlet."

"Oh, holy crows, Kay! Let's go."

Tren bolted up the wide, carved gray stone steps toward the upper halls. His long legs taking the steps two at a time. Kay pushed herself, trying to keep up. Tren was taller than her by almost a head. Kay growled and pushed herself. She knew that Tren was her partner and consort, and they weren't in competition. He didn't even learn magic like she did. But she couldn't help herself. She hated how much better he was at the physical stuff than she was. She tried to remind herself her gifts take a lifetime to develop. Kay couldn't even legally drive yet, and some of the sisters here in Mercer were hundreds of years old. It's said that Mother Mercer, Elder Valkyrie, and Elder Alysse were more than a thousand years old.

Tren slowed suddenly as he was rounding a bend in the giant staircase. Kay sprinted to catch up to him, thinking he was wearing out. She almost slammed into him as she turned the corner around the central pillar.

"Tren what the…"

The words choked in her throat as she realized why Tren had stopped at the landing. He was standing face to face with Mother Mercer, Elder Dinah, and an older black woman that she had never seen before.

Mother Mercer reached out her hand to Tren, who took it gently in his own.

"Children, good morning. Come to see our sister Bets put her skills to the test?"

Kay and Tren both nodded.

"Kay, sister Bets holds a special place in your heart as you do in hers if I heard the story correctly. Is that true."

Kay bowed her head. "Yes, Mother Mercer, Colleen, Sister Bets, was, is, my best friends' mother. I was with her daughter, Marianne, on the night Cordray took my father."

"Chen Sal." Spat the woman Kay did not know. She did not understand the words, but their meaning transcended language.

Mother Mercer smiled up at the taller woman. "Then it is good that you are here. You can offer her your love and support as she faces his trial. And it will be good for you to see what may come for you one day. Now, children, let me introduce Elder Ezili Danto."

The woman adjusted her broad brimmed hat. The smooth, dark skin of her hand contrasted against the blue of the hat in a way that mesmerized Kay,. "It is good to meet you children. You may call me Mama Rosie, most everyone does."

"It is nice to meet you ma'am, my name is Kay Bryant, and this is Tren Praktavady."

Mother Mercer pulled Tren a little closer. "Tren if you don't mind, would you walk me to the bench at the railing so we can get a good seat? I do not want to miss this."

Tren and Mother Mercer led the way, her holding on to his arm as they did. Dinah was behind them, and Mama Rosie and Kay followed. Kay had to admit she was a little jealous of Tren. She would love to walk and talk with other Mercer like that. She had noticed that every time she saw Mother Mercer with a group, she always seemed to have the consorts close to her. Often escorting her or acting as a support. But she never seemed frail or like she couldn't get along without someone's help.

"Kay, how is your training going? Who is your mentor?"

Kay started a little at the sound of her name. She had been so focused on Mother Mercer and Tren that she forgot she wasn't alone for a moment.

"Claudia Giles, I think it is going well, Ma'am. I feel like I'm learning every day."

She eyed the fading bruises on Kay's face from the lesson with the stones.

"That is good, Sister Claudia isn't exactly known for her infinite patience."

"She is tough on me for sure, but she's never mean."

Mama Rosie smiled down at her. Kay resisted the instinct to shrink from the intensity of her gaze. Most of the Elders and Sisters she had met so far shared that same motherly kindness. It was a trait that Kay had just come to associate with Mercer magic. It wasn't that Mama Rosie didn't appear kind, but there was something in her eyes. Something almost predatory. It was unsettling; she didn't hide her power like some of the other Elders seemed to. Her power was all over her. It was etched in the lines of her face, in the dark of her eyes, the set of her shoulders.

Kay could not help but wonder what her actual name, Ezili Danto, meant. Who was she? She didn't seem very motherly at all. Fierce and confident. It made Kay think of the way Colleen was when she and Marianne were little. She was never all that nurturing, not like Kay's mom. But there was something about the way she walked into every room as if she owned it that resonated with Kay. This woman had that same power in her walk.

"Something on your mind, young sister?" Mama Rosie leaned closer as they walked.

"Yes Ma'am, nothing important really, I am just stacking the list of questions for Sister Claudia the next time I see her."

"Well, why don't you lay one on me, see if perhaps I can help answer something for you."

"Yes Ma'am, again it's nothing too important. I've noticed that every time I see Mother Mercer with a group, like this, or even larger. She seems to gravitate toward the consorts and always has whatever consorts are around escort her or stay close to her and talk with her."

"You are very right, Kay. Now before I answer, let me ask you. What is it that prompts you to ask? Are you jealous of the time she is spending with Tren?"

"Of Tren? No Ma'am. Not jealousy really, just curiosity. I mean, I would love to learn from all the Elders, especially Mother. But it was just an observation."

"I can promise you Kay, over your life here, you will learn from all the Elders. Perhaps not in a formal, sit down and take lessons, kind of learning. But you will learn. Now let me ask you, why would you think that Mother gravitates toward the consorts? Really think on it for a moment."

Kay slowed her breathing down and opened up her connection to the divine. She found that when she did this, answers seemed to come more readily for her. Sister Claudia told her no one was one hundred percent sure if it was because the answers were carried on the currents of divine energy waiting to be read. Or because falling into the connection caused more neurons to fire and allowed the witch to be more receptive to her knowledge and intuition. Either way the more open you became to the connection, the more likely you would be to get answers.

When she came back to herself and looked up at Mama Rosie, the woman had her eyebrows raised, clearly waiting for her answer.

"She's empowering them, isn't she? Some kind of spell work or warding. She is helping them in some way."

"Very good Sister. Mother is often imbuing them with spell work, warding, or funneling divine energy through them with intention. Our consorts learn many skills here, but without the ability to manipulate the divine energy, they are always at risk. Mother is bolstering their physical bodies as well as their protections."

Kay grinned at her own cleverness. *I got it!* She thought. *I can't wait to tell Sister Claudia I figured it out.*

"That is a big smile little witch. Care to share?"

"Oh yes Ma'am, sorry. I have been practicing falling into my connection when I am seeking answers. This is the first time that I did that and the answer to my question seemed to pop into my head. Fully formed, like someone had written it on a piece of paper and held it up in front of my eyes. Only inside my brain. I was grinning because I was excited to tell Sister Claudia. She was telling me that we never really understood if opening ourselves allowed us to receive the answer from the flow of divine energy, or if the flow of divine energy allowed us to find the answer within ourselves more easily."

"And what do you think now Kay? Did that experience change your thoughts on it?"

"To be honest, I hadn't really formed an opinion one way or the other. I wanted to get better at it, but in my mind, the result was the most important part. What I want to explore now, when I am ready of course, is if that answer came to me fully formed like that, because I was standing next to someone powerful who knew the answer. I am curious to see if I ponder a question while isolated, and while in proximity to someone who knows the answer, does that make a difference. Even more interesting is now that a connection has been formed, say between you and I, does that mean those answers will always travel that band even if we aren't standing next to each other?"

"That is a great question. Knowing what you know now about our magic, about how we develop and grow, what do you think would be the logical answer? If of course it aligns with how, we learn most other things."

Kay closed her eyes for a moment. She raised her hand to her face and pointed the tip of her left index finger at the center of her forehead. Her finger resting down the length of her nose. As if she was pointing at the answer in her brain. Mama Rosie almost laughed out loud at how powerfully intuitive this young witch was. She gave her just another moment, and when her eyes snapped open Mama Rosie could not help but laugh. Kay seemed not to notice.

"I think it's like everything else. The art in the temple bricks and the stones in the library. The tattoos. If it is like the rest of Mercer's magic, you cannot understand it until you can understand it. I think this is the same. It makes sense that I would have to ask a question and focus on finding the answer and that tiny answer would flow from you to me. But I will be there is a lot of information flowing between say you and Mother Mercer, or Mother Mercer and Elder Alysse or Elder Valkyrie."

Mama Rosie slid a long thin arm around Kay's shoulders and pulled her close. "Well done young sister. Now, let's go watch the gauntlet before I have to tell you the rest of my secrets."

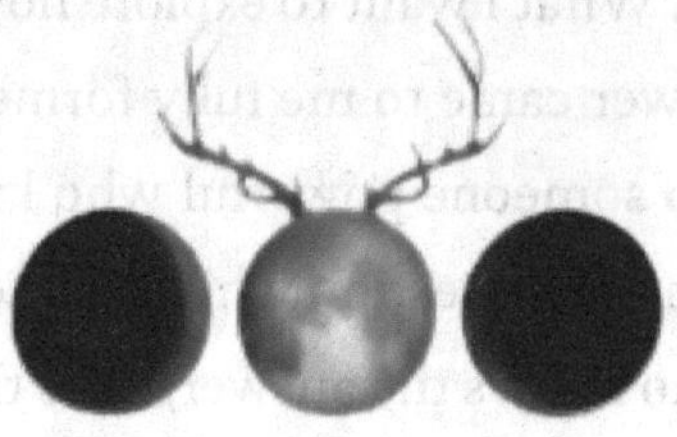

OF THINGS TO COME

Dinah knelt in the sand across from where Bets sat in meditation. Bets felt her come into the space. She felt everything in the space at that moment. She had been deep into her connection to the divine energy for more than two hours now. Feeling it move through her, informing and empowering her.

When she woke just before dawn this morning, she was gripped with anxiety. A feeling that had been so unfamiliar to her for most of her life that she still struggled with it. She had no idea what she would face today. Only that it served as a marker of sorts, an assessment of her growth and training to date. So here she had sat. She did not know exactly how long she had been here waiting, breathing, being. But she was as ready as she could get.

With the knowledge that her gifts and abilities were developing in a way that made her joining the mission in the field inevitable, Elder Dinah felt it was time to put her to the test. To see how adept she had become at the skills needed to engage the enemies of the innocent, where it was the most dangerous, face-to-face.

She did not open her eyes and acknowledge Elder Dinah; she didn't have to. She sent a greeting of admiration and respect vibrating across the connection of the divine energy between them. The brilliant band of white light as thick as Bets' forearm and streaked with jade and sapphire, the colors Bets had come to associate with her own energy, and the reds and oranges of Dinah's. She felt Dinah extend her love and concern toward her.

"It's almost time. I can't tell you much of what you're going to encounter in there. Only that you will be tested. Once the door opens you will need to navigate the gauntlet and make it to the exit.

Bets, not every test will be physical, there will be just as much aimed at breaking your emotional state as well. Know that every single person participating in the gauntlet, or observing, loves you, and wants you to succeed. But not a single person will take it easy on you. Because they want you to live—and going easy on you here will make your survival less likely when you join the mission."

Bets did not answer, she didn't need to. She continued to breathe in her connection allowing the power to flow through her every cell.

"There are many who have gathered on the observations decks to watch but you will not be able to see them through the glamour. Do not get distracted Bets, and do not hold back. All the combatants you will face are protected. You can hit them with everything you have, and they will survive it. It might hurt, but they are prepared for that. I am going to say that again. Do not hold back. They won't. I will see you on the other side sister."

Dinah rose and left Bets kneeling in the sand.

Bets felt the energy shift and the door to her left slid open revealing a short stone hallway leading to a sharp turn to the left. She could see the lanterns set into alcoves in the stone walls. She rose and began to shake the stiffness from her limbs. Her mind and spirit were as open as they could be. She released the steel baton from its hook on her hip. Took a deep breath and walked forward to meet her destiny.

The first twenty or so feet into the hallway felt like walking any other stone corridor in Mercer. It wasn't until she slipped quietly around the first corner that she felt the first tingle in her warding. A tingle that should have signaled someone was close by. It wasn't the alarm of a threat, just a twitch really. The corridor was widening as she walked along it. She considered sticking to one wall or the other, trying to be stealthy but she laughed it off. It wasn't like whoever was waiting wasn't expecting her. Still, it might not hurt to try and slip up on them before they knew she was there. That tingle again, not exactly a warning, just...

She barely got her hand up in defense as Eugene's first volley of attacks landed. His steel baton hit hers with such force that even the glancing strike rattled up her arm. She caught the twist of his body as he swept at her legs with a spinning low kick. She hopped back one step, but before she could reassess he planted the kicking right leg, continued the momentum of the spin, and launched a reverse kick that caught her under the ribs on her right side. She could not get a ward up in time to stop the kick but was able to push backward enough that it did not break her ribs when it landed. Eugene came forward. Bets knew she could not spend this kind of time on one opponent when there could be many more to come. She could also see by the look on Eugene's face; this was no longer the fatherly martial arts trainer with whom she had spent almost every morning and evening with. This was Eugene, the consort of Mercer, a weapon, razor sharp and eager for the blood of any who threatened his home or mission.

She pulled the energy of creation into her as she regained her footing, feigned a stumble backward toward the wall behind her, anticipating what was coming next. Feeling that little tingle intensify, she focused the gathered energy and launched it at the ground around Eugene's feet.

"Saldyta."

The ground at his feet froze locking him in place. At the same time, she swept her right hand, intercepting and redirecting the first three fireballs from Hannah as she stepped out from behind the glamour where she had been hiding, and attacked. Bets sent all three slamming into Eugene's chest, and he fell backward into the wall. His still frozen feet holding his legs in place while his unconscious body slumped over backward.

Hannah stalked toward her and Bets turned to face her head on. She had not expected Hannah to be one of the first people she encountered. She was powerful and had been involved in Bets' combat training since day one. Hannah starting slinging fireballs in rapid succession. Bets deflected them easily but after the third volley of half a dozen or so something felt off. Hannah knew Bets could easily deal with these. Hannah was the one who taught her how.

She has a surprise coming my way. She began not only deflecting Hannah's fireballs but also drawing a little bit of energy from each one. Using her power as a siphon she starting pulling the energy into herself. Not enough to stop them or dissipate them. She didn't want to alert Hannah to what she was doing, but just enough to add to her quickly growing power.

Bets fell deeper into her connection; she was no longer really seeing Hannah standing twenty or so feet away from her. She was seeing the space she occupied in the energy of creation. Her connections to the energy. She could also see that while she was flinging fireballs at her with her right hand, Hannah's left was at her side and Bets could see the buildup of energy there.

The warding in her mind came to life as Hannah started speaking.

"Bets, what did you do to Eugene."

Bets felt the tug at her mind, the pull of Hannah's magic as it searched for opening in the ward, a crack in the armor in order to get in and plant her poison.

"The gauntlet is over Bets, drop your warding and check on him dammit. Can't you see the holes in his chest? You've killed him. A consort of Mercer, who has survived decades in the fight, and you killed him with your ego and incompetence."

The entire time Hannah was speaking Bets could feel her words wash over her warding like a storm surge, all the while Hannah's fireballs were crashing into her physical warding. She could feel the pull of guilt over Eugene. *What if Hannah was right? What if I really killed Eugene?* The thoughts were so pervasive, so perfectly in sync with her own voice. *No, Dinah told her everyone was protected, no harm could be permanent.* That meant her warding was beginning to fail, she had to act.

The most difficult part of all of her training had not been the physical, or even the charms and spell work. Those almost came naturally to her. Way easier than she expected. For her, the hardest part had been the complex and multifaceted wards she had to learn just to function. In this moment alone, she was shielding herself from Hannah's fireball attacks with a physical ward. She was blocking her mind from the intrusion of Hannah's magical influence. She was also pouring focus and energy into a series of wards that kept her siphoning abilities in check. It was these wards that she allowed to drop now.

Bets pushed forward toward Hannah, her hands extended out, pulling all of the power she could from around Hannah and the chamber.

"Hannah, get the fuck out of my head."

Bets was becoming angry at the intrusion. The insinuation that her ego had caused her to kill Eugene. Hannah's fireballs now dissipated before they ever reached her or her wards. Bets was pulling all of the energy out of Hannah's attacks.

"Losing your temper Bets? That isn't going to help you finish the gauntlet, that's only going to prove everyone right about you."

Bets pulled Hannahs energy from her in great streams now, and at the same time used their connection to feed Hannahs influential magic back at her.

"Everyone Hannah? Even you?"

She could feel Hannah pulling back, trying to leave her mind as Bets expanded her reach, pulling more and more energy and ability from Hannah.

"You talk to me about ego, about what everyone thinks of me, yet here you are, hiding from your pain by tormenting me. If anyone killed Eugene today it was you. You sent him in first to distract me, knowing how dangerous I was, knowing my ego and incompetence. Then you gave me the ammo to kill him with."

Hannah slammed her with another volley of fireballs, but these came nowhere near her before dissipating and being absorbed into the wall of energy Bets had now built around her.

Bets was picking up speed now. Drawing more and more energy from Hannah and the room around her as she stalked forward. She could see the building of energy in Hannah's other hand, the one that wasn't hurling fireballs at her. She knew it was coming and she was ready.

Hannah unleashed a firestorm, a spinning wall of flame, like Hell's own tornado with her at its eye and spinning fiery death toward Bets.

Bets threw her head back and howled in defiance and fully unleashed her siphon. At once, all the light, flames and heat from Hannah's firestorm was gone. The corridor was black, and silent as the crypt. The air around Bets exploded in a wave of white and yellow light. Beams of it poured from her eyes and mouth as wave after wave of focused divine energy rolled from her and down the corridor. It pounded into the meager attempt at a ward Hannah had been able to construct from the small amount of the energy of creation she was able to wrestle back from Bets at the last moment. Unfortunately for her,, it wasn't anywhere near enough and she was quickly engulfed in the light of Bets' rage.

Bets was able to see Hannah as she both existed and did not exist in the same moment. Her body becoming incorporeal, as the divine energy of creation, under Bets' instruction, began to unmake Hannah Weems. A blink of darkness, a blur of something white in the glare of Bets' assault and Hannah was gone.

Bets shook her head to clear the residual power and refocus her intention. The power flowing through her was intoxicating. She felt like over the last couple of years training in Mercer, that she had made great progress. She took to learning with all the determination and focus that she had done everything else in her life. She had pulled off, what she thought at the time were some difficult, but rewarding spells. But nothing like this. She imagined that this must be what the Witch Father felt like as he created all things.

Brimming with power and confidence Bets rounded the corner in the corridor to see what challenge lay ahead.

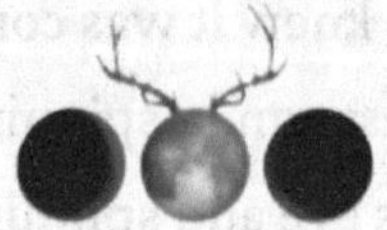

Elder Valkyrie laid Hannah Weems on the stone bench next to Eugene while Elder Dinah, Desma and Althea Lewis began the healing ritual.

"Dinah, I have to get back fast before the next contact. I am afraid our Sister Bets might put us all to the test today. A second later and no warding would have helped Sister Hannah."

"Of course, thank you Elder Valkyrie. We will be right here as we are needed."

Valkyrie began her decent back into the arena. It was her magic that was protecting the participants in the gauntlet from permanent danger. She had not expected the power that Bets had unleased. But she saw now she had to be on her guard. That was a serious attack. She almost took Hannah apart at the atomic level before she could intervene.

As she descended through the glamour into the arena she pondered. *So many things are changing. Every generation of witches grows more powerful, faster, than their predecessors. What Bets had just accomplished had taken sisters like Niri or Alysse a lifetime to master. Bets had learned it in only a couple years.* An impact that sounded like a car crash brought her back to the moment and she moved toward the sound to see what was unfolding.

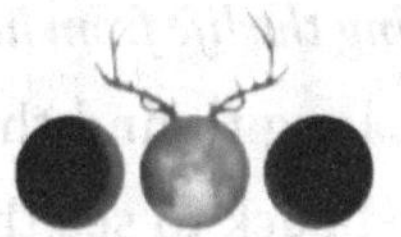

Bets felt her wards more distinctly this time. Whoever this was their attack was not hidden behind a wall of glamour. The danger was coming straight at her. The corridor ahead of her was about eight feet across but Bets could see by the flickering orange torch light that it widened out into another chamber just a few yards ahead of where she stood.

She crouched low and slid along the right wall of the corridor. Baton still in hand, and the energy of creation pouring through her every cell. As she neared the door to the corridor she heard a rhythmic pulsing. Something electrical, or hydraulic, she couldn't really tell. She extended her perception around the corner, trying to feel for whatever may be there. But she found nothing in return for her efforts. Just the steady pulse of machinery. She poured energy into her shield charm and ducked around the corner.

Of all the things she could have, or should have, expected; Edward the Fish riding atop a small locomotive engine was absolutely last on the list. He looked like a twisted version of Sir Topham Hat riding atop Thomas the Train. She nearly laughed until she realized he was barreling right at her and was not stopping. She got her baton in front of her and used it as a focal point for her shield charm just as the front end of the engine hit her. She felt herself being driven back, her feet finding no purchase on the smooth stone floor of the chamber. She did not know how far back the wall was or if she would be able to stop him once she had her back to it.

Would she be pinned? Would Edward stop when she hit the wall or would he plow right into her, crushing the life from her trapped body?

She didn't have to wait long to find the answer. Her wards were screaming, and she glanced back to see the wall was only a few feet away, she pushed harder against the train to no avail. She let him push her back another foot or two, only leaving about three feet between the front of the engine and her body when she jumped. Her feet landed on the lip of the cow catcher, and she launched herself up and onto the train, landing about twenty feet in front of where Edward sat. His eyes grew wide under the rim of top hat he wore. She was about to run toward him when a black streak sailed right at her head. She dropped prone to the top of the engine as two more black streaks followed behind it. The last in line landed on her forearm and she recognized it. A shining black beetle, about three inches long and two across. Its metallic legs clicking as it ran at her face, pinchers flexing.

Bets swatted the beetle off and jumped back to her feet, crouching low and looking around for wherever Charles and Malavika may be hiding. She stumbled back and almost fell from the front of the train as Edward reversed and turned before taking off again. Balancing herself on the cylinder as the machine picked up speed headed toward the wall on the opposite side of the chamber.

Shit, he's going to ram the wall with me up here.

She knew she would not be able to hold on if that happened and did not want to be tossed against the wall at speed. She didn't have much time to think, other than the seat where Edward sat behind some kind of control panel. There was nothing to grab on to. A perfect cylinder, resting on a shining rectangle of steel. It's sides extended down, almost covering the wheels. She saw no vulnerability, nor any handholds to climb closer to Edward. Three more black streaks flew toward her.

"Sorry Edward." She mouthed to him as she fell into her connection and found the magic powering Charles's scarab constructs. She waited until they were almost on her and then reached into the magic that Malavika had imbued them with. Fortunately for Bets, but quite unfortunately for Edward, Malavika was not actively controlling these constructs. She had given them instructions and sent them on their way. This made them vulnerable, and she took advantage of that vulnerability. Adding her own power to Malavika's spell and then redirecting it. Straight to Edward the Fish.

Two of the beetles landed on his face and one on his neck. They began their relentless chewing as soon as they did. Their tiny metallic legs digging into the flesh of Edward's face and neck as he screamed and tried to pull them off. Bets used the distraction and charged the seat where Edward was thrashing around trying to free himself from the gnawing of the scarabs. Edward saw her coming and reached for his belt. He tossed two golden orbs at her in rapid succession. The first one sailed past her as she ducked but the second hit her left shoulder in a crackle of electricity and her entire left arm went numb. She resumed her run up the cylinder as Edward managed to peel one of the scarabs off of his cheek. Taking with it a large chunk of flesh. Bets launched a kick at Edward's chest. He saw it coming but was too late to do anything to stop it as both of her boots hit him square in the chest and he went hurtling backward off of the engine. The last thing Bets saw of him was his crooked smile through the blood and gore on his face and his wild red hair spreading out around his head like a halo, as his top hat went tumbling. A flash of white just before he slammed to the ground, and Edward The Fish, was gone.

Bets slid into the seat of the engine as it barreled toward the chamber wall. She found two levers and two pedals. She pulled back on the right hand lever and stomped down on the left pedal. As she hoped, the engine slowed and veered to the right.

Now this will be fun. She thought as she turned the big machine around to try and find where Charles and Malvika were hiding.

She had only made it about twenty yards before the machine powered itself down and clanked to a stop. She hadn't felt an attack; it must have somehow been linked to Edward. It was right up his alley to put in a kill switch; in case he should be incapacitated. She hopped down from the seat and tried to get her bearings. There were three doors from the main chamber that she could see. The one she came in through, one to the right and one to the left. She found that her connection to the divine energy stopped just inside each door. Seeing no obvious way to determine which path led to her destination or if either actually did, she chose at random and headed down the left path.

The corridor was dark; a soft glow seemed to emanate from every-where and nowhere all at once. It was just enough light to navigate by, but not much else. As she moved through the corridor, Bets noticed the difference in the stone here since she had entered the gauntlet and what she had seen everywhere else in Mercer. There were no carvings anywhere here. No spell work or history etched into the living memory of the masonry. This was a bleak and lifeless place.

Bets saw the chamber opening before her. It was still dimly lit, and the visibility was almost nothing. Her steps were soft, and she slowed her movement. Extending her perception, she found she could only follow the energy of creation for a few feet around here. Something was blocking her from seeing the entire space. She moved right, staying close to the curving wall.

"Hello?"

The question came from a few feet away from her. From what she believed to be the center of the room.

"Bets is that you?"

It was Kay, they dragged her into this as either bait or a trap. Either way. She had a target now.

"Kay, keep talking baby, I'll find you."

"Please, I've been here in the dark for hours. I am tied to a chair I think. It sucks."

She walked toward the sound of her voice, concern for Kay, and anger at whoever decided to traumatize her for the sake of Bets' training overriding her initial caution."

She was twenty-five feet or so in from the wall when Kay came into the view in the murky darkness. Tied to a wooden chair, barefoot and looking only a little disheveled.

"I am here baby, are you hurt?"

Kay rolled her eyes in her perfect teenage way.

"No, just pissed. Sorry, mad. I was in bed reading a book when Sugar burst in the room and grabbed me. Didn't say anything, just dragged me here and tied me up and disappeared."

"Wait, Sugar? Sugar is here?"

"Yeah and he didn't seem happy; he didn't talk to me at all. I figured if they were using me as some kind of bait or something, like we would just hang out and wait for you, they would spring the trap and then we would all go have lunch or something. But like, he slammed me down, didn't say and word and then tied me up so tight my hands went numb. Can you untie me, I am sore and I have to pee really bad."

Bets reached again into the darkness with the energy of creation and felt nothing. But if Sugar was here that couldn't be good. Facing him made her more than a little anxious. And where was he, why hadn't he attacked yet?

"Hang tight another minute Kay. I don't know what they are planning but I am betting they will spring the trap as soon as I untie you. Let's shed some light on this first."

She focused the charm in her mind and released it with a breath. "Nur Alhayaa."

The chamber lit up and Bets felt her stomach drop. Stalking toward her, from behind Kay and to either side were the last two men on earth Bets wanted to fight. Sugar was crouched low, empty handed, but as deadly as if he was carrying a nuclear bomb. To the right Fredrick Sapp, as elegant as a dancer, armed with two short batons, glided toward her in the now glaring light.

Bets immediately backed up and began searching for options. *So, this is it, not some grand magical battle, but a fist fight with two deadly giants.*

"Alright boys, you sure this is how you want this to go?"

Neither man spoke, nor showed any facial expression as they stalked her. She had trained with Sugar, she knew roughly how he approached a fight. But she had never seen Fredrick in training or combat. She knew only that he was considered one of the few of Mercer's consorts who rivaled Sugar in his training and experience in a fight, and that both men had fought together before. She could think of no way to exploit their lack of coordination. Use one's movements against the other.

A light bulb moment hit her as the answer presented itself. Now she just needed to pull it off.

Bets took three steps back and pulled in all the energy she could at that moment. The timing on this would be the tricky part, and depended on her being able to anticipate the opening gambits of two very dangerous men.

She crouched low and circled in Sugar's direction, pouring energy into her shield charm. Sugar leapt the last ten feet toward her, rolled to the right, and came to his feet slightly to her left side and launched a series of quick punches at her. She reacted exactly the way she had been taught. She used her speed and agility to get out of his range. He stepped in closer, launching strike after strike. She deflected two quick jabs with her baton, and using a repulsion charm, pushed him back. She knew that sooner or later he would get a blow through her defense, and with his size and strength, it was unlikely she would stay conscious or alive when it happened.

But she didn't plan on fighting Sugar hand to hand, that was a losing battle. She could feel Fredrick slipping up behind her, as silent as he was he could not hide the ripple he left moving through the energy of creation. Sugar came on even harder, driving her backward, obviously thinking she was solely focused on him and looking to drive her backward into Fredrick's attack. She let him. Bets shuffled back a few more feet, spun toward Fredrick, who was reaching toward her, arms out to restrain her, brought her fingers to her lips, blew him a kiss, and whispered, "Shihai."

What normally would have been a simple charm of influence over another, when powered by the energy Bets had siphoned from Hannah's mind invasion earlier, became total control over Fredrick's mind. She had issued only one command on that blown kiss. "PROTECT." Fredrick's mind was consumed by one thought only, protect Bets at all costs.

Sugar paused in his attack, momentarily confused by Bets seemingly blowing Fredrick a kiss. His confusion became focus as he charged in.

Bets stood to the side catching her breath for a moment and marveling at the scene before her. She trained hard, and she felt confident in her physical abilities in a fight. But this, this was something different.

Fredrick spun to his left looking to flank Sugar, who easily anticipated the move, but was caught off guard when Fredrick halted the spin and launched into a series of teep kicks that came on fast. These were not meant to do damage, only create distance between the two as Fredrick set up his next attack. Sugar did his own shuffle backward now, bouncing easily on the balls of his feet and stayed ahead of the kicks. Fredrick launched a last kick straight at Sugar's midsection and when Sugar stepped easily back from its range Fredrick launched himself forward. He dropped to one knee and spun, using the momentum of the spin he cracked a baton hard against Sugar's shin.

Sugar showed no pain, but he was no longer just playing defense. When Fredrick spun again, this time the baton aiming high, Sugar jumped in close, grabbed Fredrick by the lapels and threw him off to the side. Fredrick landed as gracefully as Bets thought was possible given the situation and came on again. The batons spun in a blur as Fredrick launched into a series of strikes, all aimed at Sugar's head and torso. Sugar, with no weapons, had only his forearms, hardened by years of conditioning to block with. He took three or four blows to each forearm before he threw a hard teep of his own. Just before it landed Fredrick got a baton strike through Sugar's guard the weighted steel end of it landing below Sugar's right eye. Fredrick flew backward from the power of Sugar's kick but the baton striking Sugar's cheek made a sickening crack.

Bets winced, she knew they would be okay, but she loved these men. She had to rescue Kay while she had the chance, she turned to untie Kay but to her shock the chair was empty, the cords binding Kay to it were lying in a pile on the floor. She only had a moment to be confused before the pain set in.

Her arms were yanked violently out to the sides and up. Piercing pain shot through her hands and feet as her legs snapped together and she was lifted from the ground. She screamed in agony as she felt her scalp pierced and her stomach burned as if it was being ripped open.

She heard Dorthea's voice behind her. "Ta vasana tou Stavrou, Ta vasana tou Stavrou, Ta vasana tou Stavrou."

She struggled to focus her vision through the pain, to see anything, to think of anything other than the suffering as her body endured the pain of the crucifixion. Through the blur of agony, she saw Kay approaching, then Kay passed through some field of distortion and her sister Polly was standing before. She grabbed Bets by the throat and squeezed.

"Release him, now," she hissed through gritted teeth.

Bets was struggling to stay conscious, she wanted to show some defiance, to fight back, to win. But the pain was too much and the betrayal she felt at her sister and Dorthea causing that pain was more than she could bear. "Sleep." She whispered to Fredrick through the connection of her spell. Then her world went black.

Nothing Broken

Bets could feel the hand on her forehead. She was reminded of when she was a little girl and her mother would touch her head to see if she was feverish. She was so warm, so comfortable. She didn't know where she was or who was checking her fever, but she felt so safe here, somehow she knew that when she opened her eyes, there was pain waiting for her.

The pain of defeat. She failed her gauntlet. She had been caught and beaten by Dorthea and Polly, she had made it so far, yet she had still failed. What did that mean? A life here in Mercer, helping the twins? Researching in the vast library, cooking for the other witches as they went about their mission? Would she be allowed to try again?

She didn't want to open her eyes, she wanted to scream, to cry. She wanted to prove she still had worth, had value.

"Bets, sister, are you awake? How are you feeling?"

She took a deep breath but did not open her eyes. "Like I failed a test. Like I want to crawl under a blanket and eat junk food until I fall back to sleep."

Hannah's voice in her ear. Very close and whispering. "Well considering the crowd in this room, that might be awkward for us, love."

Bets set up and opened her eyes. The sight that greeted her made her even more embarrassed. Had everyone come to witness her failure? She was sitting on a stone bed, with a thick, soft pad. Hannah and Polly both stood next to her. It had been Polly's hand on her forehead. Hannah rubbed her hand on Bet's back, like a mother soothing a child. Dinah, Dorthea, Kay, Mother Mercer, Elder Valkyrie, Desma, and Althea were all crowded into the small room. She looked up at Polly, who stroked her cheek and mouthed, "I'm sorry."

Bets was fighting back tears. "Hannah, Dinah, I am so sorry, I failed. I tried, but I couldn't..."

Mother Mercer barked out a laugh. "Oh, Sister Bets, you think that was failure. You bested two of your mentors in even combat, nearly unmaking Hannah. You defeated your own consort soundly, and you survived an encounter with two of the most dangerous men to have ever walked among the brothers here. The only reason you were bested is you did not see through your sister's glamour in time to notice Dorthea before she caught you in one of the most painful and complex bindings we know."

Hannah continued rubbing her back.

"Bets, the gauntlet isn't pass or fail, it isn't all or nothing, it is an assessment. A way for us to truly gauge your ability and thinking under pressure. You have exceeded everyone's wildest expectations. The people in this room are here first to congratulate you, and to make sure you are whole again from your experience. If there was more room, there would be double the number of people here. As it is, there is only so much space and the people closest to you and the Elders took priority. But now that you are awake, we will give you a moment with your family, and we will all be waiting to celebrate your achievements and talk about the next steps when you are ready. I know the consorts are waiting to show their love and respect as well. I believe Stasis and Alpine have something waiting for us in the Temple. You need food and grounding, Sister. Come everyone. Let us give these sisters their space."

One by one, everyone filed out, Hannah leaned over and kissed her gently on the side of the head. "I am proud of you. You did well today." She followed Elder Valkyrie out the door. Only the Milburn family was left in the small chamber. Polly hugged her tighter as Dorthea approached.

"Bets, are you okay?"

"Yes, Ma'am, I am sore and feel kind of hollowed out. But there doesn't seem to be any lasting damage. What was that binding you used on me?"

"It was called The Crucifix Binding. It is a brutal and powerful spell. Simple to cast, very difficult to maintain even for a few moments. And of course, you felt its effectiveness. I am sorry, Bets."

"Why would you be sorry. Your job was to stop me, and you did. It isn't your fault that I didn't anticipate you and Polly hiding behind a glamour as soon as I saw the guys. Oh, the guys, speaking of, are they okay?"

"They will be, they were a little bruised up from the fight but nothing serious and neither wanted any medical. They insisted on the twins focusing on you. You lost a lot of blood from the intensity of the casting. The binding inflicts the stigmata on the target. But that is what I am sorry about. I should have never used that on you."

"Dorthea, please..."

Dorthea held up her hand in a way that told Bets she needed to say what she came to say.

"Bets, you had no way of knowing this. But my first consort was a man named Islam Medogiav. He and I were very much in love. I thought I would have him for the rest of my long life, fighting, loving and just being by my side. Instead, one day, something took over his mind. We never determined what it was. But he became dangerous, under the control of something dark and evil. I, I, I was forced to stop him myself in order to keep him from killing innocents. I thought I had healed, and had a better handle on my grief, and perhaps I did. Until I saw Fredrick, under your control and attacking Sugar, knowing that eventually one of them would get seriously hurt, or worse. Fredrick had no control other than your command, and Sugar is often on a razor's edge of violence."

She flashed an apologetic look at Polly, who merely nodded. There was no sense in getting offended over a well-known truth, when there was no offense meant. Dorthea slid her round eyeglasses to the top of her head, letting them rest upon her close cropped grey hair.

"When I realized what you had done, I lost my cool. Seeing Fredrick like that just brought back all the pain and guilt of losing Islam. There were a dozen ways I could have slowed you down without the pain."

"Well now you're just bragging."

Dorthea blinked slowly, her mind resetting as Bets' joke set in.

"You know what I mean, now don't be a brat and let me finish apologizing."

"Dorthea, I mean it. There is nothing to be sorry about. I am assuming you were told, just like I was, not to hold back. That ultimately, no permanent harm could come to anyone involved. And you didn't. I tell you right now, I learned more from the mistakes that led me to being caught in that binding than in the last six months combined. About myself, about the true nature of magical combat, and about you."

"What do you mean?"

"The very first day I was awake here, my first few hours in Mercer, I met Fredrick and Sugar and had dinner with them, Desma and Althea."

"I remember. We were both furious they got to see you first."

"I had just learned that Polly was alive and that you even existed. I mean, I knew my mom had an older sister who died in childhood.

But that was it. But when your name mentioned, the reverence that Fredrick and Sugar and the twins spoke with was inspiring. Everywhere I have gone, everyone I have spoken with, when they learn who I am, they all seem to have a story about one or both of you and the great good you have done, the innocents you have saved. I have been training with Polly for the last few months while she healed and prepared to go home permanently. But you, I have never seen you in action until today.

In my arrogance, I had begun to believe I had learned all there was for someone else to teach me, that I was ready to strike out on my own and learn as I went. Now, now I see there is a whole other dimension to our world. When no one else had even slowed me down, you stopped me without even a struggle. It was good to be reminded how much more I have to learn."

"Bets, you are amazing, and you are only going to get better. That being said, I am glad to hear that you are ready to learn some more."

Bets raised an eyebrow, hoping that this was leading up to something she could take on after a good night's sleep.

"Fredrick and I are on the trail of someone or something leaving a mountain of bodies behind it. It's tied to the monster that killed Kay's dad, or at least we think. We need another set of hands, and since my usual partners in crime are still officially benched until further notice. I wonder if you and Edward the Fish would be interested in coming out with us and assisting."

"Is that allowed? I mean, do the Elders need to sign off on it or something?"

"What did you think the gauntlet was for?" Dorthea patted her on the leg and straightened. "Now get dressed and make yourself presentable, if I am guessing right, you have a bunch of folks right outside that door waiting to tell you how wonderful you are."

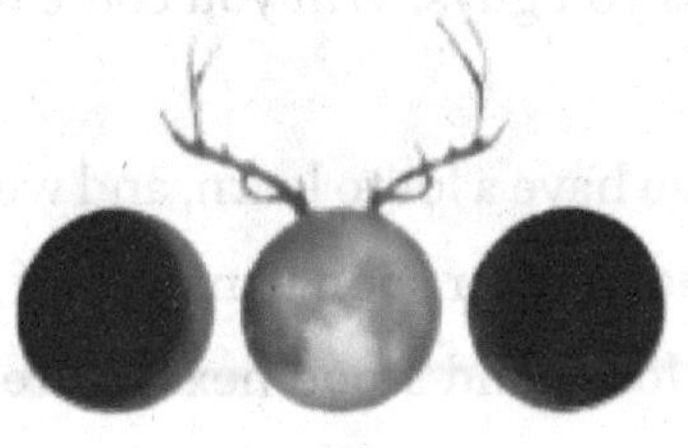

HOME

"I can't believe it's time."

M hugged Bets close.

"To be honest Sis, being here with you, and Kay has been just as healing as any of the magic, or medicine. I am going to miss you so much."

She kissed Bets on the top of the head and held her other arm out to Kay. She did not hesitate. Kay wrapped her arms around both of the sisters, as she fought back tears.

Sugar, Edward the Fish, and Tren stood off to the side, waiting their turns to say goodbye. The three finally separated. Bets held her arms out to Sugar, who swept her up in hug worthy of the giant he was. M smiled at Edward who blushed and gave a brisk bow.

After Bets was deposited back on the ground Sugar threw a giant white arm around Kay and the other around Tren.

"You guys please take good care of Edward and Bets?"

Tren looked up at him. "Yes sir," He extricated himself from Sugar's grasp and Kay took the opportunity to wrap both of her arms around Sugar and lay her head on his chest.

"I am going to miss you guys. Will you come back soon? I don't like this Sugar."

"I know Kay, but you have a lot to learn, and we have a mission to get back to. We will see each other soon I am sure of it."

Kay pulled herself loose and stood next to Tren, leaning on him for support.

Lord Seanchara stood a few feet away at the door to the library janitor's closet. "Are we all healed and ready to return to the fight?"

Sugar and M both bowed their heads. M spoke. "Yes Lord Seanchara, we are honored to have you open a doorway for us. We are ready to return to the mission. But first we have a home to rebuild."

"Then let us linger no longer. It's my pleasure to see you home. The doorway will open in the basement of your shop. Good luck to you both. Witch Father guide you on your mission."

Sugar bowed his head reverently. "Thank you Lord Seanchara."

They stepped to the open door of the closet, seeing only the small supply room through the doorway. Sugar paused and M reached up and touched the center of his forehead. A charm to help him seal his mind against the distance he was about to travel. He closed his eyes and M took his hand, and they stepped through the door.

Traveling that great a distance while aware would be catastrophic to the mind. As a result, the witch and consort have to seal off their mind from all external input for one brief moment. Because of this, if they don't step through into safety, they are vulnerable until they open their awareness again.

M opened her eyes, she knew without thinking they were not alone. They had been gone from their home from over a year; but that meant nothing. M and Sugar may not have laid the bricks of the foundation, or hammered the tresses into place, but they built this place.

Sugar must have felt it as well, and for a moment he crouched low, scanning the dark basement. She extended her perception, reading the energy of creation. It only took a moment for her to recognize them through the energy. She put a hand on Sugar's massive shoulder.

"It's all good, baby."

He relaxed and gave her a questioning look. His eyebrow arched like a cartoon villain.

"Come on, they are upstairs waiting for us. Looks like we have a welcome home party."

M did not know what to expect as she rounded the top of the basement stairs. She could feel Dorthea and Fredrick, Beck, Snow, Devlin and the twins, Desma and Althea. She knew that today would be a roller coaster of emotions. The last time they were here. Diana The Triformis had nearly gutted her and burned her insides so badly it took months to heal. She had captured and tortured Sugar for hours before M got here.

All of that had been horrible, beyond that, she had cut her off from the energy of creation. M could not feel her connection to the divine while under that spell. She could not remember anything so terrifying. Even when she thought Sugar was dead, her only thoughts were, save him, avenge him, or join him in the divine. There was no fear, there was rage, and the grief of potential loss, but not fear.

When Diana had cast that spell, M was left with no glamor, no magic, but worst of all, no connection. She could not feel anything past her own skin. While it passed, and when she woke from her coma, her connections had completely returned. It was a stark reminder of how alone she felt without them. And a reminder to cultivate all of her relationships.

To love Sugar with all of her heart.

To hold Dorthea and Bets close.

To never let her sense of duty destroy what chance she had at happiness.

To stop putting off living, counting on the likelihood of an unnaturally long life to be there when she was finally ready to start.

As they got to the landing at the top of the stairs, Sugar reached for the door handle and M grabbed his muscular forearm. "Hold on Sugarfoot."

He smiled sweetly at her, and she touched his cheeks and pulled him down into a soft kiss. "Before we get inside and everyone has our time. I love you. I am so happy that if I am rebuilding my life, it is with you by my side. Not only as my consort, but my lover and maybe, if you ever get up the courage, as my husband."

He wrapped his arms around her and her slight frame nearly disappeared into his massive body. She had never felt more safe, or more loved, than at that moment. He kissed her forehead, then lifted her lips to his. "That depends on whose blessing I have to ask for. Lord Seanchara I can do, Bets and Dorthea, that might take a little longer."

She reached behind him and squeezed one muscular butt cheek, then smacked it sharply. "Well Dorthea is right on the other side of that door so sort yourself out, scaredy-cat."

He reached for the handle and arm in arm they walked back into their lives.

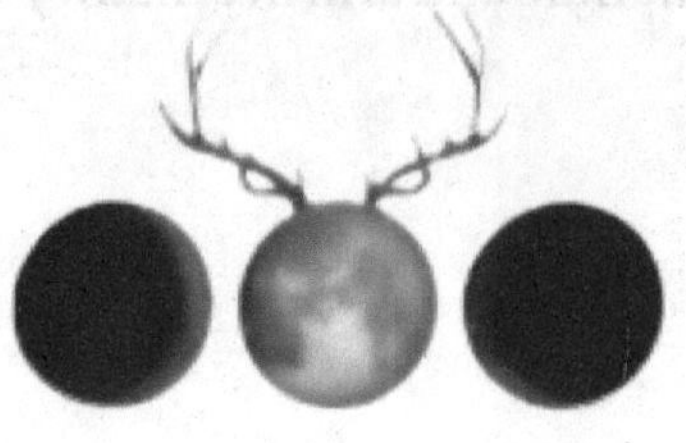

Sweet Home

"You know, Dorthea, you should maybe consider a life as an interior decorator or at the least a marketing agent for occult shops. This looks great."

M was walking through her small shop, marveling at how wonderful everything looked. To think that the last time she was here, the main area of the shop had been completely destroyed. Shelves and cabinets smashed, a rack had been affixed to one wall where Sugar was hung and tortured for hours.

But walking around her shop now, M could not tell. She stopped at a wooden bookshelf; its six shelves filled with books and statuettes. She breathed a word and the wooden shelves blurred, and when they came into focus they were made of what appeared to be human femurs tied together with leather braids.

"Shit, you know good and damn well that wasn't me. Fredrick and Devlin led the charge on all of the redecorating. Beck and Snow and I repainted and did the dirty work. Desma and Althea gathered supplies and restocked your store and personal supply of components. Not to mention Sugar's kitchen. It took us two damn days to restock the pantry. Fredrick has made a mortal enemy of the spice lady at the Soulard Market."

M stopped at Fredrick and wrapped her arms around his slender waist. She looked up into his dark eyes. "Thank you." She mouthed.

Tears welled in her eyes and her voice caught in her throat. She didn't know what else she could say. Beck and Snow were seated on the small sofa in the corner. A tea pot on the table in front of the steamed its fragrance into the air to mix with the herbs and incense as M walked shelf to shelf, wall to wall, rebuilding her glamour.

Devlin stuck his head through the beaded curtain behind the counter that led to their private quarters.

"Sugar says fifteen minutes for dinner. The twins asked everyone to wash up and head to the table."

It might have been the first time since knowing him that M did not want to kill Devlin outright. He was normally such a shit, juvenile and cocky. But he had put a lot of time and effort into helping to rebuild their home so that they didn't come home to the devastation left behind. She could never repay that kindness for as long as she lived.

Dorthea waved him over. "Thank you Devlin. Please tell them we will be right there."

"Yes Ma'am."

M shook her head, no smart ass remark, no innuendo. *Was this a different Devlin? Or was he just smart enough to know that this was neither the time nor the place to push his luck?*

Dorthea followed Beck and Snow through the curtain into the dining room. M turned to see Fredrick staring at the front door of the shop. The inner door was open, leaving the wrought iron gate over the between the shop and the foyer, visible.

"Fredrick? Is everything okay?"

He stared for another moment, M could see nothing beyond the foyer, as the door to the outside was closed and locked. Fredrick turned to her, a smile on his face that did not hide the haunted look in his eyes.

"Sorry Ms. Wildes, you know that feeling that folks describe as someone walking over your grave?"

M nodded but did not answer.

"I was just struck by the distinct feeling that I was standing on mine. I think perhaps your aunt has been a bit more determined than usual as of late, and it's time for a little vacation. But for now, let us see what that man of yours has whipped up for us."

It was her turn to cast a contemplative look his way. "My man, that has quite a ring to it doesn't it Fredrick?"

"It is a beautiful thing, Ms. Wildes, and some of us have waited a very long time to see it happen. I am honored that I am one of the people that gets to welcome you home."

"There is no one either one of us would rather be standing here when that door opened Fredrick, you are the best friend either of us could ask for. Now I am starving. Let's eat."

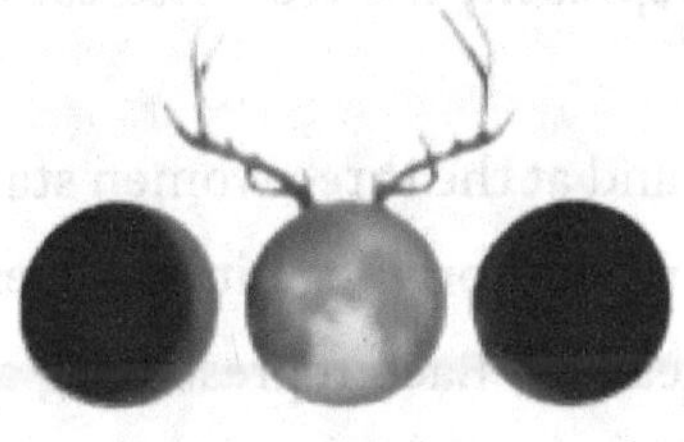

THE CHICKEN OR THE EGG

"Ladies and gentlemen, it is my pleasure to introduce to you the sponsors of Safe Women and Children ACT. Representatives LaRhonda Kelm and Harlan Rice, and Senators Rebecca Marsh and Ellen Bond."

A wave of applause rolled over the small press room. Thirty or so members of the press that normally dominated the conference room were shoved into a small corner of the room. The rest of the space was standing room only—with representatives from multiple charity organizations, and potential recipients of the ACT.

All four rose from their seats and stepped up behind the podium. Harlan Rice, tall and confident stepped up to the microphone.

"Hello everyone." His smooth Mississippi drawl slid across the room like honey.

"Six months ago, Representative Kelm and I started work on this bill, with the intention of finding a way that we could work across the aisle to benefit all of our constituents. We believed, and that belief was reinforced by the help we received, that the American people would rather have a functional government. That the voices that were screaming the loudest did not represent the true interest of the majority of the country."

Harlan swept his hand at the three women standing behind him.

"I cannot tell you what a privilege it has been to work with these three distinguished leaders. Each representing a vastly different constituency from myself and each other. The one thing I learned on day one of this project was that when you allow true leadership to shine through the bounds of the partisan buffoonery, we can really make a positive impact in the lives of every American. It is my great honor to introduce Representative LaRhonda Kelm of Illinois. Representative Kelm, they are all yours."

LaRhonda Kelm stepped forward and Harlan offered his hand, she took it and then pulled close, he whispered in her ear. "And so am I."

She smiled at him and dragged a sharp, red nail across the back of his hand as she pulled hers away. A warning and a promise of things yet to come this evening.

"Thank you Representative Rice, and thank you Senator Marsh, and Senator Bond. Without your support none of this would have been possible, and this incredible bill would not be headed to the Oval Office right now for The President's signature. What we have done here will go a long way toward providing safety and security for our most vulnerable citizens, the women, and children all over this country who have been victims of domestic abuse. With our combined efforts and advice from experts in the fields of social work, counselors, law enforcement, the Department of Justice, and the Department of Homeland Security.

We will be creating a nationwide network of resources for victims of abuse to escape their abusers, and find legal and medical advocacy. While many states have some great systems in place, they can vary greatly from state to state, and county to county. We wanted a single system, that covers every inch of this great country, and ensures no matter who, no matter where, no woman or child would be left out to fend for themselves while trying to make life for themselves free from violence."

Another round of applause from the gathered crowd. Hands and calls for attention came from the media section. LaRhonda looked across the room, briefly allowing herself to see the energy of creation coursing through the room. Connecting everyone and everything. She saw the conservative blogger angrily waving his hand around, streaks of grey and brown dominating most of the colors surrounding him. LaRhonda saw only a couple very small connections flowing from the man. *What a lonely and resinous existence he must lead.* She thought as she contemplated him for another moment. *Was he alone because of what he did and said, the divisive, corrosive energy he put into the world, or did he put that into the world because he had so little connection to the universe around him? Oh well, I might as well get the worst of it out of the way.*

"Mr. Bartholemew, you have the first question, I feel I need to remind you why we are here and that we are not deviating from the discussion of Safe Women and Children ACT."

The man rose from his chair, his considerable belly brushing the person in front of him as he did. LaRhonda could only imagine the feel of that sweaty gut brushing against her and had to keep her expression in check.

"Thank you LaRhonda..."

"Representative Kelm please." Her response left no questions to how this exchange would end if he continued to be disrespectful.

"Representative Kelm, of course." His smirk and eyeroll made Larhonda want to pull him apart at the seams. Something horrible, like The Valkyrie's Kiss, or The Spider Eats. Anything to wipe that smug expression off of his face.

"Given the scope of this project, and all of the resources necessary to accomplish something like this. How do you propose to pay for it? More taxes on real Americans? eliminating border patrols? I cannot imagine any way to pay for this kind of bloated entitlement program—and lets be real, that's what it will turn into. Without making our country less safe--or making the hard working American taxpayers float the bill so that women can get divorced easier."

LaRhonda felt the shift in the energy of the room, so many people focused on hating this man all at once. She wondered if the Lewis twins were here if they could turn this room full of social justice advocates and veteran journalists into an angry mob capable of tearing this fat bastard apart. She felt the shift in the energy from the dais behind her as well. Harlan, she knew from their many conversations, some while writing this bill, even more, whispered into the dark of her room, as they lay tangled in one another's arms. How badly Harlan hated this man, and how much he would love to take him down a peg or two.

She took the soft predictable pitch and did what she did best. She hit a home run.

"Always the fly in the ointment aren't you Bartholomew? To answer your question. No, there will be no cost to the taxpayer nor the reduction of services."

"So does the program get paid for by wishes?"

"That is the last disrespectful remark you will make, or you can pack up your toys and go home Mr. Bartholomew. I am not sure if you noticed what we are trying to accomplish or haven't been listening. But the American people are tired of this divisive, hateful rhetoric. In fact, I want you to listen, but more than you, I want everyone who can hear this to listen. It is one thing to have differing views and even differing priorities, every one of us up here has a different constituency, and our voters all have different priorities depending on demographics and region. But what they all want is a government that works for the people. And that is what we are going to give them. You can be part of that Mr. Bartholomew, or you can become another layer of irritating background noise. But you will no longer control the discourse and the narratives."

The room fell as silent as a room of a hundred or so people could be.

"Now to answer your question. What you may or may not know is that between DHS, and DOJ, hundreds of millions of dollars are seized yearly from asset forfeitures due to criminal and terrorist convictions. As a rule, the properties get auctioned off and the cash and bank accounts go into evidence or become part of departmental slush funds. The problem with this system is that departments are often reluctant to release the properties and evidence of people who are exonerated because it becomes how they pay for all the equipment and amenities that aren't in their budget and may be things that the general public would never want to see in a police budget. This redirects those funds and proceeds of people convicted of crimes to this program. So that resources forfeited by dangerous people will now be put to use improving the lives of society's most vulnerable people. Even accounting for funds and property that should be released and aren't because of clerical errors or departmental corruption. There will be more than enough funding to keep this program solvent and off the taxpayer's dime indefinitely. Are there any other questions?"

Every other hand in the press section shot up at once as Bartholomew plopped down angrily in his chair.

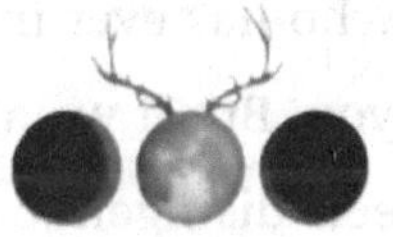

Later that night, lying in bed, with nestled into the crook of Harlan's arm, her head on his broad chest. "You know LaRhonda, for a moment there I thought you were going to step off the stage and take a swing at Bartholomew."

She pulled herself tighter to him, enjoying the warmth of his skin on hers, the smell of them together. The slight hint of his cologne, of the soap she had used to wash off her make up, the musk of the last hour of extremely intense lovemaking.

"I won't lie and say I didn't want to. I did. It's times like these that it is even more important that I keep my cool. A black woman from south Chicago losing her cool and attacking a wannabe journalist over some mean words would play into every harmful stereotype I could think of. It would give him and his ilk years of ammo. An honest journalist, just asking hard hitting, but sincere questions, attacked by an unhinged hood rat pretending to be a politician."

She felt his body shift a little, not pulling away precisely, but she could feel the change in the contact. She braced herself to hear something she may not like.

"LaRhonda, I need to be honest with you about a couple things."

Her mind raced. Here we go, he's a good man, but a white man from Mississippi all the same. She was already planning what extricating herself from this foolish endeavor of a fling would look like for her, potential fallout, damage control if he should not take it well.

"I don't know how to respond to what you just said. My first instinct is to tell you how incredibly brilliant and inspiring you are. To try and convince you that no one who has ever met you or heard you speak, could feel that way about you. But if we are being truthful, and I believe we always are, that feels disingenuous. Because no matter how amazing I think you are. I know there are always people who will never believe you are anything, but what you said."

She smiled into his chest; glad he couldn't see her face. Here she was, ready to hand him his toothbrush and demand her apartment key back just ten seconds ago.

"You're right, it would be disingenuous and thank you for being honest about not knowing how to handle it. That means a lot that you recognize that. The hypocrisy and double standard. If that man would have gotten disrespectful with you and you checked him or even puffed up at him and got a little threatening, you would have been applauded in almost every demographic. But me, or people who look like me, we have to strive for civility at all costs, even at the cost of integrity sometimes. Because there are always those who will never see us as barely more than animals."

The silence between them felt contemplative rather than uncomfortable.

"Harlan?"

He kissed the side of her forehead.

"Yes?"

"You said there was two things you wanted to be honest about."

"When Bartholomew went after you, I realized something."

He paused and LaRhonda felt his energy shift this time. He was genuinely scared or exhilarated, like he was about to jump out of an airplane or... Sometimes she hated her gifts, and this was one of them. She knew what he was about to say.

"I realized how much I wanted to step up and defend you. Not because I didn't think you could defend yourself, and not out of some warped sense of possessiveness. No school yard garbage like that. I wanted to defend you because I wanted him, and everyone there, and everyone watching, to know how much I love you. I wanted you to know how much I love you."

She fell into her connection and felt the flow of divine energy between them. She pushed her feelings down that connection, knowing that he wouldn't be able to interpret it, but he would feel the comfort, the reassurance.

There were a thousand things she wanted to say in that moment. But none of them felt sufficient to convey what she really felt. That she had loved him since the first night they spent together. That she was terrified of what that might mean for their careers, of the implications of loving someone not born to, or aware of Mercer and the magic she carried, and the risks involved. She was scared to death to meet his teenage daughters. But most of all she couldn't imagine a future for her without him in it. She rolled onto her back and pulled him on top of her. She wrapped herself around him and he cradled her head in his arm as she felt his lust rising to meet her own.

She drew in divine energy and whispered into his ear. "Harlan, say it again."

"I love you LaRhonda."

"Again."

"I love you LaRhonda."

"Oh Harlan."

He stared into her eyes, "I love you LaRhonda."

Then he was inside her, and she released her charm and wrapped them in a blanket of divine energy that carried with it all of her love and concern and hopes for the future. For the briefest moment she felt his connection to the divine open up before they were both swept up in the extasy of the moment.

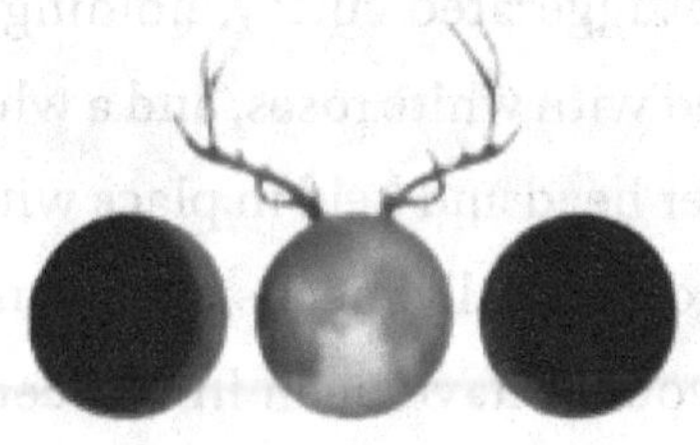

It Would Be Weirder If
We Didn't

"**G**erardo, what do you think?"

"About what? The weather, the Knicks this year? You have to be more specific."

LaRhonda tapped him on the shoulder a little harder than was necessary or polite. He was being an ass. She also knew it was because Harlan had gotten a reservation at one of his favorite restaurants for her and the girls, and he wasn't invited. He was being a brat as a result.

"Hey, stop with the hitting, lady. I don't care how important you are. You don't get to hit me because you cannot communicate clearly. Typical politician, vague questions, and even vaguer answers and all else fails, try violence."

He turned to face her laughing at his own cleverness but stopped dead when he saw her, his eyes wide and mouth agape.

"LaRhonda, you are a vision. I was jealous that you were eating at JP's without me. Now I am jealous that I won't get to see the room react when you walk in. Holy crow, I don't even know what to say."

She gave him an exaggerated curtsy, holding out the sides of her sundress. A field of red with white roses, and a white cardigan. Her locs were piled high on her head and held in place with a matching wrap.

"Thank you, Gerardo. It really means a lot to me. I don't remember ever being this nervous. I have been in Mercer since I was a kid. I have fought crooks, politicians, and the press. I've seen feats of magic that would bend most people's minds out of shape. But this, meeting Lydia, and Lexia, I am terrified. How can I have stood in the room with Elder Valkyrie and been okay, but two fifteen-year-old girls have me shaking."

"Honestly?"

"Of course, always."

"If Elder Valkyrie decides she doesn't like you, you won't have long to consider the implications before it's no longer your problem. If these girls don't like you…"

He held up his hands without finishing the statement.

LaRhonda shook her head and took a deep breath.

"How did I get here Gerardo? Do you think I am making a big mistake worse by going through with this?"

"What mistake? Being in love with Harlan, allowing yourself the freedom to follow that love wherever it may lead? I don't see that as a mistake at all LaRhonda, in fact, I see it as a wonderful idea. What is it that your scared of LaRhonda? Let's talk it through."

"What am I scared of? I am scared they won't like me, and Harlan will be forced to break things off with me. I am scared they will like me, and he won't. What if I meet them and I fall in love with them? Then what the fuck do I do?"

"Then you do your best to love them and their father, you take them shopping and support their dreams and maybe one day get to see them move on and start families of their own. Be a grandmother? Wouldn't that be a trip? Grandma LaRhonda? Or would it be Granny Kelm?"

"Sounds like a dream come true, except for the fact that I AM A WITCH GERARDO."

"You are, and a damn good one, but you aren't a general, you aren't out in the field. You are fighting our battles in the halls of congress and in the press. You are damn good at your job, but your job almost never requires you to have a violent face to face confrontation with our adversary."

"Thank you, Gerardo, but you know what I mean, it's not just the risk, but the lies. I would be building our entire relationship on a lie about who, and what I am. I don't know if I can do that. What happens if I am forced to protect myself, or you, or someone else? With the Ascension and Malleus Dei running around on witch hunts it wouldn't be out of the question to think we might be at risk someday. What happens when a year or two from now, we get outed or attacked by Malleus Dei and I have to defend myself, or you, in front of Harlan. Then what, I have built our entire relationship on lies, and a tree with no roots can't stand."

She took a deep breath. She could feel the imagined pain of losing Harlan to a deception, deep in her chest.

"So, tell him the truth. There is a precedent and a process for it. For bringing in outsiders as a resource, and he wouldn't be the first sitting member of congress to be made aware of what we do. Nor would he be the first romantic partner to be made aware of Mercer's existence and mission."

"Wait, is this something they train you guys on, what to do if your sister witch loses her mind and falls in love with a congressman?"

"Well, technically yes. One method involves petitioning the elders who then ask Lord Seanchara for his guidance. The other involves tranquilizers and a long vacation in a remote wilderness cabin."

"For whom?"

"Well, the tranquilizer is for the sister witch, the cabin is for the consort to hide after."

They both laughed, and she pulled him into a tight hug.

"Thank you, Gerardo, for all that you do for me. For all that you do for everyone. Let me get through this dinner, then, if things go well. Maybe you can walk me through the process, so I don't have to live a lie in order to be with the man I love."

"Of course, you'll just have to take him home to meet the scariest father figure in all of human history."

There was no hiding or exaggerating the look of horror on her face at the thought of Harlan facing Lord Seanchara. He was a good man, a brave man, but to stand before the Horned God of the Witches and ask for permission to love one. Maybe she was getting off easy with having to impress Harlan's daughters.

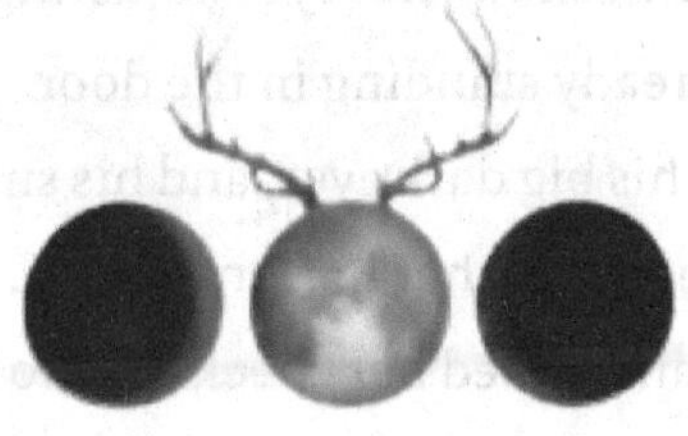

The Scariest Mission Yet

LaRhonda arrived at JP's at ten minutes before seven. She hoped to be seated before Harlan and the girls arrived. Her talk with Gerardo had calmed her nerves considerably and she had spent the twenty-minute ride here deep in her connection to the divine energy of creation. Still her stomach had rolled more than once. It was ridiculous. She had spoken on the national, and global stages more than once. Addressed rooms of ravenous reporters looking for the slightest sign of weakness. Had even had dinner with the former President and First Lady. But meeting with the two teenage daughters of her lover was nearly more than she could bear.

JP's was a wonderfully hip restaurant near downtown Bethesda. It was well known and loved among the young professionals both on and off Capitol Hill. The room was small, seating less than one hundred, not counting the patio. The décor was BOHO sheik, and the chef was an absolutely brilliant man named Corbett. She walked up the short walkway to the heavily frosted front door. Taking her last breaths of fresh air and preparing for the change in light when she stepped from the evening daylight to the dark lantern lit foyer of JP's.

As she crossed the threshold, her eyes adjusting to the dark she nearly ran over Harlan, already standing in the door.

She looked up into his big dark eyes, and his smile lit up the dimly lit foyer when he realized it was her in front of him.

He leaned in close and kissed her cheek. "Hello love." His Mississippi drawl was as familiar to her as her own voice at this point. She could smell a hint of wine on his breath as well as the spice of her favorite Azzaro cologne. She had bought him a bottle on his birthday. He of course, had continued on his long streak of impressing her by not asking at all how she had determined it was her favorite men's cologne.

"Harlan." She whispered into his ear. She peaked over his shoulder and saw the two girls approaching from behind him, followed by what appeared to be the hostess, a stack of menus in her hand. "Rice, party for the Concord room?" The hostess said with the practiced politeness of most restaurant professionals.

Harlan took LaRhonda's hand and led her toward where the hostess and his daughters had veered off down a dimly lit hallway. They emerged into a small room that LaRhonda had never seen, she didn't even know it existed. Framed, antique vaudeville posters hung on the walls, and she caught the faded scent of cigar smoke. Many of the rooms around D.C. even now, held that familiar scent of backroom deals and world altering decisions made over a glass of Glen Livet and a contraband Cuban cigar.

As the hostess laid out the menus and talked about the evening's wine and food pairing, LaRhonda took the moment to get a better look at the girls. They were paternal twins. Harlan of course, like any devoted father, talked about them constantly. So LaRhonda knew who was who. She also knew teenage girls in a way that no father really ever could. So, she knew not to rely too much on his assessment of their personalities. Neither girl was really listening to the hostess any more than she was. Lydia was certainly the bolder, staring right at her, with her white, blond hair and pale blue eyes. She was so lightly complected she could have been a Lewis. Lexia was a little more Harlan, red curly hair, dark eyes, and an adorable stripe of freckles across her nose that made her appear much younger than she was.

LaRhonda allowed herself to fall into her connection. To see the energy flowing through them. As she suspected there was a band of brilliant red and green light flowing between the two girls. And smaller ones between each girl and Harlan. She saw the tiny tendrils of connection between herself and the girls and down this she pushed all of the good intention she could. Hopeful that even if they didn't know what it was, they would feel her and be comforted.

What she had not expected was a push back. A probing. It wasn't the practiced reach of a Mercer witch. But she felt it nonetheless, from both girls. These girls were very open to the divine energy of creation. It would not surprise her at all to learn that they were or would be soon, on Mercer's radar. That might complicate things greatly. Would Harlan ever believe that their relationship was real if he found out about Mercer, then later they ended up in the family?

Harlan was speaking, the hostess was gone, she snapped back to the present moment.

"Girls, this is Representative Kelm."

"Representative Kelm, these are my daughters, Lydia and Lexia."

LaRhonda walked to Lydia and extended her hand. Lydia shook it heartily, still making incredibly intense, almost awkward eye contact. "Please call me LaRhonda, Lydia it's a pleasure to meet you."

She extended her hand to Lexia, who offered a fist bump in return. "Lexia, please call me LaRhonda, it's so nice to finally meet you."

Everyone started to take their seats. "I am sure I don't have to tell you how much your dad has told me about you. I have met a lot of proud parents in my life. But he may be the top of that particular mountain."

Lexia grinned and rolled her eyes playfully. Lydia beamed at her dad.

Lexia held her hand over her chest in a mockery of shock. "Our dad, talking a lot. I swear I have never heard such an accusation. Surely you must have the wrong man."

LaRhonda could not help but laugh out loud. Lexia's southern belle was so good it was scary and if there was one thing Harlan was good at, it was talking. There were of course many other things, many of those things she would not bring up at dinner with his daughters.

"Well, I am glad that he doesn't reserve his gift of gab just for me then. I sometimes worry after we have hung out for an evening that he might have ran out of words by the time he gets home to you and just sits mute and stares at the wall."

Lydia nearly spit out the water she was drinking. "Are you kidding? Every time he comes home from seeing you that is all we get. A play by play of all of the funny and insightful and clever things you say. For the record, we knew he was crushing on you, probably before he did. Maybe not before you did, but definitely before he did. He talks about you so much, we kind of already feel like we know you. It made coming here a lot easier."

LaRhonda glanced at Harlan, who was now roughly the same shade of red as her dress and appeared to be sweating. She reached across the table and took his hand. Emboldened by the girls' obvious approval of their relationship.

"We can always tell, can't we ladies?"

Both girls nodded knowingly. LaRhonda felt the connection between the three of them deepen.

"And if you will take a little advice from someone you just met. Don't ever settle for anyone who doesn't show you the way your dad does."

Lexia giggled quietly and Lydia stared at her dad in open admiration. *This just might work.* LaRhonda thought, as the server came into the room to take their drink orders.

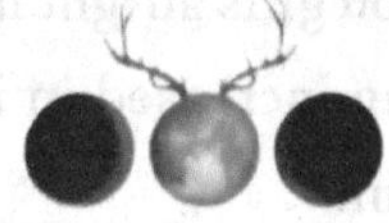

"So, now that we have the introductions out of the way, and I find myself outnumbered by beautiful and intelligent women. Can we talk about appetizers and entrées."

Harlan's face had mostly returned to its natural color.

LaRhonda took the lead.

"Well, provided no one has any shellfish allergies, I am going to strongly recommend the oysters and shrimp. Oh, and maybe, well how hungry is everyone? Ladies, are we feeling like putting some food away tonight?"

Lexia nodded enthusiastically. "We've never had raw oysters before. Are they good?"

"They tend to be a fifty-fifty thing. People either love them or hate them. There aren't too many folks, at least not where I am from, who are just okay with them. So how about a dozen oysters and an order of the collard greens and rice stuffed pastry? Then if I can make a rec-ommendation for dinner?" She held up her hands and Harlan, and the girls nodded in a synchronous movement that made her heart swell, and caused her breath to catch in her chest.

Have I really been missing out on this my entire life? Is this what a life outside Mercer is like?

"Chef Corbett is brilliant, and I would hate for you to miss out on anything. Why don't you all look over the menu and pick your idea, then we order a few different things and a bunch of plates and just pass everything around, so everyone gets a chance to try as many things as possible? Is that okay, are you girls alright if we all share?"

The synchronous nodding increased in intensity and speed as the server returned with the drinks.

Once the first round of appetizers was on the table and LaRhonda gave a quick tutorial on eating raw oysters to the girls; the conversation began to pick up speed. Lydia dove in headfirst.

"LaRhonda, is it true that you know First Lady Obama? I saw you in an article with them at a dinner, and the news always makes it sound like you are friends, but they always say that like it's a bad thing, which I don't get."

"I do know Mrs. Obama very well. President Obama and I were community organizers at the same time in Chicago, and we served in Congress together, when he was the senator from Illinois and I was a first year Representative. We do still keep in touch when we can. They are very busy, as you can imagine. But it's always a pleasure when we do get to catch up."

Lydia looked like she had just been told she had won the lottery.

"That is so cool!" She was nearly yelling, and her pale cheeks had flushed pink with excitement.

"Is she as incredible as she seems? she is probably my hero, or one of them at least. She is so iconic. Beautiful and smart and all class. I wrote a paper on her in middle school. Well, we had to pick from a list of influential women in recent history and because we are R's there weren't many left to pick from by the time I got to pick. It was First Lady Obama or Ellen DeGeneres or Simone Biles. I thought she would be the easiest to find cool information on, you know, there is a lot written about her, being she was married to the president and all. But she is so interesting even without having ever been married to President Obama. Like, that might be the least interesting thing about here and that's pretty dang cool."

"Lydia, breathe." Harlan said as he tossed an empty half shell back onto the platter. "You're going to give yourself a stroke kid."

"Oh, right, sorry about that, I just get really excited about stuff and especially about her, well her and intersectional feminism. I get pretty excited about that too. In fact—"

Lexia groaned and rolled her eyes. LaRhonda sensed that this was familiar territory for them.

"Oh, whatever Lexia, just because you don't think it's important it still affects you."

"It's not that I don't see it as important Lydia, Its that I have been your primary audience for the last two years; and every time you read something new I get a four hour lecture on whatever atrocities are currently being committed by the patriarchy and toxically masculine men. Sometimes I just want to take a bath and relax without spending every moment thinking about what is unfair in the world."

"Okay ladies, there will be time to relitigate this argument when we aren't at dinner."

LaRhonda tried not to let the smile she was feeling shine through. She didn't want the girls to think she wasn't taking them seriously. But she couldn't help but laugh at it. They were so much like their father. Smart, impassioned, charming. She wondered what their mother was like. Harlan had only ever spoke highly of her. They had split custody and seemed to get along well. She took the chance.

"So, listening to you both, you obviously learned a little from your dad. Someone I have had more than my fair share of negotiations with. But I am guessing your mom is no slouch in a debate either? What does she do for a living?"

Both girls sat up straighter. Obvious pride on their young faces. Lydia jumped in first. "Oh, mom? She's a lawyer, a really great one. She has argued before the Supreme Court a couple times. She's really smart, and yeah, she can debate almost anything with anyone. You would really like her. Wait, is that weird? That kind of felt weird."

LaRhonda snuck a glance at Harlan to see if he had reacted in a way that should concern her. He had not.

"No, I don't think that's weird at all. In fact, I hope to meet her as well someday. I mean she obviously has great taste in men and has raised two incredible daughters. Seems like her and I would have a lot in common. Although I could not imagine arguing a case in front of the Supreme Court, what an honor, and a testament to her ability. You girls should be immensely proud."

"Yes."

They answered in an uncanny unison.

Then Lexia continued. "But we have also seen you fighting it out with those nimrods in Congress."

"Lexia." Harlan admonished.

"Sorry Dad."

"But for real, it is so dope watching you check them every time they come at you. Lydia and Mom and I watched a bunch of YouTube videos of you just making people look dumb for coming at you."

Lydia hissed at her quietly and kicked her under the table.

"No, Lydia, it's okay. I expected you to be as curious about me as I was about you. You are just looking out after your dad. If I wasn't proud of the work I have done, I wouldn't do it. Sometimes, thankfully not often, it involves me checking a nimrod or two when they try to get out of pocket."

"Really, you too LaRhonda?"

"Oh, saved by the salmon." She said as they entrees began to arrive.

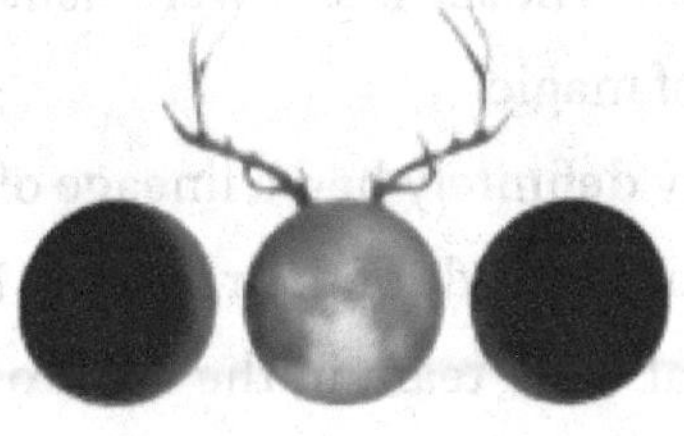

He Never Stood A Chance

More than two hours had passed since LaRhonda had walked into the front doors of JP's and into the loving arms of Harlan, and her meeting with his daughters. She had loved every moment of it. They covered every possible topic. The girls schoolwork, potential college plans, their friends, life going back and forth between their mom and dad. LaRhonda's childhood in Chicago. Her and Harlan's work on the new bill.

Every time either one of them would ask her a question, LaRhonda would feel the gentle probing that accompanied it along the connection of the divine energy that she now shared with the girls. She knew that they were not aware or in control of it. But still, it was there. They both showed potential for great magic. While anyone could manipulate the divine energy after crossing the veil of death. There was a difference. LaRhonda did not come from a line of witches. She was strong in the areas where she had spent years in practice, but it was work. She knew some of her sisters in Mercer came from long lines of witches. Some, like the Milburn and Lewis families went all the way back to

Mother Mercer herself. Those sisters were usually more powerful in almost every aspect of magic.

But these girls, they definitely had a lineage of some sort. She wondered if it was from Harlan's side or their mother. Either way, she would reach out to the social work team in the area to make sure they were being observed and protected.

With it now being well past nine and all of them thoroughly stuffed, they made their way to the front door. LaRhonda held onto Harlan's firm bicep and leaned her head against him as they walked. She heard the girls murmuring to one another behind them as she did but did not pry. She wanted them to see her affection for their father, and she hoped they were comfortable with it.

As they stepped out on to the dark street in front of JP's Harlan turned toward the girls. "Alright ladies, it is a school night. I had better get you two home."

A shot like a bolt of electricity ran up LaRhonda's spine as her wards lit up, indicating someone sneaking up on them, focused on them. She pulled in the energy of creation and began a shield charm as a series of flashes went off next to her face, blinding her for a moment.

She poured energy into the shield and pushed Harlan back, hard. She was trying to assess where the threat was coming from when she heard the familiar nasal whine of Carl Bartholemew.

"Representative Kelm, LaRhonda. You have any comment for our faithful patriots about the scandal of your affair with Harlan Rice? What's it like to be a jezebel, a homewrecker?"

"Daddy."

LaRhonda could hear the fear in the girl's voice, she didn't know who had said it. Before she could react Harlan was around her. His arm sweeping her behind him toward the girls. She could feel the rage flowing off of him in big angry waves of red heat. She fell into her connection to him and tried to push calm toward him, but either she was still too keyed up herself, or he was so angry that good vibes weren't going to be enough.

Growing up in Mercer, surrounded by highly trained warriors of all types, and training with Gerardo for most of that. It was easy for her to overlook the strength and physicality of people, men especially, not born to Mercer. But Harlan, in that moment, was a fierce as any consort she had ever met. Bartholomew kept clicking away with his camera, the blinding strobe mere inches from Harlan's face and yet he showed no signs of stopping. It wasn't until he had brushed the camera aside and was towering a good four or five inches over the troll of a journalist that he said anything at all.

"Bartholomew you need to hear me loud and clear on this."

The man tried to get the camera back in between them, but Harlan swatted it away again. LaRhonda knew a charm that could disable electronics, overloading them without physical damage. She had never cast it without preparation, but she had to try it. Or this could get even uglier if Bartholomew kept flashing that camera at Harlan.

Harlan got even louder.

"You will never get near my children again; do you understand me?"

The man lifted his multiple chins defiantly. "I will go where the story takes me Rice, and if you are going to involve your children in your affair then they are fair game."

Harlan was dangerously close to him now; his voice had taken on the determined, murderous tones of someone whose restraint is quickly failing. "My relationship, not affair, you bloated tick, my relationship with Representative Kelm is not a secret, or a scandal. We are two consenting adults in a romantic relationship. There is nothing hidden, nothing dishonest or scandalous about it. The scandal will be when I slap you, with a restraining order for endangering the lives of my minor daughters, and you are no longer allowed in the press corps on Capitol

Hill. Because you cannot be charged with a felony and get clearance to those spaces. Do you understand me?"

Bartholomew must have seen in Harlan's eyes what LaRhonda could hear in his voice. This was no longer the southern gentlemen, the voice of calm reason in a world of disrespectful chaos. This was a father protecting his children. Bartholomew had scared them all running at them with the camera flashing. But Harlan, his fear turned into an iron rod that forced his spine rigid and set his blood to boil. The two people he loved most in the world were threatened, even if in the abstract, and Harlan was a breath from violence in an effort to protect them.

"You call it what you want to Rice, But it's obvious to everyone around you that you two are crossing professional boundaries. I am sure your constituents would just love to hear about how you've abandoned your conservative values to sleep with a Chicago liberal. Not to mention I am sure they will love to vote for a white Christian dating a black demo..."

He never got to finish the sentence. Harlan reached for him, obviously looking to get physical. LaRhonda released a simple repulsion charm just ahead of Harlan making contact. Bartholomew stumbled backward three steps, just out of reach of Harlan's arm. She probably saved Harlan's career and definitely saved Bartholomew a broken jaw, or worse.

"Consider your press credentials revoked Bartholomew, that was the last line you got to cross. I hope it was worth losing what little credibility you had in D.C. You are done."

"You can't do that; you aren't in charge of the press corps Rice. You are a traitor to real Americans everywhere, and I have the pictures and now the video to bring you down, you arrogant bastard."

Bartholomew reached for the black box on his chest. *Dammit, he's wearing a body cam. Well, here's to hoping that charm worked.* LaRhonda stepped between the two men. "Harlan lets go. Let him wallow in his failure. It's late and we are all tired."

Harlan looked back at his daughters and took LaRhonda's hand leading him to them. Leaving Bartholomew staring slack jawed at them as he fiddled with the body cam.

Harlan pulled his girls to his chest and kissed each one of them on top of their head. "Are you okay?"

"Yes sir." Said Lexia.

"I think so. But Daddy, are you two going to be in trouble now? Like are there rules against you two dating or whatever you old folks call it?"

"Your dad and I declared our relationship to both of our caucus leaderships. Which isn't as much of a rule as a courtesy. Gives them the chance to look for any possible conflict of interest. But no matter the party, your dad's integrity is something that everyone agrees on. Even the most staunch liberals know him to be a fair, honest, and consistent man. That's more than can be said for a lot of our peers." LaRhonda looked around suddenly aware that she didn't drive downtown and needed to get back to JP's to order an Uber.

"Harlan, sorry, I have to head back and catch an Uber, I just realized I was walking you to your car." She laughed but even she could hear the nervousness in it. She wasn't looking forward to running into Bartholomew again. He was a pain in the ass, but he had been humiliated and there is no way to tell how someone like him would react to that.

Lexia and Lydia whined in unison. "No!"

Then Lydia said. "Dad, you really should give her a ride home. Like come on, be a gentleman."

"Of course, LaRhonda, I am sorry, I didn't realize you didn't drive here. I insist, the girls insist. Let me give you a ride home."

She pulled herself up to his side again and kissed him lightly on the cheek. "On one condition. "He arched an eyebrow at her.

"We stop by Dairy Haven on the way to my place and you let me buy, they have bacon and waffle caramel sundaes on special this week and I am dying to get my hands on one."

The squeals of delight from the girls drowned out the anxiety she felt about the confrontation with Bartholomew and worrying about telling Harlan about Mercer. Really, it drowned out just about everything else and just left an overwhelming feeling of peace and joy.

That is a feeling I could get used to. She thought as they approached Harlan's SUV.

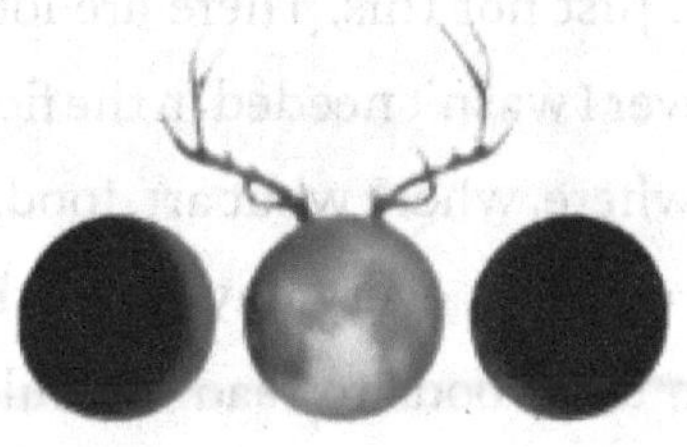

At Last

Other than the yellow police tape blocking off the front porch and door, there would have been almost no way to distinguish 114 Cardinal Dr, from 116, or 118, any of the other houses in this subdivision. Dorthea squinted against the afternoon Georgia sunshine as she looked up and down the block at the various shades of grey and beige and brown.

"Fredrick?"

Fredrick was reclined in the passenger seat of the F150 King Cab, being well over six feet tall, it was a challenge for him to get comfortable in any vehicle. He pulled the seat upright.

"Yes Ma'am?"

"You ever wonder what this life would be like? These cookie cutter houses, the manicured lawns and shrubs. Four colors to choose from, everyone has the same garbage can."

"HOAs, PTAs, mortgages, and cookouts with the neighbors? I cannot think of anything I would enjoy less."

"So, no picket fence retirement for you and someone special?"

"I did not say that. Just not this. There are lots of ways I could see spending my time if ever I wasn't needed in the field anymore. A loft in a cultural center somewhere, where what art, food, or music to consume is my most stressful decision every day. Or perhaps even something rural, a quiet place in the woods to read. I would love to learn an instrument, so that I can make music of my own. Perhaps write a memoir disguised as a fiction with an unreliable narrator." He paused.

"Javier?" She asked.

Silence filled the cab of the truck for a few seconds.

Fredrick nodded his head and smiled at her. "I would like that very much—if he is willing to have me."

"How long has it been since you've seen him Fredrick?"

"Almost a year."

"Oh Fredrick, I'm sorry. Let's get through this then take some time off—"

He cut her off.

"Sister, respectfully, the mission—"

She returned the favor.

"The mission will remain, as it always has been. But you, Fredrick, deserve to take some time for yourself. If we haven't learned anything in the past couple of years. From M and Sugar, from Mathew and Hannah. We don't know how many chances we get for even a moment of happiness. If you want to take some time, to see Javier, to go relax, to wander the streets of Paris, I don't care. I will move mountains to get you the opportunity if need be."

"Thank you, Dorthea. I appreciate your concern."

"I know that I can be a grouchy-ass sometimes Fredrick. That by driving myself harder and harder, I am inadvertently driving you as well. But I appreciate you, and I am grateful for your partnership and protection. Besides, I can totally hold down his end of the library for him if you guys want to go to Cancun or whatever."

"Sister, now you're just being insulting, I would rather burn my tie than step into a resort."

She reached across the armrest and squeezed his muscular forearm. He laid his hand over hers. They had never touched before—other than in training, and certainly never from affection. But in that moment, that reassuring calm before the next storm that was their lives in service to Mercer, it was something both of them desperately needed.

Dorthea's wards sent a slight tingle up her spine just as the movement outside her driver side window caught her eye. Approaching from a black SUV— unmarked except for the cattle catcher crash bar across the front and a discrete light bar behind the rear view mirror, was a man in a charcoal suit. His jacket was open and Dorthea caught the flash of silver from his badge, and a brief glimpse of the grip of a pistol in its holster on his right hip.

She waved a hand at him in greeting and he nodded. She grabbed the handle to jump out, and the man reached with his left hand and calmly but with no mistaking his intention leaned on the truck door. A flash of impatience made her wonder how he would react if she hit him with a concussion charm that put him on his ass. His hand moving toward his right hip made it perfectly clear how he would react.

She smiled as well as she could and hit the button to lower the window.

"Detective LaSalle?"

"Yes Ma'am."

His voice was dripping with Atlanta swagger.

"You Dorthea Milburn?"

"Yes sir, and this is my partner, Fredrick Sapp."

"And you are both P.I.'s?"

"Independent insurance investigators, working the Lewis case. Company is trying to do its due diligence before the funds get sent to the Unclaimed Properties Division. Both of them had fairly sizable policies. But given that her and the kids are deceased, and he is missing..."

"Okay, seems I was misinformed. I was under the impression you were private investigators tracking this killer for someone."

"You don't think Henry Lewis killed his family? I thought that was the prevailing theory?"

He shook his head, the sunshine gleamed off of his dark scalp, dotted with sweat.

"It was, well, it is for most people. I have been unofficially tracking this monster across four different states now. Its slow, tedious work without a task force, and not being able to travel in an official capacity. So far everyone else is looking at them as isolated cases. Too much inter-jurisdictional bullshit."

"That we can understand well. Do you think a fresh pair of eyes would help? Or two pairs for that matter? We aren't on the job, but we have been investigators for various outfits for a long time."

"I am pretty sure that's why Micky sent me to meet you guys here. He thinks you can help."

Dorthea paused a moment before remembering Michael O'Laughlin went by Micky. He was the consort of a local Mercer witch. She was a public defender, and he was a police officer.

"Yeah, Micky is good people."

"He's a mean old bastard is what he is, and you can tell him I said so. But you won't find anyone more dedicated to getting bad guys off the streets than Micky. I think that's why he sent me to you. He doesn't think we are going to be able to get this guy in any conventional way."

"Do you mind if we take a look at the information you have?"

He took his hand off of the door frame. She took that as a sign she could get out of the truck.

"I made copies of the files, let me run back to the car and grab them, then we can step inside where it's cool. How's your stomachs? Some of this stuff is pretty tough to look at."

Dorthea smiled up at him as she reached for the handle. "We will let you know if it gets too much."

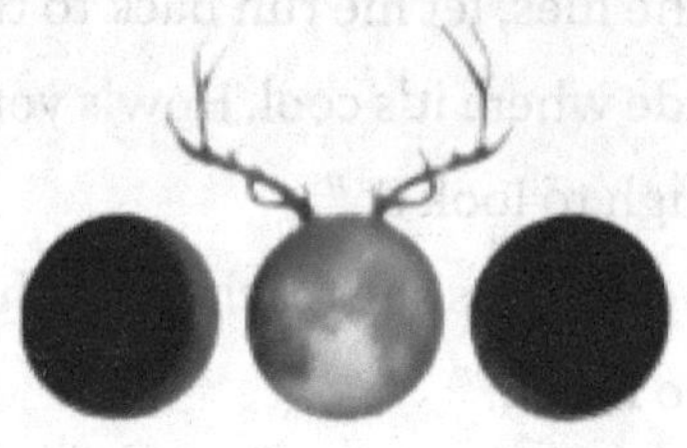

Some Things Never Change

"**F**redrick what does that third file say about the time of death?"

Fredrick flipped through pages, reading at a speed most people would question.

He finally settled on a page.

"Placing the time of death between midnight and two, although that is based on cell phone usage and some other random factors. There wasn't much left to test lividity or temperature on accurately. Dorthea, if I have to be honest, if it wasn't for the pattern we have been following the last three months, and how convinced Detective LaSalle is, I would hesitate to even connect this one with the others. The level of violence and savagery here, well it is far beyond anything else we have seen."

He pulled a handkerchief from his breast pocket and lightly dabbed the sweat from his smooth dark forehead. Not much rattled Fredrick Sapp, but Dorthea could see that going through these files had a visceral effect on him. She hated to see the hurt and sadness in his eyes when he saw what this monster had done to these families. But a little part of her was glad, not that he was in pain, but that he hadn't gone numb to the horrors of it all. That his beautiful soul was still intact. A lot had changed for her in the year since she had almost lost Polly and Sugar. A lot had changed about her. One of the biggest things had been her relationship with Fredrick. No longer did she keep him at arm's length. They grew closer every day, and she was better for it.

"So, what do we know, will you talk me through it?"

"Yes Ma'am."

Fredrick stood from the small desk in the office of the house they had rented in Navarre Florida. He slid out of his suit jacket and cuffed the sleeves on his navy blue shirt. Dorthea couldn't help but grin when his back was turned. For Fredrick, he may as well have been walking around in swim trunks and crocs. To take off his jacket and roll up his sleeves. She looked at herself in the mirror across from her seat on the leather sofa. She wore a maroon hoodie from a college she had never heard of before, a great thrift store find in her estimation, and a pair of old sweatpants, cut off above the knee to make shorts out of them.

He paced the floor as he spoke.

"Five families in three months, all the same patterns as Cordray. With the following exceptions. The fathers were all later found dead at separate locations, always an abandoned basement or garage, in one case a storage unit. Obvious signs of a summoning in every one of the locations, but nothing we can piece together or replicate, yet. The third and fourth families also included extended family. A cousin with the third family and the parents of the mother in the fourth. The violence has also escalated dramatically. This last family was essentially torn apart.

By all appearances this is either a copycat of Cordray's murders, or we are seeing evidence of the father that the tether spoke of before her destruction. Either way, we are close. This last family here in Navarre has only been dead a couple of days. With fifteen to twenty days between discoveries, we cannot be far behind them. Whoever they are."

Dorthea stood from her seat on the sofa and stretched. Fredrick arched an eyebrow at her.

"Everything where it should be Ma'am? Do you maybe need a trip to the chiropractor? We have been in the car a lot lately. Perhaps..."

"Perhaps, you should can it, Sapp." Dorthea snapped as she rotated her shoulders first the right then the left. "Besides, you're almost as old as me and six feet-forty or however damn tall you are. How are you not stiff from all the hours on the road?"

"Well Ma'am, I would venture..."

The door to the room they were standing in exploded inward in a shower of wooden splinters and sand. Fredrick was thrown forward toward Dorthea. She held out her left hand like she was catching a pass one handed, and it swung backward as she slowed the momentum of Fredrick being thrown before he could crash into the bookshelf beside her. Her right hand she threw up and shouted "beskerm liefde."

The debris from the door and the sand from outside deflected off to the sides and missed both her and Fredrick. As the air began to clear a stout looking man in a red flannel shirt stepped through the whole in the wall where the door used to be.

When he spoke, it sounded to Dorthea like the buzzing of a thousand flies under his nasal tenor.

"I cannot believe the lengths I had to go to for you to finally track me down. In the end, and this is the end you stupid bitch, all that matters is you're here now. And tonight, you are going pay for killing my daughter."

Dorthea stammered and looked around furtively as if for something to use as a weapon, Fredrick moaned in pain as he attempted to get up.

"You might want to tell tall, dark, and soon to be dead to stay the fuck down. You are both dying tonight, but if you cooperate, and tell me what I want to know, you'll die easy. If not, well, you've seen just how messy I am willing to get in order to get my point across."

Dorthea reached for Fredrick, putting a hand on his hip. "It's okay Fredrick, just do what he says.

Sensing the weakness in the gesture, the man in the flannel shirt smirked at Dorthea and stalked forward his eyes ablaze with vengeance and a promise of pain to come.

As the man stalked forward, drawing a thin blade from a sheath on his belt, Dorthea leaned protectively over Fredrick's prone body.

"I have to say, I expected a little more from you witch. Being able to trap and kill my daughter was quite a feat. She had several witch heads on her wall from previous attempts. I was honestly looking forward to more of a challenge, but seeing you here, all pathetic and crying over boyfriend there. It almost takes the fun out of it. So, I am going to make it interesting. I won't be using any of my power to kill the two of you. Just my blade here."

He held the cruel looking blade in front of his face and smiled. "Well, I might chew a little too."

He grabbed a handful of Dorthea's short grey hair and yanked her to her feet. She screamed in pain and tried to pull away. She was no match for his strength as he held her head in place just inches from his own. A look of pure panic crossed Dorthea's face as he drug the tip of the knife across her cheek, the razor edge opening a line of red.

"Ahh, there we go, is it really a party until someone starts bleeding?"

There are some things in the world that remain consistent no matter time nor place. One of those consistencies, a universal truth as it were, is that men will always underestimate women. Especially middle aged women.

Even when that man is a powerful evil entity, and even when that woman is Dorthea Milburn.

The terror in Dorthea's eyes vanished, replaced by a different expression, the smile of a warrior who knows they have won the fight before it ever started. The smile of a general whose enemy allowed their ego to dictate their actions, and will now pay the price.

"You know, it's really not."

She wiped the blood from her cheek and flung it at the wall next to where she stood. At once the spell work inscribed on every inch of this room exploded to life. Red and orange light glowed from the walls, ceiling, and floor as the warding took hold.

She held out her bloody hand to him. "Appreciate that sir, no greater source of power than the blood of the witch. Seals these wards right up. Now, Bets if you would be so kind."

As if she had been standing there all along Bets appeared in the corner of the room, Her hands were outstretched as she opened up her siphon and pulled every bit of magical energy from within the circle.

The man began to spin back and forth wildly like a caged animal.

"Weird how that works isn't it. See, no energy can flow in or out of this room now. Think of it like a Faraday cage for the divine energy. And once she pulled all of the power in the room into herself then no more can get in to replenish those of us who rely on it for our power. So, wherever you were about to run off to, I am afraid that will have to wait."

He snarled and pulled back the hand holding the knife. "You stupid bitch, you think I need power to gut all of you." He lunged forward with the blade intent on burying it in Dorthea's chest. A crunch of bone, and the blade clanging against the hardwood floor was the only sound as Fredrick's baton smashed down onto his forearm shattering it. He screamed in pain and outrage and cradled his now useless right arm in his left hand.

Dorthea smirked at him. "Might not need power, but that arm might have come in handy."

A cackle from behind the man "HA! Handy, oh that's a good one."

The man attempted to turn and look at Edward the Fish, but before he could spin all the way around he started to shake. An electric sound and the smell of burning flannel and skin permeated the air in the room as Edward's stinger sent wave after wave of electricity through his spine and into his brain.

"Handy, I'll have to remember that one. Oh, I almost forgot." He hit a button on the remote in his hand and the man collapsed to the ground flopping uncontrollably and moaning in pain.

Edward turned a dial and the man stopped flopping around. Dorthea looked at Bets.

"Are you okay, that was a big power draw…"

"You stupid fat cow, I will cut your fucking throat and AHHHHHH!"

He started flopping around again and screaming as Edward rotated a different dial on the remote. "Now you be nice to Ms. Dorthea." Edwards normal high pitched sing song voice was even more out of place and creepy in this situation than normal.

He twisted the dial back and the screaming and flopping stopped.

"Thank you Edward."

Edward beamed like a student answering his favorite teacher.

"Do you have the manacles?"

"Yes Ma'am, Ms. Dorthea, General Milburn. Ma'am."

"Just Dorthea or Sister Dorthea is fine Edward."

Yes Ma'am, sorry. Sister Dorthea."

The man now lying prone at his feet, a shining black and silver scorpion about the size of a cell phone attached to his spine. He groaned a little but made no attempt to talk or move. Edward reached for the dial again, but Fredrick grabbed his arm.

"Edward, if you would, perhaps we wait a moment or two before you light him up again. I am afraid the smell is getting a little overwhelming and I think he received your message about civility and politeness loud and clear."

"He is getting a bit stinky isn't he?"

Edward reached into a deep canvas bag on his hip and pulled out a strange looking device. A series of loops of bright white metal connected two loops of leather at one end and two loops of iron at the other. Both appeared to be covered in markings and laced through with gold and silver.

Fredrick raised an eyebrow. "How exactly do I use these manacles Edward?"

"Oh, super-duper easy Fredrick my good man." Edward bowed toward Fredrick in what everyone assumed was an imitation of Fredrick, a sincere and good natured one. His long curly hair nearly touched the floor as he did.

"You just slide the iron ones over his feet and onto his ankles, then bend him double and slide the leather over his wrists. Pull the silver chain out of the middle of the links when you have them in place and they will secure themselves. Then it's the same magical principle as this warding. No energy of creation in or out of the vessel. Since he is already drained from Bets, Bets, Bets, doing her thing. We can carry him out trussed up like dinner and escort him back to the chambers at Mercer where the elders will figure out what to do with him."

"Thank you Edward, that is brilliant. Did you design these yourself?"

"Yes sir. Bets, Bets, Bets, laid the spell work on them." He leaned in conspiratorially and whispered. "She's really good at that kind of stuff."

The man at his feet groaned again and faster than Fredrick could do anything about. Edward spun the dial.

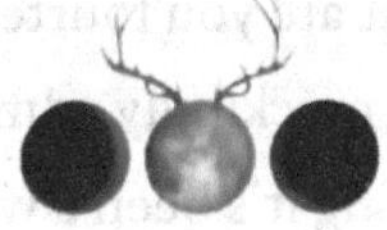

"Dorthea, do you think the elders will be able to get answers from him? Maybe ascertain his origin or if he is the only one of his kind?"

Bets was sitting on the tailgate of Dorthea's truck waiting on Fredrick and Edward to return from their trip dropping the tether's father off with Elder Beckham and Elder Daniella.

"I think whoever or whatever he is, he won't have much of a choice. If he is lucky he will answer some questions from a couple of the Elders and they will determine the best course of action. If he decides to play tough, he will end up with Elder Valkyrie asking the questions and that takes on a whole new look."

"What will happen with him? Will they execute him?"

"I doubt know. That seems like the most likely course of action. If it's possible. If even half of his bragging is correct he may be immortal or nearly immortal. Who knows what that looks like? And honestly Bets, I am just happy our part in it is done. There has been more attacks here and there on witches and their consorts."

"I heard, this last one sounded bad."

"It was, I know of Amy and John Park. Good people and good at what they do. They had made friends with the folks next door to them. They were attacked, the neighbor's husband was blown apart, Amy and woman escaped, but no one knows what happened to John. Amy and the woman were using a Belos Transport to get out and right as they vanished they saw John get attacked again.

It was a pyro and two half naked guys with giant hammers."

Bets raised a questioning eyebrow.

"Oh, holy crow Bets, what are you fourteen?" Dorthea couldn't hide the smile on her face as she mockingly admonished Bets.

"No Ma'am, I am just saying it's been a while since I have seen, held, or been hit by a giant hammer and at this point I wouldn't be mad about it."

"And that my love, is why you ended up with Edward the Fish as a consort and not someone like a Devlin or Fredrick. They didn't want to give you a second consort just to protect your first one from your need to be hit with a giant hammer now and then."

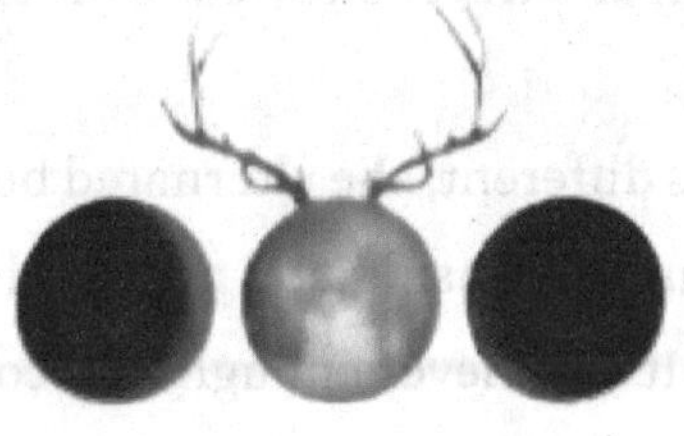

Rawr!

S itting at her desk in her office, LaRhonda was half reading a briefing from Gerardo and her team about a new house bill headed her way. It was a long and tediously written affair that was basically a twelfth attempt by this congress to defund the United States Post Office and funnel federal postal funding to the private shipping company owned by the nephew of the newly appointed chairman of the budget committee. The other half of her mind was where it had been these last couple of months, in the arms of Harlan Rice.

To say she had been distracted lately would be the understatement of a lifetime. Congress was on recess, and she had been running back and forth between her D.C. apartment and her loft in Chicago trying to stay in touch with her community. They had been spending one night a week or so together. Then every other weekend they had dinner with his girls. LaRhonda tried to be very respectful of his time with them.

What she wanted was to be selfish, to take up every minute of his free time. But she knew that wasn't realistic, nor was it healthy. But this was the first time in her life she had really been in love. Over the years she had a fling or two; casual encounters that served their purpose. But always at arm's length and never allowed to bloom into anything more serious than that.

With Harlan, it was different, she alternated between this incredible hunger to be near him she wasn't, and a breathless feeling of acceleration when she was. It was never enough, she could spend a day with him, shopping, walking in the park, eating. Then spend the entire night lying naked in his arms, feeling the warmth of him against her, talking until he began to doze mid-sentence, then listening to him sleep. But it never felt like it was enough.

She knew what it was. No matter how much she opened up, there was this part of her that she had yet to show him. The deepest, truest part of who she was had still been hidden from him. But that time was ending. She was just waiting here now. One way or another today the anxiety of lying to Harlan was coming to an end. Today she made her petition to the elders of Mercer. She would ask their permission to bring Harlan before Lord Seanchara and ask for his blessing to tell Harlan the truth. To tell him who she really was and what her real purpose in life was. She was terrified and exhilarated. If the petitions went well she would be opening up to him and hoping he understood and accepted her for who she was.

If either the elders or Lord Seanchara denied her petitions then she would be faced with the nightmare of continuing to live this lie or break things off with him. Could she do that? Could she go back to living her life without the feeling of her heart racing when she saw him walking toward her, or the smile that stretched across her face every time she heard his text notification go off.

"LaRhonda?"

Gerardo's voice brought her back to reality. She must have really been out of it. He was standing directly in front of her desk, and she hadn't even heard him come in.

"Yes?"

"It's time, they're here."

"Who Gerardo? Time for what, I thought the trip home was the only thing scheduled for today. You know we have no idea how long it will take."

"No, apparently plans have changed. They are here."

"Wait, Mother is here? With—"

His grave nod stopped her mid-sentence.

"Where, why are they here, wait are all of them here?"

"Perhaps not all, but there are several here. Enough that I am certain your question can be answered. Probably more importantly they are waiting at your apartment building. We should go now."

"Are they in my apartment?"

Could this be real, did the elders of Mercer just break into her apartment?

"I just received the call; it sounds like they are in the courtyard waiting for us. Elder Dinah said not to rush on their behalf that they are just enjoying the sunshine."

LaRhonda was on her feet, her bag in hand and headed for the door before he finished the sentence.

A ten-minute ride and she was bailing out of the car in front of her building. Gerardo would head around to the garage and park. She was shaking and her mind was racing. What would make the Elders of Mercer come to her apartment in Washington D.C.? It couldn't be a good thing. Did they know about Harlan? Were they anticipating her question? Why here? Did they expect things to go wrong?

LaRhonda made the last two stairs and grabbed for her key fob. She needed to calm herself before she walked through the front door and down the stairs to the private courtyard in the middle of her building. She had no reason to be scared. Yes, these were the Elders of Mercer, the most powerful witches in the world. But she had known these women her entire life. She had learned from them, trained with them, and taken every meal with them, since she was a young girl.

The scene that greeted her was as surreal as she could have ever imagined. The courtyard in her building was a large multi-tiered green space. From her spot at the head of the stairs leading down into it she could see almost all of it. Lounging around the flower garden like figures in a Victorian painting were some of the most powerful women to have ever lived. Elder Dinah and Elder Hirut were reclining in two bamboo hammocks side by side. Elder Yasmina, Mama Rosie, and Mother Mercer were sitting on a bench in front of the small koi pond, Mother Mercer was sipping from a paper QuikTrip coffee cup. LaRhonda had never seen one anywhere near D.C. She wondered where that one came from.

In the lower garden there was a playground with a small swing set and a slide for the building's children to play on, and a small, fenced area used for pet relief.

She could hear small children laughing and she shook her head at the sight that greeted her as one of the children screamed. "Higher friend, push me higher please."

Lord Seanchara, in a fine tailored suit was pushing two small kids on the swings while Elder Valkyrie in a pair of dark sunglasses looked on from a bench next to the nanny and another woman LaRhonda did not recognize.

"Oh children, I am afraid that if we swing any higher we will take flight. Think of how worried your parents would be if you just flew away. Would your mommy be worried if you grew wings like a bird and flew away Brianna? I know that my mother would be very worried about me if I grew wings and flew away from swinging so high."

The little girl on the swing cackled with the laughter only used by very small children when they have caught a grown up being ridiculous.

"We can't grow wings and fly friend, we aren't birds."

"Or dinosaurs." Yelled the boy on the other swing.

"Very true Jamal." Lord Seanchara grinned wide. But I bet we can roar like dinosaurs can't we?"

"Yeah!" The kids both cheered.

"Okay kids, on the count of three, lets roar our best dinosaur roar. Then I have to rejoin the grownups and doing boring grown up things."

"Awwww." The children whined in the practiced unison of siblings trying to get a parent to see things their way. "Okay, but you roar too."

"Deal. Alright, one, two, three."

"Rawr." Both kids and Lord Seanchara all gave a loud roar, and the kids gave their scariest dinosaur faces before falling into hysterical laughter.

LaRhonda was astounded.

Lord Seanchara looked to where she stood at the top of the stairs.

"Okay new friends, it is time for me to go. My friend has arrived. Now remember what we talked about. You behave for your grownups okay."

"Yes sir." The reply came from both children as they continued swinging.

As LaRhonda looked around the courtyard in disbelief all of the elders present rose and began to walk in her direction. Lord Seanchara at the back.

Elder Dinah reached her first and opened her arms. LaRhonda embraced her and whispered in her ear. "Why are you all at my house?"

Dinah held her at arm's length and looked her up and down. "Nothing to fret about dear. We just wanted to stretch our legs. Since you had asked to come before the elders today we thought it would suit everyone just as well if we came to you. Since Lord Seanchara was already opening a path we thought we would get out for an afternoon. Besides Mother loves that cheap coffee."

"A handful of Elders and Lord Seanchara popping over for tea is a bit more than I was prepared for."

"Well come on, put on some tea and let's talk, it's been entirely too long since I have seen you and I am ready to catch up."

After some shuffling to fit everyone in the elevator and getting everyone comfortable in her living room LaRhonda surveyed the gathered Elders. They were all smiling or chatting among themselves and she truly felt no cause for concern. Some brief greetings and pleasantries were exchanged before Elder Hirut began speaking. Her high-pitched voice heavy with her Egyptian accent.

"Sister LaRhonda, thank you for your hospitality on short notice, you wished to speak to us. Let us hear your business now if you would."

Lord Seanchara rose from his throw pillow on the floor. "Sounds like that is my cue, as much as I have enjoyed our sojourn, the Elders of Mercer hardly need my input, and I will take my leave. Sisters, when you need me, you can have my bride summon me and I will reopen the path."

LaRhonda held up her hand to stop him. "If it is all the same Sisters, this will concern Lord Seanchara at some point I believe. If everyone is comfortable, I will address you all together."

She looked around the room for any objections and saw only nods of approval, although the mood had obviously changed. She took a deep breath and fell into her connection to all of those present. Extending her love and goodwill to each of them.

"I have asked to speak to you today as I have come to a crossroads in my life, and need your guidance. As you all know I am currently serving in the United States House of Representatives. Earlier this year I began work on the Safe Women and Children Act. A bill designed to unify and simplify protecting abused women and children and providing resources they desperately need to escape their abusers. This bill also allows us to place Mercer contacts, or witches in positions of leadership in safe houses and resource centers all over the country to act as guardians and mentors for these women."

Several of the Elders were nodding in approval of this. Elder Valkyrie had taken her sunglasses off, her red glowing, eyeless sockets giving her a blank expression despite her intensity.

"In order to accomplish this and in an effort to calm some of the louder and more destructive voices in congress I worked alongside a coalition of two Senators and one other Representative, all of us from different parties and different areas of the country. During the course of this I began a romantic relationship with Representative Harlan Rice of Mississippi."

More than a few eyebrows raised, but more than anything LaRhonda noticed the smiles, kind and knowing.

"As our relationship has grown, I have become more and more concerned that I have built this love on a lie, a necessary lie, but a lie, nonetheless. After some discussion with my consort Gerardo, he recommended I come to you all, to petition on Harlan's behalf, that he be told the truth about who I really am and our mission. I believe in my heart that he will be a valuable partner to Mercer, and just as importantly, I believe our love should be built on a foundation of truth. So, I need your guidance on how to handle this situation, on what my options may be."

Mother Mercer spoke in her soft sweet voice. "Sister, first of all, from all of us, congratulations, on the success of your new bill, that was an amazing piece of work on behalf of vulnerable women and children everywhere. Secondly and perhaps just as importantly, congratulations on your newfound love. All of our sisters and brothers dedicate so much of their lives to our mission that it can be so difficult to find a way to fulfil our desire to love and be loved by another. Your consort was wise in sending you to us. There is indeed many cases of loved ones being made aware of our mission, there is also a precedent for cultivating contacts outside Mercer to aid in our mission. Let me ask you sister. Do you think that this man, who has captured your heart, would be not only a good partner to you, but also a good partner to Mercer? Please keep in mind that both do not have to be true for us to consider your petition."

"I do Mother, I believe that Harlan Rice is the best of men. His kindness and integrity are beyond reproach by every measure I have available to me. He truly lives the life of a servant. Believing wholeheartedly in the Christian traditions in which he was raised. He also has twin daughters who are very in tune with the divine energy. I have felt them exploring their connections more than once."

Behind LaRhonda Elder Valkyrie spoke. "Sister, do you believe someone should be observing the daughters as well?"

LaRhonda turned and gave a gentle bow of her head in acknowledgement of Elder Valkyrie. "Yes Ma'am, I do. The girls, Lydia, and Lexia, are very clearly of a Mercer lineage. I am not certain whose side it is one since I have not yet met their mother, but I believe in time both of them will find their way into Mercer."

Mama Rosie shifted in her seat on the couch. "So, a Mercer witch, falls in love with a Christian man, who has twin daughters who are likely natural witches? If that isn't the divine energy guiding your heart, I don't know what is."

LaRhonda relaxed and felt the divine energy flowing through her and into her connection to everyone here. Their love and support rode on the waves of their connections.

"I believe it is Mama. My only question now is how do we proceed?"

Mother Mercer motioned to Lord Seanchara, who was rising to his feet.

"Sister that would be my distinct honor. I will meet with this young man and take measure of him. If I sense nothing that threatens the mission of Mercer you will have my blessing and may proceed however the council advises. Being a hopeless romantic myself, my hope is that his heart is true. Should it prove otherwise, would you like me to bring it to you on a platter?"

"Thank you Lord Seanchara, my hope is that will not be necessary. But your offer is greatly appreciated."

"You're very welcome, I do need a little more information from you then I will be off." He reached forward, his eyes asking her permission before his hand made contact. LaRhonda nodded at him, and he gently cupped her cheek. She felt his gentle pull at her mind and relaxed. She saw the image of Harlan in her mind, him laughing at some ridiculous joke of his own. Then it was over and Lord Seanchara was gone.

She felt Mother Mercer's gentle hand on her upper arm as she guided her to a seat on the couch next to Mama Rosie.

"Rest a while now love, it will not take our guardian long to make his decision."

"Wait, Lord Seanchara is going to Harlan right now? I guess I thought it would be more of a meeting or petition?"

"Like bringing a boyfriend home to meet your father? I guess that would be slightly more dramatic, but also not necessary. This way, Harlan will not be aware of anything other than meeting a rather large and overly friendly fellow on the street and if he is deemed unworthy there is no risk to him, or Mercer."

"Only to me."

"Yes Sister, only to you."

LaRhonda sank back into the couch cushions and Mama Rossie but her hand on her leg to offer her support.

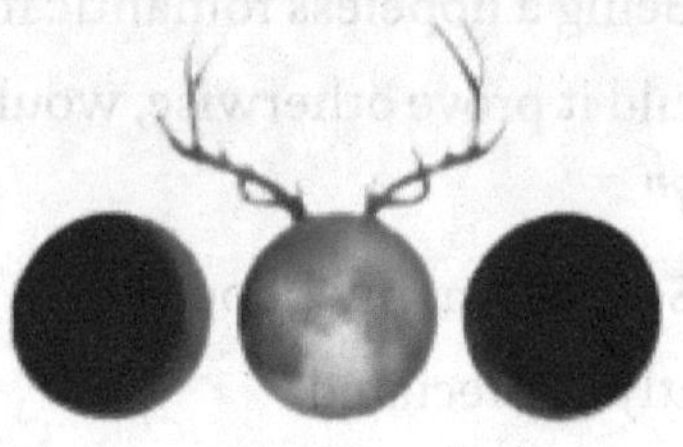

Everyone Loves Lunch.

LaRhonda found a disconcerting comfort in ordering lunch for the Elders of Mercer. It was rare for her that the magical and the mundane intersected in her world. Her work within the mission of Mercer was her work as a Representative. Sure, she had to deal with the procedural day to day life of an elected official as well as the normal fundraising and networking. No magic was used to get her elected or keep her involved with community or national politics. That was all her own work. But every decision she made in that capacity was to serve the mission. Not much magic was involved in her day to day.

But now here she was ordering sandwiches and salads for Mercer's Council of Elders, and Lord Seanchara. She wondered how long this would take, all of the Elders seemed so calm. Just chatting away about this thing or that. None of them seemed at all interested in acknowledging that the love of her life was currently being examined by an unpredictable and terrifying demi-god, and that the future of her life hung on his decision.

She paced around nervously as she waited on the delivery guy from the sandwich shop down the block, unable to sit and enjoy what should have been an incredible opportunity to commune with her elders.

A gentle hand on her shoulder made her jump and gasp. She spun and Mama Rosie was standing before her. "Come sit down Sister. You're going to worry yourself sick."

"I'm sorry Mama Rosie. I am trying to stay calm, but I feel like a kid waiting to be called to the principal's office."

"Of course you do, you have a lot riding on this. But you know as well as any of us. Lord Seanchara is fair and wise. He will look into this man's mind and spirit, and you will know the truth of him. Have you thought of how you will proceed?"

"I have, if he is accepted by Lord Seanchara, we have a weekend away planned. He and his ex-wife own a cabin in the woods in Virginia that they keep as a vacation home. They take turns during the summers taking their kids up there. Harlan and I were planning on spending a few days there over the Fourth of July holiday and I thought that would be a great time to tell him. There won't be anyone else around for the whole time we are there, and it is far enough out in the woods that if he needs some kind of demonstration to convince him that I am telling the truth, I won't be risking someone else seeing."

"And if he doesn't take the news well?"

"My hope that is if I know his heart like I think I do, he will love and support me no matter what. I think Lord Seanchara's assessment will attest to that. If he doesn't than both I and Lord Seanchara's opinion of him would be incorrect and that just doesn't seem likely."

The doorbell ringing pulled LaRhonda's attention from Mama Rosie and she called over her shoulder as she crossed the room to open the door for lunch. "Food is here everyone, I will lay it out in the dining room."

She froze as she opened the door to see Harlan, a bag of take out from Delhi Deli in his hand, in conversation with a smiling Lord Seanchara. A delivery guy stood behind them with two large boxes of food in his arms.

"Harlan, what..."

"Oh LaRhonda, I am sorry. I was stopping by your office to say hi and your staff said you were working from home today. I remembered you said you had a couple of important remote meetings today and figured you might want something easy for lunch. So, I stopped for some curry on the way and was just going to drop it off and run. Through the strangest coincidence ever I run into your friend in town from home out in front of the deli. He said you had a bunch of friends and family in unexpectedly, and he was out grabbing coffee while you waited on lunch to be delivered. I am sorry for showing up announced."

He stepped aside for the delivery guy to bring in the boxes. Lord Seanchara took them from the man and headed for the dining room. LaRhonda thanked him and turned back to Harlan. She leaned in and gave him a quick peck on the cheek and pulled back.

"Harlan, thank you for the gesture. Yes my remote meeting ended up in person with a bunch of folks from back home. No need to apologize there is just some timing issues."

He held up his hands to let her know there was no need to apologize, that he understood. When she heard Mother Mercers voice behind her.

"LaRhonda, is that the handsome man you were telling us about. Let him in girl, you weren't raised to be rude."

Harlan leaned to the side enough to see around LaRhonda.

"Oh, Ma'am, I sure did not mean to intrude on your meeting with Representative Kelm, I know how seriously she takes her time with her community."

"Well sir, now I insist. We have heard all about you, it would only be fair for us to get to meet you for ourselves."

Harlan looked questioningly at LaRhonda. She smiled and nodded, stepping to the side so he could step into her apartment. He slid his shoes off and carried his bag of food to add to the buffet already being arranged by Elder Dinah on the dining room table.

LaRhonda took a deep breath and fell into her connection to Mother Mercer who only grinned at her like a child who knew she was up to some mischief but was having too much fun to stop. LaRhonda could not remember ever being this scared for another person. These women were her family, and she loved and respected every one of them. But why did she suddenly feel like Harlan was a lamb being led to slaughter at her request?

One by one the women filed into the dining room where Harlan and Lord Seanchara were opening containers, unwrapping sandwiches, and laying out sides and sweets. How was she supposed to introduce these women to Harlan, how to explain Lord Seanchara and Valkyrie's eyes. Holy crow, this was going to be a disaster.

She heard Harlan's deep laughter, that genuine belly laugh that she loved so much. She came around the corner to see him standing between Mother Mercer and Elder Hirut.

"Well Ma'am, I can promise you I have no designs on stealing her away for Mississippi. Although I suppose that means her and I will both have to continue to win elections so that we don't have to navigate that. But it seems like with support like what she has in your community, she will be as successful as she chooses to be. Not that I have any doubt. She is beyond special, and I think everyone who has met her or worked with her recognizes that."

"That is the Lord's truth if I have ever heard it. Representative Rice, LaRhonda tells us you have twin daughters, how old are they?"

Harlan's smile could not have been wider as he started talking about his girls.

"They are fifteen Ma'am, Lydia, and Lexia. I know every parent will tell you their kids are special, and I am no different. My girls are amazing. The way they have navigated their mother and I separating, her and I both having jobs that require a lot of travel and flexibility. And of course, they think LaRhonda is the coolest human being they have ever met."

Elder Hirut touched Harlan's shoulder and LaRhonda could see the energy of creation flow through her and into him. She could not see what it was Hirut was doing to him but there was definitely some kind of charm or spell work involved.

"Ms Agash..."

"Please Harlan call me Niri."

"Yes thank you, Niri, I am sorry but if you would indulge me. Is that Amharic I am hearing in your accent?"

"Yes! It is, but I cannot remember the last time someone recognized it randomly."

"My roommate for my first two years in college was Ethiopian. Yours isn't quite the same as his, but it is close enough I recognized it."

"I am from a small village in the north of Ethiopia. But I have not lived there since I was a very young girl and that was many, many years ago. I am surprised you caught that."

"Ma'am, it could not have been that long ago."

Harlan flashed her the full wattage of his smile, his southern charm turned all the way up.

Niri batted her eyes at him dramatically. "Mr. Rice, your lady is just a few feet away, and I am far too old for you, your magic won't work on me. Now come sit with us, I want to hear all about the work the two of you are doing."

What followed was some of the most intense and nerve-wracking conversation of LaRhonda's life. But as the lunch went on she realized just how much she shouldn't have worried at all. Harlan was a kind and charming person by nature, and a highly educated politician by trade. He was just as home on the board of a symphony as he was at a county fair or a roadhouse. He could make friends and find common ground anywhere he went.

Somehow, she had forgotten that every single witch on the Council of Elders was a real live person, not just enigmatic and reclusive witches. But they were also mothers, and daughters and sisters, with friends and goals and ambitions. They had not always spent their lives within the Temple of the Mother. Some of them, like Elder Hirut and Mama Rosie were rarely there. Even Lord Seanchara, who introduced himself as Billy for some reason, was extremely personable. Spending a good part of lunch talking to Harlan about fishing for catfish in rural Mississippi. She had no idea what that was about.

Once lunch was over Harlan excused himself to help clean up with LaRhonda. Once they were alone in the kitchen he walked up behind her wrapping his arms around her waist and kissing the side of her neck. "Hey, I hope you are okay that I just dropped by unannounced. I've never done that before. I didn't mean to intrude; I was really just planning on dropping off the food for you and maybe stealing a kiss. But I could tell you were tense through lunch, and I feel like there is something I am missing here. If I disrespected a boundary, please just let me know."

She leaned into him and held his arms tighter around her. "Harlan, you are fine, it was very thoughtful, and I am in no way upset about you stopping by. There is some stuff going on that I will tell you about later and that's what has me distracted. But I promise it has nothing to do with you."

"Oh love, I may not be the cause, but if it's important to you it's important to me. You let me know if there is any way I can support. But for now, I am going to say my goodbyes and get back to the office,

I have a bit of a busy afternoon and dinner with the girls tonight. I love you LaRhonda. Let's talk soon."

She kissed him and followed him back to the living room so he could say his goodbyes, fifteen minutes later she was closing the door behind him and taking a deep breath, ready to hear the final decision from the Council of Elders on her future with Harlan.

When she returned Lord Seanchara was kneeling before Mother Mercer as she sat on the couch, they both turned her way as she walked in.

He rose and motioned her to the empty armchair next to the fireplace. When she was seated he took his place on the cushion in front of Elder Valkyrie. Mother Mercer began.

"LaRhonda, first and foremost, what a delightful man. One does not need our magical insight or the ability to read the souls of men to see he is not only kind and thoughtful but also adores you almost as much as he loves his girls. That being said Lord Seanchara has delved into his mind and spirit to search for anything that could bring harm to our family and mission and informed us of his assessment."

LaRhonda's stomach flipped and her heart was racing.

"We are in agreement that you may inform Harlan of your origins and your life in Mercer, and we request that you extend the invitation to him to become an ally to our great family. We do need you to understand, that he must be sworn to secrecy and will be watched for any concerning behavior regarding our mission. Should he decline to become an ally then his knowledge of Mercer should remain only about you and your origins. If your relationship should end, it will be up to Lord Seanchara to decide the best way to protect us from any potential fallout. We wish you the best sister and it is my personal hope that this man loves and honors you for the rest of his life. Now come and walk us out and say your farewells, we have enjoyed your fellowship and hospitality. But like you, we all have many matters to attend."

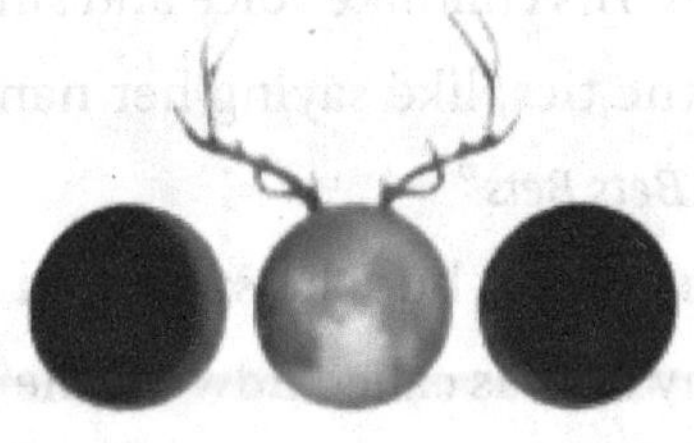

TIME TO KEEP THAT PROMISE

Bets stepped out of Edward's van and stretched, bending at the waist then straightening. She extended her arms to the sky, threw her head back and breathed in the morning air. They had driven through the night, setting out from Navarre. She didn't know precisely where they were, only that they were somewhere outside of Springfield Missouri, and that she was happy to be out of that seat.

Dorthea and Fredrick were already grabbing their bags out of the truck. Edward's white Ford Econoline van was a perfect reflection of his personality, cluttered and eccentric, but tuned to perfection where it mattered. He maintained the engine meticulously; he had upgraded every possible aspect of it. It looked like a beat up old van from the outside, but in reality, everything about it was computer tuned and intentionally designed.

Edward was an enigma to her still. An undeniable genius, capable and confident under pressure. His social skills and ability to interact with the people around him were limited at best. He as always friendly and as polite as his idiosyncrasies allowed. But he could be somewhat off putting sometimes. His childlike voice and sing song way of speaking, combined with the tics, like saying her name three times, every time he said it. *"Bets, Bets Bets"*

She had never figured out, but she supposed it didn't matter. She also did not know why he was called Edward the Fish, when she asked anyone else they said to ask him and when she asked him he just said, "That's my name, what else would I be called?"

He took his obligation to aid and protect her deadly serious, and she had come to trust him and that's really all there was to worry about.

Still, she was ready for a break in the non-stop stream of consciousness that was alone time with Edward the Fish.

The house was a small white 1960's ranch style at the end of a farm road. The home gave the distinct feeling of being old, but well cared for. A woman appeared on the porch, her long black hair cascaded over the shoulders of the white tunic she wore. She was barefoot but moved down the stairs and across the stone path with no noticeable discomfort. Bets and Edward caught up to Dorthea and Fredrick just as the woman made it to the front of the driveway.

She extended her arms toward Dorthea.

"Sister Dorthea, it is good to meet you. Thank you for coming so quickly."

"Sister Ruth, it is good to meet you as well. Thank you for having us. We are happy to help. This is Fredrick Sapp, Bets, and Edward."

Sister Ruth made her way from person to person hugging all of them. When she got to Edward she shook her head. "Edward the Fish, what on earth are you doing here? Last I heard you were up in the mountains in Tennessee. I almost didn't recognize you with all that hair."

"Hi Ruth, I was, for a while. But Bets, Bets Bets, needed a consort so Mother called me down from the cabin. Is Benny here?"

"He is Edward. He will be thrilled to see you I am sure."

"Do you think he will remember me?"

"Benny never forgets a friend Edward. He will remember you for sure. He is out back, once you all are settled I will show you. Please everyone, you must be tired from the trip. Let's go in for tea and we can talk then."

Once everyone was in the living room and settled with a cup of tea and a small array of snacks, Ruth disappeared momentarily down the hallway toward the back of the house. When she returned there was a blond woman trailing behind her. Fredrick rose at once; Edward caught the gesture and awkwardly did the same. Ruth addressed the group once again.

"Everyone, this is Amy Park."

The woman stepped around Sister Ruth and began introducing herself. When she got to Fredrick she paused, her face softened and Bets did not miss the well of sadness there.

"Fredrick Sapp, you trained with Mathew Weems?"

"I did."

"My husband John Park also trained with Mathew, he mentioned you more than once. Said that Mathew would bring you in for sparring sessions." She choked back her grief. "Said, he never understood what the word gentleman truly meant until he met you."

"I remember John well. He is a brilliant judoka, and an even better poker player if memory serves."

She gently touched his arm. "It is good to meet you; it is good to meet you all. Thank you for answering the call. Let me get a cup of tea, and I will tell you what happened."

Over the next half hour, she recounted the story of the attack and the aftermath. When she was done Dorthea began to plan.

"Amy do you have a tracker talisman for John?"

"I do, it's still warm so I believe he is still alive, but I cannot get a read on where he is. He is either too far away or its being blocked somehow."

"Okay, Sister Ruth, do you have clear quartz and Holy Basil?"

"Yes Sister, I have almost anything you might need."

"Good, Fredrick can you grab my pack from the truck? Edward, do you have any copper?"

Fredrick was already moving out the door and Edward hopped up. "Yes Ma'am, wire or sheet?"

"Wire more than likely, If I give you the dimensions can you rig us up a ringlet? It will need to be big enough to fit snuggly on Sister Amy's wrist. Sister Amy, we will build an amplification bracelet that I think can track him down no matter where he is. Am I safe in assuming that you will be joining us in hunting these bastards down?"

Amy nodded, the fire in her eyes betraying her calm expression. "I made a promise to Lord Seanchara, and I fully intend to keep it."

It was late in the evening before they had finished the physical and spell work necessary to combine Amy's tracking talisman to the ringlet Edward had fashioned for them out of copper. As soon as Amy slid it onto her wrist and Edward adjusted it, she whispered John's name into the talisman and a sad smile came over her face.

"I can feel him Dorthea, thank you. Oh, sisters he is alive, and I can feel him. He is very far and muffled like he is buried under something. But he's alive and that means we can find him. I will start packing immediately."

Dorthea grabbed her arm. "Let us make preparations, but we have been on the road for three weeks hunting a monster. None of us have slept in a real bed or had a meal that wasn't eaten in a car seat. We can leave out tomorrow but tonight we need to plan and prepare. We are talking about taking back your consort from Malleus Dei, something that has not been done before. We need supplies, and rest or we will be walking into a war with nothing."

Amy was nodding grimly, she understood, but there was no mistaking that she did not agree with Dorthea's plan. She was also wise enough to know that arguing this was counterproductive and futile. Bets made a mental note to keep an eye on her should they fail to rescue

John. A woman in this position may look for anyone she can blame, for any reason.

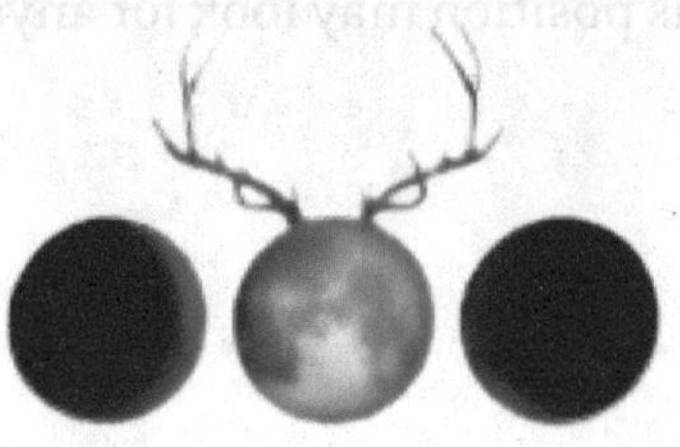

THE FISH AND THE DONKEY

Bets awoke to the strangest sound she had heard in recent memory. Loud raucous braying, that sounded like a combination of human laughter, and a donkey. No, multiple humans laughing with a donkey thrown in the mix.

She made her way to the kitchen of the little house. There was a fresh pot of coffee on the stove. Bets poured herself a cup and followed the sounds of the laughter to the back door of the house.

In a big circle pen in the back yard, Edward the Fish was being chased by an extremely large, and loud, donkey. It brayed and jumped, and he ran ahead of it. Edward had taken his flannel shirt off and was wearing jeans and a tank top as he ran around the pen waving the shirt as the donkey charged him. He let the donkey get withing kicking distance, then would jump out and over its back. Fredrick and Dorthea cheered and the donkey jumped and brayed louder.

Bets walked over to stand by Ruth, who was in a white wrap and drinking a cup of coffee off by herself. All at once Edward collapsed in the middle of the pen. The donkey was barreling right at him. Everyone looked to Ruth, who held up her hand.

The donkey ran right to where Edward lay, reared up, and collapsed next to him. It rolled onto its back as well as it could and kicked its legs into the air.

Edward and the donkey both rolled in the dirt laughing. Not a single person watching could help but to join in.

Back in the kitchen Bets was helping Ruth put together supply bags for the group.

"Ruth, can I ask you? How do you know Edward the Fish?"

"Oh, that is a long, sad story. But the short of it. There are a small number of us, witches, and consorts, who were born to Mercer. There aren't many of us right now. But Edward and I were both born to Mercer witches, while in Mercer. As was my sister Miranda."

Bets shifted, she did not particularly like where she thought this story was headed.

"Edward the Fish was Miranda's consort. She was killed trying to help a small group of kids escape a violent foster home. The neighborhood was overrun with gangs and drug dealers. She and Edward went in, grabbed the kids, and got out quick. Edward was loading the kids up in the van and Miranda was dealing with the foster mom, restraining her, when the mom's drug dealer boyfriend came in, thought they were being robbed and shot Miranda. He didn't even care about the kids being missing."

Ruth tinkered around in a drawer, not finding what she was looking for. But it gave her a moment to collect herself.

"Unfortunately, Miranda didn't survive, they did save all the kids. Edward's permanent grasp on reality also seemed to have suffered. He tried to stay in Mercer but was going a little stir crazy, he came to stay with me here, that's how he and Benny developed the little game you saw. But ultimately he couldn't find anything that helped with his grief, that is until now."

"I am sorry about your sister."

"Thank you, but it was a long time ago. Edward seems happier now than I have seen him in a long time. Just please, take care of him if you can Sister Bets. He is the best of men and this life we live has not been gentle with him.

"I will Sister, thank you."

"We should gather everyone for breakfast. Amy is getting impatient, and I fear her need to rescue John my override her manners and her common sense with your aunt."

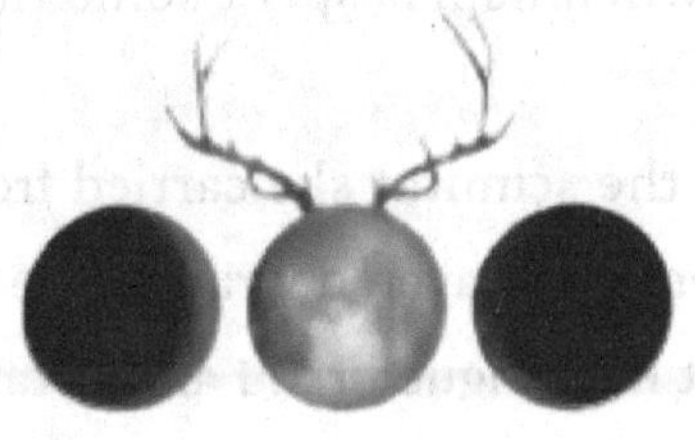

Like Father, Like Daughter

"You know that I am not afraid of the dark, bitch. I can smell you, all three of you. Oh yes, you are old aren't you, very old, but not as old as me."

The man shifted in his bindings. The iron shackles holding him tight, and keeping the energy of creation out, clanked against the cold stone floor.

"Come on, you fucking cows, say what you came to say, ask your questions, and let me be, or get close enough I can snap your fucking necks. I don't much care either way. You know eventually you will make a mistake, and I will start eating my way out of here. Once I am free of these shackles, there isn't one of you powerful enough to stop me."

Torches lit up around the stone chamber at Niri's command.

"What a foul mouth this one has on him. Elder Hirut, I am not sure we can have a civil conversation with this one yet. He seems... angry. Perhaps we let him relax for a hundred years or so, then revisit after that. He seems powerful enough to last. We can just seal up the chamber and come back when he has spent some time mediating on his manners."

Hirut was pulling the scimitar she carried from its sheath on her belt. She adjusted her many layered wrap as she did. "I agree Mother, perhaps I can cut out his tongue first. I am certain we can put it back when it is needed or give him a pen, or maybe an iPad to communicate with."

"I told you bitches I will eat my way out of this room; I will kill all of you worthless..."

The wet thump echoed in the chamber as Elder Beckham slammed her brass knuckled fist into his jaw. Two more thumps as she attacked his ribs, and the clicking of teeth hitting the floor as he spit them out in an attempt to catch his breath.

"Thank you Sister. He was getting really rude."

"Of course, Mother. Elder Hirut, there is a lot less in the way now if you want to remove his tongue."

Niri held up her hand. "I don't think that will be necessary now, do you sir?"

His voice was slurred and garbled around the broken jaw and blood gushing from his gums.

"Stupid cow, I am going to nail you to a wall and make you watch while I eat every child I can find here. I will slaughter the whole fucking bunch of you."

The man thrashed and pulled at his bindings. The leather creaked and the chains banged off of the stone floor. Suddenly, he went very still, and Niri felt a change in the room as Elder Valkyrie stepped out of nothingness to appear beside her.

The man fell to his knees, his bloody face touched the dirty stone of the cell, and he spoke, with his eyes still on the ground. "Bismil-lahi-ir-Rahmani-ir-Rahim, it is you, if these witches be your charges then my humblest apologies. I did not know, none of the host know. Please Shining Star, be merciful sister."

All four women stared at the man, who had gone from threatening to eat them all, to groveling for mercy in a puddle of his own blood and teeth.

Elder Valkyrie turned to Niri, "Mother, any idea what this one is on about?"

"Not a clue. Only that, a moment before you arrived, he was all threats and bluster, even after Beckham knocked his teeth out and broke his ribs. It seems he thinks he knows you."

"It appears so. It also appears his knowledge is one-sided."

"Elder Valkyrie, perhaps you and I can take our leave and let Elder Hirut and Elder Beckham secure this monster until he feels more co-operative?"

"Of course."

She held out her hand to Niri who grasped it without hesitation, and they stepped together through the energy of creation to arrive a moment later next to a bench in the flower garden overlooking the Temple of the Mother.

"Thank you Valkyrie; can you sit with me a moment among the flowers?"

"Something on your mind, Mother?"

"A thought, perhaps; do you know who that monster is?"

"Only that he was captured by Sister Dorthea."

"When the monster Cordray was finally captured and destroyed, his daughter, his tether, claimed to serve a dark father. That she was the power behind Cordray, and her father was greater than her. This is that dark father."

Valkyrie only nodded her understanding.

"Even among the strange and unknown, there are universal truths, and that monster was struck by a genuine terror the moment your presence became known. He was shaken to his black core. He truly believed you to be his executioner and was resigned to whatever fate you had for him. Only a moment before, he was telling the three of us he was going to torture and eat everyone here. He had no fear of our power at all."

"What are you saying, Niri?"

"That maybe therein lies the answers you have sought for as long as I have known you. Should we summon Lord Seanchara, ask him to intervene and look into the man's mind or what passes for it?"

"You are wise as always Niri, and thank you for your endless friendship and counsel. I will speak to my love about it. Will you be warding the cell against intrusion?"

"Yes, but nothing that Lord Seanchara will not be able to pass."

"Good, I will let you know what I find. Do you mind if we keep this between us until we know something for certain? Then I will bring what I find to the Elders for knowledge and discussion, should there be anything to discuss?"

"I believe that makes the most sense. Do you have time for tea? I would love to take tea here in the flower gardens. I am sure Stacis or Alpine would be happy to bring us something."

"I think that sounds lovely."

The two women sat very still for a moment, staring at the impossible flower garden. The tiered rows of planters overflowing with every blossom in creation, and many that have not existed for a millennium or will not exist for another.

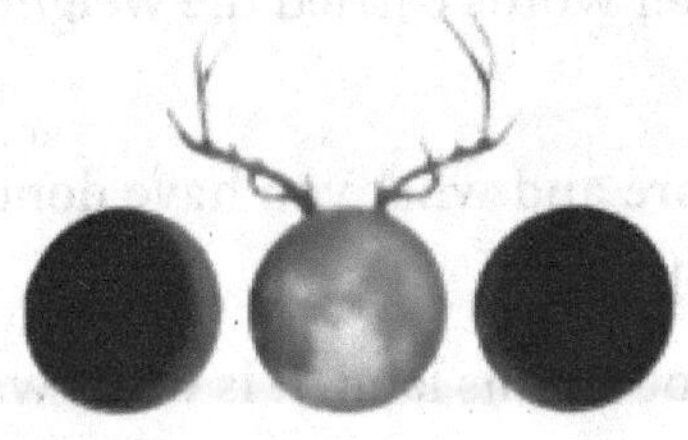

Something About Her

"**I** can feel you there, Sister."

His words were garbled around his broken teeth and jaw.

"I apologize for my condition, your charges have bound me, and I cannot heal or shed this form as is respectful. I pray you will forgive me the trespass."

Elder Valkyrie stepped from the space in front of the shackled man. He was kneeling and when he saw her he bowed his head, bending until it touched the ground.

"I cannot believe, after all these centuries, it is really you. Some thought you were destroyed, others though, like me, never lost faith. The father would not speak of you; in fact, he has not spoken since your disappearance."

Elder Valkyrie leaned back against the cold stone wall opposite the man and slid down until she was seated before him.

"I do not know what you are talking about. Please lift your head so that I can look upon you when we speak."

The man did not move.

Her eyeless sockets glowed red.

"Lift your head!" Her words carried the weight of her magic, and he snapped upright.

"I know who you are and what you have done, how long have you been murdering families?"

"Since I stepped foot on this land. It is why I was created."

"To murder innocents?"

The man looked at her, seeming somewhat confused.

"Why do you call me sister? You are not of Mercer that much I can discern."

"We are of the same order, although you were the greatest among us. Can you not see through this disguise? I can see you beneath the cloak. Is it the damage to your eyes? Why have you not healed them?"

"My eyes are not your concern. Telling the sisters here the truth of your origins and why you murder innocent families is your concern. Understanding that imprisonment or death are your only choices here, that is your concern. And explaining why you think you know who I am will go a long way toward making that decision as painless as possible for you."

He smiled at her, his wrecked gums showing beneath the twisted grin. "You don't remember do you? You have no idea who you are."

At that he bowed his head again and began humming a melody, she did not recognize it, but it somehow felt familiar.

Not Awkward At All

"Harlan are you sure we are going the right way? I thought you said only another hour?"

"Really LaRhonda? Who was it that has asked to stop once for snacks and twice for sightseeing?"

"Okay, that's totally true, but still, I would not be an effective passenger princess if I didn't distract the driver and complain about the time, now would I."

"Please explain to me how the strongest, most independent woman I have ever met suddenly becomes a brat when we start a road trip?"

"Really, a brat? Maybe I show you just how much of a brat I can be when we get in."

She slid her hands over his thigh and rubbed him through the thin material of his trousers, feeling him stiffen under her delicate touch.

"Ma'am we are about two minutes from the driveway and if you keep that up we aren't unpacking until much later."

"Sir, did you think I was letting you drag me out into the woods to pretend camp for a weekend. I want you to myself where no neighbors can complain about the noise."

"Oh, so you wanted me where no one can hear me scream? That sounds a little ominous—and totally worth the risk."

The sound of his phone ringing through the car's speakers interrupted the moment and his ex-wife's name and photo appeared on the dashboard display.

"Oh boy" he said. "That isn't awkward at all. Sorry LaRhonda, I better grab this, she doesn't call me often it might be about the girls."

"Of course, go ahead."

He pushed a button on the steering wheel and Heather Phelps-Rice's smooth southern drawl poured out of the speakers.

"Har, hey."

"Hey Heather, just so you know I am in the car with Representative Kelm, and you are on speaker. Sorry we are driving. What's up."

"Oh, Representative Kelm hello, sorry to intrude. The girls have told me a lot about you."

"Ms. Phelps-Kelm, it is good to finally talk to you, you have some wonderful daughters as I am sure you know. I was hoping once the school year started, and the girls are back in town you and I would be able to meet up."

"Well Harlan, that is kind of why I am calling. I hate to do this, but something came up with work, and I am in a bad spot. Janice is out of town, and we were supposed to be spending the weekend with my mom. Now I have to make an emergency trip to like three different states in two days and my mom can't come until Sunday. Is it possible for the girls to stay with you until mom flies in?"

He glanced at LaRhonda, obviously conflicted. But she already knew what the answer had to be. She smiled and nodded her head enthusiastically.

"Of course, but I am not home. We are headed to the lake for a long weekend and weren't coming back until Tuesday. Will your mom be able to rent a car and come out here to grab the girls or will I need to bring them back to town?"

"Mom can come get them. I am so sorry guys, I didn't know you had a weekend away planned."

"No need to apologize, these things happen. Can you get them to me?"

"Yeah, I will be there at about 5:30 this afternoon, is that okay?"

"Sure thing."

Bringing the car to a stop in the driveway; he looked to LaRhonda.

"I am sorry babe, I really am. I will make it up to you."

She was unbuckling her seat belt and shook her head. She grabbed his hand and pulled it up her thigh, sliding it under the hem of her flowered blue dress.

"That only gives us about three hours of privacy. You better start right here and now if you are going to cram a weekend of making it up to me into the next three hours."

Like any good southern gentleman. Harlan obliged.

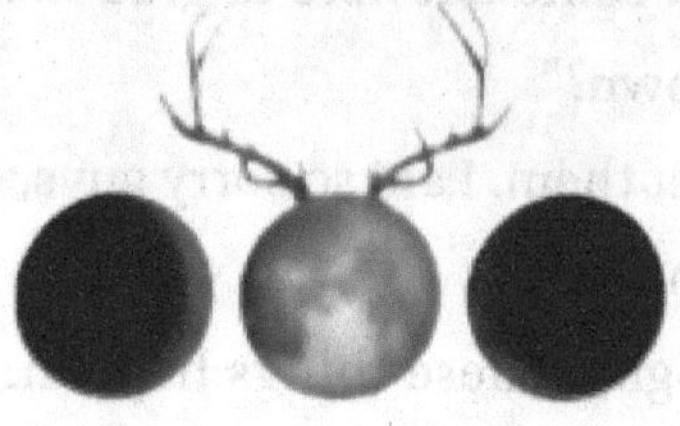

Hold Close Those You Love

LaRhonda watched as Harlan finished bringing in the last of their bags. What had started in the driveway on the front seat of his SUV, then on the hood, then continued on the chaise in front of the fireplace, then the master bedroom, and the shower, had just concluded for the third time on the porch swing.

LaRhonda stretched and tried not to think too much about everything they had done over the last couple hours. If nothing else, that man was thorough and committed when he began a task. The girls would be here with their mother in about a half an hour and it was going to be awkward enough meeting Harlan's ex-wife while still glowing from being bent over furniture that she was certain Heather had picked out at some point. It would only make it worse if she was still seeing the look on his face as she knelt before him on the porch swing, when they shook hands for the first time.

She went to the bathroom on the first floor off and checked herself in the mirror. She had managed to keep her sundress in one piece somehow and had located her undergarments so that she wasn't essentially naked when the girls arrived. She grabbed her makeup bag and started touching herself up. She searched her connection to the divine energy, she could feel Harlan, upstairs now putting the bags away. She felt the energy flowing through the woods all around her. It was beautifully refreshing. She had never spent much time in the woods, she was a city girl from Chicago and other than D.C., that is where she had spent most of her life.

Not many opportunities for communing with nature where she was from. But standing here now, feeling the difference in the flow of energy when it was devoid of people. She was a bit jealous of her sisters who spent most of their lives in places like this. She knew there was at least one family of Mercer women whose entire existence was in places like this. She had heard about their strange gifts, traveling through the root systems of trees and mycelium, keeping wild animals as familiars like the witches in fairy tales. She had always felt a bit sorry for them. Standing here, now, she realized the power and healing in it.

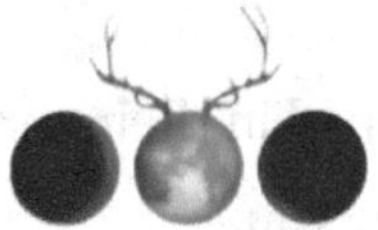

Heather Phelps-Rice's Audi pulled around the corner of the drive just as Harlan was walking out of the door behind her. She had laid out some snacks, a meat and cheese tray and had a kettle on for tea and had been out here for a few minutes awaiting the girls arrival.

She had felt them just before they hit the driveway, they were apprehensive, both of them. She thought she understood. They were torn between their excitement about seeing her and their dad, and their loyalty to their mom. They somehow felt like it was a betrayal to like LaRhonda when their mom was around. LaRhonda was determined to put them at ease as much as possible. She whispered to Harlan as the car was coming to a stop.

"If I can, I am going to invite Heather in for a few minutes, I want to meet her, and I want her to feel comfortable with the girls being here with me for a weekend."

"LaRhonda, she thinks very highly of you already."

"That's good, but please, I need this too."

"Of course. Thank you for being so understanding, I love you."

He started down the stairs without waiting for a response, LaRhonda didn't need her connection to Harlan to know he was excited about seeing the girls.

The girls came barreling out of the car before it was even fully parked. Lydia made it to Harlan first wrapping him in a tight hug, Lexia wasn't far behind, barreling into them both hard enough to nearly knock them over and she joined. LaRhonda slid down the stairs and past the hugging three. The girls looked up from their dad and acknowledged her as she passed.

"Hi LaRhonda." They pipped in their perfect unison.

"Hi Ladies, it's good to see you."

She continued toward the car as Heather Phelps-Rice exited the driver door. Two things struck LaRhonda at once. First, photographs did nothing to capture the truth of this woman. She was tall, with blond hair and blue eyes that were so bright they didn't look real, almost like painted doll's eyes. She was strongly built; she wore tight jeans and sandals and a sleeveless black blouse and there was no mistaking the muscular build of her body.

The second thing was that there was no longer a question of where the witch line ran in the twins family. This woman radiated power. There was no way that she wasn't on Mercer's radar. This was like standing next to one of the elders. LaRhonda extended her feelings of goodwill and excitement at meeting her through the energy of creation and got nothing in response. This woman was not a witch, but she damn well could be, a great one at that.

Heather turned her gaze on LaRhonda, and her smile beamed as she extended her hand. "Representative Kelm, it's wonderful to finally meet you."

"Ms. Phelps-Rice, please call me LaRhonda. It is great to meet you as well."

"Thank you, and please call me Heather. I have to say, I love that dress. The girls said you were one of those women who could just make anything look like it was made for you, and they were not lying."

LaRhonda felt her cheeks flush. *Wow, lawyers.* She thought. *Thirty seconds and already she has me off guard and flat footed.* "Thank you. I am afraid the girls have too small a sample size to judge from, and I am just good at picking clothes that keep these curves at bay. Will you stay a few minutes, I laid out some snacks and have a kettle on for tea? I would love to chat while the girls are getting settled."

"That would be lovely, before we get inside. Thank you again for letting them interrupt your time away with Harlan. I know it can be difficult to get any down time in with him."

"No need to thank me at all. I was looking forward to this weekend, but I knew from the beginning that Harlan was a dedicated and devoted father. And I am sure you won't find this at all surprising that your girls are just wonderful, and the only thing that could make a weekend away with him better is getting to see them too. How about you and I head in, and we let Harlan get the girls settled?"

"Sounds perfect."

As the two women headed toward the house, LaRhonda felt her wards tingle. She scanned the woods around them quickly, extending her feelings through the energy of creation. She felt nothing, just that momentary warning from her wards that something was amiss, that someone was focused on her from afar, then it was gone.

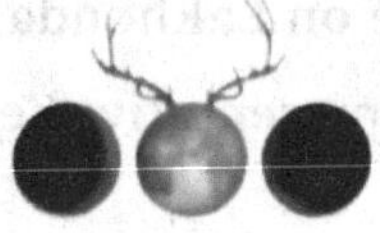

Under most circumstances LaRhonda would protest being up before sunrise on a Saturday morning, But Harlan had done it right. He had woken her up just before dawn, and led her, clad only in a cotton camisole and boy shorts out onto the balcony from the master bedroom. The sides of which were six foot wooden lattice with creeping vines but facing directly east there was only a small three foot wrought iron railing. She protested only for a moment as he handed her a cup of fresh coffee and motioned toward a seat at the small table, where there was already a bit of fresh apples, grapes and cheese waiting on a silver tray.

They sat in silence for only a moment or two in the pre-dawn grey, her wondering exactly why he was dragging her out here for coffee and fruit this early without saying a word. Before she could ask, the morning exploded in color as the sun broke the horizon. Whoever had designed this house had made sure the two master balconies on the second floor lined up perfectly east and west. So that you could watch the sunrise in the morning and the sun set at night over the tops of the trees surrounding the house. It was brilliant and beautiful, and any irritation she may have felt about Harlan waking her up so early without telling her why, had disappeared instantly when the sun burned its way across the horizon.

Harlan leaned over and kissed her on the side of the neck and whispered in her ear. "Stay here, enjoy the sunrise for a moment or two, I am going to run us a bath so we can start the day off right before the girls get up."

LaRhonda smiled up at him, this beautiful man, who had stolen her heart so completely. "Harlan is this balcony completely private from the rest of the house?"

"It is."

"Okay, yes, please get a bath started, come back and get me when its ready."

She rose and slid her shorts down over her hips, stepped out of them, and pulled her camisole over her head. She desperately wanted to feel the sun on her naked body. Another product of growing up in the city, she had never been naked outside before. She stretched allowing her body to flow from one movement to another. She had always loved yoga, and this felt like heaven. The cool morning air on her body, the sun bathing her, the energy of creation flowing through and around her as she let her body guide her through the movements it needed. Her mind and body were clear and focused, she knew it was time. She was going to tell Harlan today. After the girls were up and moving she would ask Harlan to take her for a walk and when they were alone she would tell him everything. The attack, Mercer and her birth into it, their mission, her role, and power. His invitation not only into her life but into the work of Mercer. She already knew the charms she would use to demonstrate to him that she wasn't crazy or messing with him. Both of them were simple but dramatic and she could modify them enough to give him whatever reassurances he needed.

The only thing she needed to worry about was if he reacted badly and asked her to leave or took the girls and left her here. But in her heart, she did not think that was possible. That was fear and doubt talking, not the reality of who she knew Harlan Rice to be.

Breakfast with the girls was as much fun as LaRhonda could remember having in recent memory. Harlan cooked, and Lydia played DJ, while LaRhonda and Lexia danced and offered both cooking and musical critique and advice. The girls laughed until all of their sides were hurting at Harlan's antics with the pancakes. According to Lexia, Harlan had always been ridiculous in the kitchen. "Making more jokes than food," had been her statement.

Afterward Harlan announced a trip to the lake. The girls were instructed to clean up after breakfast and change into their swimsuits. There was a private lake about a quarter of a mile through the woods only accessible to the three homes on this property. He and LaRhonda went upstairs to change and were going to head down while the girls were getting ready.

"Harlan, I have to ask you something."

He had just stepped out of the ensuite clad only in some grey trunks. "Is it about my incredibly masculine swim trunks or how good I look in them? Because I know that's a tough one to get your head around."

She rolled her eyes and smiled. "No baby, I am serious. Is there anywhere we can talk privately before we swim with the girls?"

His face turned serious in an instant, and he was crossing the space between them, eyes soft but jaw set as if ready to take a punch. "Is everything okay?"

Seeing where his head went she responded immediately. "Of course, I just have some important things to ask you, and I was planning on talking to you about it this weekend. I am thrilled the girls are here, but I really don't want to wait any longer to have this conversation."

"Sure, let's get them down to the lake then you and I can walk the path. I already know they are just going to swim out to the water slide dock and sun themselves most of the time. Both girls swim like fish, so we don't have to stay right on top of them the whole time and unless you are planning on yelling at me for something they won't be able to hear us."

"Harlan." She put her hand on his chest to hopefully calm his racing heart and softly kissed him on the mouth. "Everything is okay, I promise this isn't a bad conversation. Just a necessary one."

Back in the kitchen, everyone was dressed in swimsuits and beach wraps, LaRhonda doled out the items to be carried. Harlan had a small drink cooler and his lawn chair. LaRhonda had the picnic basket, Bluetooth speaker, and another small cooler with some popsicles. The girls handled the beach towels, picnic blanket, and their own water bottles.

The girls led the way out the back door and down the path behind the house. LaRhonda was once again amazed by the peace and security. They didn't even bother to close the back door or lock it. Just let the storm door swing shut behind them. More and more the mantra of "*I could get used to this,*" played in her head when she was with Harlan.

She was walking close to Harlan as he was trying to get the girls involved in singing some song that LaRhonda did not recognize. They, of course, were having none of it. That just made Harlan all the more determined. LaRhonda could hear two birds chirping wildly, engaged in some intense communication she could not interpret but found beautiful, nonetheless. The forest they were cutting through was dense and lush. The smell of trees and moss was intoxicating. The girls disappeared around a corner, and Harlan leaned over and pulled her close with his free arm. She stopped and looked up at him. He gave her a hard kiss on the mouth, before walking on, pulling her with him.

"The lake is right around this corner, it's gorgeous, I can't wait for you to see it..."

"Daddy."

The scream from the girls ripped through the trees at the same time LaRhonda's warding lit up. Not the tingle of someone watching or noticing her. But the red hot lightning bolt that came only from imminent danger. Harlan was already running and LaRhonda had to push hard to keep up.

As they rounded the corner any hope of being able to help, or there being some kind of mistake that just startled the girls fled LaRhonda in a flash of real fear. Maybe the first real fear since her last night before she had awakened in Mercer.

Standing in the middle of the trail about ten feet in front of the twins were two men. Men she didn't know, but whose description had gone out to every Mercer witch and their consorts. One blond, one with black hair, shirtless, covered in tattoos, and each carrying a giant hammer.

"Carpenters." The word hissed through her lips like a curse before she could control herself.

The blond man spoke, "Oh, look here Levi, these girls is almost as pretty as us. And since the witch knows who we are, that should save us some fuss. Look at me, a poet and I didn't know it."

Harlan looked at her in confusion and said something, but LaRhonda could not hear what it was. Her mind was racing, a whirlwind of memories from funeral songs and relayed stories. These men were deadly when evenly matched. She was on her own.

LaRhonda pulled in the energy of creation, whispered a prayer to the Witch Father, and sent out a silent cry for help through the bands of her connection. She screamed, "Harlan, get the girls out of here now," as she unleashed a torrent of fireballs aimed at the blond brother. The first one hit him square in the chest and knocked him back; the next two were deflected by his brother's hammer.

To their credit Harlan and the girls did not hesitate, they all took off toward the house.

LaRhonda kept screaming as she followed. "Run, get to the car, and get out of here now. I am right behind you."

She could hear the brothers coming in pursuit, she knew if they caught up to her she was dead, she didn't want to die, but she knew that at least they were only here for her. Harlan and the girls rounded a bend in the trail, around two large trees about twenty yards ahead. Her heart sank when she heard the girls start screaming, and something heavy hit the ground.

No, no, no. Her pleas echoed in her mind, *they aren't witches, leave them alone.* She rounded the bend and saw Harlan on the ground his face bloodied, a muscular blond man stood over him, fists already covered in what she assumed was Harlan's blood. The girls were behind the man, kneeling in front of a tall red haired woman, holding a staff with a golden cross at its head. The woman was chanting in a low quick rhythm. LaRhonda could not hear her words, but she could feel the ripple across the energy of creation. This was a spell or charm she was laying on the girls. Neither girl made a sound nor moved a muscle.

LaRhonda froze, there was no way she could save Harlan or the girls in time to keep the other one safe. She fell into her connection, searching for an answer. Her wards lit up again and she spun to face the threat. She got her left arm up to her ribs in time to keep the blow from Levi's hammer from caving in her chest completely. She landed hard in the rotten foliage, her shattered arm and broken ribs screaming in protest. She tried to roll onto her stomach, determined to crawl to Harlan, to try and protect him any way she could.

From behind her, she heard the blond brother, "Oh girl, you messed up good with this one. Jebediah, is her man dead yet?"

LaRhonda sobbed knowing there was nothing she could do now. She kept crawling toward Harlan, determined to at least die at his side.

"Not yet Asher, one of you guys want to bring a hammer? Make it quick for him?"

LaRhonda made it to Harlan and laid her head over his. They would have to kill her first. She tried focusing the energy of creation, any kind of charm or spell of protection, and found the fear, and the pain in her arm was too much, she couldn't focus.

Asher spoke again from above her this time. "Sonya dear, would you and Jeb take those girls back out to the truck, we will dispatch daddy and the witch here and join you in just a moment. Say your goodbyes girls, big things are coming for you, it's time to leave this life behind."

A shuffling and LaRhonda heard the girls in their strange unison, "Bye Daddy, Bye LaRhonda."

LaRhonda wanted to scream, to cry, to blow up and kill all of them. But she didn't have the power or focus. She had never been a warrior; she knew how to fight. But her magic was in influence and well-being. She was a healer and an organizer, that's why she went into government work. But now, that work was going to kill the man she loved and steal the children she wanted most in the world to protect and there wasn't a damn thing she could do about it. She felt again for her connection to the Mercer witches. *Please, if anyone can hear this, they are killing me and Harlan Rice, and taking his children somewhere. Please save his children, Mother, Elders, Lord Seanchara, anyone please help.*

She heard the man above her lift his hammer and pulled her face tighter against Harlan's, shielding him as best she could. She could not look; she hoped only that he would never awaken to see his fate or that of his girls. She whispered to him. "I am sorry love; Witch Father guide us as we join the energy of creation in its eternal journey."

She kissed his bloody face as the hammer swung.

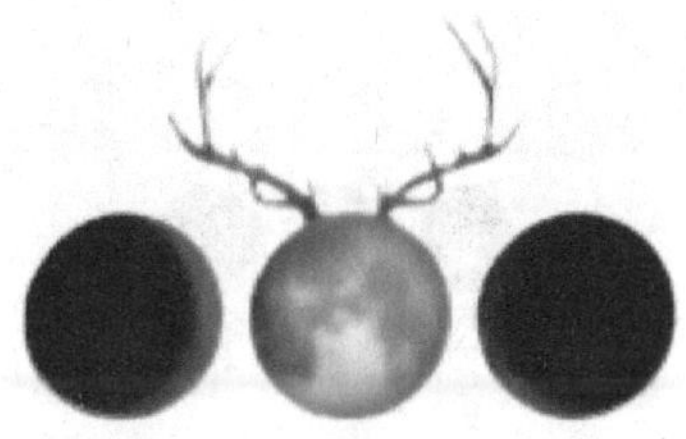

None Asked, None Given

A wave of power rolled over LaRhonda, and she heard Asher Carpenter grunt as his body was blasted into a nearby tree. Chaos erupted all around her, and she rolled over to try and sit up and see what was happening. She heard the commands as she did.

"Amy, Fredrick, Edward, save the girls and bring back John. Bets you are with me. No quarter. The Carpenters do not leave here today."

LaRhonda didn't recognize the voice giving orders, but she could feel their movement through the divine energy and recognized the power of Mercer Witches. These were sisters, powerful sisters. She tried to push herself to her feet, she needed to join in the fight, to save the girls for Harlan and Heather. Her left forearm was crushed, and her ribs hurt so badly that she thought she might pass out. She called on the divine energy for healing and strength but no matter what her will or desire, her body was just too badly damaged to continue, and she fell to her side.

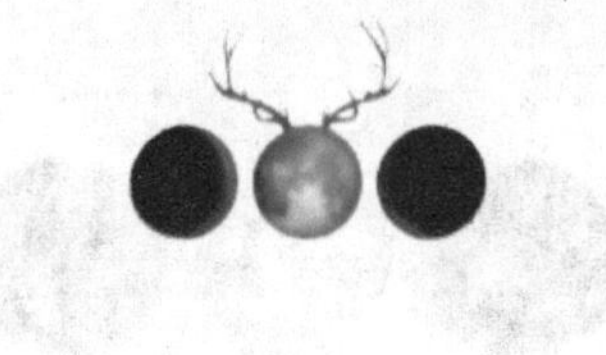

Amy saw Fredrick fly past her, then quickly veer off the trail. Trusting in the consort, even though she did not know him personally. She knew his reputation and Dorthea's; and knew John's fate and hers were in the best of hands. From the angle he ran off she guessed he was going to try and cut them off on the trail ahead, drive them back toward her and Edward. She sped up and Edward kept pace.

They rounded the bend in the trail, Amy breathing heavily from the run. She took the scene in all at once. The twin girls were on their knees in the middle of the trail. The tall red headed woman stood in front of them, the golden cross on the head of her staff blinding in the afternoon sun. She looked up as Amy and Edward rounded the corner and whispered something to the girls.

Behind the woman, Amy saw an explosion of movement in the trees. Her heart dropped as she saw him. His blonde hair was cut to the scalp, he looked somehow thinner, and less present, yet more intimidating than she had ever seen him.

"John." She couldn't help but scream. He did not respond or act as if he even heard her as he threw a series of short fast kicks at Fredrick. She started to run to him, to try and bring him out of whatever had captured his mind. The sounds of the girls screaming and Edward yelling her name brought her back to the fight at hand.

Amy spun to help Edward and the girls when she realized it was the girls that Edward needed help with. He was backing up quickly down the trail. Trying to cover his face the best he could while both girls were on attacking him with the rage rarely seen in anyone other than teenage girls. One sister had a handful of his long, curly hair and was yanking his head back and forth. The other was slapping at him with both hands.

"Amy, help, I don't know. Help."

Edward was stammering, obviously at a loss on how to deal with the kids without hurting them. Mercer consorts were trained for a lot of dangerous situations, but deescalating teenage meltdowns was likely not in their wheelhouse.

Amy saw the red headed woman, her staff raised toward Edward and the girls, her eyes closed. It was her; she was the one controlling the girls actions. Was it her that had brainwashed John? Had they just found the key to The Ascension's mind control? If so, it was ending right here and now.

Amy ran toward the woman, drawing a dagger from her belt and beginning a charm to silence the woman before she could do any more damage.

The tall woman turned on Amy as she approached and swung the staff in her direction.

"God is our refuge and strength, an ever present help in trouble."

Amy felt the first wave of the woman's spell roll over her, crashing against her wards.

"Therefore, we will not fear, though the earth give way and the mountains crumble into the heart of the sea."

Amy tried to push through the spell. Feeling it as the woman attempted to control her mind. Amy could still think, still had her own will. But it was like swimming through mud. Pushing her own will into the world was becoming more difficult.

"Though the waters foam and the mountains quake with their surging."

Amy found herself wanting to sleep, to surrender control, to let go, to let God decide her fate and John's.

It was that last thought that steeled her mind and strengthened her wards against the intrusion. She found her connection to the energy of creation. Drew it in, breathed in her connection to all of her sisters and all of the sisters come before. She felt her connection to John, thin and ragged though it was. She focused her rage. *This bitch, this bitch is the reason John isn't running to her side, sweeping her up in his strong arms and telling her he loves her.*

"There is a river where the streams make glad the city of…"

She did not get finish the line before Amy broke free and screamed her own charm.

"Be burnos, be liezuvio."

The woman fell instantly into silence. The waves of power crashing against Amy's warding ceased immediately. Her anger, however, did not abate. Dagger in hand she lunged toward the woman, fully intending to cut the woman's foul tongue from her mouth. To rip out her heart if necessary. Whatever it took to get her John back to her. As she slashed the woman managed to get her staff up and sweep it across, deflecting Amy's attack enough that the dagger buried itself in her right shoulder instead of the woman's throat.

The woman swung the staff back across her body and caught Amy on the side of the head with the golden cross. Amy rolled to her left moving with the blow. It probably saved her a concussion at the least. She continued the roll and came back to her feet as the woman darted off the trail toward the lakeside.

Her mission was clear, while she wanted this woman dead; but she had to first rescue the girls, then John. Her anger would have to wait. With this she turned to help Edward. Both girls were now seated on the ground crying. Edward was standing awkwardly over them, obviously trying to comfort them.

The girls seemed safe for a moment, so she turned her attention to John and Fredrick. She sprinted toward the clearing where they were engaged. She had trained with and fought beside John Park her entire life. She knew just how seriously the man took his training and his hunger to constantly improve his skills.

It was also evident in only a moment of watching that he was completely outmatched by Fredrick Sapp. Having only known him by reputation until just a few days ago. Amy had been completely taken with Fredrick's charming refinement, his manners and knowledge of all things related to Mercer lore. She had almost forgotten that he was widely considered one of the most dangerous of the consorts and had been partnered with Sister Dorthea Milburn for a very good reason. He towered over John, but beyond that, there was a grace and efficiency to his movements. Every move John made, Fredrick seemed to already be there, not only anticipating John's attacks, but also his response to Fredrick's counters. Amy watched only for a moment, mesmerized by the two warriors. But she knew Fredrick was holding back. He didn't want to injure John, but if John kept getting more and more frustrated and grew more desperate in his attacks it was inevitable that Fredrick would have to respond in kind and eventually John would be hurt.

"John." She called as she ran toward them. He showed no sign that he heard her. "John, dammit look at me."

Still, he stayed completely focused on her. She wondered if the spell the woman had cast on him was still working on him, did she have to cast it continuously or now that she was gone was it still going. Amy needed to stop this now.

She focused on her connection to John, a band that at one time had been a brilliant column of orange and green connecting them no matter where they were. Now it was a thin line barely visible to her. She pushed her love for him down this connection. Begging him to feel her there, to hear her cry for him to return to her.

John was launching a roundhouse kick toward Fredrick who had already slid back and away from the strike, when he turned to look at her. He stopped stalking toward Fredrick and started toward her.

"John baby, look at me."

He shook his head like he was trying to shake a pest away.

"John, it's me, its Amy, come on baby. I know you're in there."

He frowned; she recognized the look. It was the look he got when he was trying to solve a problem. *There he is.* The thought caused her heart to soar. He was really in there.

He reached for her, she stepped forward. A flash of movement as Fredrick moved behind him. His hand flashed toward John's neck, as fast as cobra strike. The small pendant in his hand delivering a powerful dose of tranquilizer as it struck the muscles in the side of John's neck.

Amy screamed, "No goddammit Fredrick, he was back."

Fredrick caught him as he collapsed.

"Amy please, he will be fine. But now is not the time to risk him losing the fight with whatever is controlling his mind. We can get him to Mercer, and they can help him, but now we have more sisters in danger. We need to go."

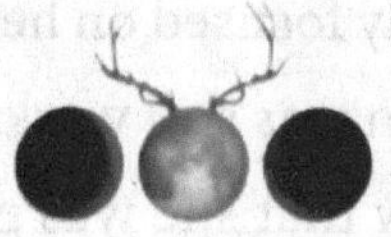

Bets saw Dorthea kneel next to the black woman on the ground covering the man. His face was a bloody mess, and she could see the woman's left arm was badly broken. She didn't need magic to guess it was from one the hammers.

Asher Carpenter was crumpled against the base of a tree, his hammer a few feet to his side. Levi cocked his head toward her. His expression gave away nothing. But he started toward her, hammer swinging like a pendulum in front of him. Bets backed away drawing in power, being here, in the woods, the energy of creation felt amplified. Dorthea's orders had been simple and to the point. These men died here today.

Bets unleashed her first charm as Levi closed in. He was picking up speed and allowed the hammer to swing first to the left in front of him, its giant polished silver head pointing at the ground. Then back to the right, instead of sending it back left like he had done, he continued the swing back to the right, toward his trailing leg. The hammer swung up and over his shoulder as he prepared to bring it crashing down on Bets.

"Saldyta." She yelled and the ground swallowed both of Levi's feet and he tumbled forward with the momentum. He snarled and pushed himself upright using the hammer. He put the head of the hammer on the ground and rested his hands on the end of the handle. Palms up they formed a bowl and he whispered something into them.

Immediately another Levi Carpenter, this one not trapped by the earth started moving in from Bet's right. His hammer slung over his shoulder. She heard something to her left and turned her head to see two more Levis stalking her way from about twenty yards out. She started to back away as the three Levis began to circle her. She heard a thumping sound and saw the Levi that was buried up to his shins in the ground was swinging his hammer from right to left, almost like a golf club. Digging up big chunks of earth with each swing. He was trying to free himself. She wasn't worried about squaring off with him, even if he should break free. She was more concerned that these other three may turn out to be tangible and not just illusions.

Bets focused on Levi digging himself out. She could see the energy of creation flowing through him and all around. She could also bands of it flowing to the other three Levis. But unlike any other connections she had seen. Those ended abruptly at each one of the replicas. They did not pass through or return the energy. She quickly understood.

She opened up her siphon abilities. Seeing the energy used to cast these replica illusions, she pulled, hard. She felt the power drain from the illusions, and they began to fade. She kept pulling.

Pulling from him was different than she had felt pulling from other Mercer witches, even different from the monster they had just trapped. This was like a layer of energy wrapped around him. Not necessarily flowing through him. She felt like she was unraveling a ball of yarn instead of drinking from a well.

She could see the veil of energy thinning, and something different, no, someone different underneath it. Like there was a man inside, and they had somehow draped another man over the top of him like a tapestry and held it in place with the energy of creation. Beneath it she saw the man come in to focus. His hair was still black, but he had no tattoos, his eyes were kind but fearful. It was strange to see the outer body of Levi Carpenter, swinging the giant hammer, the blank look of dispassion on his face. But underneath she could see the other Levi, his face confused, his body gaunt and looking malnourished, his eyes imploring her to help. She pulled harder and the and the veil between the two thinned even more.

She could hear the hammer pounding the ground, but her focus was entirely on the man underneath. So much so that she didn't notice the blond man limping toward her, his hammer raised over his head.

Not until he started screaming as Dorthea's spell hit him. Bets could hear her chanting and see the waves of energy roll off of her, as she walked by her. Hands held out at her waist, head back to the sky.

"North, South, East, West, a web of light to bind him best, East, South ,North, West, grind his bones to bring his death."

Bets could see the energy envelope him, the web pattern of light wrapping him like a mummy. He screamed and twisted frantically, trying to escape. But the web only tightened.

Levi began frantically pounding at the dirt trying to dig himself free. But Bets' spell just kept forcing the dirt tighter around his feet as he did, the hole filling faster than he could dig it.

She saw movement back toward the trail. She saw Amy walking with two young girls on either side, leaning heavily on her. Edward and Fredrick were behind them carrying a man, she guessed was John Park between them.

Asher Carpenter writhed on the ground, the web of light now covered his face, and his screams of pain were muffled. A sickening crunch of bone as the web constricted and he stopped his struggling. Dorthea stopped her chanting and ran back to the people on the ground. Bets turned back to focus on Levi, and he had stopped swinging his hammer. He now stared blankly at Asher's still form on the ground. She didn't believe he could see the web of light that had crushed the life from his brother. But see it or not the result had been the same.

Levi dropped his hammer. Bets didn't know if it was the shock of seeing his brother dead, or exhaustion from trying to dig himself free or from the battle of the man inside Levi struggling to break free from whatever power was holding him there. Either way the fight had gone out of him.

Behind her the two girls were kneeling in the dirt next to the bloody man. Amy and Dorthea talking to the other woman, who Bets now recognized as a sister witch. She did not know her name, but she could feel the connection and see the power move through the woman. There was something else about her, something familiar but Bets didn't have time to figure out what it was. They needed to help the injured and get John, Levi, and Asher back to Mercer. There was much to learn.

Amy began laying a healing charm on the man on the ground, while Dorthea wrapped the woman's injured arm. Fredrick and Edward were loading John onto a back board in the rear of Edward's van. One of the teenage girls broke off from what was presumably their dad and hugged the woman.

"LaRhonda, what's going on, who were those people? Why did they attack dad, is this because of his job?"

She hugged her with her good arm. "No baby, this has nothing to do with your dad, and he is going to be okay, these people are friends and they will get him healed."

LaRhonda Bets repeated the name in her mind two or three times before it clicked. LaRhonda Kelm, the representative from Illinois. The one who is always on television fighting with the hardcore right wingers.

"Sister Bets, if you would be so kind as to release your spell. We will get this man secured for transport."

Bets saw Fredrick and Edward standing on either side of Levi Carpenter. The man's head hung low and his body slack. She had no fear of him escaping the two consorts. Just as she released the spell, she heard a crack like a giant tree limbing breaking and a flash of brilliant white light as she was thrown to the ground.

Bets scrambled to her feet. She heard the kids crying and saw everyone else also on the ground or trying to get back to their feet.

"What the ..." she heard Dorthea from behind her.

The red headed woman with the staff stood on the trail about twenty yards from where Bets lay.

With the ringing in her head Bets could barely make out her screaming. "And the angels of the lord did lay God's wrath upon them."

Just behind Levi, a sphere of white light appeared towering over Fredrick and Edward who had both made it back to their feet. Bets heard Dorthea behind her, "Guys, get out of there, now!"

Fredrick and Edward both took off, each running in a separate direction as the light began to take form. Vaguely human in shape, brilliant yellow and gold with streaks of the purest white. The creature had to be eight feet tall. From its back, spread out what could only be wings. Each wing was longer than the creature was tall. Bets had never dreamed something like that could be real. Even after hearing the accounts from the raid on the church camp.

Bets felt the wave of power as Dorthea unleashed an assault on the creature. Concussive force like a car crash slammed into it, yet it showed no signs that it even noticed the assault. It raised its arms high in the air above its head and Bets felt the ground beneath her begin to shake. Not just the ground. Everything, like all of creation was vibrating with the sound that came from the monster. She could see Fredrick off to her right, down on his knees, hands clasped over his ears. She could not tell if it was her vision that was blurring or if Fredrick himself were becoming blurry. She tried to focus. She had to get some kind of warding in place. But the roar of sound felt like it was vibrating her every cell. She sensed Dorthea standing beside her. She reached through the energy of creation, feeling for her, hoping she would understand what she was asking, and began pouring what energy she could into a wall of warding. Anything to give them a moment to regroup. Dorthea must have realized what she was doing. She could feel Dorthea pouring energy into her spell. Bolstering Bets warding, expanding it, adding layers.

Slowly the roaring subsided as they got the warding in place. She could still feel the vibration through the energy of creation, but the wards helped her to focus. They shielded Edward and Fredrick as well. She risked a glance back and the sister witch was sitting up now, leaned heavily against the injured man. The girls were huddled around them. All of the taking comfort in one another.

She looked to Dothea and mouthed "what the fuck." Dorthea shrugged and said, "Get to the cars, we have to get out of here."

The world tumbled sideways as the creature swept its wings toward them. Bets felt the power blast right through her wards.

Bets was still struggling to determine what parts of her were touching the ground and how best to get back to her feet when she heard Dorthea yelling.

"Fuck you, you'll have to kill me first."

Bets focused her vision and found she could only do that by closing her left eye. She didn't have time to assess why. Fredrick was nowhere she could see. Edward was laying on his back; half wedged beneath his van. Dorthea was standing alone. All of her power pouring into a shield wall. For a moment Bets could not believe what she was seeing. Tentacles of light stretched out from the creature. One of them was wrapped around Asher Carpenter, another was dragging Levi by the arm. Bets watched in morbid fascination as Asher was seemingly absorbed into the light surrounding the monster. Two more of the tentacles of light crashed against the wall held in place by Dorthea's will. Behind her Bets could see, the two kids, Amy, the woman Kelm, and the man who had been badly beaten but now seemed to be coming around.

Levi was also absorbed into the light. He made no sound, but Bets could see the look of serene comfort on his face as he was dragged into the sphere and disappeared.

She made it to her feet and felt along her connection to Dorthea; she could feel the divine energy flowing from her into the shield wall and Bets added what power she could to it.

Dorthea nodded in acknowledgement. Bets could now feel the power of the creature. Wave after wave of energy slammed into the wall as the tentacles of light tried to force their way past the barrier. Bets reached out with her siphon. If she could weaken this monster, while they held it at bay, it might mean the difference in getting out of here in once piece.

As soon as Bets began to pull she recognized the layers of energy, the same that lay wrapped around Levi Carpenter. She pulled a little harder, channeling it back into the shield. For one brief moment, the being in the light came into focus.

More than eight foot tall with a flowing mane of white hair. The creature wore a golden wrap of some sort that hung open in the front. Bets could see the pale hairless flesh as smooth as marble. No marks, no muscle definition, no genitals. Just a smooth facsimile of a human body. The face too, was blank and expressionless. The face of a doll or automaton. The face of a machine.

In a blink the image was gone, replaced by the glowing monstrosity. It raised its wings again and Bets braced for the impact. This time when it swept them forward Bets and Dorthea were both thrown back past where the others were scattered in the dirt and leaves.

It blasted through their shields as if they weren't even there. The tentacles of light stretched out toward the group and Amy tried to get a ward in place, but another wave of power sent her rolling back. The girls began to scream, and Bets heard Dorthea swear again.

"Dammit no."

Both girls were now caught in those bands of light and being dragged toward the creature. They screamed.

"Daddy, help, please."

The man scrambled toward them and Bets could see LaRhonda attempting a spell.

Dorthea and Amy were on their feet and Bets saw Fredrick darting in from the side. He was almost to the girls. They just needed to buy him a second, then he could grab them.

Bets focused on a repulsion charm, anything just to slow it down. Her spell seemed to have no effect as the monster kept dragging the screaming girls. A fireball shot past the girls and slammed the creature in the chest.

As a result, it raised its arms over its head and roared again. The sound dropped Fredrick where he stood. LaRhonda collapsed protectively over the man reaching for the girls. Amy and Dorthea both had their hands over their ears. Bets began to wretch violently. She opened her eyes just in time to see the two girls screaming in terror as they were pulled into the light of the monsters body.

With the same thunderous crack that had heralded its arrival, the creature, the Carpenters, and the children were gone.

"Lexia, Lydia." The man on the ground was wailing in agony. LaRhonda was crying.

A wet thumping sound from the tree line and Bets tried to focus on what threat was now manifesting.

A choked cry and another thump and the sound of a body being dragged through the brush.

Edward the Fish came crashing through the trees dragging the red-haired woman by the arm. Her golden crucifix staff was somehow strapped to his back. He looked like a crusader of some sort. And Bets had never been happier to have him as a consort than in that moment.

The woman seemed to come out of her daze and looked up, making eye contact briefly with Bets, then she started to struggle, pulling against Edward as he dragged her behind him like luggage.

He spun on her and punched her hard in the jaw, then followed up with another hard punch to the gut.

"Not your kids you monster. Where are they?"

Another punch to the gut and the woman moaned and tried curling up to protect her vulnerable and damaged torso.

He shook her hard by the arm and drew back to hit her again. Fredrick grabbed his arm and Edward spun on him.

"Edward, please."

Edward shook loose of Fredrick's grasp. Bets had never seen him like this.

He yanked the woman up by her arm. She stumbled to her feet crying out. Edward grabbed her collar in both hands and brought her face just an inch from his and screamed again.

"Where are they? Bring them back right now."

Fredrick put his hands on Edward's shoulders and started talking to him. Bets made it to her feet and ran to his side.

She put her hand over his as he gripped the woman's collar.

"Thank you Edward, I've got her. Please help Fredrick with the others. We have people hurt."

Edward released the woman who fell in a heap at Bets feet. Bets had every intention of continuing the interrogation that Edward had started. Her plan had been to give Edward some distance so he didn't continue to devolve and maybe cause permanent damage before they could get their answers. And had the woman even looked the slightest bit relieved or contrite when she looked up at Bets, she may have. Unfortunately for her, she chose a different route.

The woman was sneering at Bets when she turned to look down at her.

"It doesn't matter what you do to me. The Seraphim have them now, they will burn the evil out of them and purify them for the Lord's work."

The smug look, the threat to the children. Bets had enough.

"An Haken Hangen." Bets whispered as she thrust her hands toward the woman.

She screamed as she was lifted off the ground. Her flesh stretched at two places on her abdomen and on top of each thigh, as the invisible hooks of the spell held her suspended.

Bets heard Dorthea exclaim behind her. "Shit."

Bets rotated her hands and the woman spun in air until she was level with Bets' gaze. Her head hanging limply upside down, just a few inches from Bets' face as she struggled against the hooks holding her in midair.

Bets pulled in the energy of creation and a ball of white hot light began to form between her hands. She moved it close to the woman's face, and she began to scream from the heat.

"Where are the children? Did you think you were being saved? They left you, abandoned you to pay the price. Where are the children?"

Bets felt movement to her side and saw Dorthea and LaRhonda standing together. Not moving to stop her, just watching. She lifted her hands, pushing the fiery heat a little closer to her face. "Where?." Closer and the woman screamed again.

"Where? Where? Where?"

"Where did they take them, how do we get them back?"

The woman tried shaking free, but Bets could see the blood running from the magical hooks embedded in her flesh as they tore deeper. Finally, she spoke through the cries of agony.

"The Seraphim have taken them; their names were on the list. The Lord has marked them for Ascension. There is no getting them back now. You cannot fight the Seraphim, no one can. They are God's strongest warriors, angels on earth."

"Where?" LaRhonda screamed at her.

Bets pulled in more energy, determine to ramp up the fire, when Dorthea touched her shoulder.

"Let's get her secured for transport. As much as I sure we all want to rip her apart. We must let the Elders play their part and get information out of her if they can. And it looks like our sister here may need some help explaining some things."

Behind them Harlan Rice stood stock still and staring at the back of LaRhonda's head. The betrayal and pain on his face evident to everyone there.

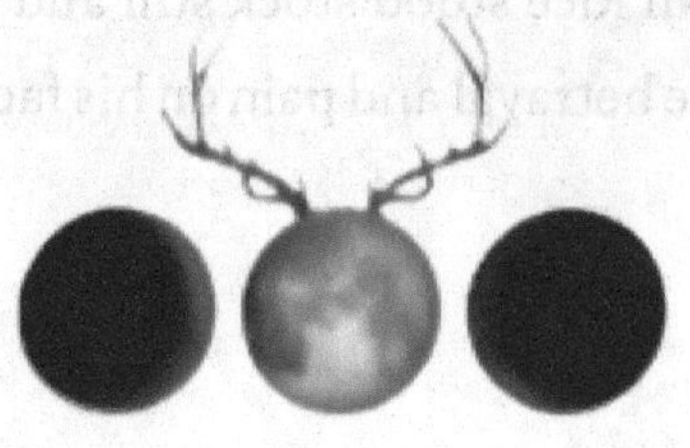

I Shall Not Want

"LaRhonda, what the hell was that? Where are my kids, who the fuck are these people?"

Harlan was angry and scared and picking up speed in his questioning without ever giving LaRhonda a chance to answer.

LaRhonda was seated at the dining room table in the lake house. Dorthea was tending to her arm. Already the healing magic and first aid were bringing the pain under control and allowing her to focus her thoughts. She could see Harlan was holding it together by a thread and at any moment that thread might snap. Unfortunately, he was in the worst possible situation. His children had been abducted, and there wasn't anything he could do about it.

Dorthea raised an eyebrow at her. Her meaning was clear, *should I shut him up?*

LaRhonda shook her head.

"Harlan, please love. I do not know where the girls are or I promise we would already be on the way there. There are some things I need to tell you. I am going to need you to be patient and listen to me."

Dorthea tapped her on the shoulder. "Sister, do you think that's wise considering the call that's being made right now?"

Bets and Amy were out back with the consorts, John, and the red haired woman. They were setting up a summoning of Lord Seanchara. Dorthea did not think breaking the privacy and secrecy of Mercer was a good plan on any day but definitely not when Lord Seanchara was moments away from being summoned.

"Sister Dorthea, under any other circumstances you would be correct. But I petitioned the Elders and Lord Seanchara himself last week. Harlan and I are in love, and I received their blessing to tell him the truth of who we are and to seek him as a partner to myself and to Mercer."

Dorthea nodded. "I understand. You have my love Sister. I will be outside if you need anything."

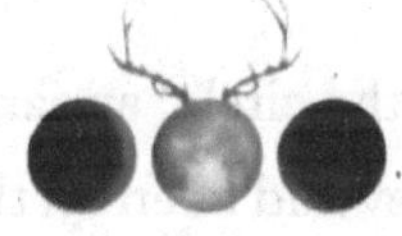

Thirty minutes later LaRhonda and Harlan emerged from the house. Dorthea and Bets both looked up. Bets was happy to see the two of them holding hands. Both of their eyes were red rimmed with tears. Harlan's face was bruised and swollen but Amy and Edward had tended to the worst of the damage and none of it was likely permanent.

Dorthea waved them over to the circle in the grass on the side of the driveway. Bets moved to the side and allowed LaRhonda a place between her and Amy. Fredrick offered Harlan his hand and helped him to kneel on a mat next to Edward before taking his own place behind Dorthea. Gerardo had been called and was ready to meet them wherever Lord Seanchara sent them for a doorway.

Dorthea addressed the group as a whole. "In just a moment I will begin the summoning. Edward, Harlan and Bets, you have all met Lord Seanchara but since this is your first summoning, please, remain silent unless he addresses you directly."

Harlan looked extremely confused, LaRhonda held up a hand, and addressed Harlan.

"The man you met as Billy, at my apartment, is Lord Seanchara, the guardian of Mercer. He is the only one that may open up a doorway to grant access to the city. He can change shapes and is for all purposes a God. Just be patient Harlan and don't give in to despair. We will get the girls back, but this is the first step, and everything must be done in order."

He nodded, but did not respond. Bets got the distinct impression that he was still processing, questioning everything he had learned. She knew that feeling well.

Dorthea turned back to the circle, apparently satisfied her instructions were understood. They had been on the road for eight days since capturing the tether's dark father. Still Dorthea showed no signs of fatigue or burnout. *Is this what her life was like?* Just running from one rescue to the next, day after day of do or die. No wonder she was so revered among the Mercer women.

Dorthea whispered a word under her breath and all nine bowls around the circumference of the circle burst into flames. A flash of brilliant white light and Bets caught a glimpse of the beast, the form that Lord Seanchara first appeared to her in. Another flash and she saw The Stag of Red Mountain, the Horned God of the Witches. Tall and naked except a small fur around his waist. An expansive crown of antlers upon his head. Another flash and he stood before them. In a fine tailored suit, his shaggy brown hair hanging over the collar. His bird's head walking stick was cradled in his left arm.

"Sisters." He looked around at the group kneeling before him.

"Oh, I see, Representative Rice. My sincerest apologies."

Harlan made no sound but nodded gravely.

"No time to waste, we will dispense with the formalities. Representative Rice, this might go much faster if you would allow me to bring some of our Elders here to conduct the interrogation of this woman. Would you allow that? Can we use your place here to start the search for your precious daughters?"

"Of course, uh, Lord..."

"Seanchara, and I apologize for the deception at our first meeting but now that you are aware of who and what your beloved is and the potential danger that brings, I am sure you understand its necessity."

"Yes sir."

Bets could hear the waver in his voice. This poor broken man. She could feel the guilt and despair that threatened to smother him.

"I will return in a moment or two, allow me to collect Elder Valkyrie and whomever else is at hand and I will bring them straight through. After that I will open a doorway so that we can get John Park back to the chambers of the veil and determine what the next steps are."

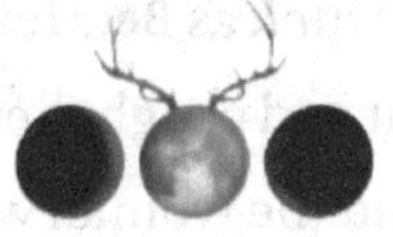

Dorthea turned to Edward and Fredrick, gentlemen, would you bring that self-righteous monster to the house so can make a space for the

Elders to work. Fredrick can you throw me my supply bag? I want to lay down a circle as well, so she stays cutoff.

The red-haired woman was on her feet and awake, although she did not appear to be in good mental health or physical. Bets was shocked at the beating Edward the Fish had put on this woman. She knew she shouldn't be, Edward was as trained as Fredrick, or Sugar, or Eugene or any other consort. His personality quirks did not make him any less dangerous either. He was still a consort of Mercer, and the protection of the innocent at any cost was part of his very being.

As they marched the woman past the circle of summoning, Fredrick and Edward flanking her on either side. She came suddenly alive and bolted. Fredrick missed her completely, and Edward reached for the back of her shirt, but she was too fast.

Unfortunately for her escape attempt, she chose a route that took her through the circle.

A slender arm, as pale as marble and covered in tattoos shot from the void and caught her around the neck. A gurgling sound as the woman was lifted from her feet and Elder Valkyrie stepped into view. She held the woman aloft by one delicate looking but clearly powerful hand. He long black nails dug into the flesh at the sides of the woman's neck and blood had begun to trickle down. Elder Valkyrie's eyeless sockets flared red, and she whispered something under her breath and tossed the woman like a dirty shirt at the nearest tree.

She did not slam into the trunk as Bets feared, but at the last moment the branches of the tree bent and caught her. They formed together like the web of a giant spider, and the woman was as caught in them as any bug would be in the spider's web.

Valkyrie was on her then, he nails like the claws of an animal slashing and digging. In a moment, the woman's face was bleeding from several deep scratches, and her shirt was a tattered bloody mess hanging off of her. Deep gouges across her abdomen and rib cages bled freely.

"Do you know how long I have wanted one of you to pay back for your crimes against us."

The woman did not respond directly but Bets could hear her prayer.

"He maketh me to lie down beside still waters."

Valkyrie yanked a handful of hair from the woman's scalp.

Harlan rose to his feet. "Hey, is that the only…"

Valkyrie spun on the group. Bets could see the energy around her looked as if it was on fire. Like Elder Valkyrie's rage had lit it aflame.

"Consorts, take him inside now."

There was no hesitation from Fredrick or Edward and if either of them took offense at being ordered around like children they did not show it. There were times to express your opinion, but interrupting Elder Valkyrie was not one of those times.

Fredrick leaned over to Harlan as he took his arm.

"If there is anyone who can figure out where your daughters are, it is Elder Valkyrie, but it likely won't be pretty. Let's wait inside."

After they were in the house Elder Valkyrie held out her hand to Bets. Blood dripped from her nails and her silken white wrap was soaked in it and clinging to her body.

Bets did not hesitate; she stepped forward and took Valkyrie's outstretched hand.

"Come sister, stand before her, and open your connection. Feel the energy flowing from her. Feel the spell she is trying to cast using scripture as the component."

"Yes Ma'am, I can see it."

"Good, now. I want you to see the energy flowing from you in a great big net. Focus your siphon and capture everything I am forcing out. I am going to force the information out of her. Block out all things physical and focus only on reading the truth as it leaves her body."

"Yes Ma'am."

Bets did as she was told. She blocked out all external stimulus. She forced herself to only see in the energy of creation. She could see the woman in front of her, just like Levi Carpenter, she could see a woman beneath the woman. A woman who appeared to be sleeping beneath wrapped layers of divine energy. Like it was somehow gluing the false person over top of the real one.

Bets could vaguely hear screams as felt the energy flow from the woman...*SONYA*. Bets froze. That was the woman's name. Sonya. No that wasn't right, Sonya was the name the Seraphim had given her.

A picture appeared in Bet's mind of the monster made of light that stole the girls. Her name had been Sarah, Sarah Summer, Summerfield maybe, or Summerlot. But then the Seraphim remade her.

Bets saw again the layers of energy wrapping this woman's body and mind. Holding the mask that was Sonya, in place over Sarah.

More screaming from a distance. Sonya was awake and feeling the pain. But Sarah seemed fast asleep. Another wave of energy rolled from Sonya to Bets along the connection, pulled by Bets' siphon. She saw three men laid out on stone slabs and she was immediately reminded of The Chambers of the Veil. Two of the men were obviously the Carpenters, although they had no tattoos. But the third, could this be Leroy Lewis. Yes, a giant with jet black hair and blue eyes, like a negative image of Sugar. At the head of every slab stood one of the Seraphim, bands of light and energy extending out from their hands and wrapping around each man as they lay deathly still. She could feel Sonya's elation as she watched what she thought of as The Ascension.

This was it, this is how they brainwashed them, and how they imbued them with power. She watched as Sonya left the room. She could feel Sarah beneath the memory, screaming to be set free. Stone corridors and a spiraling staircase that seemed to go on forever. Bets ignored the screams of agony trying to break through the connection, Elder Valkyrie at work. *Keep going, I am almost there.* She was not repulsed by the thought of this woman's torment. She hated that there was an innocent woman seemingly trapped underneath but the woman in charge of this *vessel*, that wasn't her word, had harmed the innocent and nearly murdered a sister witch and had stolen her lover's children.

One more turn and Sonya was standing in a great chapel, the banner across the top of the stage read, "The Church of The Ascension," and "Memphis welcomes all international delegates."

Bets pulled herself out of the connection and yelled "Got it. I've got the bastards."

Elder Valkyrie had Sonya's head by what was left of her red hair. Bets had a hard time looking at the damage done. By the slack way that she hung on the web of branches Bets could tell she had passed out.

"Elder Valkyrie, a moment with you and Sister Dorthea if I may?"

"Of course, sister."

They met Dorthea a few feet away from the circle.

"First, I have it. The Church of The Ascension in Memphis. That's where they will take the girls. Second, and maybe just as important. I know how they are changing people. I know what they did to Leroy to turn him into Bishop, same with the Carpenters, and our friend Sonya here. More importantly, I think I can undo it, if the two of you will help me."

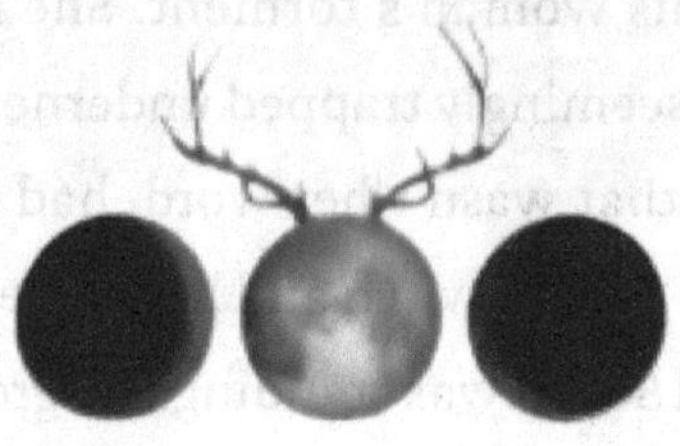

PULL THE THREAD

As Harlan made it into the back door of the kitchen with Fredrick and Edward close on his heels, he tried not to think about the sounds of the red-haired woman screaming. The last few hours had been just about all his mind could take. The chase through the woods, the beating at the hands of that blond man. Losing the girls to that monster made of light. LaRhonda's admission of being a witch, Lord Seanchara. All of it.

Not only had Harlan's body been broken, everything he thought he knew about the world was wrong. Every lesson in Sunday School, every bible story that he had based his life on, was a farce. If there was a God, the closest thing to it was now standing in his kitchen in a three-piece suit drinking a cup of tea, while his wife ripped a woman apart with her bare hands in Harlan's backyard.

He looked around the room for LaRhonda, wanting to be near her right now. His shoulders dropped and he inhaled and exhaled slowly and deliberately as he saw her. He spoke quietly enough that he was certain she could not hear him.

"I suppose I should get used to strangeness like this."

LaRhonda was levitating two feet above the floor, seemingly suspended in a cocoon of light between two extremely tall, pale women. They turned to look his way, and he realized he was looking at twins. His heart broke for his girls, how scared they must be. Slowly they lowered LaRhonda back to the floor, her bare feet landing as soft as a whisper on the hardwood floors of the dining room.

As one, they held out their hands to him, beckoning him. He hesitated only a moment before moving toward them. LaRhonda's eyes opened she smiled at Harlan, she held out her left hand, and he took it in his own. Only then, realizing that her left arm had been smashed, pulverized by a giant hammer only two hours ago.

Healers, he thought to himself, and twins, like his girls. Then he was warm in LaRhonda's embrace. Her soft lips touched his own and for a moment he forgot everything. The sound of screaming from the backyard suddenly stopped.

Everyone looked toward the back door of the house, anticipating what may come next. A minute passed with Harlan standing there in LaRhonda's arms. Fredrick and Edward stood silently next to Lord Seanchara, who had stopped sipping his tea and just thoughtfully held his cup in front of him.

The back door crashed open, and Bets, Dorthea, and the woman they called Elder Valkyrie came into the room. Valkyrie walked straight to Lord Seanchara, and he laid his cup down on the counter and spread his arms wide. She leaned into him, her head on his massive chest and the blood from her tunic staining the front of this suit.

"Are you okay, love? Is it done, do we have what we need?"

"All and more, I am afraid, Sister Bets here proved quite useful in an interrogation, and may have unraveled one of their secrets. But we will need some assistance in proving her theory.

Will you all join us outside? Where is Amy Park?"

Edward straightened, "Out in my van with John, Elder Valkyrie, would you like me to retrieve her?"

"Yes, please Edward, and consorts."

Fredrick and Edward both nodded in respectful acknowledgement.

"You did well today, thank you both for being willing to lay your life on the line for your sister witches."

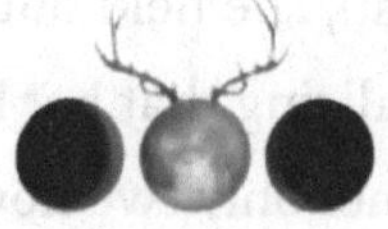

Back outside, the group stood in front of Sonya as she hung on the web of branches. Bets could see the damage was very serious. Sonya was bleeding from multiple wounds, most of her scalp was bare and bloody from her hair being ripped out. One arm was obviously dislocated, and the collar bone broken on that side.

Bets stood directly in front of her. Dorthea, Amy, LaRhonda, Desma, Althea and Elder Valkyrie stood in a semicircle around Beta also facing Sonya.

"I am sure when you look you can see what I see, there is a woman beneath the woman here. It was the same with Levi Carpenter.

A layer of energy surrounds the person inside and seems to act like a sort of binding agent for the person they laid over top of the original."

Bets looked around at the gathered witches, all of them nodding in agreement.

"It does not appear that this process is voluntary, it seems to be something brought on by the monsters that we battled here and that

Dorthea's raiding party ran into at the church camp last year. They call them Seraphim, and she, at least, truly believes them to be Angels.

When I tried to siphon the energy that was binding Levi, I could feel it start to unravel, but then it would snap back. My belief is that if I can pull a single thread of it and hand that thread off to one of you. You can act as an anchor, and I will repeat the process until we can all just pull and unravel the energy like a ball of yarn."

Elder Valkyrie spoke grimly. "And if it doesn't work?"

"Then this poor woman will finally be at peace, and we will know to try something different to save John."

No one had any further questions.

Bets fell completely into her connection and looked at the group gathered around her.

She knew she should feel terrified. Here she was, barely two years into her craft and attempting something never done before in the presence of Elder Valkyrie, Dorthea, and the Lewis twins.

Instead, she felt exhilarated and challenged. Was this ambitious? Yes, but she was Colleen Elizabeth Milburn, failure was never an option for her.

She only paused to acknowledge for a moment the flash of her old self.

Bets found the energy surrounding Sarah and holding her within Sonya. A woven tapestry of golden light, each layer knotted and twisted around her spirit over and over in a complex pattern.

Using her siphon, she picked and pulled until at last she found it. A thread to grasp. Like a surgeon, she delicately grasped this thread of light and power and pulled. Her hands raised slowly above her head, and she backed up toward the left side of the semicircle, and as gently as handling a baby bird, she handed that thread of light to Dorthea. It shifted colors when it touched Dorthea. After a horrifying moment when she felt like she pulled too hard, or too fast and the thread would snap back, it was secured. Dorthea smiled at Bets as she went back to work finding another point at which to peel away the energy.

After nearly two hours of slow deliberate work each witch gathered was holding onto a binding thread of energy and all could see the woman beneath the mask that was Sonya. She was a slight, mousy woman with light brown hair and a cartoon mouse tattooed on her right arm.

Bets had been slowly siphoning the energy down the thread held by each witch. She was exhausted, drenched in sweat. Her clothes clung to her, and her hair was plastered to her face.

But now it was time for Sarah to save herself.

Bets called to the consorts

"Fredrick, Edward, it's time. We must wake the woman within. I know you cannot see her, but she is there.

Please stand to either side, lay your hands on her, let her feel your warmth, and Fredrick, call her back.

We don't know her, but her name is Sarah, just call her name, tell her that her family is waiting for her here. That she can have her life back."

The consorts did as instructed. Bets could see Fredrick leaned close and whispering to the scalped woman. Bets continued to unravel the energy. Each time she drew a little more out, the corresponding witch would tighten her grasp on her thread, and she would continue around the circle. Now she could feel Fredrick's call vibrating down the energy of creation. She could feel him calling Sarah to attend.

"Sarah, sister, it's time, you have loved ones waiting for you. But you have to push through. They've made a lie of you; you're not the person they made you out to be. Awake now Sarah, awake and push through to us. We are all waiting to meet you."

Bets could see the woman's spirit rolling and twisting inside her prison. She could feel her fear and rage as she pushed against the veil that held her. Bets pulled hard with her siphon, trying to help Sarah break free.

A scream of anguish and a crackle like electricity arcing, and Bets landed hard on the ground.

She tried hard to clear her head; she could hear crying from Sarah and the bustling sound of movement all around her. Something was happening, she...

A searing pain behind her eyes and a voice screaming in her ear, no, in her head. *"Evil, all of them, kill the witches, the Lord will not allow this blasphemy to continue. Contact Malleus Dei, you must escape."*

Bets rolled onto her belly, trying to push herself up to her feet, but she could not move. She lay there face down and the voice in her head. Sonya's voice kept screaming, raving. She could feel hands on her, and a voice whispering through the haze of Sonya's rage.

"Bets, come back. You did good, and rest is coming, but not now, and not here. Your sisters need you."

Desma's voice cut through the din of Sonya's screaming in her head. She felt Dorthea's strong hand on her back and could smell the wild forest smell of Edward the Fish as she was half carried, half guided into the house and led to a couch. The last thing she remembered before drifting off was Dorthea's calm, flat voice. "I don't care if it's her fault or not, if she doesn't come back to us, I will kill that girl myself."

Bets tried to tell her she would be okay, that she didn't need to worry. Then Sonya started screaming again, and Bets couldn't stay awake any longer.

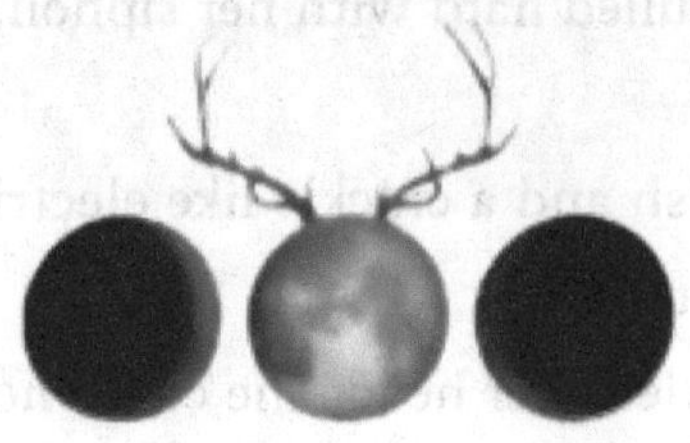

Pick Up The Pieces

Bets woke to the sound of someone talking nearby.

"I'm sorry Ma'am, I wish I knew more. I was with my dad, he is a minister at a small church in Springfield, Missouri, and then I woke up screaming out there in the yard with youns. I wish I could tell you more. That I remembered more. But I don't."

Bets did not recognize the voice, but a fair guess said it was Sarah. It was dark in the living room where she had been sleeping. She could see light pouring in from one of the side doors, so she made her way into the kitchen.

She squinted against the light as she came around the corner. Dorthea, Desma, and Althea were seated at one end of the table. Sarah, looking somewhat healed, was at the other. Gone were the bare bloody patches of scalp. Replaced by what looked to be a few days growth of ginger red hair.

Dorthea was on her feet immediately as Bets rounded the corner into the kitchen.

"Bets come here, how are you feeling?"

The look of concern on Dorthea's face was very real.

"I, I think I am okay. I'm starving, and I smell bad, but other than that I think I am in one piece."

"Do you remember what happened?"

"I do, but I think I need a shower first and something to eat before I relive any of that. Dorthea, I am a little unsteady, could you come with me to get my clothes out of the van so I can change?"

"Edward and Fredrick have the van and are making a quick trip to deliver everyone to where they need to be. But I brought your bag in, let me show you where, and get you settled. ladies, if you would excuse us, and could we trouble you to set out some snacks?"

Desma and Althea nodded in unison. Even after more than two years around them, Bets could not tell them apart.

Once they made the landing at the top of the stairs, Dorthea led Bets into a small bedroom. Bets saw her bags there, along with some of Dorthea's things.

"Are we staying awhile?"

"Harlan said we could use this as a home base for a few days while we rally the troops to get his daughters back. I just saw you walk up the stairs, I am guessing this has nothing to do with you being a little unsteady."

Bets flashed a smile her way.

"That is correct. What is the deal with Sarah? Does she remember anything at all that can help us? Does she know what happened?"

"Not a damn thing. She remembers leaving bible study on a Sunday evening in May of 2022, then waking up three years later in the yard out back."

"Fredrick has already confirmed her story. She was the daughter of a pastor of a small church in Springfield, Missouri. She was reported missing by her mother when she didn't come back from her normal weekend at her dad's house. By the time the police got involved the father was also missing. Parental abduction was assumed. Of course, after a couple years went by, everyone involved but the mother claimed the father must have killed her then himself. Although no bodies were ever found."

"So, what is the plan for her? Do we just turn her loose after all this? Send her back to her mother?"

"I am afraid not; she will need to be kept under close observation. We have no idea what the lasting effects might be, or if Malleus Dei may come back to retrieve their lost member. We cannot let that happen."

"What about John, should we get started unraveling him? I am sure Amy will be thrilled to have her husband and consort back."

"It is already happening. Elder Valkyrie has arranged the whole thing back in Mercer. Bets, what about you? You went down hard, and we could all hear Sonya screaming though you."

"As far as I can tell, she's gone. I am hearing nothing. I think it was just a misstep on my part. I dropped my wards to pull harder and help Sarah free herself. But when she broke through I was still connected and puling hard, and I pulled the construct that was Sonya into myself. What is the plan from here?"

"From here, you shower and rest up. The twins are putting everyone back together again. LaRhonda Kelm is taking Harlan to meet with her consort, Gerardo. They cannot seem to track down the twins' mother anywhere. She was supposed to be on a short work trip, but they said she is never without her phone. Fredrick, Edward, and Amy are escorting John back to Mercer, so that they can start the process of unraveling him. When they get back with word from the Elders on how to handle the Sarah situation, we will go from there. In the meantime, we need to get a plan together to get the twins back from The Ascension. The only question now is, surgical strike and rescue or massive attack?"

"Ugh, okay, I will leave that to my betters and get my smelly ass in the shower. Just let me know what we need to do next."

Dorthea hugged her close. Bets relished the contact. She knew that there was more turmoil just around the corner.

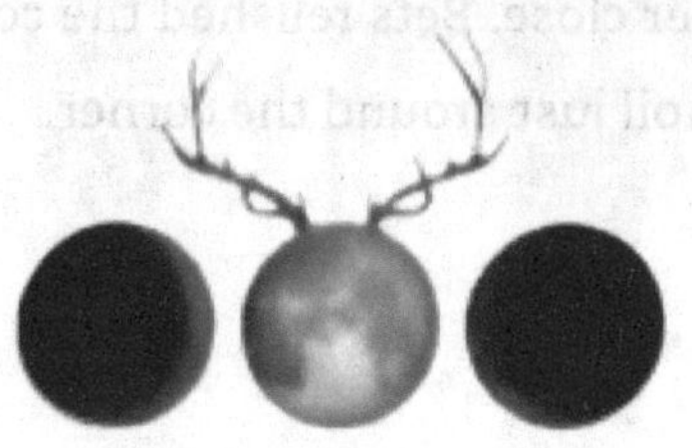

Like There Was Another Option

The early evening sun was shining through the windows in The Temple of The Mother. The colored glass cast a reddish glow over the room.

"And Dorthea, what is your recommendation? If you were to be asked to lead this operation."

Dorthea stood from her seat at the end of the table. She knew that her being asked to lead the mission to rescue Harlan Rice's daughters and any other innocents currently being held by The Ascension, was more likely than hypothetical.

"Thank you Mother, a small team, quiet and fast as possible. We have no idea who all is at this building. The last thing we want to do is drive up a body count in downtown Memphis."

"I think we are all in agreement on that. I also believe that is why they moved their operation into the heart of a major city. They are aware we are far less likely to come out in force and risk innocent lives, and exposure for our sisters and brothers. How many sisters and brothers do you think would be effective?"

"It's impossible to know for sure. I will not speak for anyone else. I would be happy to go, I think having Sister LaRhonda along would make getting the girls to trust us a lot easier. We don't know what they are enduring and they may be very reluctant to participate in their own rescue if they think it is a trick. I would like to have three to four sisters and their consorts total besides myself."

Niri turned side to side addressing the gathered witches and elders. "Does anyone else have any thoughts to the contrary? Or are we all in agreement?"

Heads nodded all over the dining hall of the Temple of the Mother.

"Good, Dorthea please assemble a team and send word when you are ready to strike out so that we can have Lord Seanchara open a doorway."

"Yes Mother. I do have one further request."

"Of course, ask away."

"I would like the permission of the council of Elders to have my niece join us. Pardon me, both of my nieces. Polly and Sugar have been convalescing more than a year, and I am sure they would relish the chance to get back out into the mission."

"I think that is a reasonable request, give us an hour to discuss and we will send word. Are you staying with Sister Bets?"

"Yes Ma'am."

"Then that is where we will find you when a decision has been made."

It took nearly thirty minutes for everyone to file past Dorthea and say their hellos and good lucks. When almost everyone else was gone Bets approached.

"Alright General Kenobi let's get some food in you. Besides, I have a surprise waiting back at my place."

Dorthea raised an eyebrow at the Star Wars reference but did not give Bets the satisfaction of a response.

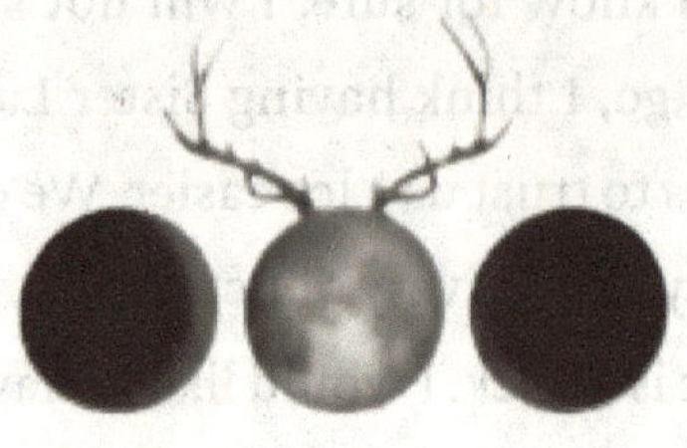

A Breath

"**S**ister Dorthea, Fredrick!"

Kay bounded across the courtyard behind the house she shared with Bets as she saw the group approaching.

Dorthea held out her arms. "Come here young lady, let me look at you. My goodness Kay, you have just shot right up haven't you? And those connections. Is there anything you haven't learned yet young lady?"

"Well." She drawled. "I still can't fly, haven't been able to turn Tren into a hippopotamus, or a parakeet. Can't cook like Sugar and still have to climb on the counter to get the cookies that Bets thinks she hides from me. Oh, and Sister Claudia thinks I am the dumbest thing since Crocs, but other than that I am all aces."

Dorthea scoffed. "Still can't fly, and she has the gall to call herself a witch. If Sister Claudia ever tells you you're doing a great job be very afraid. She's a hell of a teacher, but she's not giving away validation like some sweet old grandma."

Kay shrugged. "Come on, your surprise is inside."

"I thought you were my surprise."

"Not hardly, now can I give Fredrick a hug or are you keeping me all to yourself."

"I would say that is a question for Fredrick, far be it from me to offer consent on his behalf." She winked at Kay. "Look at me being all woke and progressive."

Fredrick spoke from behind her. "While your progress as a social justice advocate is admirable Sister. I am enthusiastically consenting to getting a hug from Miss Kay."

Kay leapt the five feet between them and Fredrick caught her as if she weighed no more than a newspaper or a kitten.

"It is good to see you well young sister. I am eager to meet your consort as well. Sugar speaks highly of him."

"Tren is pretty rad Fredrick, I think you'll like him. I know he is hoping to meet you. Sugar talks about you all the time and Tren got to train a lot with Sugar. I think anyone that Sugar respects as much as you. Tren knows you have to be cool."

"May we all be so lucky to have friends as good as Christopher Lewis one day."

As they entered the back door of the house Dorthea was nearly overwhelmed by the sounds of people busy in the kitchen and the smells of food cooking. Tren was leaning against the wall next to the back door and when Dorthea walked through the door he straightened immediately. "Sister Dorthea, Tren Praktavady, it's an honor to meet you." He held out his hand. She shook it briefly.

"Thank you Tren, seems like you have your work cut out for you, keeping Kay safe will turn out to be a full time job I fear."

She flashed Kay a smile that would have looked perfectly at home on a lioness who just spotted a lone gazelle. Kay rolled her eyes and loudly addressed the room. "Hey everyone, look who I found wandering around."

The small group turned almost as one.

Dorthea recognized Amy Park at once. It took a moment longer to realize she was looking at John. He had started to put on a little weight and his bruises and cuts from his fight with Fredrick had mostly healed. He rose and headed her way. Behind him, Sarah was cooking in Bets' small kitchen. Dorthea could not tell what she was working on, but the smell had Dorthea's stomach growling.

John stopped in front of her. "General Milburn, thank you for all you did to bring me back. Amy has gotten me up to speed, and I will forever be in your debt."

"There are no thanks necessary Brother. Watching each other's back, keeping each other safe is just being part of our great family. If we spent all of our time thanking each other every time one of us saved another's life, we might never get anything else done."

"That's fair and wise, Ma'am, nonetheless, we cooked for you. Hopefully, you will join us and let us show our gratitude even if it isn't necessary."

"Of course, John, and you are welcome. My apologies, it wasn't my intention to dismiss your gratitude. It has been a long couple of weeks, and a meal and some fellowship seems like it might be exactly what I need."

"Then let's get you a seat and some coffee." He motioned her over to the table and turned to Fredrick.

They said nothing for a moment and seemed to be frozen in time as they stared at one another. John stepped forward and wrapped Fredrick in a hug so tight it caught the larger man off balance.

He spoke quietly. "Brother I can never thank you enough. I don't remember any of it. But you know if I was in control of my faculties that never would have happened. Amy told me how restrained you were, which is evidenced by my standing here in one piece."

"I knew you were not yourself, and it was Amy calling to you that brought you out of it enough for me to get the drop on you with the tranquilizer. Which, you should definitely have Edward the Fish set you up with a couple before you go back to the field."

"Thank you Brother. All I know for certain is I wouldn't be standing here if it weren't for you and Sister Dorthea."

He released Fredrick, who laid a hand on his shoulder. Come, I heard someone say coffee and I think that sounds like a wonderful idea.

John and Fredrick had pulled tables together in the courtyard so that everyone could sit together and eat.

Dorthea sat at one end of the table listening to the conversation unfold. Fredrick and John were telling Tren and Kay stories of training with Mathew Weems. The children, of course, were enrapt. Fredrick especially, was as gifted a storyteller as Mathew had been, it was a wonderful tribute to the man that they continued telling his stories. She heard his funeral song in her mind.

"Eighty-nine years, the enemies of the innocent fell beneath his blade."

"Eighty-nine years, he held the hands of the frightened as they faced their biggest fears."

"Eighty-nine years, he taught his brothers and his sons, the ways of our family."

"Now, our brave brother has fallen, protecting the ones he loved from a monster in the night."

As it would always be when she thought of him. The memories of his deeds, of his life within Mercer would live forever and therefore so would he. She wondered who would sing her funeral song when the time came, Polly maybe, or Bets.

She had heard more funeral songs in the last two years than in the last two decades combined. Too many brothers and sisters had fallen at the hands of Malleus Dei and The Ascension. She wondered sometimes if they wouldn't be served by an all-out assault. Just walk up to Jim Meadows, turn him to ash where he stood, then pull his entire operation apart. Yes, there would be risk of exposure, but it is not like the witch who did it couldn't just disappear into Mercer and never leave. A small price to pay for dismantling the evil that is The Ascension.

She knew that was frustration, not wisdom, speaking. It did not change the fact that some part of her, the part that was made of the same stuff as her mother, wanted to do it. Wanted her and the rest of the Elders to walk into that chapel and level it and all of the bastards in it who have hurt her great family. It wouldn't take more than a handful. Mother Mercer, Elder Allysse, Elder Hirut, Elder Valkyrie, that would likely be all they needed. Set Bast loose to hunt down any stragglers and that would be the end of The Ascension.

But even now, as angry as she was, they knew that not everyone involved was there voluntarily, that many of them may not even be aware of what they are doing, or who they really are.

Should Sarah, John, and Leroy all die because Reverend Meadows and his ilk have declared war on anything non-Christian?

What would that make them, except the monsters they claim to be fighting against? No, they needed to fight this the same way they always do. If it requires more attrition, more blood on the altar of righteousness in order to bring this threat down without sacrificing the innocent then so be it. That was what they signed up for. She would happily open all her veins, give every drop if meant one innocent life was spared, that had to include those poor souls taken by the Seraphim and The Ascension.

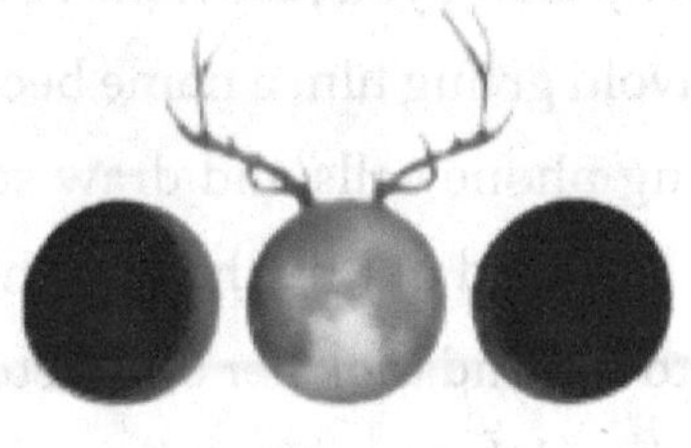

SHAKE THE FOUNDATION

"LaRhonda, what the hell am I supposed to do here?"

Harlan was pacing back and forth in her dining room.

"Harlan, we are going to find them, I promise you. They cannot hide from this group that is hunting them. You saw what they are capable of."

"That's not what I am talking about LaRhonda. You will find my daughters. Or did you forget that I am the ranking member on the Armed Services committee and very close friends with Sec Def? If I don't have an answer within forty-eight hours, I will call in Seal Team Six if I have to. I am getting my daughters back."

He had every right to be pissed, and terrified, she did not begrudge him the bluster. Although they both knew that it wasn't likely how things would play out. She could only imagine how angry and helpless he was feeling right now.

"I know Harlan, I am sorry. We know where they are, Dorthea is meeting with the Elders now. They will have a plan together quickly. Harlan, the people behind this are influential and respected in the evangelical world. They..."

"Who LaRhonda, why won't you just come out and say it?"

She was trying to avoid giving him a name because she was worried he would start making phone calls and draw some really unwanted attention to himself. She held out her hand to him, and almost automatically he walked to her and took her outstretched hand.

Oh good, at least he doesn't hate me enough to refuse my touch.

She was having a harder and harder time seeing a way where this ended with the two of them together. Even if she got the girls back to him unharmed. Why would he stay with her? He was convinced and more than likely correct, that their association with her was what got them kidnapped.

She led him to the couch and sat down. He sat down next to her. As soon as he did, he leaned his head on her shoulder. She draped her arm around him and pulled him close.

"LaRhonda, I just want my daughters back, I want to go back to how it was supposed to be. The girls safe in their beds, you on my deck doing yoga. God was in heaven. You know the worst part of this LaRhonda? I don't know what to do. Normally, in a situation like this I would be on my knees crying my eyes out in prayer. But who am I praying to now? The guy that was in my kitchen drinking tea. Everything about my life has been a damned lie. My parents aren't in heaven waiting for me to arrive. My parents are rotting in the fucking ground LaRhonda. Everything I have ever stood for is a lie and not knowing that has gotten my kids taken from me and there isn't a damned thing I can do about it."

Her heart broke for Harlan. She hadn't even considered how much his faith was a bedrock for him. How much it held him together, and now it was broken. It had taken her less than a day to destroy this beautiful man. What a fool she was, to think she could ever be with someone like Harlan. And her foolishness, may have gotten his children killed, and it has certainly changed him irrevocably.

"LaRhonda, I am exhausted. I need a shower, and I need a couple of hours of sleep. But I am scared to be alone, I am scared I am going to wake up, and you will be gone too. Will you come with me upstairs? Will you stay close, so I don't panic?"

"Of course, Harlan. Let's get some rest. The council will come to a decision soon, and we will be getting your girls back, and I know you will want to be rested and ready when they come running in."

He sobbed into her shoulder. She pulled him close and gave him his moment. Her heart was also broken, she loved Harlan, she loved the girls more than anything. But this was not her time to mourn. She needed to be ready. At any moment, the call could come. While she was confident that Dorthea and the Elders would come up with a plan to rescue the girls and that no force in the Witch Father's existence could stop her from going along. She also knew there was a real chance that the girls were already lost to them. Or that she would not survive the conflict. She was not a warrior, and she knew the reality of it. Had Dorthea and Bets not come to her rescue; she would have died under that hammer.

Just as she felt Harlan relax and melt into her, the doorbell rang.

They both jumped at the sound. He straightened, and she pulled herself up and crossed the floor to answer the door.

Gerardo pushed through the door before LaRhonda could even open it all the way.

"Harlan." He held his arms out wide. Harlan embraced him.

"I've good news and good news for us, and really bad news for someone else."

LaRhonda looked at him impatiently. This was not the time.

"We are going right now to get the girls. Like grab a go bag and get your ass to my car, Kelm."

"Okay, so what's the other good news and bad news."

242

D.O. SCISSOM

"Dorthea Milburn and her niece are leading the rescue, with you and me in tow. All of that is very bad news for whomever is holding your daughters, Harlan. These are very dangerous witches. Oh, and Elder Dinah is waiting downstairs for Harlan, he is going with her to a meeting place for us to bring the girls when we get them back."

LaRhonda smiled and relaxed visibly. "Where is Dinah?"

"Downstairs, parked next to me. Grab your stuff and meet me at the front door, guys. Chop, chop."

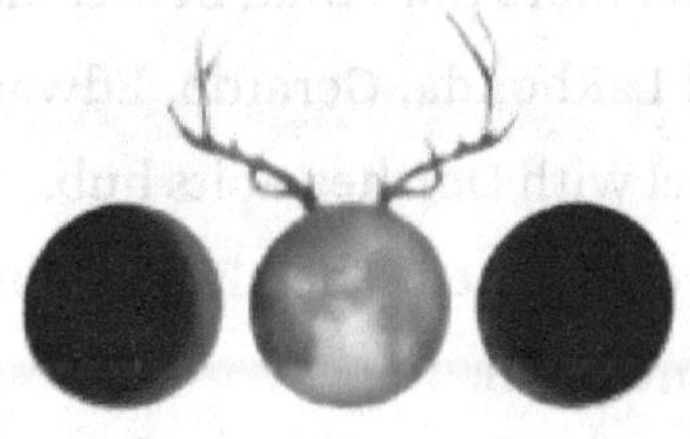

PROVE ME WRONG

"**F**redrick, what are you seeing?"

"Looks like a single security guy at the front desk. Although there are two rather unassuming looking gentlemen just lounging in one of the waiting areas. From their builds and demeanor, I am guessing they are part of the same group that was guarding the camp."

"Okay, make your way back here and we will get started."

A few minutes later Fredrick pulled up in the dark blue delivery van. He immediately began changing out of the safety vest and t-shirt that he had been forced to wear as part of the disguise.

Bets was, as always, charmed, and impressed by the care that Fredrick took with his appearance, even when they were getting ready to head into a potential fight.

Dorthea began the connection ritual. When she got to Bets, she leaned in close touching the ground crystal, herbs and blood to Bets' forehead then sealing it into place with the spell.

Immediately Bets felt the connection come alive between her, LaRhonda, and Dorthea. This was different than the normal connections. This was a direct line of communication, as clear as walkie talkies, only silent. And more than that, Bets could feel what they were feeling. As if her and LaRhonda, Gerardo, Edward and Fredrick were spokes around a wheel with Dorthea at its hub.

The connections were formed. The plan was in place. They just had to wait as the sun went down.

In Bets' mind there couldn't be a better time. On a Tuesday evening the building should be empty of anyone not directly involved in church operations or The Ascension. In a further stroke of luck Meadow's Ministries was holding a big church service up by St. Louis. So, most everyone involved wasn't even in the state tonight.

As the sun dropped below the horizon and dusk began to creep over the world they pulled into the parking lot across the street from the delivery door at the back of the chapel. Dorthea parked her SUV on the opposite side of the lot so that if one of their vehicles got blocked in, it wouldn't trap both.

They had the city building plans, which only showed a small utility room in the basement. But more importantly they had Bet's memory of seeing the building through Sonya's eyes. They also had the small locator charm made from the girls' hair.

LaRhonda and Gerardo would follow Bets and Fredrick in the back door. Bets and Fredrick would clear out any opposition either coming in or leaving the building while LaRhonda and Gerardo focused on finding the girls. Dorthea and Edward would remain in the vehicles and ready to either extract or back up wherever they were needed. The mission was simple, get the twins, and any other innocents they found, out of the building as fast as possible. And avoid a fight with whomever is there if they can.

Fredrick led the way across the street Bets fast on his heels and Gerardo and LaRhonda running to keep up. Bets threw a quick charm up at the camera over the door. Just a quick fog of static, while Fredrick scanned them into the delivery door with the key card he had stolen from the desk of the security guard while he was fumbling through his fake delivery earlier in the day. It was one of the few benefits unconscious bias and residual racism. It didn't take much acting on Fredrick's part for the white security guard behind the counter to assume Fredrick was too dumb to be a threat of any kind.

As they passed through the door and it closed behind them Bets released the fog charm. She didn't want to arouse any suspicion by disabling the camera completely. The four crept quietly down the institutional hallway, barely making a whisper of a sound on the blue and white tile. As they passed a series of doors Bets noticed the watercolor handprints and crude crayon drawings, along with bible verses. *The children's Sunday school classrooms,* she thought, as they passed by one darked doorway after another. She did not like the open doorways of every darkened classroom they passed but felt nothing through her connection to the divine energy. She relayed the need for caution while passing the doorways to the group.

The only way she knew to get where they were going was a spiral staircase at the back of the chapel. Fredrick was leading the way through the utility hallways and classrooms. But once they hit the stairs they would let LaRhonda guide them to the girls.

Fredrick stopped just in front of a green wooden door. LaRhonda and Bets slid to the front. Each one extending their perception along the energy of creation. Bets felt no one present on the other side of the door. She quietly opened the handle and one at a time the group slipped into the back of the chapel.

Crouched low, the group slid silently between the pews and across the width of the chapel to the stone door Bets had seen in Sonya's memory.

As they approached the door LaRhonda pulled the location charm from her pocket. She whispered each girls name into it. She turned to Bets as she opened the door. "They are here. I can feel it pull."

"Good, everyone get ready. We may encounter no resistance, or we may find all of Malleus Dei and the Seraphim."

Fast and quiet the group descended into the halls of the ascension.

As they came out of the staircase into a small stone chamber lit with wall sconces designed to look like gas lanterns Bets heard Dorthea in her mind. *"Is everyone in one piece? Have you found the cells yet?"*

Bets focused on her connection to Dorthea *"No Ma'am, but LaRhonda is tracking them now, we are in the halls under the chapel. Should have them shortly."*

Bets saw LaRhonda ahead of her nodding in agreement. They heard whispering ahead and the group slowed. Bets felt Fredrick slide past her in the hallway. As silent as a cat and crouched low he moved past LaRhonda and disappeared around the corner ahead of them. Bets reminded herself to trust in Fredrick, this was exactly the kind of thing he was trained for. A few seconds later LaRhonda, Bets and Gerardo rounded the turn to find Fredrick still crouched and looking into an open doorway. He was closing the door softly as they passed him, Bets caught a glimpse of two distinct sets of legs piled up in the center of the floor before the door quietly clicked shut. She wondered just how he was able to take them both down with no sound. For a moment, she also wondered if they survived the ordeal.

LaRhonda glanced back at Bets and nodded toward the end of the hall, then took off quickly. They hit a junction in the hallway and LaRhonda led them to the left and down another set of stairs. Bets could feel the presence of people ahead in the energy of creation. She could not tell who or how many. As Bets and LaRhonda emerged from the bottom of the stairs side by side they ran into two men dressed in blue trousers, and white button down shirts. These were the same guys from the church camp, or at least part of the same group.

The guy on the right reached for a radio on his belt and LaRhonda let loose a quick charm. "Boule Yo" The radio melted in his hand before he could speak a word. Snap of a baton and the guy fell in a heap at her feet.

Bets spun and kicked the second guy directly in the solar plexus, doubling him over. She reached out as he fell, tapping him in the center of the forehead and unleashing a small concussion charm. His head snapped back, and he did not move after landing on the floor.

"Hello." A small, scared voice called from up ahead.

"Lydia." LaRhonda gasped as she sprinted ahead.

Bets signaled to Gerardo to stay and watch the hallway behind, and Fredrick to sprint ahead. LaRhonda stopped at the darkened doorway. Bars covered the opening. But the room beyond was pitch black.

LaRhonda whispered into the darkness. "Lydia, Lexia, are you okay?"

Bets did not know which girl answered. "LaRhonda? Is that really you? We are here. Please get us out."

"Okay, I got you girls, are you together."

From the darkness two voices, in unison, "We're here LaRhonda, there are others here too. But we are chained up, in the dark. No one can move. Please, our mom was here but they took her out and never brought her back."

Bets felt her connection to Dorthea. *Dorthea, we found the girls, there are more than just the two of them. It appears their mother was also here but was taken from holding at some point recently. We are going to break everyone out we can find.* She felt Dorthea's acknowledgement.

Bets spoke up. "Everyone cover your eyes. I am going to get some light in there and if you've been in the dark for a while it may hurt."

Some shuffling and several voices replied. "Okay. We're ready."

Bets dug in her hip bag for a small piece of quartz and a piece of moonstone. She held them together between her palms and rubbed them against each other and whispered. "Mother Moon we seek your light, guide us to our home. Mother Moon defeat the night, your light upon these stones. SOLAS NA GEALAI!"

She tossed the now fused stones through the bars and into the darkened room and the glow of the moon lit up the space beyond. In the soft twilight Bets could see roughly a dozen people lining the walls of the room at intervals, spaced out so they could not touch one another. Each one appeared to be shackled with a leather strap on their right wrist and left ankle. The straps were held in place by a pad lock. She spotted the twins at the same time as LaRhonda cast a charm to force the lock open.

The barred metal gate swung open on its hinges and LaRhonda and Bets stormed in. Bets sent the message to Dorthea. *"We are in, we are going to set them free and come running, looking at roughly twelve, maybe more. Be ready. I want to try and find the girl's mom if I can. Once everyone is headed out safe to you I will double back."*

"Stay with Fredrick, Bets. I understand your concern and if you all see her, grab her if you can. But do not go alone into a building where there may be Seraphim, Malleus Dei and who knows who else."

Bets stewed on the reprimand for only a moment before responding. *"Yes Ma'am. Signal the guys to head back to us to regroup please."*

Dorthea didn't respond but Bets knew she got the message. She ducked into the room behind LaRhonda, who ran straight to the twins. Bets started at the first person she came to.

A middle aged man with a shaved head and a tribal tattoo across his throat stared up at Bets as she approached. "I am going to set you free, just wait at the door with my friends. We have a van parked outside we will get you home."

He said nothing but nodded.

She grasped both locks, the one on his ankle and the one on his wrist. She felt the charm build inside her gut and pushed it out with a breath. "Negare." And the locks both clicked open.

He took her outstretched hand, and she hauled him to his feet. From his slow, unsteady gait she wondered how long he had been down here, chained up in this cell.

She continue down the line.

LaRhonda was holding both twins in her arms and crying. The girls were sobbing loudly into her shoulders.

Bets heard them ask about their dad, then she moved on. She let them have their moment. "LaRhonda move toward the door, I can get the rest out."

LaRhonda did not hesitate, she pulled the girls toward where Gerardo and Fredrick had everyone gathered at the entrance. Bets hoped she could stay focused, they were moving a big group of what were essentially hostages through enemy territory.

There were two people at the back of the room—a squat powerful looking man of mixed race. In a tank top, his muscular arms and shoulders were covered in faded tattoos. And a strikingly beautiful woman even in this low light and strange circumstances. Bets only paused a moment to look at her perfectly symmetrical features and the cast of the moonlight on her dark skin. Then she came back to herself and grasped both locks.

Three things happened in the same moment as she grabbed the locks to cast her charm.

She realized the woman's restraints were not locked.

He wards lit up, signaling the kind of danger that meant an attack was eminent.

Moses Myman, Jim Meadows chief of security and right hand man, wrapped the chain he was pretending to be shackled with, around Bets' neck and yanked her off of her feet.

Bets warding going off in the split second she realized the woman was not actually secured to the wall, allowing her to get a hand in between the chain and her neck, was likely the only thing that kept her neck from being broken as Moses whipped the chain back and forth.

Bets choked out the word "Help." As best she could. And while no one heard it, it reverberated through her connection to Dorthea, and was relayed through Dorthea to LaRhonda, Fredrick, Edward the Fish and Gerardo.

Bets fought to keep her hand in place as the man put a foot on her back and pressed her face first into the floor as he pulled up with the chain. The woman began laughing and kicked Bets hard in the ribs. She felt her ribs crack with the impact and the man pulled up even harder, trying to separate her head from her body. She heard a dull thump, then a crack of skull hitting the stone floor as the woman fell only a couple inches from her. Her brown eyes glazed in death just inches from Bets' face.

Then the pressure was gone, and she rolled quickly to her back.

She could not believe her eyes for a moment as the short man had grabbed Fredrick by the lapels and slammed him hard into the wall. Keeping the much taller man off his feet he pulled him back and slammed him again. Like he was trying to push Fredrick through the wall. Bets could not believe how strong he had to be. Fredrick was a good six inches taller than the man and she knew just what a capable warrior he was.

When the man pulled Fredrick back to slam him into the wall again he kicked off of the wall and propelled himself toward the man. The man tried to stop Fredrick's momentum and slam him backward into the stone again. He used the change in direction to snap his right knee up and catch the man under his chin. Bets heard his teeth click together and he released Fredrick who launched a series of quick punches to the man's ribs and abdomen.

The man staggered back trying to catch his footing and mount a defense. Bets could not risk Fredrick being injured by this man, even if she had faith in his ability. She focused the energy of creation into a single bolt of electricity. Not quite a lightning strike but more powerful than a taser. The bolt shot from her outstretched hand and connected directly with the man's temple. He hit the ground in a crackling shaking pile.

Fredrick's eyes went wide. As he helped bets to her feet and they headed toward the door.

"I must say, I appreciate the save there Sister. But I can smell that man's brain cooking from here. Was that your intention?"

"No, I didn't think I put that much behind the casting. It felt like something juiced it up. But we will have to figure that out later. If they were hiding in here they likely knew we were coming or at least saw us come in. Let's go."

They met LaRhonda and Gerardo at the front of the group.

"Okay, LaRhonda we need to move these people out of here. But if that is any indication we need to be ready for company along the way. Fredrick can you lead the way? Gerardo stay on his heels with the group. LaRhonda, let's put you and the twins in the middle to run off any possible interference. I will be right behind you all. Okay everyone be as quiet as you can. It's not far to the staircase and the van and we are going to get you all home safe."

Fredrick slipped ahead of the group silently acting as a scout. The group began to move, the first of them had just reached the bottom of the stairs when Bets heard it. In the labyrinth of hallways, it was impossible to tell what direction it was coming from.

Ping

Ping

Ping

The sound of a hammer striking stone.

Ping

Ping

Ping

Then the voice. The weird accent that sounded like someone imitating a southern accent that had only ever heard bad imitation of a southern accent.

"One little, two little, three little witches."

Ping

Ping

Ping

"I'm gonna burn their brooms and give them stitches."

"Shit, let's go." Bets whispered to the group.

To Dorthea through her connection. *Carpenters. I think Asher survived.*

"Collect their heads and leave the rest in ditches."

Ping

Ping

Ping

"Hey ho, Halloween is here."

Bets was halfway up the stairs when her warding went off. She spun just in time to see Asher Carpenter creeping silently up the stairs behind her on all fours like a cat.

"Ahh witch, you caught me being a sneak. That don't matter much. You aren't leaving here alive. Wait, I recognize you. Where is the old bitch you was running with? I need a little payback for her killin' me."

Bets said nothing but cut loose a repulsion charm aimed right at his chest as he was standing up straight.

He got his hammer up just in time, holding it across his body in two hands like a staff it seemed to absorb the blast.

"Oh, Youse ain't getting me like that again. Now come here nice and easy so I can smash your pretty face in."

Bets could feel the group as they made the top of the stairs. Then a panicked message from Fredrick through Dorthea. We have trouble in the chapel; Bets get them up here now."

Bets turned and ran up the stairs after the group. Dropped a darkness spell over the staircase behind her as she did. Hoping to slow Asher down even a little so she could regroup with her people before the fight started.

Out in the open chapel Bets looked around. LaRhonda and Gerardo had the folks they rescued up against the far wall of the chapel. Some of the pews had been hastily moved to block the door they came through.

Standing in the center of the room was Levi Carpenter, shirtless, in just a pair of basketball shorts and sneakers. He stood in contrast to the tall black man beside him in a heavily decorated purple robe. The man's locs nearly touched the ground. Asher Carpenter made the top of the stairs behind her, and she spun to face him. Directly behind him was the strong man from the cell who had fought Fredrick, apparently recovered from his electrocution at her hands. His shirt was missing as was a big chunk of his hair.

If there was a single lesson taught among the witches and warriors of Mercer when it came to conflict. Once the decision was made that violence was the only option. Death comes for the hesitant.

Fredrick was a blur as he launched himself at Levi Carpenter. Baton in his right hand, long knife in his left he spun, becoming a whirling dervish of death. The man in the robe next to Levi held his hands above his head and a ball of flame formed there. He launched it at the group along the wall. LaRhonda redirected the fireball back at the pyro and it dissipated about six feet ahead of reaching him, as he prepared another attack.

Asher and the other man ran toward Bets. She held out a hand and yelled "Cia bet ne toliau." Both men froze under the weight of her spell. But she could feel them pushing against her. She had enough of both of them. Of all of this bullshit. She was done, tired of them hurting her family and destroying innocent lives. She dropped the shield spell and stalked straight toward Asher, holding his eyes in her gaze. She needed this to be powerful, so she wanted to be as close as possible. He tried to speak, to look away, but Bets' will was strong and she held him in her gaze until she was only a couple of inches from him. She heard Gerardo yell her name, and LaRhonda started toward her. She ignored them, and the warning from Dorthea in her mind. She grabbed Asher Carpenter by the back of the head and pulled his face to hers. She kissed him hard on the mouth and when she pulled back she whispered "Shihai."

Asher froze, unable to move from Bets' spell. Until she gave the command. "Protect us Asher, prove your love to me."

The man behind Asher was yelling at him. "Asher, what are you doing. Kill her already." He took another step toward Bets. Asher smiled, his white teeth shining in the dim light of the chapel. Then he spun full speed and slammed his hammer into the side of Moses' head. Blood sprayed like a fountain from the impact and the man fell at Asher's feet. Asher spun back to Bets, winked at her, blew her a kiss, and ran off to where his brother was fighting Fredrick.

Bets turned to the LaRhonda and Gerardo, who were now on either side of the pyro and dodging fireballs in between getting their own hits in.

"Come on, let's go, out the front if we have to, we can circle back to the cars."

The group started moving toward the front of the chapel as Bets heard the first clang of steel ringing against steel as Asher Carpenter attacked his brother Levi.

"Fredrick, let's go!"

Fredrick obliged, momentarily enrapt by the sight of the two Carpenters spinning their dance of death toward one another.

Just as the group reached the doors, Bets' biggest fear was realized. The whole of reality began to shake.

"Seraphim." Bets hissed and sent the message to Dorthea.

Her only response was, *"Get low and stay away from the doors."*

Bets moved everyone back from the doors and motioned for them all to get down. A fireball shot past her head as LaRhonda deflected another one.

She started to rise, to go help them deal with the pyro and get clear and the doors of the chapel exploded inward. What Bets saw next made her heart soar and filled her with hope despite the sound of the Seraphim approaching. Out the front door of the chapel Bets could see three vehicles lined up, Edward's van, Dorthea's truck, and a red SUV. For a full second she had no idea who the SUV belonged to, until Sugar came crashing through the debris of the doors and charged full speed toward the pyro.

In his defense, he did manage to get a couple of fireballs off as Sugar stampeded toward him. Unfortunately for him, they did about as much damage to an enraged Sugar as a mosquito bite and within a moment Sugar was on him. Two quick punches to the head and the pyro was crumbling. Sugar caught him on the way down and spun like a discus thrower. He tossed the pyro a full twenty yards across the chapel and into the pews.

Polly came through the open doorway and started waving people on. Fredrick and Sugar were bringing up the rear when about a dozen men armed with batons and tasers and dressed in the strange gear of the camp guards.

Behind them as if they were ascending from the bowels of hell. Two Seraphim rose into the center of the chapel. Their wings outstretched, their arms skyward in praise. One of them looked to the Carpenter brothers locked in a deadly combat thanks to Bets spell. A humming sound that seemed to come from the air around the Seraphim and both brothers froze mid swing.

Bets could hear Fredrick and Sugar running hard behind her, Sugar yelling the whole time. Get them in the cars we have to go now. Don't stop, go, go, go."

All three vehicles were open, and people were piling in. Dorthea's truck sped off first, its bed loaded down.

LaRhonda, Gerardo, the twins and two other people jumped into Edwards van and slammed the doors and his tires smoked as he stomped the gas. Polly was already in the passenger driver seat. Bets jumped in the front passenger seat. Polly had the hatch open and the SUV rolling as Fredrick jumped into the back seat.

"Sugar come on." Polly was screaming. Bets saw him darting for the back of the SUV, two of the camp guards behind him. One launched his baton at Sugar's head. Bets held her breath as it sailed by him to clatter uselessly on the ground. Sugar jumped and landed on the tailgate and the entire SUV lurched to one side with his weight and momentum.

The SUV tore down the street behind Edward's van; she could just make out the taillights of Dorthea's truck as she rocketed ahead toward the interstate. They were going to haul ass toward Southern Illinois as fast as possible. There was a doorway there that Lord Seanchara could easily open, and they all felt like the pursuers would never follow them that far.

Three blocks from the church the first of the white vans marked Church of The Ascension pulled up behind them. Two more were close behind them. Bets was concerned they weren't going to make it to the interstate. Or even worse they would attract the wrong kind of police attention. Dorthea turned off of the main drag and onto a smaller side street that headed into the park. She seemed to be leading their pursuit somewhere away from the populated parts downtown.

Once the last pursuing van had turned onto the street behind them Bets reached out to Dorthea through their connection.

"Dorthea what's the plan here? They are on us pretty hard, three vans, no idea how many people."

"I know, I am leading them into this park, at least here, in the dark we have a chance to keep it off of any official radar. But it's going to be a fight, and we have a lot of innocents to protect."

Bets glanced in the side mirror, watching the approaching vans. She reached out with the energy of creation, trying to feel their numbers, to get a sense of what they were up against.

That was how she was able to feel their approach before she saw them. Two glowing white masses streaking past the vans as Polly swung the SUV into the parking lot of the park. Bets realized what was happening just as one of the Seraphim plowed sidelong into the SUV throwing it into the air.

The world turned sideways, then spun right again. Bets braced for the impact with the ground, and she felt Polly casting a spell. Their turn slowed and they eased down on the ground. *One day, I will be half the witch she is.* Bets turned to her sister to tell her just that only to see her staring out the driver's side window a look of terrified confusion on her face.

"Out of the car, now." Fredrick yelled from the back seat.

Bets could not get her door to open as that was where the Seraphim made initial impact with the SUV. She slid over and climbed out of Polly's open door. By the time she oriented herself Bets realized they were no longer in the park in Memphis. She looked around, confused until she recognized the land, and more than the land, she recognized the energy, his energy.

She opened up her siphon and pulled it into her, confirming what she already knew.

"Stag's Grove." She whispered and Polly reached out and took her hand as the three vans began to empty out. The church guards looked around as bewildered as she felt until they saw the burning white light of the Seraphim. They stood side by side, their giant wings stretched out behind them, their arms raised to the heavens. But before them, between them and the three vehicles full of Mercer witches and the rescued hostages, stood Lord Seanchara and Elder Valkyrie. He was as tall as the Seraphim, his antlers spreading out more than two feet on either side of his head. He wore nothing but a fur wrap around his waist, and in his hands a club of gnarled black wood, at least as long as Bets was tall. The handle of the club, a living raven's head, just like his walking stick.

Elder Valkyrie stood beside him, she wore only her silk wrap, upon her head, woven into the intricate braids flowing down her back was her crown, the triple moon, but in her right hand a slim curved sword the likes of which Bets had never seen. Deep in her connection Bets could see the storm raging within that blade. Lightning and thunder, raging wind, and pounding rain. *The Sword of The Storm*. The phrase popped into her mind unbidden and unaided.

There he is, the guardian of Mercer, The Horned God of the Witches. The Stag and his Mother Moon. Bets felt a swell of pride beyond what she could have ever imagined, and any despair she had felt about the arrival of the Seraphim was gone, replaced by a sense of absolute righteousness. There was no doubt in her mind they would prevail and save these innocents from whatever fate The Ascension had in store for them.

Behind the Seraphim the church guard gathered with Levi and Asher Carpenter at their head. Gerardo, Sugar, Edward, and Fredrick all approached where Lord Seanchara and Elder Valkyrie stood side by side facing the Seraphim. She glanced back to see Dorthea and LaRhonda, walking up on either side of her and Polly. Two sisters she did not recognize were herding the hostages through a doorway, one at a time. One guiding them, one touching them on the forehead just before they stepped through. Blocking their minds from the maddening distance they would travel in just a step.

The Seraphim roared and all of creation began to shake. Elder Valkyrie ran her hand over one of the tattoos on her arm and the sound ceased immediately.

Lord Seanchara spoke. "Did you think my children were unprotected?"

The Seraphim did not respond.

His voice roared and his face reddened. The air around him shimmered with the power of his outrage.

"Did you think you could attack my charges with impunity, steal their children, and not face consequences?"

Bets felt the tension rising all around as he screamed at the Seraphim.

"Did you think you were the only monsters in this world?"

He leapt the twenty yards toward one of the Seraphim and the battle was joined.

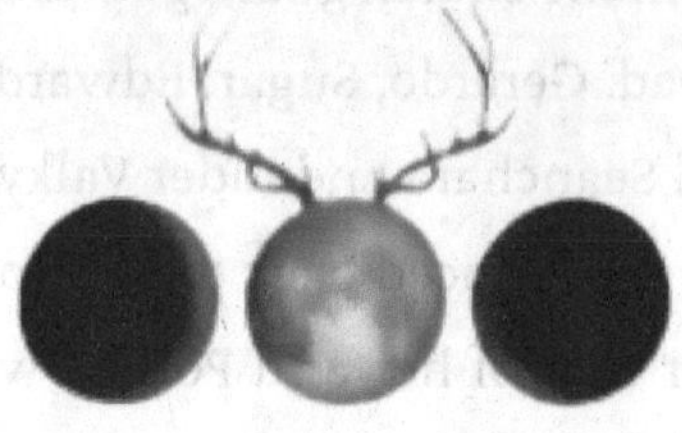

Battle At Stag's Grove

Three fireballs streaked across the field and slammed into the group of guards closest to the vans. Bets threw up a shield as two flash bang grenades came sailing toward where she stood with the rest of the Mercer witches. She was worried about them deflecting to where Lord Seanchara and Elder Valkyrie were engaged with the Seraphim. But she realized that while she could make out where they were as they danced around one another in the air. All four combatants seemed to be moving in and out of focus. She caught a glimpse of light as Elder Valkyrie's sword struck the shoulder of one of the Seraphim, then they both vanished into a blur.

She focused on what she could actually see, which was Edward the Fish running headlong into a group of three of the guards. She sprinted after him, trusting all of her sisters and brothers to keep one another safe, but Edward was her consort and her friend.

He tossed a taser ball at the three men, they scrambled thinking it was a grenade of some sort, and they weren't totally wrong. Two of the three managed to get out of range of the ball as it released its storm of electricity. The third was not so lucky and became the lightning rod for enough voltage to bring down a rhino.

Bets leapt past his smoking corpse and brought her baton down on the back of one man's neck before he could escape, the first man to run turned back to help and caught a boot under the chin from Edward the Fish for his troubles.

He yelled over his shoulder as he ran by her. "Did you see that Bets, Bets Bets, kicked just like Fredrick."

She took off in pursuit of Edward, preparing her next spell.

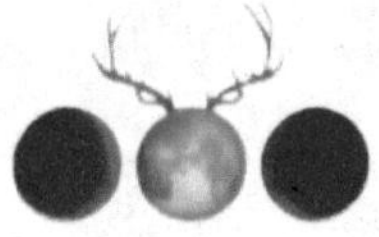

Sugar leveled the first guard with a single punch to the side of his head. The man's neck snapped with the force, and he dropped to the ground in a pile. He fell to the ground and rolled as Levi Carpenter's hammer swung where his head had been a moment before. Had that swing connected it would have likely ended Sugar's life. Sugar continued the roll and pushed off hard as he rolled upright again. His powerful legs pushed him higher than one would expect a person his size could jump and Levi's low swing at his knees missed its mark as well.

Sugar backed away a few steps allowing Levi to reset his swing and plan his next move. Not something he normally would have done. But Levi couldn't see what Sugar saw. A slight shimmer in the air behind him as his sister witch stepped from behind her glamour.

Levi must have sensed her presence at the last moment and spun to face her.

M.M. Wildes punched upward with both fists, as she did her twin push daggers slid into Levi's neck and under his jaw on either side. He froze, and blood spurted from the severed artery and gushed from the vein on the other side. He turned instantly grey and collapsed in front of her.

M withdrew her daggers, took a deep breath, smiled sadly at Sugar, and disappeared behind her glamour again.

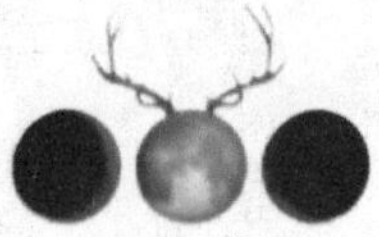

Bets heard Asher Carpenter's scream from across the grove. She located him, running toward one side, away from where Gerardo and LaRhonda were engaged with several of the church guards, and handling them with ease. She clocked his trajectory and saw his target. Sugar was squaring off with three of the guards; but just behind him, lying still and grey, was Levi Carpenter.

Sugar kicked one of the guards hard in the chest and he flew backward several feet, Bets could not hear the crunch of bone when the man's sternum caved in from the blow, but she didn't have to, in order to know that it did.

He did not see Asher Carpenter grab up his brother's hammer in his left hand and sprint toward Sugar, a hammer in each hand. Bets could not get to him to stop him, but she knew she had to give Sugar a fighting chance, she couldn't let this man sneak up on him blind.

She didn't have a chance to get a spell or charm cast before Asher was on Sugar. But Asher did not have a chance to land a blow before Fredrick landed a hard side kick to his ribs, sending him staggering several feet back.

The man did not stop. Tears flowed down his cheeks as he whirled and spun, the two hammers trailing one another, certain death for anyone who strayed too close.

Bets was running across the grove toward them as Sugar and Fredrick fell into sync around him. Darting in and out between the swinging hammers. Sugar with his big, curved blade knife darted in only to have the blade swiped aside by the swing of the hammer. Sugar danced back out before the next hammer swung around. Fredrick was turning a circle around him the other way. For almost a moment Bets felt sorry for the man. Then she remembered all the sisters and brothers hurt or killed at the hands of these bastards.

He spun toward Fredrick and thrust the head of one of the hammers at his face, Fredrick dodged easily but Asher had used the maneuver to hide his real target and spun fast, his body falling back at an angle to increase the leverage as he swung at Sugar.

Sugar did not duck or dance out of the way but leaned closer catching the hammer under his arm and continuing the rotation, he grabbed Asher's hair, and flipped the man over his hip, slamming him into the ground with a force that should have broken him in half.

Sugar bounced up immediately and as Asher was rising to his feet Sugar punched out with his giant fist and landed directly on Asher's spine just above his shoulder blades.

Bets was about twenty feet away and heard the crack of Asher Carpenter's spine with the first blow, the second sounded like a baseball bat hitting a chunk of roast as Asher collapsed paralyzed to the ground.

Sugar did not pause, he grabbed both hammers in one hand, and Asher's long blond hair in the other and dragged the screaming man toward the two sisters that Bets did not recognize who were obviously guarding the doorway. "*Leroy.*" She thought as she realized Sugar was taking Asher alive to try and find his brother. She did not envy Asher in that moment, knowing just how far Sugar was willing to go to find his little brother.

In The Name Of God,
The Most Gracious, The
Most Merciful

V alkyrie was not her name; she knew that now. Neither was Brigid, Freyja, Bride of the Eternal, or The Mother Moon. When she felt the danger to her sisters and brothers, she could not explain it. It just slammed into her spirit. Where they were, the pursuit, and the fact that they would all die at the hands of the Seraphim.

It took nothing for her to convince Seanchara to open the doorways, in an instant they found the group fleeing the chapel in Memphis, and as the Seraphim attacked they brought the whole menagerie to Stag's Grove. While she appreciated the energy here and knew it would empower her allies to be in this place.

It did not strengthen her.

It would keep the damage off of the busy city streets and minimize the risk to her beloved family. But she realized as soon as she stood before the Seraphim, she did not need the energy of Stag's Grove to slay these monsters. These were her creations, she brought them into existence, and now she would kill them as well.

As Seanchara attacked, all four combatants began to shift between the planes of reality. One of the Seraphim, they had no names or identifying marks, just as they had no identity beyond soldier, attacked her. It swiped its great wings and a wave of energy swept over her. Rather than throw her backward, it empowered her, and she threw her arms open and embraced the change. She felt herself grow even more powerful, and as it charged her, she lunged with Kilij Shuurga, The Sword of The Storm, loosing its lightening as it struck the Seraphim on the shoulder, right at the crease of its invisible armor.

The beast raged and flew at her; she grabbed it and for a moment they reentered the physical plane before existing for a moment as two beings of pure divine energy then re-materialized just beyond the physical realm.

She saw Seanchara, her beloved Horned God, as he slammed his shoulder into the other Seraphim throwing it yards across the astral field of his grove before it righted itself. She saw the smile on his face as he realized he was once again more powerful than his adversary. He would make quick work of the Seraphim, she would need to do the same to the one she was fighting, for now that she remembered, truly remembered her who she was, and her purpose here. She knew she had no time to waste.

In her moment of distraction, watching her beloved, and sifting through a millennium of lost memories, the Seraphim attacked. It launched itself at her. Its powerful hands finding her throat and its wings wrapping around her, pulling her tight to it. It was strong and pulled her close. It's strange, featureless face did not change as it crushed the life from her. She heard Seanchara scream her name, the name he knew. Then she heard her true name being called from beyond the veil separating the realm of the physical and the realm of the divine.

"Shining Star of the Morning, First Light, it's time, fulfill your destiny, protect my children. Slay their enemies."

For the first time in more than two thousand years, she spoke in the divine tongue to her true creator.

"Father, the only enemies I see are my own creations, and those who bring your banner to the war."

"Bismillahi-ir-Rahmani-ir-Rahim, my blessed child, my sword and shield, do what you were created to do. I command it. Have no doubt your path is true and righteous, and all of creation will celebrate when you are done. Now, slay this monster of yours and be about your holy work."

Then it was gone, the divine presence. But her memories were not. The Seraphim felt her go limp and pulled tighter, meaning to crush the life from her. A being of pure purpose, with no thought beyond whatever it was bidden to do, it could not reason, it could not sense when danger was near. It knew only the drive to fill its divine mandate.

It did not know how to react when Elder Valkyrie screamed and cast it off of her. A blazing white and gold light emanated from within her, and her wings emerged from her back. Their twenty-foot expanse glowed with holy fire and her Sword of The Storm crackled with lightening as it took the head of the Seraphim, covering her with its blood. She said a prayer of thanks to her creator and the power of the song reverberated through all creation as The Shining Star of the Morning, the first and most beloved angel, drifted slowly back to the physical plane.

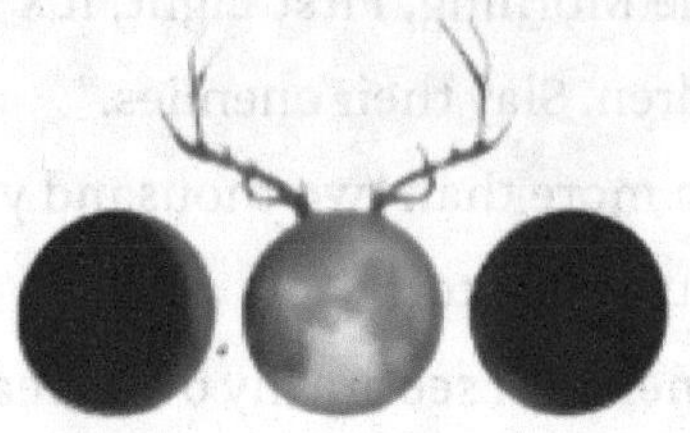

A Destiny Revealed, A Promise Fulfilled, A Return To Red Mountain

Seanchara surveyed the devastation around him. Not only in the metaphysical realm where he and his bride had done battle with the Seraphim; but also, in the physical realm. He could see the tears in the divine energy. Ugly scars ripped through the flows of the infinite.

The Mercer witches could see the divine energy as it flowed through the physical realms, interacting with creation. Even they could not see what he saw, all apparently except one. The one who stood before him now. The head of her defeated foe resting on the ground at her feet. His bride, his beloved Valkyrie. Looking now, like her namesake. Long braids soaked with the blood of her foe. But the part of her he was staring at, the part that inspired this feeling of betrayal at her hands once again, were the massive, illuminated wings that stretched from her back. They shined with white and gold light so bright he could barely look at them. He could feel the power radiating from them, and from her. Not through her, like it did every other Mercer witch, and not even like him. This power came from her; she was its source.

He bowed his massive head, his crown of antlers dipping low in her direction. "Well, my love, it seems even after all this time you still have your secrets."

He tried not to let his heartache show.

She held out her hand to him, the light of what seemed like a thousand passing stars reaching for him. When she spoke, her voice resonated at an infinite number of frequencies all at once.

"Seanchara, my love, please. Give me a moment to try and get myself under control. I can see the hurt and anger in your eyes. I promise you, if you can be patient with me for just a moment all will be made clear to you. You will see that my heart is and always has been yours, and true."

He felt her words move through him in waves, waves of love and yearning, of reassurance and peace. It terrified him, and he had never been afraid. Not in the thousands of years that he could recall his existence. Until just now.

The wings folded behind her and began to fade from view and the light emanating from her began to dim. Both of them were still covered in blood from the battle she motioned to the fountain near the edge of the clearing.

They walked slowly, side by side. He did not pull away from her, nor did he rage or scream his heartbreak. She asked him for the time to explain, and he owed her that. For more than a thousand years of love he owed her at least the chance to explain. As they walked his form shifted. When they reached the fountain he slipped out of his furs, and she dropped her thin linen wrap. Together they slipped naked into the fountain. It's cool, clean water rinsing away the battle and fatigue from them both. She approached him, with confidence, not caution. She did not fear him, but there was only love on her face and in her touch as she wrapped her arms around his neck and pulled him close to her so that she could feel his body pressed against her.

"It's time, my love, please."

"Of course. You have been more than patient with me, and I can see the hurt and mistrust all over your spirit. Do you mind if I lay my head on your chest while I tell you my story? I fear if you do not accept the truth of my tale, I will see it on your face, and my heart would tear in two."

He kissed her gently on the side of her head and began to ladle water over her braids with his cupped hands. Rinsing the blood and dirt from her glorious hair.

"Could you see lover? Could you see what I am?"

"Yes, I saw you, is that the real you, did I finally see you after all these centuries?"

"That is me, but I need you to believe me that it was only in the last year or so that I began to suspect there was more to my origins than I knew. And not until now did I truly remember who and what I was. This is not a secret I have kept from you, but rather a secret kept from myself. What I cannot say is by whom, whether it was me or my creator that hid my truth from both of us. Please, tell me you believe me, look into my spirit Seanchara, you can see the truth of what I say."

"I will not. I told you that I would trust you to tell me your story, it is not trust if I am constantly verifying it by looking into your mind. I will hear your story as your husband and friend, not as the guardian of Mercer."

"Thank you. Do you remember the day we met Seanchara?"

"The battle at the pass. I was a wild God then, as savage as the people that worshiped me. Niri had just begun to cry out to the Witch Father for his aid, and he had yet to send me to her."

"Oh, you were a savage and glorious God. I woke for the first time across the field from that battle. My first memory, my first vision, was of my horned God decimating his enemies. Laying low any that would threaten your charges. A victorious song upon your lips as you sprayed the air with the blood of the wicked.

I knew nothing that led to that moment. And up until recently I have never known my origins. We always assumed I was a creation of the Witch Father, same as you. And in a way that is true, but it's so much more than that."

He picked her up in his arms, cradled her body next to his and in a blink they were in their little cottage on the side of Red Mountain in Alabama. Laid out on a pile of furs in front of a roaring fire. He rolled onto his back, and she snuggled close to him. Still not looking at him. She spent a moment breathing in the smell of him, aware that at any moment he could decide his patience had run out and she may be without his love again. The last night they spent together, before her betrayal the first time, was in this cottage; during the time of the choosing at The Red Mountain Pentecost Revival. She hoped their return here wasn't symbolic.

"Are you, a Seraphim, like them? Whatever they are?"

"I am not a Seraphim; I am of an order even greater than them. Like you, I was my father's first born. The guardian he anointed to protect his flock. His first born and most favored."

"What are you saying mother?"

"I am the shining star of the morning. The first light. I am his most beloved and most feared among his chosen. I was sent here by my father to protect his creation at all cost. Even from themselves."

"So, you remember your creation at the hands of the Witch Father?"

"No, my love, I remember the arrival of The Witch Father. I was already named before he sat foot on this world."

"I don't understand. How can you be older than the creator of all things?"

"I don't know Seanchara, only that I was at peace at my father's side when I became aware of The Witch Father. My father did not name him an enemy, only that his actions would one day lead to destruction. I asked to slay him in that moment, and my father refused. He said that I was to live among his people, to know them, to love them, and when the time came, I would see the true danger, and I would know how to act."

"What brought your true nature out today?"

"The danger Seanchara, our sisters and brothers would have fallen at the hands of the Seraphim. Nearly mindless beasts, they were created only to serve, not to think or question or even survive on their own. They are foot-soldiers, created for a war that has yet to pass."

"Created by your father? For what war?"

"No love, they were created by me. The Seraphim were my army before I was cast out to live among the humans. Although I no longer recognize the purpose that drives them, they were my creations, driven by a force I could not discern."

She rolled off of him and sat up facing the fire. She had prepared herself for a rebuke and it had yet to come. She did not want to let down her guard, but staying on this knife's edge was killing her. She felt him shift and he slid up behind her wrapping his arms around her and pulling her into him. His long legs stretched out on either side of her, and she could feel him warm against her back. His heat, different than the heat of the fire on her face and breasts.

"So now you know. You were created by a father, older than The Witch Father. His first and most beloved angel. If I am not forgetting my Sunday School lessons, that sounds like the God of the Christians and his angel Lucifer. Is that what you are telling me love? That after centuries of seeing all we have seen. The Christian God is real? The bible was true, and I am in fact just a demon?"

"No." She said a little more forcefully than she intended.

"No." She softened her tone. Fully aware of her power and its effects. "The Christian Bible is exactly what it has always been and nothing more. Just as there are parts of it based on people we know personally. There are parts of it that carry some half-truths or misunderstood truths. But you are as you have always been. The guardian and harvester of Mercer, the protector of the innocent. You are also my one true love, my heart and soul. None of that is changed. The only thing that has changed is I now know from whence I came and what my true role in our mission must be."

"Then tell me love. What are you to do?"

"We, Seanchara, we are going to protect the father's children from their biggest threat."

"How?"

"First we must return now to our family, there is much still to do before we can continue."

"Continue how my love?"

"We are going to kill the Gods, Seanchara, all of them."

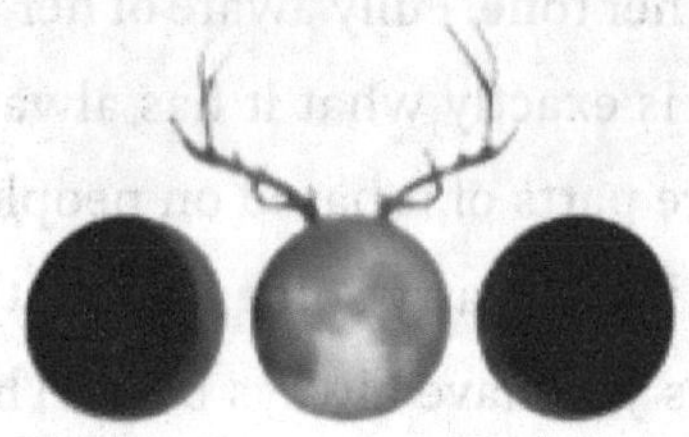

A Feast of Friends

As the sounds of battle died down Bets surveyed the landscape of Stag's Grove. All of the guards from the church were either lying out on the grass or zip-tied kneeling faced in a circle. Edward the Fish was walking around them waving his hands, and yelling. He appeared to be lecturing them on something. She could not help but smile in spite of the grimness of the situation. Edward had proven himself to be a valuable partner to her in every way. His inventions have saved the day a couple of times now. He was seemingly tireless. His fearlessness against both the Carpenters and Sonya, and the Seraphim.

Yet here he was, lecturing the Ascension guards, like a child whose classmates weren't following the teachers instructions. What a wonder he was. She reminded herself to thank him, to tell him how much she appreciated him when they found a moment of reprieve.

LaRhonda Kelm, and Dorthea were tending to Gerardo, who was sitting up but appeared to have a nasty cut on his scalp and he looked as if he had lost a lot of blood.

Sugar, Polly, and Fredrick were searching the dead, and their vehicles. She wondered for a moment how they were supposed to get all of the cars and bodies out of the grove. Surely Lord Seanchara would not want these evil men rotting in his grove and their cars polluting this perfect land.

"How very right you are Sister Bets."

She turned at his voice, Lord Seanchara and Elder Valkyrie stood before her. Him in a brown tunic and some kind of breeches and her in a light crimson wrap. They both seemed strangely composed and at peace considering the battle that was just waged.

"I will oversee the removal of these vehicles to a place somewhere more appropriate, and when everyone is back safe in Mercer, I have some friends that will help see to the dead."

He nodded over his shoulder to his left and Bets looked to the tree line of Stag's Grove. She could just make out the shadows sliding through the trees. Some small, some large, and something rustled the branches high up in a tree. She looked back at Lord Seanchara trying to hide her shock at the thought.

"Sister I do not know what drove these men to follow the path that they did. I am no fool, and I am sure that many of them were just following the path of their elders or doing what they could for a paycheck. I can say for a fact, they were not all evil people. I can also say for a fact that I cannot just drop a dozen or so dead bodies on the steps of a church in downtown Memphis. As heartless as it may seem, Stag's Grove is protected by more than just magic, and as you can see, many of its guardians have gathered out of curiosity or a desire to offer a greeting and commune with the other denizens. When you have finished your work here. They will begin theirs and cleanse this beautiful place of any evidence that the men of the Ascension were ever here."

"Thank you, Lord Seanchara, I understand. I trust you are both well after your battle with the Seraphim. You disappeared from our sight almost immediately, but I feel safe in assuming since you are standing here and they are not continuing their threat, that you were victorious."

Elder Valkyrie spoke this time, leveling her eyeless sockets at Bets. You are correct, those two Seraphim are no more. But there will be more, of that I can guarantee. Now let us finish our work here so that Lord Seanchara may continue his."

She leaned up and kissed him on the cheek and walked past Bets on her way to where everyone else was gathered. Bets bowed respectfully toward Lord Seanchara and followed.

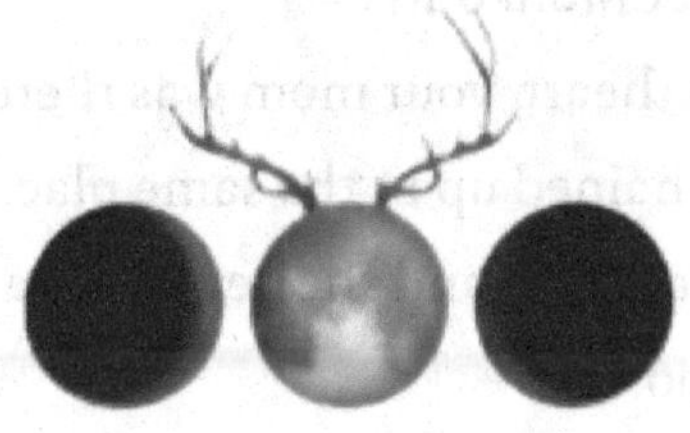

A Lesson In Love

"**D**addy."

The sound caused Harlan's heart to drop, and he couldn't hold back his tears any longer. The stampede sound of them running toward him brought back fifteen years of memories with the twins, and he braced for the impact of their bodies, and the nostalgia as they crashed into him.

"Oh girls, I love you so much. Are you okay? I am so sorry."

"Daddy, LaRhonda and her friends, they saved us, did you know she was magic? Did you know there were actual angels, and they are mean? Did they get mom out?"

The girls were firing questions so fast Harlan could barely tell who was who, and it didn't matter at the moment. All that mattered to him was that the girls were home safe to him. Everything else could wait.

He saw several more people being led past them, all of them in varying states of exhaustion. His heart went out to all of them. His girls had been gone for days; he could not imagine them missing for years, like some of the people seemingly had been.

Lydia pulled back from the hug.

"Daddy, did they get Mom out?"

"I don't know sweetheart, your mom was there? You talked to her?"

"We did, she was chained up in the same place we were for the first day, then they took her away and she never came back. Is she okay, did LaRhonda save her too?"

"We will find out as soon as LaRhonda and her friends get back."

Elder Dinah approached. Harlan Rice was usually quick to get the measure of someone. She had fooled him at LaRhonda's apartment at their first meeting. He had since discovered that it was intentional and apparently magical. On the drive, then the weird walk through several tunnels and hallways to get to this place, she had let her guard down a little more. Shown him who she really was, and Harlan would trust her with his life.

"Hello girls. My name is Dinah, are you okay? Are either of you hurt physically?"

The girls answered in unison. "No Ma'am."

She reached for them and almost on instinct they both walked to her. Harlan was amazed, Lexia especially was slow to warm to strangers. But they just walked right into her arms. *Like magic,* he thought.

Dinah hugged them tight to her, then one by one held them at arm's length and looked them in the eyes.

"Okay girls, looks like you are physically okay, maybe we get some food in you and a shower. Someone here smells like they were locked in a basement for days."

The girls both rolled their eyes and Lydia snorted. "Yeah, Lexia, take a bath once in a while."

Lexia shrugged. "Anyone who has issue with it can chain themselves up in a basement waiting on killer angels to eat you or whatever they are doing and see how they smell when they come out."

"LaRhonda!" Both girls screamed and ran across the room.

Harlan felt his shoulders relax as he saw LaRhonda and Gerardo enter the small room. She paused only a moment, then ran toward the girls, sweeping them both up in a hug so tight it knocked all three of them off balance, and they fell in a pile to the floor. Harlan started toward them; Dinah stepped in front of him.

She whispered in his ear.

"Give them a moment please, I don't know what the future holds. But I know the coming days won't be easy, and once the relief wears off, there will be a lot of big emotions flying around. Especially if LaRhonda couldn't save their mother. I need you to understand a couple of things."

Harlan narrowed his gaze on Dinah, curious as to where this conversation was heading.

"The day we met you in the apartment, two weeks ago."

He nodded.

"That was LaRhonda asking us for permission to tell you who she really was."

"She told me."

Dinah held up her hand.

"I know that, but do you know what it means?"

He had no answer in his mind that made sense.

"She loves you so much, that she was willing to risk the rebuke of the only family she has ever known. She loves those girls so much that she was willing to do anything to make sure your relationship was built on truths. So, there is the thing. If you want to walk away from that, it is your prerogative. No one can tell you how you should feel about it. And if that's the case, a quick visit from Lord Seanchara and you and your girls won't remember a thing outside of you dated Representative Kelm briefly, and it didn't work out."

He nodded without breaking eye contact.

"But beyond the implications of a very heartbroken LaRhonda suffering for something she did not cause. I want you to consider something. Every single case we have of The Ascension kidnapping someone. That someone was destined to join our magical family one day. Your girls come from an old line of witches. I can smell it on them. And since their mother was also taken. I will bet that she does too."

"While I don't doubt you, the irony would be incredible. Her family are mostly religious zealots. Like, we have had to be careful what exposure the girls had to her mom and her mom's family because of it."

"It wouldn't be the first time. My point is this. You need to have a plan if you walk away from LaRhonda, especially if it's because you think she caused this, or proximity to her did, and they come back for your girls."

Harlan looked across the room at LaRhonda, back on her feet now and hugging the girls close to her and rocking back and forth.

"Dinah, thank you for everything. I mean it. But I am not going anywhere. I may not be magic, but I don't back down from a fight. A fight to keep bad people from hurting the innocent, a fight in the halls of congress, or a fight to keep the people I love the most safe and happy. If you'll excuse me, my girls have monopolized enough of LaRhonda's time, and I need to get to her before she collapses."

He turned to go and she grabbed his arm. He spun to face her, and the grandmotherly woman, who was all smiles and hugs, was gone. This was a different woman standing beside him, a powerful woman, a woman who had seen the secrets of the universe.

"Harlan, you need to prepare yourself and the girls. They took her mother for a reason. Likely to perform whatever they do that lays another person over the top of them. We have no way of knowing what may become of her, or who, or what she will be when they are done."

Harlan nodded his understanding, and she released his arm with a smile and a squint of her steely gray eyes.

He did not look back as he made his way to LaRhonda and the girls.

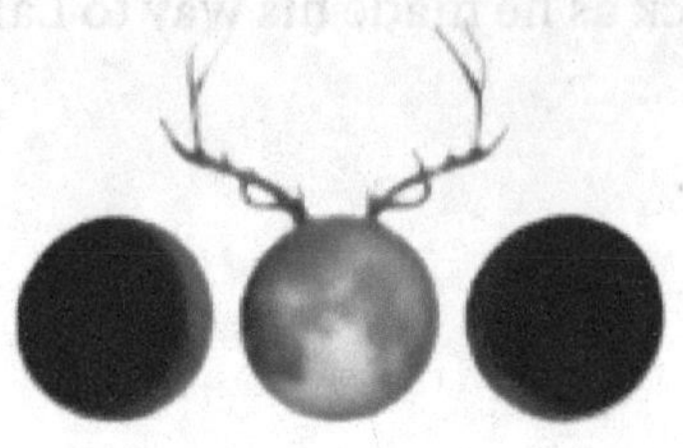

DAN MF'N THOMPSON

Big Pimp Daddy From Cincinnati

Dan Thompson slid his F150 into the one spot on the side of Van Dyke avenue that didn't look to be riddled with broken glass and garbage. He double checked his GPS and threw the truck in park, squinting at the small sign on the run down brick two story across the street from where he parked.

How his wife even found this place he wasn't sure. He had tried to Google the business name when she showed him the card, and they had zero digital footprint. The only way he found it was from the address on the business card. He asked her about it, and she was as vague as ever. He thought maybe she was a little embarrassed about her newly found spirituality and didn't want to tell him.

But either way she had dropped about a hundred hints that her anniversary gift should come from there. So here he was, parked outside what looked more like a crack house than a business. He glanced at the card then back at the small sign on the wall of the business. M.M. Wilde's, Tarot and Beyond, that was the place.

"Alright, Fuck it, let's go, if it keeps Judy from whining." He said to the dash of his truck as he pulled his bulk from the behind the steering wheel.

The front of the store looked even worse close up, he opened the gated door and walked in. The foyer was exactly how he expected it to look. Old worn hardwood floors, the overwhelming smell of incense, and something else, something that smelled forbidden or dangerous.

Dan already knew what the inside would look like without opening the door, cramped, cluttered, no sense of marketability or organization. Candles, rocks, essential oils, some old books, and those ridiculous tarot cards Judy wanted.

Why couldn't she order the damn things from Amazon like everyone else?

"But, Dan, they are more accurate when they are a gift." He mimicked what he thought of as her "whiny Judy" voice. She was probably blowing the middle aged, pony-tailed loser who ran the place and that's why she sent him here.

He always just assumed she was having affairs. Not that she had ever given him a single reason to believe it; but because he was always attempting to. He had even managed to have one or two over the years, before he traded his good looks for a ridiculously high salary and a ton of disposable income.

Now he scratched that itch with weekly blowjobs from a rotation of hookers, and a monthly outlay for a higher end escort. He always paid a little extra for them to pretend he was picking them up from the hotel bar where they met. Like they had randomly met him and couldn't refuse his looks and charm.

Whatever, if she wants to get railed by a nasty old wanna-be cult leader more power to her. Maybe her fat ass will fall in love and leave me in peace.

With that he stepped into M.M. Wilde's Tarot and Beyond.

Whatever his expectation had been before opening that door, it was gone the second it shut behind him. The room he walked into looked like it belonged in a different building. The walls were a light grey, pillars of light shined down in various places on both objects and plants.

He saw beautiful crystal towers, statues of every shape and material depicting figures he could not name if his life depended on it. A spiral staircase, its center a winding bookshelf packed with books ascended into what appeared to be the heavens, this did not make sense, how could this building be this big inside and yet so small and dilapidated outside?

He turned twice more, and the room seemed different with every rotation, he saw shelves in places where there had been bare walls only a moment before. He spun again trying to orient himself. He tried to find the door to use as a point of reference, it seemed to be on the opposite wall from where he was. His head was spinning, and he was reaching for his phone for some kind of assistance when he heard a voice behind him.

"Can I help you, Hun?"

He turned around and ended up turning a full 360 degrees back the way he was just looking to find the source of the voice.

The woman behind the counter might have been the most beautiful woman he had ever seen. Her hair was raven black and hung to her shoulders, her pale skin was dotted with freckles. He could not see her eyes from here. But her smile radiated from across the room. He stepped closer, she was wearing a sleeveless vest-like top, and both arms were covered in full tattoo sleeves, one arm a jungle scene with several birds; and the other a rose vine from shoulder to wrist, with more blooms than he could count.

A movement to his left caught his eye and he turned to see a small metronome click clacking its pendulum on a shelf next to a bunch of old unmarked books.

Had that been there a second ago? He had to get a hold of himself.

He looked back to the beautiful woman behind the counter and now she looked like a desk at study hall, covered in small independent tattoos with no visible theme or continuity. Just random words and crudely drawn pictures, he bumped into a small shelf and looked down to see what he ran into.

When he looked back she was wearing a blue flowered sundress, her hair had shifted to a shimmering red, not that dyed, mall goth red, but that deep rich red that's only passed through generations of beautiful women. Her arms were mostly bare, just a small rose tattoo on her right shoulder and an evil eye on her left forearm.

"Hey sweetheart," she drawled. "You look a little poorly, if I must say sir, and it's not a good look on a man as handsome as you. You wanna have seat there on that sofa and I'll bring you a cup of tea or water or something?"

Dan looked to where she had gestured, there was a small loveseat and coffee table a few feet from where he was standing. But that didn't make any sense, only a second before he could have sworn there was a glass display of some rocks or crystals or whatever, right there. He walked quickly to the loveseat before it disappeared on him and sat down. His head swam and his eyes kept blurring like he was having a hard time focusing.

He kept trying to form words, but even thoughts seemed to escape him. He felt, somewhere deep in his mind, like he should be panicked, there was some word here he was supposed to be scared of, but he could not find it.

"Sir, here's some tea, it should help your head."

Her voice was close and had that soft, demure, tone that he loved. He glanced up and she was on the other side of the table, bent forward placing a tea service tray on it directly in front of him. Her hair was black again and she was wearing that vest, like corduroy, over a flowing skirt.

He could see down her top the way she was bent over and her small pale breasts swayed gently with her movement, then realized he was staring down her shirt and shot his eyes up, her smile was dazzling white and her lips pale, soft pink.

He imagined those lips working their way down his chest. He looked her in the eyes, such a beautiful blue, turquoise, aqua, he didn't know, he was horrible at that kind of thing, but it didn't matter. He fell into them, imagining the feeling of her perfect lips, engulfing him, while he stared into those endless pools of blue.

He blinked and realized she was now sitting next to him, and he had a cup of tea in his hand and was shaking. She was sitting on the edge of the love seat, leaned forward at the waist and shuffling a deck of cards. The side of her skirt had come unwrapped, and he could see her entire right leg all the way up the hip. She didn't seem to be wearing anything under her skirt, he could see he tattoos covering her calf and down onto her bare foot, her thigh appeared to have a bloody crucifixion scene. Very graphic and very gruesome.

He stared at the tattoo on the top of her hip for a moment before he realized what he was looking at. A handprint, a big red handprint colored as if it was a burn scar.

After a second or two he understood the orientation. The print was laid out as if a giant or at least someone with giant burning hands had held onto her from behind. The alignment was perfect, if she was bent over in front of you that is exactly how your hand would grip her hips during sex. He imagined her bent over front of him, his own hand gripping on the spot where this hand had left its burning mark on her.

He saw in his mind her blue skirt bunched around her waist as she pushed herself back on to him. He saw the difference between his own hands and the hands that these tattooed burns represented, how big had this man been that left these marks. That had claimed her with such authority that she felt the need to wear his claim for the rest of her life. He felt her breath on his ear, hot and close, her lips brushed against the outer lobe.

"You should feel the marks he left inside me."

Dan's head rocked back against the couch and his body stiffened as he orgasmed. In his mind, he entered this beauty on the seat next to him, and somehow she expelled him into the vastness of the universe. As if she was a portal, leading to infinity. He dwelt among the stars for moments and eons, ceasing to exist but becoming infinite all at once.

As if this moment, this meeting was really what his entire existence had been leading up to, all the things he had experienced were just a prelude to meeting M.M. Wildes.

"Sir, I have your total here, one hundred fifty-nine dollars and seventy-two cents. I put them all in one bag, or if you want I can gift wrap them for you separate, so she will have more to open on the big day!"

Dan looked around, startled, he was standing a couple feet from the counter, the pretty redhead was back on the stool behind the counter. Smiling at him with that eager to please, do anything smile he was used to seeing from hookers when they saw the Rolex and bill roll he always made sure to flash them before he paid for their services.

After the disorientation of the last few minutes, it felt good to be back in charge again, and he was in charge, despite that little daydream, hallucination or whatever.

He was Dan fucking Thompson and this little counter girl, owner of the shop or not, should be grateful he was thinking about fucking her at all, much less the offer he was about to make. Maybe change her life in exchange for letting him leave his own mark on her.

"And that's everything in the bag?" He asked her as he made his way closer, his eyes on her. She glanced into the bag and nodded then added.

"A candle magic starter set, a mortar and pestle, two incense packs, The Crone's Book of Charms and Spells by Valerie Worth, By Rust of

Nail and Prick of Thorn by Althaea Sebastiani, make sure she starts with that one. Oh, and a Wildwood oracle deck; she is going to love that one. I used it myself for a long time."

She extended the bag toward him, and he used the opportunity to reach with his left hand, show off the Rolex a little. He brushed his hand, almost absently, over hers as he took the bag, then extended his right hand with his Platinum American Express, sure it wasn't a Black Card, but she wasn't likely to know any better.

As she was running his card, he pulled a business card from his holder, grabbed a pen from the fake skull on the counter, he flipped it over and jotted down a number. When she turned back with his card and receipt, he smiled wide and held out his hand with his business card.

"Ms. Wildes, I was thinking, I have been in the market to diversify my investments a little. Looking at what you've done with the inside of this place compared to the outside of the building and I cannot help but wonder what you could do with a nicer building, and a really high budget. I can only imagine the kind of place you could create for your customer base if you had someone to bankroll a much nicer piece of real estate and provide you with the capital to expand."

Now that he was in pitch mode and not losing his mind seeing and feeling things that could not have been real, he looked like a pig eyeing a meal. His cheeks were red, and the skin of his balding scalp shined bright. He eyed her up and down, she was pretty, but there was nothing that special about her, just a cute little red head in a sleeveless vest and blue skirt with some flowers or some shit embroidered on it. She should feel lucky he was bothering with her at all. But she was cuter than most of the hookers he picked up, so he would throw out the bait, let her stew a bit, and avoid her first call or two, until she was desperate. Then he would draw up a fake contract and let her imagine all the possibilities over dinner, then see if he could get her into a hotel room for the signing and post contract celebration.

He was willing to bet that with a couple drinks and some promises of getting her a new building, getting her naked would be no problem.

Even if she demanded they sign before giving it up, he had pulled enough shady deals like this to throw an escape clause or two in there, so that unless she was a lawyer, she wasn't likely to catch them. She stared at the card and then took it from him.

"Wow, thank you Mr. Thompson." She said, as she ran around the counter and threw her arms around his neck in a tight hug. He could feel her small tight muscular body pressed against him. As she pulled back, her lips brushed against the side of his neck. His vision swam again and for a moment all he could see was black.

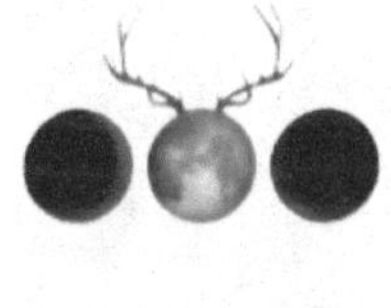

When his eyes focused again he realized he was standing at the curb, in front of the building, facing his truck. He held the shopping bag with Judy's gifts in his left hand and his truck key fob in his right. He had no idea how long he had been standing here or how he got there.

He turned and looked back at the building and the closed sign was in the front window and the barred gate was pulled shut across the front door. He glanced at his watch, 6:45 pm, that was not possible. He had arrived at a few minutes past four, and the sign on the wall of the shop said it closed at five. There was no way he had been standing out here on the sidewalk looking like an idiot for an hour and forty-five minutes.

He started across the street to his truck and realized he felt something cold and damp brush his left thigh. He looked down at the wet spot, quite large wet spot, on the front of his slacks. He had actually came in his pants at some point. He stomped across the street; he was going to put her bag in the truck then go pound on the door and demand some answers. They must have drugged him or something, he checked his wallet and bill roll, all there. He had already seen his watch and keys and his phone was resting where it always was, in his left back pocket.

As he reached the truck he started to feel even worse, like he had a wind blowing through his skull and the din from it was making it hard to think. He closed his eyes and tried to focus, to remember, but all he could see in his mind was her, M.M. Wildes, smiling widely and brushing her lips against his skin, and the storm was calm for just a moment.

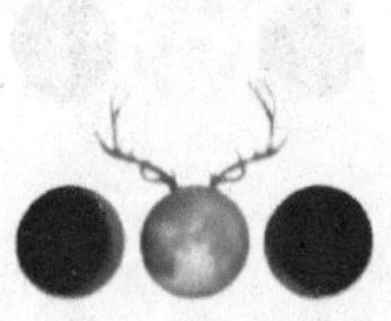

M.M. Wildes sat on a stool perched behind the counter. She was watching Dan Thompson's little internal dilemma play out on the video monitor under the counter. He was exactly what she had expected, although the business angle was something she was surprised by, she didn't expect him to offer to help expand her business. But it makes sense, an ugly troll like that, he doesn't have looks to rely on, so money is the next best thing in his mind.

She wasn't at all confused by his reaction to her glamour. Under any circumstances, it could be disorientating. If you ran into her at a grocery store or gas station, you might notice something off about her hair color or question if the tattoo you were seeing was the same one you saw a second before.

In her sacred space, with her intention behind it and a good dose of hash burning on the brazier as you came in through the foyer, and the hypnotic click of the metronome. She was a constantly shifting, color changing work of art. The longer he stood in her presence, the deeper the spell dug into his mind. A few minutes, she could make almost any man desire her uncontrollably, Dan Thompson had stood before her mesmerized for more than two hours.

If he wasn't institutionalized by the end of the week it would be surprising.

"Do you think maybe you laid that on a little thick, love?"

She spun on her stool to face him.

"On Dan fucking Thompson, big pimp daddy from Cincinnati? I thought I took it easy on him, all things considered."

"Took it easy on him? That guy's gray matter was a bowl of pudding by the time he left here. I have never seen you put it on someone like that before. What the hell did he do? Did I miss something?"

"I met with his wife Judy before..." She trailed off.

She didn't need to say before when, before Bets, before Leroy, before they were both butchered and nearly killed by Diana The Triformis. Before Malleus Dei, the Seraphim, Before they stopped fighting how much they were in love.

"And he is what, some kind of abuser?"

"Serial cheater, kept her home, wouldn't let her work, or get an education. Now he makes all the money and lords it over her. Add to his constant hiring of prostitutes, dangerously young prostitutes, I think were her exact words. She just wants out and wants out clean. I had almost forgotten about her with everything else that went on. But she contacted me last month, right after we came home, and said she was ready. She had tried to forgive him, to move on with her life and find some comfort in the stability but could not make it work."

"So, you fry his brain as punishment for being a lecherous douchebag?"

"No, I just needed him to fall for me, to plant the seed that he is willing to give up anything to be with me. Let him think he is calling the shots, but the whole time that spell is grinding away at his will. Give him time to cook, and he will not only ask Judy for the divorce himself, but he will be willing to give her anything she wants. As long as he thinks he can get closer to being with yours truly."

"I don't really like the idea of this guy getting so obsessed with you that he is willing to burn his life down. Not when we don't really know anything about him."

"Dan Thompson? Did you not see him lover, he's a fucking toad. I could handle him with no magic, and you know it. Don't start getting overprotective on me Sugar. There's no place for that here."

"M, my entire job description, and magical mandate is to protect you at all costs. Remember? Even if it means my life, I must protect my sister witch as she fulfills her mission. So, it's not overprotective, its doing what I have spent my entire life doing. And he may look like a toad, but toads can be poisonous. You make a guy like that insane and you have no idea how he will react."

She slid her hand inside his vest, rubbing his bare and muscled abdomen beneath the worn hand sewn leather. She could feel his emotions coursing through her. His concern and confusion but most of all, his love for her.

"I promise Sugarfoot, I will be careful. I will reach out to Judy and help connect her with one of our lawyers, they love stuff like this. In the meantime, I will defer to you where safety is concerned. You're right of course. It's always been your job to keep me safe, and I guess, I just needed to feel like I was back in control. My ego needed the win, and I was worried about you becoming overprotective given our new circumstances."

"That's fair M, let me research this guy and keep an eye on him. I am as bored as you, and the trail on Leroy has gone cold until the elders can get some information out of Asher Carpenter, and I need something to do with my time besides dust the shop and bake bread."

"Speaking of which." M stretched the words out dramatically. "That took it right out of me, what's for dinner?"

"Anything you want M, name it. You can go run a bath and recharge while I cook."

"No sir, I think that you might be right and it would be safer if I am not alone until we do our research on Mr. Dan Thompson. So, you can cook and I will watch and talk, then after dinner we can both take a bath, and you can help me ground myself."

Sugar leaned into her until his lips brushed the outside of her ear. His whispered response to her suggestion was filled with promise.

The End

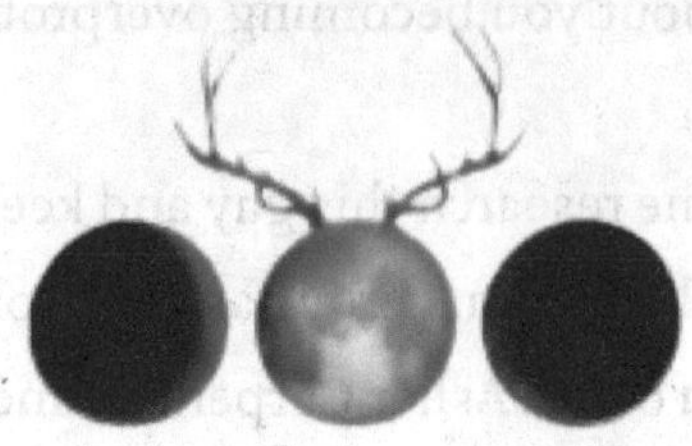

About The Author

Punk rock bastard son of country folk healers and big tent evangelicals.

Neo-Pagan and keeper of the Aging Elvinian Psycho Vaudevillian Vibration.

D.O. lives in the Midwest where he experiments with taming wild animals with string band instrumentation, and roasting meats, between writing novels.

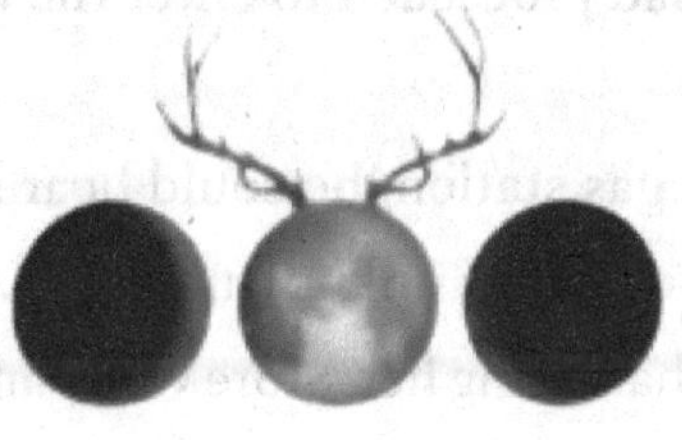

Notes From Detective Alexander LaSalle

On The Case Of Henry Leroy Lewis And Family

First interview with Henry Leroy Lewis, WM 39, complainant claims he and his family are being stalked, and harassed by gang members due to an altercation that occurred Feb 3, 2021.

According to Mr. Lewis' statement, reports filed and verified by responding officers and court records. On the evening in question Mr. Lewis and his wife Amber had been to a happy hour function for her office. Mrs. Lewis does not drink, Mr. Lewis said he had three or four beverages at the function, then on the way home they stopped for gas, and he wanted a six pack to drink a couple more at home, Mrs. Lewis drove. This was confirmed by the gas station surveillance footage as well as witness statements.

Mr. Lewis proceeded to fill up their vehicles gas tank at the pump while Mrs. Lewis went inside to use the restroom and grab the beer for Mr. Lewis. After a few minutes had passed and Mrs. Lewis had not emerged Mr. Lewis had proceeded to enter the gas station to look for her.

Upon entering the gas station, he could hear several people yelling and his wife crying. Four men, unknown to Mr. Lewis, had surrounded Mrs. Lewis and were harassing her. Store video and witness statements corroborated.

Two of the men had physically restrained Mrs. Lewis, one behind her with his arm around her waist, the other in front with his hand around her neck. According to her statement and the statement of one Marlene Bond, on duty clerk at the store, the four men had propositioned Mrs. Lewis to leave with them, asking her to share her beer with them and asking if she had ever "partied" with four men at once.

She tried to ignore them, when they persisted, she told them her husband was right outside, they threatened to "take her to the bathroom and take turns while he beats on the door and cries."

This is her directly quoting the men, and corroborated by the witness statement. Upon seeing his wife restrained Mr. Lewis attacked, he claims to have little or no recollection of the altercation once it began, surveillance video shows Mr. Lewis punching two of the men a single time, and them falling either unconscious or unable to return to their feet.

It is significant to note here that Mr. Lewis is perhaps one of the largest men I have ever personally seen. His driver's license records his height at six feet, eleven inches and weight at three hundred and ten pounds. I would say Mr. Lewis has a very low body fat percentage. He is extremely well muscled.

Hearing the first two men drop, the man in front of Mrs. Lewis turned around to face Mr. Lewis. Mr. Lewis grabbed him by his shirt collar and groin, squeezing hard enough to rupture both testicles in the process and picked him up over his head and slammed him on the floor hard enough to fracture his clavicle.

The last assailant released Mrs. Lewis and ran for the exit. Mr. Lewis did not pursue but did jump on the assailant at his feet.

Note: at this point I am not sure if this person should be referred to as an assailant, or victim. Mr. Lewis jumped on to the prone victim and proceeded to punch him in the face and torso. Fracturing his skull and collapsing his sinuses, both orbital bones fractured, several ribs and his sternum. If I would have seen the x-rays of the victim without context, I would have said car crash, no safety belt or airbag.

Mr. Lewis was questioned and released at the scene, all evidence was gathered, the officers and state's attorney agreed that while Mr. Lewis could have technically stopped after slamming assailant three on the ground, any reasonable person could have assumed an ongoing threat to himself or his wife. The first two assailants suffered severe concussions, the third was in a coma for three weeks before passing away from his injuries, the fourth was not identified, nor would the assailant one or two give up his identity.

Mr. Lewis claims that he has noticed he is being followed by strange vehicles, has received several phone calls where no one is on the line. On two occasions he has returned home from running errands with his family to find his front door open, and most recently, 09/18/2021, his dog, terrier mix age 4, white with brown spots, went missing and has not been found. Mr. Lewis believes this to be revenge for the death of one of his wife's assailants.

Upon investigation, the three known assailants:

William P. Cunningham WM 22- Currently awaiting trial on assault charges relating to this case and a felony driving under the influence charge. Current location Macon county jail.

Terrell M. Jones BM 24 - Currently incarcerated on parole violations stemming from this incident and a failure to report address change and a possession of weapons. He is remanded to Illinois Department of Corrections for no less than 4 years for his parole violations and that is with these assault charges pending.

David Skaggs WM 26 - Deceased due to injuries sustained during this assault on Mrs. Lewis. Unknown assailant BM early to mid-twenties, 5'10" - 6', slender build, wearing dark jeans, a blue hoodie, and white sneakers. An unknown assailant jumped the fence to the north of the gas station and disappeared into the neighborhood.

Of the three known assailants, none of them have any known gang affiliations, all have extensive criminal histories but none of it gang related. Skaggs (deceased) does have one brother (working as a nurse in Utah) when contacted as next of kin, brother wanted nothing to do with burial or dealing with the affairs of Mr. Skaggs. One sister, who went missing and has been presumed dead since 2002, at the age of 12. Case has been closed since 2004, investigating officers were able to find no sign of her. She disappeared while walking home from school. Skaggs' mother passed away shortly after, Father was unknown. Mr. Lewis was advised at this point to continue being vigilant and to record any further strange or threatening occurrences and report them to me immediately. It is my opinion that these things are unrelated, unless there is something happening here that I cannot see yet, there appears to be no connection.

Detective Alexander La Salle

Notes on Case #7757821L Continued harassment and potential stalking of Henry Leroy Lewis and family after the assault on his wife Amber.

See previous notes for case history to date.

On 09//08/2021 The Lewis family dog went missing from their home. The four year old terrier was in their fenced in the back yard where it spent a good majority of its time. The fence was locked from the inside and did not appear tampered with, nor was there any obvious signs of how the dog left the fence. Mr. Lewis was convinced it was related to his wife's attack and his defense of her. I was not sure at first as I have found no evidence to link any of the known assailants injured by Mr. Lewis to any known criminal organization or family members that might be looking for revenge.

Amber Lewis and their two children Deanna (f age 8) and Christopher (m age 5) went to visit her mother in St. Louis over the weekend of September 17-19. Mr. Lewis plays on a rec league rugby team, so he did not join them for the trip. (personal note, I played rugby in college, and I cannot imagine coming up against this guy in a scrum or trying to tackle him.)

He returned home the afternoon of the 18th after his match and found a large Amazon box on his porch; he was not expecting a delivery but said his wife would often order items without mentioning it and it did not seem unusual. He brought the box in and went about his day. He said that he showered and had a light dinner then called his wife to check in on her and see how her visit was going and say hi to the kids. During the course of their phone call, he mentioned the package and asked if he should leave it upstairs or take it out to her workshop. Mrs. Lewis makes custom furniture and has a workshop in the back of the home. She told him she was not expecting any shipments or packages and asked him to read the shipping label. When he examined the shipping label he found it was not a standard Amazon Shipping label but was handwritten on a piece of notebook paper. It was also not addressed to his wife. The name on the address was his childhood nickname. According to his statement there is no one living who would know him by this name or has ever referred to him as such. It was a name he was called by his older brother who passed away in a drowning accident when he was 12 years old. He has never mentioned the nickname to anyone, including his wife.

Mr. Lewis immediately opened the box and found a large leather bound photo album; he opened the album and on the first page was a picture of his wife in their bed asleep, a pink collar was seen laying on top of her sheet. The collar he claims belonged to their family dog. One the following two pages were almost identical pictures of his children in their beds with the collar.

On the fourth page was a handwritten note that said, "See you when I get back from Ol' St. Louie."

Mr. Lewis immediately contacted me, and I sent a patrol car there to sit with him and secure evidence until I could arrive. Mr. Lewis has a doorbell camera but the part of his porch where packages are normally left isn't visible. He claims he has been meaning to buy a secondary camera, but they live on the end of a quiet Cul de sac and security has never been an issue for them.

All evidence is being processed and so far the only fingerprints are unreadable smudges and a couple clear prints from Mr. Lewis.

St. Louis County Police have been notified of the situation and potential threat to Mrs. Lewis and their children. They are returning a day later than planned and by a different route then they would normally take, just to be cautious.

We will continue to monitor the situation but unless evidence points to someone, there is not a whole lot we can do at this point but wait.

Mr. Lewis is investing in an alarm system for the house and stepping up his security in general.

It is clear now that there is some kind of direct threat to the Lewis family, I am just not entirely convinced it is related to the incident at the gas station.

Det. Alexander La Salle

Final notes on Case #7757821L Continued harassment and potential stalking of Henry Leroy Lewis and family after the assault on his wife Amber.

See previous notes for case history to date.

Case is now being turned over to Homicide and missing persons. 10/10/2021

10/4/2021 I received a call from Mr. Lewis that the harassment/stalking had resumed after three or so weeks of no contact. Mr. Lewis claimed that Mrs. Lewis had been out shopping and when she returned to her vehicle there was a box on the front passenger seat that she did not recognize. Confused, she opened the package. The box was filled with photographs of her and the children, shopping around town, eating at restaurants, playing at the park and in their backyard. There were also printed advertisements for every single funeral home in Atlanta. Mrs. Lewis panicked and rushed home before calling the police.

Mr. Lewis contacted me directly after Mrs. Lewis returned home and informed him about the package. He did not remove it from the van and left it in place for me to retrieve. I drove to their home that afternoon and retrieved the package, the box and its contents are currently logged in evidence under the homicide case number. It was very clearly a threat toward Mrs. Lewis and the kids.

A couple notes: All of the photographs appeared to our techs to be cell phone photos taken with a quality phone camera and printed on a home printer on standard printer paper. Same with the advertisements for the funeral homes. All of them seem to be printed from the individual business websites or social media pages on a home printer.

Notes on Case #7757821L Continued harassment and potential stalking of Henry Leroy Lewis and family after the assault on his wife, Amber.

See previous notes for case history to date.

As of today, 11/30, this case is now considered an open homicide investigation.

On 11/29 at 14,:25 Mr. Lewis called to report that his wife had taken the kids to the mall to do some shopping that morning and had not returned or answered his calls, so he went to the mall to look for them. He found her van in the mall parking lot. Unlocked, the kids' coats were still in the seats, and his wife's purse, shoes, and cell phone were lying on the driver's side floorboard. They were nowhere to be found.

Immediately after his call, mall security was contacted, and the mall was locked down under a code Adam protocol.

The mall was searched, none of the three were found, nor were they seen on any mall surveillance cameras. There was no camera coverage in the parking lot.

17:45 Mr. Lewis was dropped off at his house by uniformed officers. He was extremely upset and agitated. I contacted Mr. Lewis at 08:30 on 11/30 to update him with our plan for continuing the search for his missing family.

After two hours of attempting to contact Mr. Lewis by phone I drove to his residence to speak to him in person.

Upon arrival at 11:00 I found the front storm door unlocked and the primary front door standing open. I knocked several times and received no answer. Looking in through the storm door I could see the dining room, three chairs had been overturned, the table was turned on its side and broken glass could be seen on the dining room floor. At this point I announced myself and entered the home.

The inside was in complete disarray. Furniture broken and turned over. Every room appeared to have been ransacked.

There were multiple stains and drag marks that appeared to be blood trails. So much in fact that it did not seem likely that the person bleeding would have survived if it all came from one person.

I called in for assistance, analysis, and support.

Units and two other detectives arrived with crime scene technicians around thirty minutes after my arrival.

While we wait for forensic analysis we can safely assume that no one who has lost that much blood could still be alive without medical intervention.

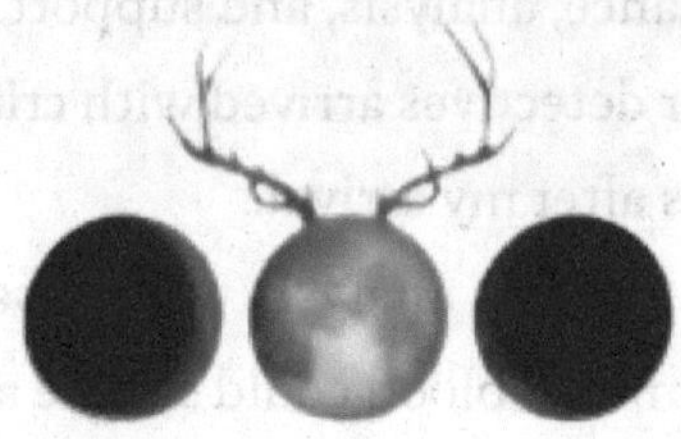

Preview From The Mercer Witches Book III

"Ladies and Gentlemen, Reverend Jim Meadows."

The roar from the crowd was staggering. The main room at the Gateway Center, plus the supplemental seating they had opened up from the side rooms put the head count at close to seven thousand people. Every single one of them were on their feet and singing praises to the lord when Jim Meadows took the stage and made his way to the pulpit.

Jim Meadows did not look like a stereotypical television evangelist as he strolled across the stage. Athletic and handsome in a way that would catch the eye in jeans and a t-shirt. In a tailored suit, made up for the cameras, there were many who felt like he could have gone into acting or modeling just as easily as the ministry.

His black hair was stylishly short but not severe. Every single thing about the man appeared cultivated and practiced. Every seam lay perfectly in place. Right on cue he emerged from the side of the stage, the spotlight tracking his graceful movement across the ivory and scarlet stage. From his mark on the side of the stage to the exact spot behind the glass pulpit, he never changed stride.

"Brothers and sisters, amen."

"Amen." Sang the choir.

"Brothers and sisters, amen."

"Amen." The call from the crowd combined with the choir drowned out the band.

"Join me now, brothers and sisters, as every head bows and every eye does close. Let us thank our father for this opportunity to fellowship."

A hush fell across the room.

"Father, we come to you today, seeking your grace and salvation. We thank you, Father, we thank you for this chance for us to come together to worship in your most holy name. We come singing praises and seeking your face. Reach down Lord, lay your hand on our hearts father, open our spirits to your message, allow us to see you, to praise you, and to call upon your holy name. Amen."

"Amen."

"Brothers and sisters, we have something special in store for you today. Today marks the beginning of a new era, a new healing in the world. Today, is the day we will see God's glory revealed in a way not seen since the days of Moses. Today is the day that God has chosen to send his most devout and blessed among the world. To share his message far and wide, to leave no doubt of the miracles and blessings that he pours out on his faithful."

The reverend grabbed the microphone from its stand on the pulpit and began to walk across the stage.

"For the last three years, we at Meadows ministries have been hard at work, and hard at prayer. Three years ago, God reached out and put his hand upon my heart. He led me to a group of people, people from all over the world, from all walks of life, and every background and from many churches. Now we are finally able to announce the fruit of this work."

Meadows walked to the edge of the stage. He perched right on the edge and stared out over the crowd, as if looking for something over the top of the audience.

"Brothers and sisters, I want to introduce you to our partners in this endeavor. Margarite Miller, from the Fellowship of the New Covenant. Mickey Carver, from Outreach Christian Church. Blake Ridwan from New Light Consolidated Baptist Ministries. Tyus Melous from Church of Christ. And last but never ever least, Mary Ellen Jennings from Church of the All Mighty Rock."

One by one the partners walked across the stage, waved to the crowd, and took a seat behind the pulpit.

"Brothers and sisters, I have one more introduction to make. In our prayers and meditations, we have discovered, the Lord wants us to push ourselves, to trust in him, and to give ourselves over to his blessings and designs completely. That is just what we have done. From our combined congregations, rises a new church, a new body of Christ. Done are the days of our denominations working at cross purposes or looking for minor differences in belief or scriptural interpretations. Now is the time of Ascension, we are joining together to seek God's face and feel his blessings rain down upon this world. It is through the Church of The Ascension that we will accomplish this; through these young people, we will see God's miracles poured out over this world in a way that has not been seen since Jesus Christ himself walked this earth."

Murmurs rippled across the crowd as Meadows let the information sink in.

"The body and soul of this new church will not be this leadership you see on the stage. We are facilitators, and intermediaries, handling the logistics and business of the church. But the real driving force behind this, are God's chosen warriors, are his Faithful Ascended. It is my absolute honor to introduce you to the two young people who will be leading the charge as we take the word of God into this world and let the healing begin. Brothers and sisters, the future of the Church of Ascension and of all of our combined ministries. Derrick and Paula Bringwald."

The two young people walked from each side of the stage. They both wore white robes like those of a monk or friar. Derrick's was trimmed at the collar and cuffs with crimson and silver, Paula's with black and gold. They walked to the podium, where they were met by Reverend Meadows. He hugged each of them in turn, then took a seat next to Margarite Miller. Paula pushed the hood of her robe back, revealing her pretty face and chestnut hair. Derrick walked to the front of the stage without her.

She spoke softly.

"Brothers and Sisters, the time has come for healing, the time has come for victory over sickness and death, the time has come for God's grace to pour out over us. I give you, the Faithful Ascended."

From every corner of the great hall and even the extension rooms, Close to one hundred hooded figures poured in, immediately a low rumble could be heard above the gasps and exclamations of the crowd. A chanted prayer, the words indistinguishable, like an electric hum.

Paula held up her hands and the only sound in the room was the low hum that seemed to accompany the Faithful Ascended.

"Brothers and Sisters join us in prayer and lift one another up as God's healing begins here and now."

She closed her eyes and the stage, where she was, grew even brighter.

"Father, we thank you for this blessed day..."

The first wave of power rolled over the room. It did not originate with any one of the single members of the Faithful Ascended but rose like a thunderhead, building pressure within the room, fed from the prayers of each Faithful Ascended and drawing from the energy of creation flowing through every person in attendance.

"We ask that you reveal your grace and healing to us Lord, There are those here who need healing Father..."

A sound like thunder shook the massive room. A woman in the crowd yelled, "Hallelujah, he is risen."

"All the glory to you Father, hear your faithful as they call out..."

Three rows from the front of the stage, a man spit out his dentures on the floor in front of him. When his wife touched his shoulder to let him know so he could pick them up before anyone else noticed, and he embarrassed himself, he turned and smiled at her with the brand-new teeth that had just grown in his seventy-four-year-old mouth.

BOOM. The thunder shook the room again.

"Lift the pain from your children, Lord, hear their cries and let your love pour out onto..."

On the left side of the stage was a special cordoned off area for folks who had to be brought in on walkers or wheelchairs. Above the chanting and the rhythmic booming, a voice cried out. "Look at God, look what God has done."

The twenty-five people who had been seated in this area were all up on their feet. They danced and jumped like children, even though some were well into their eighties.

"Show your children father, help us, bring us to your breast Lord and let us praise you with the heavenly host."

The band started into a fast, thrumming instrumental and the room erupted. Wave after wave of power rolled through the room as tumors shrank, bones mended, mental illness cleared and vision corrected itself.

Everyone on the stage was on their feet dancing and praising God.

The Ascension had begun.

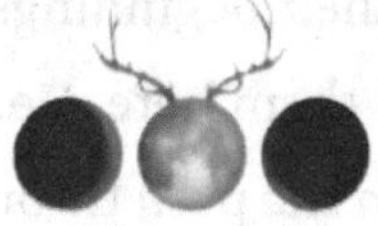

Just outside of Omaha Nebraska, The Fellowship of the New Covenant had set up their tent revival in a large natural amphitheater in Pleasant Point Park. They were expecting a big turnout tonight and everyone had been hard at work preparing for the service.

In the mess tent, Darrell Ray and Alexis were watching on a laptop as Jim Meadows introduced the various members of the Church of the Ascension. He smiled as Margarite walked across the stage and took her seat. She was as beautiful as ever. She had been spending more and more time away from the Fellowship, attending the meetings with Meadows ministries and the others. Preparing for this moment.

Darrell understood the calling on her heart, but he still felt some sadness at her absence, and perhaps a little jealousy as well. He could not help but worry sometimes, after all, when she was with him, they spent all of their time with the Fellowship. Town to town, in the little caravan of cars and vans and the new box truck. Living out of tents and bringing the gospel to the people one city at a time.

It had been their dream, but now when she went to see Reverend Meadows and his team. She stayed in the nicest hotels; she had a driver, catered meals, and one of the richest ministries in the country seeing to her every need. Not to mention Reverend Meadows himself, he doted on and complimented Margarite openly, in front of Darrell and everyone else. Darrell could only imagine what he was like when they were alone.

He tried to push that out of his mind, he knew that was not of God, that jealously had no place in a healthy relationship and that his wife, if nothing else, was as faithful as a person as he had ever met. Now at least, Darrell remembered their beginnings, who they had been, what they had done that had led them here. He closed his eyes and prayed silently for God to show him the path through this insecurity.

Alexis screaming brought him back to reality.

"Jenna! Look Brother Darrell, it's Jenna. What is she doing there? Why didn't sister Margarite say anything?"

On the screen, Meadows had just introduced two of the Faithful Ascended, as Derrick and Paula Bringwald, but Alexis was right, it looked just like Jenna, too much to be anyone else, unless she had a twin. The man next to her, holding her hand and leading her to a place behind the pulpit, that looked like Anthony Watkins, one of the first kids to be touched by the spirit at one of their earliest services.

Darrell Ray could never forget him. He was called by God for great works and threw himself into studying the gospels, then he was just gone. Taken by Mr. Bishop as part of the harvest. But now he was on stage with Jenna and Margarite. Why hadn't Margarite mentioned that she found the kids living under different names?

He touched Alexis on the shoulder.

"We don't know anything for sure yet, Sister. Let us pray until we can get in touch with Margarite, I am sure she will have answers."

He closed his eyes and asked God, once again, to drive the jealousy from his spirit so that he could discern his will with clear eyes and a pious heart.